"Abani's poems are the most naked, harrowing expressions of prison life and political torture imaginable. Reading them is like being singed by a red-hot iron."

—Harold Pinter

"*GraceLand* teems with incident, from the seedy crime dens of Maroko to the family melodramas of the Oke clan. But throughout the novel's action, Abani—an accomplished poet who published his own first novel at Elvis's tender age of sixteen—keeps the reader's gaze fixed firmly on the detailed and contradictory cast of everyday Nigerian life. Energetic and moving . . . Abani [is] a fluid, closely observant writer."

—*The Washington Post*

"Ambitious . . . a kind of small miracle."

—John Freeman, *The Atlanta Journal-Constitution*

"It is to be hoped that Mr. Abani's fine book finds its proper place in the world. . . . [Abani's] perception of the world is beyond or outside the common categories of contemporary fiction, and he is able to describe what he perceives compellingly and effectively. . . . The novel is a reflection of the chaos that reigned in Nigeria . . . on the broader tension between tradition and Western culture in postcolonial societies [and] on the trials a boy must face to become a man. . . . [Abani captures] the awful, mysterious refusal of life's discrete pieces to fit."

—Tim Marchman, *The New York Sun*

"An intensely vivid portrait of Nigeria that switches deftly between rural and urban life."

—*The Boston Globe*

"Singular . . . Abani has created a charming and complex character, at once pragmatic and philosophical about his lot in life. . . . Observes the chaotic tapestry of life in postcolonial Africa with the unjudging eye of a naive boy."

—*The Philadelphia Inquirer*

"The imagery of the book is tremendous . . . a mesmerizing glimpse at a polarized society with an unbelievable ability to function. . . . Abani's debut is spectacular, and may be just the spark today's Nigeria needs to undergo its own revival in stability, progress, and culture."

—*The University of Wisconsin Daily Cardinal*

"[Abani's novel is] deeply concerned with how Western colonialism transformed Africa in ways both major and minor. . . . Abani masterfully gives us a young man who is simultaneously brave, heartless, bright, foolish, lustful, and sadly resigned to fate. In short, a perfectly drawn adolescent. . . . Abani's ear for dialogue and eye for observation lend a lyrical air. . . . In depicting how deeply external politics can affect internal thinking, *GraceLand* announces itself as a worthy heir to Chinua Achebe's *Things Fall Apart*. Like that classic of Nigerian literature, it gives a multifaceted, human face to a culture struggling to find its own identity while living with somebody else's."

—*Minneapolis Star-Tribune*

"*GraceLand* is a grotesque, painfully hilarious look at the dark underground world of Lagos, Nigeria, and it brings back vivid memories of an urban culture seemingly always on the verge of a complete societal breakdown. Chris Abani's riveting novel is an unrelenting focus on blight, squalor, savagery, and violence. It is a superbly written, structurally fascinating work, and I found myself captivated by the hilarity of some of the scenes, often as I found myself on the verge of tears. It is a stunning debut by an immensely talented writer."

—Quincy Troupe, author of *Transcircularities* and *Miles and Me*

"The next wave . . . of Nigerian literature."

—*America Magazine*

"Beautifully written, perceptive and painful . . . A serious and poignant novel about the problems in the postcolonial era in Nigeria."

—*Altar* magazine

"This is a new kind of book. We will look back on its publication as a watershed moment in the history of postcolonial literature. It is, as the best of such novels are, hybrid, monstrous, exilic, an indictment of the global terrorism of capital, yet it is also something we have not seen before. In Elvis we meet an African man who suffers incandescently, who watches others suffer more, yet emerges not as another tragic masculinity, but as that rarest of creatures, a hero. This is Chris Abani's gift, to transmute the harrowing into the transcendent. Believe it: Elvis is redemption."

—Wendy Belcher, author of *Honey from the Lion: An African Journey*

"The novel is not just a politically charged coming-of-age story, but a tale of an entire nation's loss of innocence represented in the life of one boy. And it is this thematic largesse and the stylistic demands to which Abani rises that puts *GraceLand* in the league of novels like Czeslaw Milosz's *The Issa Valley*, Oë, and even Márquez, each of which tries to describe the loss of an old world in the face of a new one. . . . *GraceLand* is an overwhelming novel, and may well count as a major work of literature."

—*The Seattle Sinner*

"Disturbing but hysterically funny, *GraceLand* is a poignant work of innocence robbed by endless corrupt and brutal forces."

—*India in New York*

GRACELAND

GRACELAND

Chris Abani

PICADOR

FARRAR, STRAUS AND GIROUX

New York

www.picadorusa.com

Picador® is a U.S. registered trademark and is used by Farrar, Straus and Giroux
under license from Pan Books Limited.

For information on Picador Reading Group Guides, as well as ordering, please
contact the Trade Marketing department at St. Martin's Press.
Phone: 1-800-221-7945 extension 763
Fax: 212-677-7456
E-mail: trademarketing@stmartins.com

Designed by Patrice Sheridan

Library of Congress Cataloging-in-Publication Data

Abani, Christopher.
    GraceLand / Chris Abani.
        p. cm.
    ISBN 0-312-42528-7
    EAN 978-0312-42528-9
    1. Elvis Presley impersonators—Fiction. 2. Fathers and sons—Fiction.
3. Lagos (Nigeria)—Fiction. 4. Teenage boys—Fiction. I. Title.

PR9387 .9 A23G73 2004
813'.6—dc21   2003012705

First published in the United States by Farrar, Straus and Giroux

10 9 8 7 6 5 4

Delphine, Stella and Daphne

whenever, wherever, whatever

These are the words of lovers, of dancers, of dynamite singers.

These are songs if you have the music.

—AMIRI BARAKA, *BLUES PEOPLE*

Book I

It seemed almost incidental that he was African.

So vast had his inner perceptions grown over the years . . .

—BESSIE HEAD,

A Question of Power

2:30

ONE

))))))

This is the kola nut. This seed is a star. This star is life. This star is us. ?

*The Igbo hold the kola nut to be sacred, offering it at every gathering and to every visi-
tor, as a blessing, as refreshment, or to seal a covenant. The prayer that precedes the
breaking and sharing of the nut is: He who brings kola, brings life.* ?

))))))

Lagos, 1983

Elvis stood by the open window. Outside: heavy rain. He jammed the
wooden shutter open with an old radio battery, against the wind. The
storm drowned the tinny sound of the portable radio on the table. He
felt claustrophobic, fingers gripping the iron of the rusty metal protec-
tor. It was cool on his lips, chin and forehead as he pressed his face
against it.

Across the street stood the foundations of a building; the floor and
pillars wore green mold from repeated rains. Between the pillars, a
woman had erected a buka, no more than a rickety lean-to made of
sheets of corrugated iron roofing and plastic held together by hope.
On dry evenings, the smell of fried yam and dodo wafted from it into
his room, teasing his hunger. But today the fire grate was wet and all
the soot had been washed away.

As swiftly as it started, the deluge abated, becoming a faint drizzle.
Water, thick with sediment, ran down the rust-colored iron roofs,
overflowing basins and drums set out to collect it. Taps stood in yards,
forlorn and lonely, their curved spouts, like metal beaks, dripping rain-

water. Naked children exploded out of grey wet houses, slipping and splaying in the mud, chased by shouts of parents trying to get them ready for school.

The rain had cleared the oppressive heat that had already dropped like a blanket over Lagos; but the smell of garbage from refuse dumps, unflushed toilets and stale bodies was still overwhelming. Elvis turned from the window, dropping the threadbare curtain. Today was his sixteenth birthday, and as with all the others, it would pass uncelebrated. It had been that way since his mother died eight years before. He used to think that celebrating his birthday was too painful for his father, a constant reminder of his loss. But Elvis had since come to the conclusion that his father was simply self-centered. The least I should do is get some more sleep, he thought, sitting on the bed. But the sun stabbed through the thin fabric, bathing the room in sterile light. The radio played Bob Marley's "Natural Mystic," and he sang along, the tune familiar.

"There's a natural mystic blowing through the air / If you listen carefully now you will hear . . ." His voice trailed off as he realized he did not know all the words, and he settled for humming to the song as he listened to the sounds of the city waking up: tin buckets scraping, the sound of babies crying, infants yelling for food and people hurrying but getting nowhere.

Next door someone was playing highlife music on a radio that was not tuned properly. The faster-tempoed highlife distracted him from Bob Marley, irritating him. He knew the highlife tune well, "Ije Enu" by Celestine Ukwu. Abandoning Bob Marley, he sang along:

"Ije enu, bun a ndi n'kwa n'kwa ndi n'wuli n'wuli, eh . . ."

On the road outside, two women bickered. In the distance, the sounds of molue conductors competing for customers carried:

"Yaba! Yaba! Straight!"

"Oshodi! Oshodi! Enter quickly!"

Elvis looked around his room. *Jesus Can Save* and *Nigerian Eagles* almanacs hung from stained walls that had not seen a coat of paint in years. A magazine cutting of a BMW was coming off the far wall, its end flapping mockingly. The bare cement floor was a cracked and pitted lunar landscape. A piece of wood, supported at both ends by cinder blocks, served as a bookshelf. On it were arranged his few books, each volume falling apart from years of use.

By the window was a dust-coated desk, and next to it a folding metal chair, brown and crisp with rust. The single camping cot he lay on was sunk in the center and the wafer-thin mattress offered as much comfort as a raffia mat. A wooden bar secured diagonally between two corners of the room served as a closet.

There was a loud knock, and as Elvis gathered the folds of his loin-cloth around his waist to get up, the lappa, once beautiful but now hole-ridden, caught on the edge of the bed, ripping a curse from him. The book he had fallen asleep reading, Ralph Ellison's *Invisible Man*, fell from his side to the floor, the old paperback cracking at the spine, falling neatly into two halves as precisely as if sliced by a sword.

"Elvis! Elvis! Wake up. It's past six in de morning and all your mates are out dere looking for work," his father, Sunday, said.

"What work, sir? I have a job."

"Dancing is no job. We all dance in de bar on Saturday. Open dis bloody door!" Sunday shouted.

Elvis opened the door and eyed him. The desire to drive his fist through his father's face was old and overwhelming.

"I'll just wash, then go," he mumbled, shuffling past Sunday, heading for the backyard, passing Jagua Rigogo, who stood in the middle of the backyard cleaning his teeth with a chewing-stick, preparing for his morning ablutions and the clients who would soon start arriving to consult him on spiritual matters. He reached out and squeezed Elvis's arm as he passed. Elvis turned to him, opening his mouth to speak.

"Before you speak, my friend, remember, a spiritual man contain his anger. Angry words are like slap in de face."

Elvis took in Jagua's dreadlocks, gathered behind him in a long ponytail by a twisted tennis headband, and the distant red glare of his eyes. He didn't have his python with him, and Elvis wondered where it was. Probably asleep in the cot Jagua had salvaged from one of the city dumps, and which sat in the corner of his room. Merlin, his python, slept in it, comfortable as any baby.

"Jagua. I . . ." Elvis began, then stopped.

Jagua smiled, mistaking Elvis's resignation for control.

"Dat's de way," he said.

Elvis just sighed and silently fetched water from the iron drum sunning in a corner of the yard. He snatched his towel off the line and entered the bathroom, trying not to touch the slime-covered walls and the used sanitary pad in the corner. How did they come to this? he wondered. Just two years ago they lived in a small town and his father had a good job and was on the cusp of winning an election. Now they lived in a slum in Lagos. Closing his eyes, he rushed through his morning toilet. On his way back inside to get dressed, he passed his father in the corridor again.

"Are you still here?"

Elvis opened his mouth to answer but thought better of it.

The road outside their tenement was waterlogged and the dirt had been whipped into a muddy brown froth that looked like chocolate frosting. Someone had laid out short planks to carve a path through the sludge. Probably Joshua Bandele-Thomas, Elvis thought. Joshua was the eccentric who lived next door and spent his days pretending to be a surveyor.

Elvis and his father lived at the left edge of the swamp city of Maroko, and their short street soon ran into a plank walkway that meandered through the rest of the suspended city. Even with the planks, the going was slow, as he often had to wait for people coming in the opposite direction to pass; the planks were that narrow.

While he waited, Elvis stared into the muddy puddles imagining what life, if any, was trying to crawl its way out. His face, reflected back at him, seemed to belong to a stranger, floating there like a ghostly head in a comic book. His hair was closely cropped, almost shaved clean. His eyebrows were two perfect arcs, as though they had been shaped in a salon. His dark eyes looked tired, the whites flecked with red. He parted his full lips and tried a smile on his reflection, and his reflection snarled back. Shit, he thought, I look like shit. As he sloshed to the bus stop, one thought repeated in his mind: What do I have to do with all this?

Sitting on the crowded bus, he thought his father might be right; this was no way to live. He was broke all the time, making next to nothing as a street performer. He needed a better job to come. He pulled a book from his backpack and tried to re current inspirational tome, a well-thumbed copy of Rilke's *Young Poet*. He read books for different reasons and had them where he was: one in his backpack, which he called his on-the-r book, usually one that held an inspirational message for him; one by his bed; and one he kept tucked in the hole in the wall in the toilet for those cool evenings when a gentle breeze actually made the smell there bearable enough to stay and read. He opened the book and tried to read, sitting back as far as he could in the narrow seat. He hated the way he was being pressed against the metal side by the heavyset woman sitting next to him, one ample buttock on the seat, the other hanging in the aisle, supported against a standing stranger's leg. Elvis shifted, careful of the loose metal spring poking up through the torn plastic of the seat cover. Giving up on reading, he let his mind drift as he stared at the city, half slum, half paradise. How could a place be so ugly and violent yet beautiful at the same time? he wondered.

He hadn't known about the poverty and violence of Lagos until he arrived. It was as if people conspired with the city to weave a web of silence around its unsavory parts. People who didn't live in Lagos only saw postcards of skyscrapers, sweeping flyovers, beaches and hotels. And those who did, when they returned to their ancestral small towns at Christmas, wore designer clothes and threw money around. They breezed in, lived an expensive whirlwind life, and then left after a couple of weeks, to go back to their ghetto lives.

But for one brilliant moment, they dazzled: the women in flashy clothes, makeup and handbags that matched their shoes, daring to smoke in public and drink beer straight from the bottle; and the men, sharp dressers who did not rat on you to your parents if they caught you smoking. They let you take sips of their beer and shoved a few naira into your shirt pocket.

Lagos did have its fair share of rich people and fancy neighborhoods, though, and since arriving he had found that one-third of the city seemed transplanted from the rich suburbs of the west. There were beautiful brownstones set in well-landscaped yards, sprawling Spanish-style haciendas in brilliant white and ocher, elegant Frank Lloyd

Wright–styled buildings and cars that were new and foreign. Name it and Lagos had a copy of it, earning it the nickname "One Copy." Elvis had read a newspaper editorial that stated, rather proudly, that Nigeria had a higher percentage of millionaires—in dollars, not local currency—than nearly any other country in the world, and most of them lived and conducted their business in Lagos. The editorial failed to mention that their wealth had been made over the years with the help of crooked politicians, criminal soldiers, bent contractors, and greedy oil-company executives. Or that Nigeria also had a higher percentage of poor people than nearly any other country in the world. What was it his father had said about statistics?

"If you have it, flaunt it; if you don't, flaunt statistics."

He had been fourteen when he arrived in Lagos two years before, miserable and unable to fit into school, where his small-town thinking and accent marked him. The differences did not seem that obvious, but they were glaring to the other kids—he'd never played cricket at school, his experience of the movies had been with old dubbed-over silents and the Americanisms he knew were old and outdated. Where the other kids used slang like "cool" and "hip," he was limited to cowboy lingo like "shucks" and "yup" and "darn those rustlers."

So he cut school, spending long periods of time on a deserted beach, not too far from the ghetto of Maroko where they lived. He practiced his dance routines for hours to the sound of his little radio. At first the sand slowed him down, making his movements jerky. But he persevered until his moves appeared effortless. Subsequently, when he danced on smooth surfaces, he seemed to float. The beach was also refuge to the homeless beggars moved on by the police; always polite, they offered to share their "tickets to paradise." Elvis always refused the marijuana, but the smell hung in the hot air, and it soon became difficult to engage fully with the reality around him.

A man arguing loudly in the back of the bus intruded on his thoughts and reminded Elvis of his first molue ride. Molues were buses unique to Lagos, and only that place could have devised such a hybrid vehicle, its "magic" the only thing keeping it from falling apart. The cab of the bus was imported from Britain, one of the Bedford series. The chassis of the body came from surplus Japanese army trucks trashed after the Second World War. The body of the coach was built from scraps of broken cars and discarded roofing sheets—anything that could be beaten into shape or otherwise fashioned. The finished product, with two black stripes running down a canary body, looked like a roughly hammered yellow sardine tin.

The buses had a full capacity of forty-nine sitting and nine standing, but often held sixty and twenty. People hung off the sides and out of the doors. Some even stood on the back bumpers and held on to the roof rack. The buses wove through the dense traffic so fast they threw the passengers about, and caused those hanging on to sway dangerously. An old man on the bus had told him that the spirits of the road danced around the buses trying to pluck plump offerings, retribution for the sacrilege of the road, which apparently, when it was built, had severed them from their roots, leaving them trapped in an urban chaos that was frightening and confusing. Elvis never knew whether these spirits inhabited a particular road or all roads, or what they looked like. But the old man's story sounded so plausible it had stayed with him.

Elvis yawned, closed his eyes and rested his head on the cool metal side. Suddenly a man in the front got up, rapped his knuckles noisily on the roof of the bus and cleared his throat.

"Good morning, ladies and gentlemen."

His voice had a curious ring to it.

"We get new product for sale today call Pracetmol. It cures all pains, aches and fever caused in de body. If you look at de package, you will see dat de expiry date is December eighty-three. Dis is a new drug from de white people's labs and plenty research done go into it. It is manufacture in Yugoslavia. In dat country dey call it narcotics and it is costing plenty money. We in Star Advertising Agency with head office in Orile Lagos have been choose by de makers to promote dis drug in Nigeria. Today you can obtain your copy at cheap rate from me. Due to and because of advert purpose, dis packet containing twenty tablet is costing only one naira. If you check any chemist it is costing three naira dere. Buy your own now, for mama, papa and childrens too . . ."

Elvis tried to tune out the voice of the drug vendor but could not. Luckily the vendor got off at the next stop and Elvis watched him cross the road and hop onto a bus going the opposite way, relieved that he didn't have to listen to him all the way to Iddoh Park. Sitting back, Elvis closed his eyes again, and just as he drifted off, the insistent calling of a mobile preacher woke him. The preacher was wearing a grimy, threadbare white robe and unkempt dreadlocks; he had a Bible in one hand, and in the other a huge bell with which he punctuated his ravings. He must have gotten on when the drug vendor got off.

"Repent, I say. I am a voice crying out in de wilderness. Repent and come unto de Lord before it becomes too late. I saw a vision from de Lord and he did reveal many things to me. Listen—I say, listen," he said, reinforcing his ranting with loud and generous peals from his bell.

"De Lord says de only road to salvation lies in de Yahweh Adonai Latter Day Prophetic Spiritual and Messianic Church of God and His Blessed Son Jesus of Mount Carmel. Amen. Listen, brethren, I am de representation of dis wonderful Church of God and I call on all who will be saved from damnation to visit us on Sundays near Ojo bus stop and see miracles happen. Witness de power of prayer, de lame shall walk and de blind see. Listen . . ."

Elvis couldn't take any more and got off at the Bar Beach stop. It was a nice day, not too hot, with a nice breeze coming off the ocean, and he thought he might make some money off white expatriates and the odd tourist tanning on the beach. They were always surprised and pleased to see an Elvis impersonator here, particularly the Americans, who were often quite generous. He crossed the hot sand of the beach that abutted the Hilton Hotel. As he walked toward the makeshift raffia changing stalls, he noted who was there.

Sprawled on a deck chair was a heavyset man with a gargantuan stomach on which sat an open book. The sun was burning the skin around it and Elvis wondered if the resulting white patch would contain any of the text. A harried-looking woman with red hair and skin reddening to match chased after three excited children, ranging from around five to nine. In her hand was a white smudge of sunscreen, and with her distracted expression, she looked as though she suddenly realized she was holding a bodily secretion. Her husband (if he was her husband) was dozing on another deck chair, which was missing a leg. With every snore it tottered precariously but, defying the laws of physics, remained upright. An elderly couple stood looking out to the horizon, hands cupped against the glare of sun on water as though looking for their lost youth.

Meager pickings, he thought, as he ducked into a stall and shed his street clothes. He slipped into the white shirt and trousers, pulled on the socks and canvas shoes, and jammed the wig down on his head. He couldn't see himself properly in the small pocket mirror he carried. In Iddoh Park, his usual spot, he had come to rely on the glass shop fronts for his reflection. He hoped he looked fine. He rummaged in his bag for his can of sparkle spray. He couldn't find it, so he began pulling everything out of the bag, including a journal tied with string. Its leather binding was old and cracked.

Elvis paused for a moment and untied it, flicking quickly through the pages as though in search of a spell to find the lost sparkle spray. His fingers traced the spidery writing. It was his mother's journal, a collection of cooking and apothecary recipes and some other unrelated bits, like letters and notes about things that seemed as arbitrary as the handwriting: all that he had inherited from her, all that he had to piece her life together. He stared at the page he had opened it to and read the recipe as though it were a fortifying psalm. Closing the journal with a snap, he retied it and returned it to his bag with the other items he'd taken out.

Although he found the sparkle spray, when he tried to use it, he realized he'd run out. He shook the can angrily and depressed the nozzle repeatedly. There was a tired hiss of air, but no sparkle. With a defeated sigh, he turned to the small tin of talcum powder stuck in one of the pockets of his bag. He shook out a handful and applied a thick layer, peering into the mirror. He was dissatisfied; this was not how white people looked. If only he could use makeup, he thought, the things he could do. But makeup was a dangerous option, as he could be mistaken for one of the cross-dressing prostitutes that hung around the beach. They were always hassled by the locals, and often beaten severely. Besides, Oye, his grandmother, used to say in her Scottish accent, "Dinna cry about tha' things you canna change." Pulling on his gloves, he grabbed his bag and stepped out.

As he walked over to the foreigners, unable to tell the tourists from the expatriates and embassy staff, he noticed that one of the hotel security guards was spraying water from a hose onto the beach. It seemed odd to Elvis, and the only thing he could think of was that it was meant to cool the sand near the foreigners.

They stopped what they were doing to take in his approach. The gargantuan-bellied man sat up, unread book sliding off his stomach. The sleeping husband woke up with a start, promptly falling to the sand as his deck chair finally gave out. The harried woman stopped chasing the children, who gathered around her legs as the wraith that was Elvis drew closer. Even the old couple had given up the search for their youth to watch him.

"Welcome to Lagos, Nigeria," Elvis said.

He put his bag down and took several steps away from it, the freshly watered sand crunching under his heels. He cleared his throat, counted off "One, two, three," then began to sing "Hound Dog" off-key. At the same time, he launched into his dance routine.

It built up slowly, one leg sort of snapping at the knee, then the pelvic thrust, the arm dangling at his side becoming animated, forefinger and thumb snapping out the time. With a stumble, because the wet sand, until he adjusted to it, sucked at his feet, he launched into the rest of his routine. It was spellbinding watching him hover over the sand, movements as fluid as a wave, and it was some time before any of the foreigners moved or spoke.

"What d'ya think he's doing?" the gargantuan-bellied man asked, turning to the father prone in the sand.

"I don't know."

"Does he work for the hotel?"

"I don't know."

"So what d'ya think he wants?"

"I think he's doing an Elvis impersonation," the harried woman said.

"He doesn't look like any Elvis I know. Besides, ain't that wig on back to front? Do you think he speaks English?"

"Don't they all?"

"Hey, son, what do you want?"

Elvis stopped.

"Money," he replied.

"Like a tip?"

"Anything you want to give."

"I don't have any money," the harried woman said. "But I have some chocolate. Have you had chocolate before?" She reached into her bag and held a Hershey bar out to him.

"No thank you, madam," Elvis said.

"Hey, Mom, that's mine!" one of the kids said, grabbing the Hershey bar and running off.

"Bill! Bill!" she called, setting off after him.

"Say, son, are you going to stand there all day?" Gargantuan Belly asked.

"Do you want me to dance some more?"

"No! No!" Gargantuan Belly said.

"I don't think he's gonna leave until he gets some money," Prone Husband chimed in.

"Here," Gargantuan Belly said, reaching into the pocket of his pants lying in the sand. "Take. Now go, vamoose. Before I set the security guard on you."

The guard, who had been watching silently, put down the hose when he heard himself referred to. Elvis took the two naira; it hardly seemed worth it. His bus fare cost more.

"No dollars?" he asked.

"Dollars? Beat it, son. Go on, vamoose."

Elvis watched the guard approaching and, with a sigh, picked up his bag and headed away to the bus stop. Chocolate indeed, he fumed. He got to the bus stop just as a molue was pulling up. He waited for a rather generously proportioned woman to get off. She paused in front of him, taking in his clothes and wig and the talcum powder running in sweaty rivulets down his face.

"Who do dis to you?" she asked.

But before he could answer, she turned and walked away laughing.

Elvis strolled down to the ferry jetty as a cold wind began to blow. It had been a long day, and between Iddoh Park and Bar Beach he had barely earned enough to get a good meal. It was hard eking out a living as an Elvis impersonator, haunting markets and train stations, as invisible to the commuters or shoppers as a real ghost. This evening he had found himself dancing frantically against the coming abruptness of night, but nobody paid any attention; they all wanted to get home before the darkness brought its particular dangers.

The nocturnal markets on the beachfront came alive and the flickering oil lamps winked like a thousand fireflies. He wandered aimlessly through the jostling crowd of people, wondering if they were all human; markets were supposed to be the crossroads of the living and the dead.

He chose a cheap gutter-side buka and ordered a wrap of pounded yam and egusi sauce. He thought wistfully of Oye's cooking as he hurriedly ate the tasteless food. He missed her. Comfort, the woman his father had moved into the house, never gave him food. It was hard to think of her as the evil stepmother, because she didn't always feed her own children, all three of whom were under ten and lived with them. He bought a few wraps of moi-moi for his stepsiblings and rapidly left the hustle and bustle of the market behind.

Negotiating the ghetto plank walkways with care, he made his way home. One wrong step could cause him to lose his footing and fall headlong into the green swampy water that the ghetto was mostly built on. Raised on stilts like some giant millipede, the walkways' many legs were sunk below the surface.

"Where have you been since morning?" his father grunted at him.

He was sitting on the front veranda with some neighbors, slowly getting drunk on palm wine and talk. Elvis noted who was there. Jagua Rigogo with his dreadlocks and his pet python, Merlin, wrapped around his neck (Elvis returned the snake's deadeye stare and lost). Joshua Bandele-Thomas, head bent, sipped on his glass of palm wine, avoiding eye contact with Elvis. Even Madam Caro, who owned the bar down the street, was there. Maybe she had brought the palm wine.

Elvis regarded his father contemptuously, trying to remember why he had feared him for so much of his life. A muttered greeting thrown casually over his shoulder as he entered the house was his only reply. He met his stepsiblings in the corridor, where they sat playing a game of Ludo.

"Good evening, brother Elvis," Tunji, the oldest one, said.

"Good evening, broder!" Akin and Tope, the two younger ones, chorused.

Elvis grunted, barely looking at them as he gave them the moi-moi before continuing out to the backyard. He did his best to avoid them, not wanting to get too involved. He knew it was unfair, but it was his way of punishing Comfort.

Just to annoy her, he strolled over to the kitchen, where she sat gossiping with some women. The laughter died on her face when she saw him.

"Good evening, Ma," he said. He was met with stony silence. "Is there any food for me?"

"Look at dis mad boy O! Since morning he go out only to walk around. Him don come back, the only thing him can do is to find food. Get job like him mates he cannot. Oga sir!" she said, addressing Elvis. "I wait for you until I give dog your food. Food no dey for you." As if to confirm this, the family mongrel licked his empty plate with a scraping sound.

Sighing, he turned and left the kitchen. "God, I hate her," he muttered under his breath as he walked away, contemplating setting her aflame with the smoldering remains of the charcoal fire. He didn't know why he bothered; he only ever succeeded in annoying himself. He lay on his bed and tried to read. But he couldn't concentrate and soon dozed off.

The cold breeze coming in through his open door woke him. He could see his father outside on the veranda, sitting in a drunken stupor, oblivious to the biting-cold sea breeze, head inclined at an impossible angle. Flies hovered over pools of spilled sweet palm wine, crawled into his nostrils and over his bald head. Joshua and Madam Caro had left. Jagua Rigogo lay asleep on a bench, boa in a pile on his belly.

The rage when it came surprised him. He slammed the door so hard, plaster rained from the lintel. He heard his father fall off his chair with a startled yelp, but it brought him little comfort.

Anger
Problems?

▲▲

BITTER-LEAF SOUP AND POUNDED YAM
(Igbo: Ofe Onugbo Na Nniji)

INGREDIENTS

From his moms journal?

Bitter leaf
Palm oil
Crayfish
Salt
Hot peppers
Cooked oxtail beef or chicken and its stock
Ogiri
Uziza
Stockfish
Dried fish
Yam

PREPARATION

Wash the bitter leaf repeatedly until it no longer exudes green foam. The bitterness is in the chlorophyll. Cooking is always a good time for healing, so you must wash your pain, rinse and wash again until you too have washed out your bitterness in the green bile.

Next, heat some palm oil in a pot and add the crayfish, salt and peppers. Fry for a while, then add the stock from the meat with some water. Leave on a medium heat for about fifteen minutes before adding your spices, in this case, ogiri—an alkaline not just for the soup, but the soul as well—and uziza, which tones down the ogiri while letting the pepper burn hot. Next, add the meat, stockfish, dried fish and then the bitter leaf. Leave to cook for another twenty minutes. Boil the yam in chunks. It is cooked if it passes the fork test. Pound it in a mortar until it has the consistency of soft dough. Eat by dipping balls of pounded yam in the bitter-leaf sauce and swallowing.

TWO

)))))

We worship in different ways. With wine, the flow of worldly sweetness; with alligator pepper seeds, the hot and painful trials; with nzu, the sign of peace; with water, the blessing of the holy spirit; with blood, the essence of all life; with food, to fill the hunger of gods; with prayers, to allay the wrath of demons. But greatest of all this, is the offering of kola in communion, the soul calling unto life.

The Eucharistic qualities of the kola-nut ritual are clear. There are close parallels to Catholicism, as there seems to be some kind of transubstantiation involved in the kola-nut ceremony, similar to the communion wafer in the Catholic ritual of mass. There is the invocation of a supreme deity, the reference to the kola nut as representative of life and by association, the implication that the consumption of one was equal to that of the other.

)))))

Afikpo, 1972

Elvis had no idea why his father had summoned him to the backyard, away from the toy fire engine he was playing with. He had no idea why he had been asked to strip down to his underwear, or why Uncle Joseph first strapped a grass skirt on him and then began to paint strange designs in red and white dye all over his body. But he was five years old, and had learned not only that no one explained much to him, but that it was safest not to ask. Uncle Joseph had a habit of expressing his impatience in slaps.

His mother, Beatrice, stood in the shadows, leaning on a door-frame for support. She was ill and had been for a while. Whatever was

His mother
still alive

going on must be important, Elvis thought, if she had gotten out of bed for it. She had a sudden coughing bout and would have fallen over had Aunt Felicia not caught her and led her back in.

"Mommy! Mommy!" Elvis called, struggling to get to her.

"Stand still," Sunday said, pulling him roughly by the arm. He stumbled, but steadied himself against his uncle. Near tears, he watched Beatrice retreat into the house. He looked around for Oye, but she was nowhere to be found. Instead he saw his teenage cousins, Innocent and Godfrey, and a gaggle of other boys ranging from ten to nineteen. This group was made up of young men from the neighboring hamlets that had come to welcome Elvis on his first step to manhood as dictated by tradition, and as part of the ritual they would form a retinue of singers. The truth was, they were only there because they hoped that they would all be treated to good food and plenty to drink. Sunday noticed Elvis's attention straying and realized that he was looking for his mother and grandmother.

"It is time to cut your apron strings," he said to Elvis. "Dis is about being a man. No women allowed."

"Easy, Sunday," Joseph said.

"Easy what? Dis is why he has to learn early how to be a man, you know?"

"I know, but easy."

Elvis stood still throughout the exchange as Joseph continued to paint.

"Eh, Joseph, I have some White Horse whiskey, let me bring it?"

"You need to ask?" Joseph replied with a chuckle.

Sunday got up and went in the house to fetch the whiskey from his private hoard in his bedroom. From the house came the quiet protest of Elvis Presley's "Return to Sender" played at a low volume. As soon as Sunday was gone, Elvis started asking questions.

"What is happening?"

"Today, Elvis, you are going to kill your first eagle."

"But I'm too little."

"Don't worry," Uncle Joseph said, laughing.

"But why must I kill the eagle?"

"It is de first step into manhood for you. When you are older, de next step is to kill a goat, and den from dere we begin your manhood rites. But dis is de first step."

Sunday returned shortly with the whiskey and two shot glasses. He sat down with a grunt and opened the bottle. Holding it over the ground, he poured a libation, while Joseph responded at appropriate moments. Joseph took the proffered shot glass and downed the whiskey in one gulp, snapping the empty glass out to his side, allowing any errant drops to water the ground. He grunted and grimaced.

"Ah, Sunday, dat na good brew dere. Pour me anoder."

"Don't finish my good whiskey. Dis stuff is not kaikai."

When Joseph finished painting Elvis, he sent his son Godfrey out to summon the male elders. While he was gone, Joseph handed Elvis a small homemade bow with an arrow strung in it. On the end of the arrow, pierced through its side, was a chick. It was still alive and it chirped sadly. There was a line of blood from its beak that ran into the yellow down around its neck. The blood was beginning to harden and stiffen the feathers into a red necktie.

"It is alive," Elvis said.

"Of course it is. You just shot it," Joseph replied.

"I didn't."

"You did," Sunday said.

"Is this an eagle chick?" Elvis asked.

Joseph laughed. "Elvis, you funny. No, it is chicken, eagle is too expensive."

Elvis stood there holding the bow and arrow, with the helpless chick as far away from him as possible. He did not want the blood touching him. He tried not to make eye contact with the dying bird. When the old men assembled, Sunday passed the whiskey around and the men took swigs straight from the bottle.

"Do we have a kill?" they asked in Igbo, all speaking as one.

"Yes, we have a kill," Joseph replied.

"Was it a good kill?" the old men asked.

"Yes," Sunday answered.

"The father cannot speak," the old men said.

"Yes," Joseph said.

"Where is the kill?"

Joseph pointed and Elvis stepped forward. The old men smiled and looked at one another.

"In our day it was a real eagle."

"Let's just get on with it," Sunday said.

The old men glowered at him. Then, one by one, they walked up to Elvis and blew chalk powder in his face. They anointed his head with oil and, taking the bow and arrow from him and passing it to Joseph, they spat in his palms and muttered a blessing for him. Then they walked out of the compound.

Innocent, at fifteen, was Elvis's eldest cousin. Elvis knew that Innocent had been a boy soldier in the civil war that ended two years before and that when Innocent slept over at Elvis's house, he woke up in the middle of the night, screaming. Oye told him that Innocent screamed because the ghosts of those he had killed in the war were tormenting him, and if he, Elvis, didn't behave, Innocent's ghosts would torment him too. Other than the war story, Innocent and Godfrey, who was thirteen, were virtually strangers to Elvis. He admired them from a distance with their towering Afros and platform shoes, but as teenagers they didn't have much to do with him.

Innocent bent and lifted Elvis up onto his shoulders. He felt very grown-up sitting up there, seeing the world from that high. Uncle Joseph handed the bow back to Elvis and they followed the old men out of the compound, accompanied by the group of young men, who now joined the procession, singing.

They followed the old men up the road, singing the praises of Elvis as a great warrior and hunter. The road headed away from the square, toward the farms and ritual spaces. It was unpaved and lined by trees Elvis knew simply as bush mango trees. They grew in straight lines. He once asked Oye how come wild trees could grow in such a straight line.

"They don't, laddie," she said. "In tha olden days, criminals and murderers were buried alive, standing up. A flowering stake was driven through their heads and they became the trees. Tha's why tha fruit is so sweet."

She cackled at his horrified expression. Beatrice had intervened. "Mama! He is only five."

"Children are never too young to hear tha truth. You know why tha criminals were killed tha' way? Redemption. In death they were given a chance to be useful, to feed fruit-bearing trees. Do you understand?"

Elvis shook his head.

"Don't worry, someday you will."

But Elvis couldn't walk past the trees without feeling the ghosts of the criminals reaching out to him, and neither could he eat the tasty fruit. High up on Innocent's shoulders, he felt the leaves brush his face like hungry fingers, and he was really glad when the old men turned off the road and into the bush. They soon came upon a huge iroko tree that served as the clan shrine. The old men stopped and, taking the bow and arrow from Elvis, approached the tree. They freed the chick, tying it upside down to a branch next to others that were in several stages of decay. They hung like grotesque ornaments on a Christmas tree. The old men plucked a tail feather from the bird and stuck it in Elvis's hair. They cut the tree bark and, dipping their fingers in the sap, traced patterns on his face. And then it was over. Sunday picked Elvis up and held him close to the decaying birds. Elvis turned away from the smell.

"Don't turn away from death. We must face it. We are men," Sunday said.

forshadow?

Elvis turned to him, tears brimming.

"But it stinks."

"So does life, boy. So does life," Joseph said. "Come, Sunday, leave your son to join his mates. He is a man now. Come, we still have to finish dat whiskey."

Sunday nodded. He looked at Elvis for a long moment before putting him down.

Turning to Innocent and Godfrey, he told them to watch over their cousin, and then he left with Joseph. The group of singing boys followed them, intent on joining in on any festivities. Innocent picked Elvis up and carried him on his shoulders as they walked back to the house. He stopped at a kiosk just outside the compound.

"Why are we stopping?" Godfrey asked.

"Ah Elvis done taste him first blood, so as a man, he must drink with men," Innocent replied.

Ordering beers for himself and Godfrey, he opened up a cold bottle of Fanta for Elvis.

"How you dey?" Innocent asked him.

"I was afraid," Elvis replied.

"Dat's how dese things are. De trials of dis world things come as surprise, so you must have a warrior's heart to withstand dem. Dat's why your papa no tell you about today. You understand?" Innocent said.

Elvis shook his head and took a sip from his soda.

"Leave him. He is a child," Godfrey said. "Dere is time for such talk later."

Innocent nodded and took a swig of beer. Sitting on the counter in his grass skirt, drinking his Fanta and watching Godfrey and Innocent tease the girl behind the counter, Elvis felt like a man.

▼▼

ASPILIA (AFRICANA) LATIFOLIA *OLIV. ET HIERN*
(Igbo: Uranjila)

This is a scrambling herb covered with bristles, commonly found in old farm-lands and open places in the forest. Its leaves are almost triangular in shape, and have broad, saw-edged margins. It produces star-shaped yellow flowers and its fruits are seedlike, tiny and hard and have a ring of short bristles.

The leaves and flowers, when crushed, are applied to wounds to stop bleeding, healing them quicker. A little salt and lime juice added to the sap of the crushed leaves, and dropped into the eyes, remove corneal opacities and other foreign bodies, clearing up vision.

THREE

))))))

With your finger on the King's head, trace the star. See? The lobes fall where its reach points. This is the first truth.

The King's head is the kola nut's apex, or head. The star is the design of lines clearly imprinted on it that determine the number of lobes the kola nut will have. This number is the key to the Igbo mathematical system. This number holds the truth of the clan.

))))))

Lagos, 1983   Elvis - 16 years old

A pale watery sun rose over the ghetto of Maroko. The place was already abuzz with life. People hurried out to the bus stops to get to work, and the ferry dock was packed tight, yet the two ferries that spanned the lagoon between Maroko and the marina of downtown Lagos were sitting about fifty feet out in the water, with no passengers on board.

The plank walkways, which crisscrossed three-quarters of the slum, rang out like xylophones as a variety of shoes hurrying over them struck diverse notes. In the mud underneath this suspended city, dogs, pigs, goats and fowl rooted for food. Somewhere in the vicinity, the congregation of a Spiritual-Church belted out a heady, fecund music that was a rhythmic, percussive background to their religious ecstasy.

Elvis had decided to find steady work, as he couldn't depend on his dancing to bring in a regular income. It wasn't that he was giving up on his dream to be a dancer, he rationalized; it was more like he was deferring it for a while. Maybe with the money he earned, he could save up to go to America. That was a place where they appreciated dancers. Besides, he thought, remembering his humiliation the day before, it wasn't as if he was enjoying it anymore. Anyway, his father was out of work and drinking again, and Comfort wasn't too happy supporting everyone.

He walked over to Madam Caro's Bar and Restaurant, a rather grandiloquent name for the shaky wood-and-zinc shack perched on the edge of a walkway, hanging over the swamp. Regulars often had to be fished out by the teenagers hanging around. Of course, there was an exorbitant charge, but when you were drowning it didn't matter. It was even rumored that on slow nights, the youths pushed people in.

Madam Caro, who lived across the street from Elvis and his family, was one of those women that traditional society couldn't peg into a role. Too big for that world, she seemed at home in the urban anonymity of Lagos. She was nearly six feet tall and had the girth of a baobab tree, or very nearly. Her skin was the black of onyx and her eyes, which missed nothing, were hard, although when she laughed they lit up.

There was a good chance that his friends would be in the bar, Elvis thought. He was eager to run into Redemption. It sometimes seemed like Redemption knew everyone, heard everything and could procure anything, for a price. Elvis hoped that Redemption would help him for free, as he was broke. Besides, they were friends.

He'd met Redemption at school when he first arrived, which in itself was a lucky break, because Redemption was hardly ever in school. He'd turned up maybe twice a month with gifts for the teachers and the headmaster, who always bumped him cheerfully to the next class. Redemption had been pulling a reluctant goat and balancing a bundle of yams precariously on his head when Elvis had torn past, nearly knocking him over, late as usual.

"Hey, stop!" Redemption shouted in a tone that froze Elvis. "What is de hurry?"

"Sorry. I'm late."

"Well, if you help me pull dis stubborn goat to de headmaster's office, I will make things all right for you."

That was how their odd friendship began. Elvis adored Redemption, deferring to him as if he were the elder brother he'd never had.

For Redemption this offered the possibility of something he desired most, acceptance. It was Redemption who hooked Elvis up with the spots at the beach and in Iddoh Park where he danced, and kept the hoods off him as he began what Redemption referred to as his "dancing career." It was also Redemption who prompted Elvis to leave school and give his art his all. Elvis hung on his every word, listening as Redemption told him, at every opportunity, of his plans to leave for the United States.

"States is de place where dreams come true, not like dis Lagos dat betray your dreams," Redemption would say. "It is full of blacks like us, you know, American Negroes wearing big Afros, walking with style, talking anyhow to de police; real gangsters," he continued.

"Uhumm."

"Dat's right. Dese gangsters drive 1965 Ford Mustangs, you see. Like cowboys."

"I thought cowboys rode horses?" Elvis would challenge, already knowing the answer.

"De horse is dere, on de hood of de Mustang. Same thing."

As he walked in, Elvis cased the room. Even though it was early, the bar was nearly half full. Gloria Gaynor screamed "I Will Survive" from crackly loudspeakers. Elvis saw Sergeant Okoro, the policeman who lived in the same tenement as he did, talking to Madam Caro. She fished deep into her bra and took out a lot of banknotes. She peeled some off and handed them to him. He crumpled them without looking and stuffed them in his shirt pocket. Elvis thought Okoro appeared a little nervous.

Redemption was not there, Elvis noted, but his father's friend Benji was. Benji didn't have a job and earned a living by hooking people up with others seeking a service or a favor or a thug. His connectedness came from being a permanent fixture, and he had once bragged to Elvis: "If you wait long enough, de world comes to you." Elvis glanced at his watch. It was eight a.m.

"Good morning, Uncle Benji," Elvis said, sitting across from him and ordering a jug of palm wine.

"Ah, Elvis! It is good to see you. How can I help?" Benji replied, filling his glass from the fresh jug of wine.

"Uncle Benji, I need a job."

Benji took a deep drink, emptying his glass. He refilled it before he spoke.

"I thought you are a dancer, no?"

"Yes. But there is not enough money to survive. I am barely making enough to feed myself."

Benji drank deeply again and tried to fill his glass from the empty jug. Elvis took the hint and ordered another jug.

"Well, dis is what your father was afraid of when he did not want you to dance. Do you remember? I mean, at your age, since you are not in school, you should be helping with de house."

"My father is an out-of-work drunk, so what does that make his advice?"

Benji bristled.

"Your father is a good man who has lost his way. Show respect, what is wrong with you?"

Elvis bowed his head apologetically. Benji sighed.

"But a son must not go hungry under a father's roof, even if dis is Lagos. I will speak to your father," he offered.

Elvis put his hand on Benji's wrist, stopping him from filling his glass from the new jug.

"Don't speak to him. I need a job."

Benji licked his lips and looked from Elvis to the jug and back.

"All right," he said. "Go and see Jimoh, he will give you a job." He gave directions rapidly and ignored Elvis's thank-you as he shakily poured more wine.

The food seller who came round at lunch with a steaming cart was never late. There was a loose agreement between her and the workers with regard to credit: as long as she got paid when they did, it was fine. The workers on the construction site were a steady source of income for her.

Lagos was littered with sites like this one, because new high-rise apartment complexes and office blocks were going up seemingly overnight. Elvis was glad for the job, which Benji had gotten for him despite the fact that he had no experience and was not trained in a particular trade. But he was strong and willing, so the foreman had put him to work as a general laborer. His duties included mixing concrete, molding cinder blocks and generally fetching and carrying for the masons and carpenters as needed.

Lunch was Elvis's favorite time, not because of the small respite from work, but because it was only at lunch that he really saw the people behind the bodies that slogged through the day's work, tight-lipped and taciturn.

They were a curious mix. Happy, buxom women who carried cinder blocks on their heads to the upper levels, their fat shaking as they exploded into laughter at some joke. There were also masons with cement-dusted bodies and carpenters strutting with leather tool belts and young girls who should have been spending their weekdays in school and their weekends at home, grooming and giggling as they gossiped their naive knowledge of men. Instead they had hands of used sandpaper, the backs wrinkled, the palms scoured and calloused. They sat or lay back in the shade of trees that survived the site clearing, or in the shade of the half-finished building. Invariably there was a radio playing and the station of choice was hotly debated. The younger workers wanted the stations that played Wham!, Sade, Duran Duran and Peter Tosh, and the older workers wanted more indigenous music. It was a careful game of give-and-take. What Elvis loved the most, though, was that there was always someone dancing. He would lie back and watch the dancers, a book open, his attention divided between the two activities. Even when he wasn't concentrating, he loved the musty smell of old books.

He had a crush on one the girls, Angela, who told him that when she took her pay home, her father seized it, blowing it on alcohol. Unsure why she told him, and feeling somewhat helpless, he had pressed a five-naira note into her palm. She looked down at it, surprised, then kissed him quickly, tucking the money into her bra.

He watched her practiced ease as she fended off the groping demands of Okoro, the chief mason, who reached out and grabbed her breasts as she passed him. A smack across the face, received in good spirits, put him in place. But Elvis fumed silently. She came and sat down beside him.

"Hey, Elvis," she said.

"Why do you let him touch you like that?" he said.

"You dey jealous?" she asked.

He ignored her.

"Listen, if I fancy him, I go pretend say I no see him hand. Dat na extra money."

"Shut up," Elvis said softly. "That is sleazy."

She was silent for a while, and he glanced at her, trying to read her face.

what?

"No, Elvis, not like dat. If I want I go let am touch me, no be sleazy thing, na practical thing—like feeding goat or tending chicken. Is only you men dat make it more dan dat," she said finally. Then, getting up, she walked over to where the older women sat.

Heading home from work, Elvis crossed the lagoon and went for a walk under the sweeping flyovers. A shantytown had grown underneath them peopled by petty traders, roadside mechanics, barbers, street urchins, madmen and other mendicants. He paused to watch, noting that despite the streetlights coming on around the National Stadium across the way, and the head- and taillights of the traffic that marked night's approach, the energy of the bridge city was unflagging. He bought a bottle of Coca-Cola from a child hawker and sipped slowly, his eyes following the child's fading figure as she called out: "Coca-Cola! Is a cold! Come buy!"

He often wondered how he would frame moments like this if he were a director making a film. What shots would he line up? Which wouldn't make the final edit, ending up on the cutting-room floor? It frustrated him to think this way. Before he read the book on film theory he had found in the secondhand store, movies were as much magic to him as the strange wizards who used to appear in the markets of his childhood. Now when he watched a movie, he made internal comparisons about what angle would have been better, and whether the watermelon shattering in the street of a small western town was a metaphor for death or a commentary about the lack of water.

He took in the young girl leaning against a lamppost. Her lithe body in the pool of light appeared somehow inappropriate. And the tire vulcanizer who was sitting before his wavering flame, waiting for a customer and reading a book on quantum physics through cracked glasses with total concentration—probably a professor down on his luck, Elvis thought. He watched a thief stalking a potential victim with all the stealth of a tiger. The intended victim, a young woman with a backpack hanging from one shoulder, seemed unaware. When the thief pounced, however, she caught him with a stunning blow across the head, raising her voice to call, "Ole! Ole! Thief!" Everyone around her reacted immediately to the call by throwing any hard object they could. Some young boys chased after the fleeing man. They carried a tire they'd picked from the pile by the vulcanizer. In Lagos, vigilante justice was common, and the popular mode of execution was the necklace of fire—a tire around the neck doused with petrol and set on fire. Luckily, the thief escaped by jumping onto a passing bus, his jeers fading into the distance.

Elvis threw the empty Coke bottle on the ground and turned to continue home. A beggar accosted him, springing out of nowhere, his one eye glittering insanely. The other socket, empty, gaped red and watery as his gnarled claws closed over Elvis's hands and his mouth opened in a toothless grin. A long scar, keloidal and thick, ran from his neck, up across the empty eye socket and into his hairline. Against the man's dark skin, it looked like a light brown worm.

"I dey very hungry," he said.

The beggar took in Elvis's confusion and labor-dirty clothes and, deciding he wasn't going to get anything from him, moved off.

Elvis came alive. "Wait!" he called.

The beggar stopped and turned.

"Wait and I'll share a meal with you," Elvis said.

The beggar nodded and smiled. Together, they walked over to an open-air buka, sat down on the rough benches next to night workers and policemen on break and ordered. Elvis studied the beggar as they ate together in silence. His nostrils were distended, perhaps from years of ramming snuff up them with his thick forefinger. His hair was a mess of matted brown dreadlocks, yet he was clean, and his old clothes appeared freshly washed. His dreadlocks had a smattering of white, and Elvis guessed he was in his late forties or maybe early fifties.

After dinner he looked up at Elvis. "Tanks."

Elvis nodded.

"What's ya name?"

"Elvis."

"Like de musicman?"

Elvis nodded. "And you?"

"Mhm, well, I am known as de King of de Beggars," he replied. "But my parents name me Caesar Augustus Anyanwu. Big name for poor man is good magic."

"Not so good," Elvis muttered. The King of Beggars laughed, head thrown back, his one eye caught savagely in the light. A big rat scurried across the floor, stopping to turn a curious stare on Elvis, causing him to shiver. The King noticed it and threw an empty Coca-Cola bottle at it, making it scurry for cover.

"All dese bukas no get hygiene," he said. "But no worry, germ has no authority in black man belly."

Elvis laughed along at the old joke. There was a moment of awkward silence. Finally Elvis asked:

"Do you live here?"

"Yes, here in Bridge City."

"I guess that's why you became a beggar."

"Someone does not become a beggar; we are made beggars."

"Is there no work you can do?"

"I beg. Dat is my work."

"But where is your pride?"

"I cannot afford it," Caesar said, laughing.

Elvis chuckled hesitantly. There was another protracted silence. Breaking it, the King got up.

"I mus' go, but I am sure we go meet again, Elvis de musicman," he said.

Elvis smiled and watched the King disappear into the darkness, then turned and headed home. What a strange fellow, he thought.

The rest of the night was a restless one for Elvis. To start with, his room was leaking: not tame drip-drops but a steady stream of water that filled the bucket placed in the middle of the floor in a few minutes. He gave up trying to empty it, and as it overflowed, he settled down and prepared to be flooded out. It wouldn't be the first time. The steady dribble of water provided a soothing background to fall asleep to.

Just as his first snore broke through, he was woken by steady splashes in the water. Rats swimming in the flooded room. One clambered up the iron leg of the bed and onto his foot. He lashed out, sending the rat flying across the room to crash with a sickening thud into the opposite wall. There was a dull plop as its lifeless body fell into the water that had overflowed from the bucket and coated the floor in a pool.

Elvis finally settled into an uneasy sleep, dreaming he was drowning in a rat-infested lake and every time he tried to swim to safety, the rats would drag him back under the waves. He struggled and spluttered but couldn't get away from them.

He woke with a start to find himself lying in the water on the floor, staring into the bright eyes of a rat that was using one of his sandals as a raft to float around the room.

YAM PEPPER SOUP
(Igbo: Ji Minni Oku)

INGREDIENTS

Yam
Salt
Palm oil
Desiccated crayfish
Dry fish
Curry
Fresh bonnet peppers
Ahunji

PREPARATION

First, peel the yam and cut it into chunks. Next, put in a pot of water, add a pinch of salt and put it on to boil. When the yam is soft, take off heat and drain. Put another pot of water on to boil. Add about three dessert spoons of palm oil, the crayfish, the dry fish, and a pinch of the curry, salt and fresh peppers. Pull the fresh ahunji apart and drop the shredded leaves into the mixture. Leave to cook for about twenty minutes. Bring off the boil, dish the spicy sauce into a bowl containing the boiled yam, and serve.

1:29:55 [handwritten]

FOUR

))))))

We are all seeds, we are all stars.

There are several stages in the rites of passage for the Igbo male. Of prime importance is the understanding of the kola-nut ritual. At the heart of the ritual is the preservation, orally, of the history of the clan and the sociopolitical order that derives from that history.

))))))

Afikpo, 1974 *Elvis is around 7 years old* [handwritten]

It had do with the smell of damp loam, the green shade of Gmelinas, the way the light caught a tomato by surprise, making it blush deep, or the satisfaction of earth worked between the fingers that made Bea- *Mother still alive* [handwritten] trice return to her little garden in spite of the doctor's orders to stay in bed and rest. This was more relaxing than any rest, she thought as she weeded the plant beds until they shone.

Oye watched over her from the back porch where she sat chopping spinach for dinner. She never scolded Beatrice the way Sunday did when he reminded her of the doctor's orders. Oye tried hard not to intervene in those fights, in deference to her daughter's request, but she could not hide her distaste for her son-in-law. Oye called out to Elvis. He was playing with his ten-year-old cousin Efua in the sandpile at the corner of the house. The sand was there so the mason could use it to fabricate cinder blocks for the new bathroom extension he was building.

"Bring some water for your mother, child," Oye said as Elvis ran up to her, Efua hard on his heels. Oye took her presence in with a smile and a shake of the head. "And be careful. I canna tell why tha both of you have to fetch a cup of water together," she added.

Elvis and Efua returned with a frosted glass of water from the kerosene fridge. Oye intercepted them and sent them back to the earthenware pot half buried behind the kitchen that held water cooled by the earth and enriched by the sweet herbs Oye dropped into it daily. When the children returned with the right water, Oye called Beatrice to take a little break. Beatrice obliged her mother. She drank the cup of water even though she wasn't thirsty. She could hear Elvis and Efua squealing as they played some game in the front yard. Probably hop-scotch, their favorite. After a few minutes of rest, she returned to work on the plant beds.

Each bed was carefully arranged in geometric regularity, each stem and leaf carefully loved and tended. Beatrice was only truly happy amid the rows of green pepper stalks ripe with yellow and red fruit, in this place perfumed with curry leaves and thyme and that most fragrant of herbs, ahunji.

"Elvis," Beatrice said, surprised to see him suddenly standing in front of her. "I thought you were playing with Efua."

"Uncle Joseph called her."

"Okay. Do you want to help me with de garden?"

"No."

"Okay den. Go sit with your granny." *Oye = grandmother*

Elvis looked over to where Oye sat. He loved his grandmother, but she had a Scottish accent, picked up from the missionaries she had worked for, and he didn't always understand what she said. She sometimes lost her temper when he asked her to keep repeating herself, threatening to turn him into a turtle like the two she kept in an earthenware bowl of water. She was a witch and he believed she would do it.

"No."

"All right, sweetheart. I'll be done in a minute," Beatrice said. She had been sick for a long time and wasn't always well enough to play with him, so she felt guilty about using her able time this way, to work on her garden. But she needed this.

Elvis, at seven, was too young to understand his mother's obsession

with her garden. Bored, he picked up a stick and began to play with it.
At first it was an airplane, then it was a machine gun, then a sword.
Beatrice looked up and saw what he was doing.

"Put dat stick down, Elvis, you will hurt yourself," she said.

He ignored her and instead began whacking the tomato plants
with the stick, scattering leaves everywhere.

"Stop it before I spank you!"

The leaves were still flying when she lashed out and caught him
across the buttocks. The cry welled up, choking him with the shock of
it for a moment, before a wail broke free. She relented and pulled him
close, holding him to her breast until he calmed down.

"I'm sorry," she whispered. "But you were destroying my plants."

She tried to explain to him that the neat beds, the soft crumbly
earth, the deep green of the okra, the red and yellow peppers, the delicate mauve flowers of the fluted pumpkin, were important to her in
ways she had no words for. He didn't understand, but was content to
bury himself in the deep aloe scent of her hair and the damp of her
sweaty brow.

"You should tell him about tha operation, lass," Oye said. "He's a
strong lad, he'll be okay. You have to prepare him. You dinna have
much time left."

Oye and Beatrice were out on the front veranda, Oye in a wicker
chair that creaked and groaned with every breath she took, as though
the weight of her were unbearable, and Beatrice lying on a raffia mat
on the floor, a light blanket wrapped around her. Beside her, Oye had
set a steaming mug of some herbal infusion. Beatrice was not quite
sure what it was for or how Oye expected the herbs to achieve what
chemotherapy hadn't. She rubbed the sore scar tissue where her left
breast had been, glad to be free of the prosthetic with its tightness and
infernal itch.

It was late and the night was cool. Across from their compound,
they could see lights bobbing about across the street as people just
back from their farms prepared a late supper. It was an arduous life,
complicated by the fact that they had all just emerged from a three-

year civil war in which most families lost members vital to the rebuilding of their new lives. Women were missed more than men, because they made up the main work force. Beatrice was glad for the education that allowed her to earn her living as a primary-school teacher. Or used to, anyway, before she got sick.

A coconut shell of smoldering coals seemed to float by unassisted in the dark, the person carrying it lost in the deeper blackness.

"Remember when I had to carry coals from neighbors' houses back to ours to light de hearth as a child?"

"Yes," Oye replied. "You were so scared of tha fire," she added with a chuckle.

"It was hot and dangerous."

"I know, lass, but we couldn't afford matches in those days."

"I will miss dis place, Mama," Beatrice said.

"Yes, lass. But we'll call you back to be reborn into tha lineage again."

"As a boy next time!"

"Why? They are such limited creatures."

"But wanted."

"I always wanted you."

"I know, Mama. But remember de songs dat de women would sing when a boy was born? Ringing from hamlet to hamlet, dropped by one voice, picked up by another until it had circled de town. And de ring of white powder we would wear around de neck to signify de boy's place as head of de family."

"We sing for girls too."

"Yes, Mama. A dirge. Mournful, carried by solo voices until all de town was alerted of de sadness of de family. And de ring of powder we wore was around de elbow to show the flexibility and willingness to work hard of de woman. When I come back, it will be as a boy. You know dat's de only reason Sunday hasn't taken another wife. Because I bore him a son."

"Hush, lass, you need your strength, but tell your son tha things he should know."

They didn't speak for a while, the silence broken only by the call of wild dogs in hills far in the distance, the shrill of crickets, the throaty blues of frogs and Beatrice slurping the hot herbal infusion.

uncle

"Mama, do you think dere is something strange with Joseph and Efua's relationship? Since his wife died he hasn't been right. Why do all de wives die young in dis family?"

"Which question do you want me to answer, lass?"

"Never mind," Beatrice said, as a shadowy figure approached, swinging a flashlight back and forth.

"Who's tha'?" Oye called out, her hand reaching into the folds of her lappa for the knife she always carried there. Used mostly to cut herbs, its blade was a sharp enough warning to any mischief-maker.

"It is Joseph, Mama."

"I'm not your ma," Oye said.

"Good evening, Joseph," Beatrice greeted him. Things were awkward between them since Joseph made a pass at her on her wedding night.

"Evening. Is Sunday home?"

"You know where he is. Since I became ill he lives at dat bar downtown."

"So he's at de bar?"

"Are you stupid, son?" Oye asked.

"Good night, ladies," Joseph said, turning to leave.

Not long after Joseph left, Beatrice hauled herself up from the mat and headed inside.

"Good night, Mama."

"You need to tell your son about tha sickness, Beatrice. You need to prepare him."

"I am preparing him, Mama. I am teaching him things dat useless school cannot. I have taught him to sew, to iron, to cook, to read and to write at a level beyond his age."

"Yes, lass. But it's not enough."

"Good night, Mama."

"Good night, child. Be here in tha morning," Oye replied.

When he woke from the nightmare Elvis stumbled out of bed and made his way sleepily to his mother's room. His parents didn't share a bedroom, though his father sometimes came to sleep in Beatrice's room. Elvis guessed he had nightmares too, and judging from the sounds his mother made, he guessed his father's nightmares transferred to her.

He could always tell when his father was in Beatrice's room. His slippers, left outside the shut door, were a clear sign to stay away. When he saw them, Elvis would make his way to Oye's room, which was outside the main house, next door to the kitchen. The short trip across the dark yard was terrifying, so he only went to Oye's when he had to.

He opened his mother's door and, in the dim glow from the storm lantern in the corner with its wick turned nearly off, felt his way to the bed. His fingers grazed the small blue Bible she kept on the nightstand. Next to it was her journal, bound in worked leather that smelled of things old and secret. He loved watching her write in it, and he would fetch it for her, inhaling the deep scent of it, thrilled that she trusted him not to look in it. And he never did. He lingered by the nightstand, touched the journal, rubbing his hand over the cracked leather binding.

Beatrice woke up to go to the bathroom. As she stood up, the lappa covering her slipped off, revealing her nudity. Before she could cover herself, Elvis saw the emptiness where her breast had been.

"Elvis! What are you doing here?"

"I had a bad dream, Mama."

She saw the look of something nameless on his face.

"Come here," she said.

He ambled over and stood in front of her. She sat down on the bed so they were the same height.

"Do you know what is happening to me?" she asked.

"Sure," he replied. "You are ill. That's what Oye says."

"Granny to you!" she chided. "Yes, I am ill," she continued. "I have cancer."

"What's that?" he asked.

"Dat's when your body begins to fight you. So de doctor cuts away de angry part and hopefully you get well."

"Was your breast fighting you?"

"Yes."

"So now it has been cut away, are you better?"

"The doctor is not sure. It might have spread."

"The anger?"

"Yes, de anger," she replied.

"Why is your body angry with you?"

"I don't know."

"Will you still have any children?" he asked.

She laughed uncomfortably.

"Why do you ask dat?"

"Well, you'll need your breast to feed them."

"I still have one."

They both laughed at this. Then, seeing that his attention was riveted on the rumpled scar tissue, not quite healed in parts, she took his hand.

"Would you like to touch it?"

"Will my body become angry too if I touch it?"

"No, silly."

He nodded and she placed his hand over the torn flesh. He moved it up and down, intrigued by the texture. She closed her eyes against the tenderness; then gently she pulled his hand from her.

"Come, get in bed now and sleep," she said.

"What do you mean, she doesn't have a breast?" Efua asked.

"I swear to God. She doesn't."

They were lying in the shade of some mango trees that grew in a clump by the river. They could hear, further upstream, the sound of women talking as they fetched water and washed vegetables and roots for cooking; downstream from them, the squeals of children swimming and the shouted warnings from the adults in their separate bathing sections, the men closest to the children, the women round the bend, hidden by shrubs. A boy ran up the hill glistening like a fish, all sun and water. At the top, he yelled and ran downhill at speed, disappearing from view halfway down the slope. The sound of him cannonballing into the water carried up to them. Elvis and Efua loved it here: close enough to everyone to feel part of things, yet far enough away so that they could be alone. Efua looked back from the river and the antics of the children to Elvis. At ten, she was only three years older than he was, yet her eyes looked ancient. Oye often cautioned her about her closeness to Elvis. It is unnatural for cousins to be as close as they were, always together, Oye would tell her.

Elvis caught her look and put down the mango he was eating.

"What? Why are you looking at me that way? I washed it before I began to eat it."

She smiled and lay back.

"Nothing."

"I'm telling you, she had no breast. She said the doctor cut it off because it was fighting with the rest of her body," he went on, thinking the look had something to do with her not believing him.

"Dat sounds painful," she said, massaging the small bumps on her chest. He looked at her and laughed.

"How would you know? Those things are not breasts."

"How many breasts have you seen?"

"Some."

The older women, in their fifties and sixties, often walked about with their chests bare. Even Oye did it. It was a custom that the British had not been able to stamp out in spite of fines and edicts, and one that the Catholic priests were happy to indulge. So he had seen his share of breasts, but he didn't feel the same tightness in his chest when he saw them as he did when he saw Aunt Felicia changing, or when Efua's tight buds brushed against him.

Efua stood up and stepped out of her dress and panties, standing naked as the tall elephant grass that grew around them.

"What are you doing?"

"Going for a swim," she said. "Coming?"

Before he could answer she was off and running, breaking the water in a clean slice. He watched, wishing he could swim that well. Shucking off his clothes, he was naked in seconds and went into a running jump, splashing into the water beside her. She squealed and slapped water into his face. They fought for a while; then, tiring, they lay back and paddled, trying to see who could stare up at the sun's glare longer. Near blind, they rolled over and trod water, playing water drums, their hands slapping the water in time.

"I'm getting out," she said, shivering.

He stopped slapping the water and stood before her. Her arms were held in a prayer pose, fingertips brushing her trembling lips, arms, like the wet wings of some rare river bird, between her breasts. He stared transfixed at her hardening nipples. Reaching out, he touched one of them, the way he had touched his mother's blank space. But this wasn't his mother, and this space wasn't blank. Efua's lips parted and he suddenly couldn't breathe. Where his mother's skin had the consistency of old, cracked leather, this felt more like the smoothness of a taut mango.

"Stop," she said, not moving.

He dropped his hand back into the water and they looked at each other oddly for a second; then he was slapping the water into her face and she was squealing with laughter and running for the bank. Dragged back by the water, every movement happened in slow motion.

"Be careful," Beatrice said to Elvis as he put the battery-powered record player down. "I just bought dat record player."

"I'm doing my best, stop picking on me," he said.

"Stop complaining and put on some music," Efua said.

"Shut up, you!"

"Both of you shut up!" Oye said.

"Guess what we are going to listen to?" Beatrice asked.

"Elvis," Efua replied. "We always listen to Elvis."

Beatrice laughed and set the plastic disk on the record player. The needle scratched the edge a few times as though undecided, then launched into the throaty call of Elvis Presley. Beatrice grabbed Elvis and began to dance with him. Her illness made her movements slow, although it wasn't hard to see they were once fluid and smooth. Dropping Elvis's hands, she grabbed Efua and pulled her up. Soon all three were dancing, watched by a laughing Oye.

It was dusk and the purple stain of night was deepening slowly. Lamps and electric lights, in scattered patterns, were coming on in the houses around theirs. From their veranda they could see the whole town unfolding like a jigsaw puzzle. The sicker Beatrice got, the more often she held these impromptu little music-and-dance sessions. There were soda and cookies and smoked meat on the table and they stuffed themselves with food and laughter and dancing.

Somewhere in the house a door slammed. Oye and Beatrice exchanged looks. Then Sunday walked out onto the veranda. He stopped by the record player and yanked the needle off the record. The kids stopped dancing.

"Why did you do dat?" Beatrice asked.

"What is wrong with you people? What are you celebrating? Your death?"

"Sunday!" Oye cautioned.

"Shut up, witch. I am not afraid of you!"

Elvis and Efua ran to hide behind Oye's skirt and Sunday turned back to Beatrice.

"By de time I come back, I want dis nonsense over! How will you get well when you don't listen to de doctor, you don't listen to me? Do you want to die?"

"Sunday, dere are children here," she replied.

He looked at her and raised his hand to strike her. It hung in the air between them as if he couldn't remember what he meant to do with it. With a sigh he wiped his face.

"Beatrice, see de kind of man I am becoming? Shit!"

And then he was gone, clumping loudly down the steps. The silence on the veranda followed him down the path until he disappeared from sight.

Edith Piaf groaned from the record player, settling like deep night over the veranda. In the flicker of storm lanterns, Oye and Beatrice sat sipping hot tea. Elvis sat on the mat on the floor next to his mother, while Oye sat in the wicker chair.

"Why is my father always so angry?" Elvis asked.

Beatrice smiled and ruffled his hair.

"He didn't used to be dat way. Not when I met him. He was full of life, and we would dance all night and he made me laugh all de time."

"Tha' was just in the beginning, when you were too blind to see him for what he was," Oye said.

"Mama! You never liked him."

"Uhum."

"It's dis sickness. It has infected him too."

"Does that mean his body is angry with him too? Will it start fighting him?"

"No, Elvis," Beatrice said. "It's your father's spirit dat is fighting him."

"And he's losing," Oye said, spitting into the darkness.

"Mama! Elvis, read your book. I have to write some things."

Beatrice had her journal open on her lap, pen poised to write. Elvis nodded and silently returned to the book he was reading.

It was about nine p.m. and Efua had been sent home. From the veranda they could see a line of farmers returning from the fields, which were located on communal land several miles from town and worked from before dawn to well after dusk with hoes and other manual tools. Elvis closed his book and watched as Beatrice wrote down a recipe for an herbal treatment that Oye was dictating to her. He watched her spidery handwriting spread across the page as though laying claim to an ancient kingdom.

"This is what the plant looks like," Oye said, handing her a plant. "Draw it next to the recipe. So you won't forget."

"What are you doing?" Elvis asked.

"Your mother is getting ready for her next life."

"By writing?"

"Yes, laddie, she is writing down tha things she wants to remember in her next life."

"Dead people don't come back, except as ghosts," he said.

"Yes they do, laddie."

"But Father Patrick says—"

"Oh, tha bloody church!" Oye exclaimed.

"Mama!" Beatrice said. Turning to Elvis, she said: "Don't argue with your grandmother."

"Yes, Ma," he said, his face wearing a sulky expression.

"Come closer," Beatrice said, pulling him close and handing him a pencil. "Here, draw next to me."

As he bent over the page next to his mother, his crude picture emerged next to her sophisticated one.

▼▼▼▼▼▼▼▼▼▼▼▼▼▼▼▼▼▼▼▼▼▼▼▼▼▼▼▼▼▼▼

ACHYRANTHES ASPER *L.*
(Igbo: Odudu Ngwere)

This is a weed common to abandoned farmlands, with a varied appearance and many branches, and can be a woody shrub or a climber, morphing shape, some healers say, depending on its mood. Its leaves are thin, smooth and ovoid in shape, covered sparely with coarse hair. Small green or pink flowers are borne on common stalks that droop when full. These stalks look and feel like the tails of small lizards, which is what their Igbo name means.

The root, macerated in water, can be applied to relieve scorpion stings. It can also be used to help stunted or crippled limbs grow back straight because it contains the regenerative power of lizard tails. Some witches claim the flowers can help you forget the sting of a broken heart when dried and drunk like tea. The dosage must be carefully monitored, however, as too much can prove harmful.

2:00:00

FIVE

)))))

We do not define kola, or life. It defines us.

The kola nut is used in divination by dibias to discern the path of the petitioner. The dibia always asks the petitioner to bring an unbroken pod of kola nuts. The dibia then mutters an incantation and smashes the pod against the floor or a facing wall. The kola nut that lands at the dibia's feet is the one used for the divination.

)))))

Lagos, 1983 Elvis around age 16

Elvis was dressed for work in an old T-shirt and pants. He stood by his desk, checking through his backpack to make sure he had everything he wanted. He took out Rilke's *Letters to a Young Poet*, replacing it with the paperback of the Koran he'd bought off a street vendor. He wasn't a Muslim, but with the constant violence between Christians and Muslims, he wanted to see for himself if the Koran called for the death of infidels. He walked over to his bed and pulled his mother's journal from under his pillow. He had taken to sleeping with it there after Jagua Rigogo had suggested that it was the perfect way to contact her spirit in his dreams. It hadn't worked so far, but it brought him comfort to have it within reach. He often fell asleep rubbing his left fingertips against the worn leather.

There was a low knock on his door.

"Come in," he called out.

Comfort's son Tunji stood in the doorway. He was holding a red shirt.

"Brother Elvis," he began, employing the moniker of respect. "I iron your shirt for work."

Elvis opened his mouth to say that he hadn't asked for an ironed shirt and that it was impractical to wear a freshly ironed shirt to a job as a laborer on a building site. But Tunji seemed so sincere he just mumbled his thanks and took the shirt. As Tunji turned to leave, Elvis stopped him. Reaching into his pocket, he pulled out a one-naira note and handed it to him. Tunji accepted it gratefully.

On his way to work, Elvis stopped at Madam Caro's to get some breakfast. Seeing his already drunk father seated at a table pontificating, he moved on. Sunday's public drunkenness was hard for Elvis to watch. Although Sunday had always turned to alcohol when life became hard, back in their hometown there had been some dignity to his drinking. Perhaps it was because for the most part it had been conducted in the privacy of their house.

As he approached another buka, Elvis saw a man standing outside, begging the owner for food. The owner's heated response was attracting a small crowd. The man grabbed hold of the plate of food the owner was about to serve and desperately tried to wrench it from her, but she held on tightly. As they struggled for it, the plate gave way and fell to the floor, spilling food everywhere. The man pounced on it, triumphantly scraping rice and dirt into his mouth.

Elvis smiled, mentally celebrating the man's victory, small as it was. He entered the buka and sat down at one of the tables. Watching the man shoveling rice and dirt into his mouth tugged at him, and he counted the money in his pocket, doing some quick arithmetic. Satisfied that he could spare some, he called the man inside and ordered a steaming bowl of soup and fufu for him.

The man bolted the food, eating so fast his hand was a blur as he shoveled balls of fufu into his mouth. Apparently unaffected by the heat of the food, his prominent Adam's apple bobbed up and down like a piston. Finishing, the man drank deeply from a jug of water on the table, belched and let out a long-drawn-out sigh. He sat back and smiled at Elvis.

"If you need something, any time, just ask for me, Okon," he announced.

forshaddow

Elvis nodded distractedly. It seemed like every mendicant in Lagos was able to help him, first the King of the Beggars and now this man.

Okon grabbed Elvis by the hand.

"I dey serious my friend, nobody knows tomorrow. Remember—Okon."

Elvis looked from the intense eyes to the grip on his arm.

"Sure, Okon."

"Dat's me."

As he left the buka and walked to the bus stop, Elvis realized that nothing prepared you for Maroko. Half of the town was built of a confused mix of clapboard, wood, cement and zinc sheets, raised above a swamp by means of stilts and wooden walkways. The other half, built on solid ground reclaimed from the sea, seemed to be clawing its way out of the primordial swamp, attempting to become something else.

As he looked, a child, a little boy, sank into the black filth under one the houses, rooting like a pig. Elvis guessed it was some form of play. To his left, a man squatted on a plank walkway outside his house, defecating into the swamp below, where a dog lapped up the feces before they hit the ground. Elvis looked away in disgust and saw another young boy sitting on an outcrop of planking, dangling a rod in the water.

reminded him of his mother

Looking up, Elvis saw a white bungalow. Its walls were pristine, as though a supernatural power kept the mud off it. The small patch of earth in front of it held a profusion of red hibiscus, pink crocuses, mauve bachelor's buttons and sunflowers. The sight cheered him greatly.

Elvis stayed late at work, and it was dark when he got home. He sank gratefully onto the shrieking springs of his bed.

Without knocking, Comfort stormed into his room. He found it hard to think of her as his stepmother, not only because she was not really married to his father, but also because her attitude wasn't maternal. He had often wrestled with not knowing exactly what to call her, and how to think of her. Sometimes she and his father fought so much it seemed inevitable that they would separate. In fact his father had

(verbal)
Abusive
Father/husband

thrown her things out into the street a few times, demanding loudly that she leave, as she was no better than a harlot and a Jezebel. At other times they seemed very much in love, and during those times, public displays of affection, embarassing for Elvis and his stepsiblings, were common between Sunday and Comfort. She and Sunday lived in a solid impermanence that was confusing for him.

She had been a neighbor in a nearby tenement when Elvis and Sunday arrived in Lagos, and although his father was fleeing bankruptcy and a loss at the polls, Comfort somehow thought he had prospects; he was, after all, educated and had been a Board of Education superintendent. She began to woo him, and at the time, Elvis. Back then she allowed Elvis to call her Aunt Comfort instead of ma'am, and she cooked elaborate dinners for him and his father. Then, a few short months after this romance started, she simply moved in with them, bringing her three children, two boys and the youngest, a girl. Elvis didn't understand why, as she had the bigger place, while he and his father had a small two-bedroom apartment. He figured it would perhaps have been a blow to his father's ego to have to move into a woman's place. It seemed to Elvis that she just appeared in their home. He went to school and when he got home, she and her children were there. No explanation was ever offered him, and no one consulted him. But then, why would they? He was only a child.

As soon as she moved in, all the niceness vanished and he learned quickly that she had no time for anyone but herself—not his father, not him, not even her own children. Elvis initially forgave her abrasive manner because he thought she might shake his father out of his slump. And when Sunday began to go for job interviews, Elvis thought she had done just that. But he turned down the one firm offer he received when he found out that Comfort had bribed a member of the hiring committee with sex. Her nagging and their constant fighting drove his father further away from any career and deeper into drink. Their relationship had never made any sense to Elvis. He could not figure out why she had been attracted to his father in the first place, and why she stayed, except to torment them all. It had been Redemption who put it into perspective for him.

"A divorced woman with three children in dis society? Shit, dat's a hard life. She needed your father to give her some kudos. Dat's all. Simple. Now nobody can call her a harlot or wonder which man is supporting her. She only wanted de respectability dat being with a man can bring."

At the time, Elvis thought perhaps Redemption was right; but if that was indeed all she wanted, why was she so mad, so clearly disappointed?

"Who cares? I've told you, dat's all shit," Redemption had said. "Dat's bullshit," he had repeated for emphasis.

"Elvis, when you go pay rent?" Comfort asked. Her voice, several octaves above normal, coupled with her stern demeanor, suggested she was expecting a fight.

"Good evening," he said.

The implied insult over her lack of protocol did not go unnoticed.

"See dis small boy O! Don't cheek me, just pay rent."

"But this is not even your house," he responded. "It is my father's."

"Does ya father have a job? Does he pay de rent? Pay or pack out," she said.

"How much?" he asked. He did not have the energy for this.

"What?" Her reply betrayed her surprise. Either this tirade was not about the rent or she had expected more of a fight.

"The rent, how much?" he repeated.

"Three hundred naira," she said.

He counted out the money from the roll held together with an elastic band and carried in his pocket. Handing it to her, he returned the rest to his pocket. She took the money and folded it into her bra and flounced out. He lay back and shut his eyes.

He was just about to drift off when his door squeaked open on rusty hinges. He sat up. Comfort was back, and when she did not move from her place at the door, Elvis looked at her with raised eyebrows, the way he remembered Roger Moore doing in *The Saint*.

"Ya papa no dey house," she said.

"I know," he replied. "So?"

"Elvis, I dey fear. He drink too much. More than before."

"What are you afraid of?" he asked.

She shrugged. There was some silence. Then she spoke, her voice breaking slightly.

"Ya papa no love me."

Elvis yawned. He couldn't care less whether his father loved her or not.

"Na ya mama he love. Every night when he dey sleep, him go call her—'Beatrice, Beatrice, soon, soon.'"

Elvis sat up.

"I dey fear say ya papa want to kill himself with drink," she went on.

"My father hasn't got the courage to do that," he said.

"He want to kill himself to join ya mama. Only you fit help him."

"Me? He doesn't love me either, how can I help him?"

"Elvis," she said, catching hold of his arm. "I never talk to you like dis before. I beg you be like son to him."

Elvis was a mess of conflicting emotions. He'd been pretty sure that he hated his father, and now he had this strange urge to help him. He didn't believe his father would actually kill himself, but he knew Sunday certainly had self-destructive tendencies. But why was Comfort telling him all this? What did she expect him to do? He felt the walls closing in on him. He shrugged off her hold.

"This is nonsense. I am going out now, excuse me," he said, standing up and walking past her.

He had no idea where he was going, but after a while he realized that unconsciously he'd taken a bus to one of Lagos's oldest ghettos, Aje. It was nothing like Maroko. It had no streets running through it, just a mess of narrow alleys that wound around squat, ugly bungalows and shacks. It occupied an area the size of several city blocks, and the main road ran to a halt at either side, ending in concrete walls decorated with graffiti. This was where Redemption lived.

It took Elvis a while to find Redemption's tenement, a squat bungalow with rooms built around a paved courtyard. Across the street was a kiosk that sold everything from cigarettes by the stick to candy and liquor. In front of it, a man sat on a bench picking a tune out of a guitar

whose appearance belied its rich tone. Stopping, he bought two beers
and headed down the long corridor to Redemption's rooms at the back.

"Madam, bring me one bottle!" Sunday shouted. "And one for
everybody here!"

He hadn't left the bar since he got there early in the morning. He
looked around for Benji, but he was not there.

"Em, Mr. Philanthropist, before you give anoder person drink, pay
for de one you done drink."

"Haba, madam, why are talking like dis? It is me, Sunday de ty-
coon. When my numbers win lottery I will make you rich."

"You never win lottery since de past twenty years, so why you go
win it next week? Please pay me money."

"Madam, dis is me, don't be like a sourpuss."

"Who are you? Money for hand, drink on de table. Simple."

"Hah! dis woman wicked O!"

"I am wicked, eh . . ."

"Ah, not you, madam, I mean my wife."

The madam of the bar smiled. She was very ready to extend credit
to all her customers, who were mostly poor and unemployed anyway.
But even her generosity had its limits, though she understood that they
had come to drown their sorrows in her watered-down alcohol. They
needed her and she needed them; they drank, she sold. If she was
owed, she owed the palm wine supplier, who owed someone else;
everyone owed someone these days, it was the vogue. But she needed
to crack the whip from time to time just enough so that her customers
did not take her for granted.

"Madam, how about one bottle on my account?"

"Which account? Dis place look like bank to you? Cash sale only."

Sunday gazed stubbornly at the palm wine seller, who in turn tried
to stare him down, but Sunday was used to this. They played it out
every night and the palm wine seller always lost. He felt confident of
victory. It was only a matter of minutes.

"You want to drink but you have no money," she said, her resolve
already weakening.

*   *   *

"We've got to start thinking beyond our guns," Redemption said, slamming down his checker piece and picking up the three he had just killed.

"Damn!" Kansas said as he watched his pieces leave the board.

Elvis took a swig of beer. "What guns?"

"What guns?" Redemption repeated, his eyes never leaving the board. "Don't you remember dat film, *De Wild Ones*?"

"*Wild Bunch*," Kansas corrected, taking one of Redemption's pieces.

"You're sure it's not *Wild Ones*?" Redemption said.

"Want to bet?" Kansas asked with a crooked smile.

Redemption recognized the confidence in the smile and declined.

"But what has this got to do with my father and me?" Elvis asked, sounding more than a little frustrated.

"Crown me, crown me king!" Kansas shouted as he won.

"Fuck dis," Redemption swore, getting up and letting someone else slide into his place. He had just lost ten naira. They were sitting in the backyard of Redemption's tenement, where there was a money game every night. Kansas and Redemption were the usual winners, making enough to pay their rent.

"See how your constant distraction cost me money?" Redemption said, sitting down next to Elvis on an upturned bucket. He reached for Elvis's beer and took a deep drink.

"Ten naira is chicken change to you. I need advice," Elvis said, wresting the beer bottle back and draining it.

"But talking is thirsty business," Redemption said.

"Please, I just bought you a bottle of beer. You know I don't have that kind of money. I am a laborer."

"Okay, okay. Let me treat you," Redemption said, handing money to one of the kids hanging around the game. "Go and get me two beers."

"Three!" Kansas shouted from his game.

"Three," Redemption repeated to the kid.

"Four," someone else shouted.

"Your mother!" Redemption shouted back. "So remember what I just said?" he continued, turning back to Elvis.

"Something about thinking with guns from *The Wild Bunch*."

Redemption shook his head.

"I said we got to think beyond our guns. See you spend your whole life fighting with your father and no time on making your own life. What will you do when he dies? Fight yourself?"

good thought

"What of you?" Elvis asked.

"Me too. I spend my life hustling for small money, staying one step ahead of de police. But I will not do dat all my life. You see, I done read Napoleon Hill and as a thinking man, and with de grace of God, I go be millionaire before I reach thirty."

"So what is your plan?"

"What's dat thing they say on dat TV show?"

"What show?"

"*Bassey and Company*, by Ken Saro-Wiwa."

"I don't know."

"Dat's why you are poor. Bassey always says, 'To be a millionaire, you must think like a millionaire.'"

"So something someone said on a television show is your plan?"

"Dis Elvis, you no get faith. Television is de new oracle. No, I go show you my plan."

Redemption looked around carefully. Satisfied that everyone's attention was centered on Kansas's game, he reached under his shirt and pulled out a pouch attached to his neck by a heavy chain. Unzipping it, he pulled out a crisp green passport.

"See dis?" he said, opening the passport.

"What?'

"Dis," Redemption said, passing the passport to Elvis. "Visa to States."

Elvis held the passport and stared at the colored stamp inside it, unable to fathom its importance. Redemption saw the lack of comprehension on his face and explained.

"With dis stamp inside my passport, I can go to United States, act inside film and make millions."

"I see," Elvis said, not quite seeing but liking the possibility of being in a film with the real Elvis. "How did you get it? I know the pass-ports are easy to come by, but an American visa? I heard people wait months outside the embassy and don't even get an appointment."

Redemption laughed.

"You are asking original area boy how I get de visa? I use connec-tion, de same way I go get movie deal."

Elvis nodded gravely, though he couldn't take Redemption seri-ously. It sounded like another mad scheme; and anyway, from the back issues of the show-biz magazine *Entertainment*, which he often read at the United States Information Service Library on Victoria Island, he gathered that getting into films was hard enough for American profes-sional actors—so what chance did Redemption stand? Still, Elvis said nothing. He had been using the USIS Library for about a year, having found out about it from a flyer he saw at the local library, which had so few books he had to pace his borrowing so as not to finish them all too quickly. Apart from the endless old tomes on chemistry, physics, elec-tronics and philosophy, the local library had an anthropology section that only had books with the word "Bantu" in their titles—like *Bantu Philosophy* and *Bantu Worldviews*. Something about the word "Bantu" bothered him and made him think it was pejorative. Maybe it had something to do with not ever hearing that word used outside of that section in the library. The only other books there were treatises on Russian and Chinese culture and politics. These came either printed in bold glossy colors or in badly bound volumes with the fading print slanted on the page as if set by a drunken printer or as though, tired of the lies, the words were trying to run off the page. So it had been with some relief that he spotted the USIS flyer on the bare cork bulletin board.

He gave the passport back. It seemed to him that everyone wanted to leave for America. Just last month, he overheard his father say Aunt Felicia was leaving for America in a few weeks to meet her husband, who had lived there since the late sixties. He had come back to meet and marry Aunt Felicia in an arranged wedding a year before, although neither Elvis nor his father had gone back to Afikpo for the ceremony. Elvis couldn't afford to; Afikpo was nearly eight hundred miles away.

He mused over his mixed feelings. His fascination with movies and

Elvis Presley aside, he wasn't really sure he liked America. Now that the people he cared about were going there, he felt more ambivalent than ever.

"Listen, Elvis, stop living like dis, you know? If you are going to do dis dancing thing seriously, den do it. Join proper concert troupe and tour de country. I hear dere is money in dat. But if you just wan' to annoy your father, den you are wasting your life."

Elvis looked hard at the floor while Redemption spoke. He had thought about the dance troupe route, especially when he saw a good troupe featured on television. But he was afraid that he wasn't good enough. There was a positive side to not trying at something: you could always pretend that your life would have been different if you had.

"On de oder hand, if you want to make more money for less work, let me hook you up," Redemption continued.

"What makes you think I am doing this to annoy my father?"

"I don't. Listen, I wan' go beat dese amateurs, tomorrow is rent day."

He then got up and went to rejoin the game of checkers, and as Elvis left, he heard Redemption raising the stakes.

Pensive on the bus ride home, Elvis did not pay too much attention to the cars that in spite of their speed wove between each other like the careful threads of a tapestry. The motorways were the only means of getting across the series of towns that made up Lagos. Intent on reaching their own destinations, pedestrians dodged between the speeding vehicles as they crossed the wide motorways. It was dangerous, and every day at least ten people were killed trying to cross the road. If they didn't die when the first car hit them, subsequent cars finished the job. The curious thing, though, was that there were hundreds of overhead pedestrian bridges, but people ignored them. Some even walked up to the bridges and then crossed underneath them.

Elvis was pulled back to the present as the car in front of the bus hit someone. The heavy wheels of the bus thudded over the inert body, spinning into another lane. Elvis winced and turned to the man next to him.

"We are crazy you know. Did you see that?"

"Uh-huh," the man grunted.

"Why can't we cross with the bridges? Why do we gamble with our lives?"

"My friend, life in Lagos is a gamble, crossing or no crossing."

"But why not even the odds a little? Did you know that they have soldiers standing on the islands in the middle of the roads to stop people from crossing the busy roads instead of using the overhead walkways?'

"Ah, dat's good," the man said.

"Yes, but that's not the point. Why do we need to have soldiers there to tell us it is dangerous to cross the road?"

"I don't understand."

"If you cross the road without using the overhead bridges, you increase the chances of being hit by a car. Simple logic, really."

"So what is your point, my friend? We all have to die sometimes, you know. If it is your time, it is your time. You can be in your bed and die. If it is not your time, you can't die even if you cross de busiest road. After all, you can fall from de bridge into de road and die. Now isn't dat double foolishness?"

Elvis stared at him, shook his head and went back to staring out of the window.

Outside, the road was littered with dead bodies at regular intervals. "At least take away the bodies," he muttered to himself.

"Dey cannot," the man interjected into his thoughts. "Dis stupid government place a fine on dying by crossing road illegally. So de relatives can only take de body when dey pay de fine."

"What about the State Sanitation Department?"

"Is dis your first day in Lagos? Dey are on strike or using de government ambulances as hearses in deir private business. Dis is de only country I know dat has plenty ambulances, but none in de hospitals or being used to carry sick people. One time, American reporter dey sick in Sheraton Hotel, so he call for de ambulance. De hospital tell him dat he must book in advance and dat de nearest available time is de following Tuesday. When de hotel staff insist, talk say de man was about to die, de ambulance department told dem dat dey only carry dead people for a fee as part of funeral processions. If de man was alive, dey suggest make de hotel rush him to de hospital by taxi," the man continued, laughing.

"How can you find that funny? That is the trouble with this country. Everything is accepted. No dial tones or telephones. No stamps in post offices. No electricity. No water. We just accept."

"Listen, my friend, anybody rich enough to afford telephone in country where most people dey fight for survival, dey should have de decency to wait for a dial tone."

Elvis could hardly wait for his stop and trudged home wearily, shoes ringing out on the walkways. It was late and much of Maroko was asleep, awash with moonlight. In the distance a woman sang in a sorrow-cracked voice that made him catch his breath, stop and look around. In that moment, it all looked so beautiful, like a sequence from one of the films he had seen. Then the silence was broken by the approach of menacing steps. He turned and saw several figures coming toward him.

"Hey!" one of them called.

Alarm bells went off in Elvis's head and he took off at speed, trying to keep his balance on the walkway. The figures chased him for a while, their laughter following him. He did not stop until he got home and slammed his door behind him.

Redemption was right; he had to think with more than his guns.

THE CALL TO PRAYER (ISLAM)

God is most great. God is most great.
God is most great. God is most great.
I testify that there is no god except God
I testify that there is no god except God
I testify that Muhammad is the messenger of God
I testify that Muhammad is the messenger of God
Come to prayer! Come to prayer!
Come to success in this life and the hereafter!
Come to success!
God is most great. God is most great.
There is no god except God.

2:35:24

SIX

◆◆◆◆◆

The shape is always traced by a divine finger. Look always to the King's head for the star. It never lies.

The ideal kola nut has four lobes, which join at the nut's apex, in the shape of a star. The four-lobed kola nut is rare. The most common is two-lobed. The number of lobes, determined by the line running across the kola nut's apex, determines what kind of person the petitioner is.

◆◆◆◆◆

Afikpo, 1976   *Elvis is about 9 years old*

Friday. Under the stern but amused gaze of Oye and the excited, not-missing-anything nine-year-old intensity of Elvis, spread on raffia mats on the veranda, Aunt Felicia and her friends settled down to prepare for the weekend and the parties they wanted to attend. The formal year-long mourning period for Elvis's mother had just ended. The entire family had performed the full rites, with the exception of his father. Igbo men didn't mourn women publicly. It was considered bad taste.

The giggling girls had an air of excitement about them that blew through the mustiness of their grief with a welcome freshness. Gone were the unkempt hair and black clothes, and it seemed to Elvis that he had only just become aware of color, seeing it everywhere and in everything, vividly. From the radio in the corner, the Reverend Al Green crooned, "I'm so tired of being alone, I'm so tired . . ."

The girls plaited their hair into wild and wonderful shapes: sensuous cornrows that disappeared on the horizon of the head, holding the promise of love; straight fingers reaching up to graze the face of the sky; bangs that fell in spiral caress around their faces, or natural locks interwoven with cowrie shells and bits of silver and gold. Aunt Felicia had invented a plait called Concorde, complete with a *Concorde*-shaped aircraft taxiing down the crown of the head to the nape. She and her friends swapped makeup tips, tweezed eyebrows into thin whispers, hot-combed their hair into burned flat runs or Afro blowouts that eclipsed the sun every time they walked by, suffering as they singed, pulled, tied and yanked. Shaved hair from armpits and legs fell in among giggled methods of birth control, the most popular being to drink a bottle of bitter lemon after sex.

"Kills de sperm," Aunt Felicia said.

Elvis longed to try on their makeup and have his hair plaited. Aunt Felicia finally gave into his badgering and wove his hair into lovely cornrows. One of the other girls put lipstick on him. Giggling, and getting into the game, another pulled a minidress over his head. On Elvis, it fell nearly to the floor, like an evening gown. He stepped into a pair of Aunt Felicia's too-big platforms and pranced about, happy, proud, chest stuck out.

Looking up, he saw his father, Sunday, coming up the path. Aunt Felicia and Oye took in Sunday's approaching figure with alarmed gasps and then looked back at Elvis's cornrowed hair, painted face and dress, but it was too late. Elvis had kicked off the platforms and was halfway down the steps running to meet Sunday. He thought that somehow his father would like him better with the new hairdo. Sunday had not been the same since Beatrice died and he'd lost all interest in his son, except to reprimand or punish him. Sunday stopped and squinted as Elvis approached, face changing in slow degrees from amusement to shock and finally to rage.

Elvis ran straight into the first blow, which nearly took his head clean off. As he fell, his father grabbed him with one hand, steadying him, while with the other he beat him around the head, face, buttocks, everywhere. Too shocked to react, still out of breath from his sprint, Elvis gulped for air as his father choked him. Suddenly, Oye towered beside them. Sunday glanced at the steel of her eyes and dropped Elvis like a rag. She caught him, enfolding him into her as he sobbed himself into unconsciousness.

When he came to, he was cocooned in Oye's soothing and healing smell. His lip was cut and he couldn't see out of one eye, but he could hear his father ranting in the backyard, giving Aunt Felicia a rough time.

"No son of mine is going to grow up as a homosexual! Do you hear me?!" he shouted at her.

Elvis could not hear her mumbled response.

"When you have your own children, you can do what you like. But Elvis is my son. Son, not daughter . . ."

Aunt Felicia's voice cut him off.

"Don't interrupt me when I am speaking—otherwise I will beat de living daylights out of you!" he screamed.

"Sunday!" Oye called.

There was silence from the backyard as Sunday stamped out front.

"Stay out of my life, witch!" he shouted at her.

In one hand, flush with his thigh, was an open razor, its metal honed to a cruel edge. Oye took in the razor with a glance and, putting Elvis down slowly, rose to her feet. Never taking her eyes from Sunday's, she reached out and pincered her fingers into a vise around his scrotum. He screamed in pain and dropped the razor.

"Don't you ever threaten me, laddie," she said quietly.

"I was not threatening you," he whispered through tears. "I only want to shave de boy's head."

"Fine. But if ye hurt him again . . ." She smiled sweetly, letting go of him.

He sighed into the floor and squatted there panting.

"Put on your slippers," he said to Elvis between gasps.

Elvis stepped into the plastic-and-foam flip-flops. He stood, waiting for his father to tell him what to do next, his breathing fast. Picking up the razor that he had dropped, Sunday stood and led Elvis by the hand out to the back. As they left, Elvis looked pleadingly at Oye. She smiled reassuringly at him and looked away. The echo of his flip-flops slapping the cement floor filled her mind.

When they got out back, Sunday pulled up a small stool for Elvis. "Sit dere," he said gruffly.

Elvis sat. His father walked across the yard to the kitchen in the corner and lifted the large kettle of water that was always smoldering over the slow-dying coals. Elvis watched, shifting from side to side. Next, his father pulled a metal pail across the floor and began filling it with steaming water from the kettle. It reminded Elvis of the preparations made for plucking chickens, and as soon as his father's back was turned, Elvis got up and began to tiptoe away.

"Sit back down," his father said without turning round.

It was the quiet way in which he said it that had Elvis bolt back to the stool and sit down. He continued to watch his father as he mixed some cold water into the hot, testing the mixture with his elbow before bringing it over.

"Now sit still so dat I don't hurt you," he said.

Elvis nodded. Humming under his breath, his father mixed up some shaving foam in a cup and then, with a painter's flourish, began to apply it with a brush to Elvis's head. Elvis, eyes closed, began to tingle all over, like when the barber's electric clippers buzzed lightly over his scalp. Once he had applied the foam, Sunday pulled up a chair and held Elvis tightly between his knees to keep him from making any sudden moves.

When the razor made contact, it buttered through the cornrowed hair with a sandpaper rasp. The pull of it was like the rough lick of a cat's tongue, and Elvis felt himself relaxing into his father's body.

"Stupid child, make sure you don't fall asleep," his father said gently. "For your own good," he continued under his breath. "I'm only doing dis for your own good. It's not easy to be a man. Dese are trying times. Not easy."

When he finished, he washed Elvis's scalp in the leftover warm water in the pail. After drying it, he applied palm-kernel oil. When he was done, he turned Elvis around and, holding his face in his hand, spoke slowly.

"I don't want you spending any more time on dat veranda."

*   *   *

It was afternoon and the sun slam-dunked onto corrugated-iron roofing and concrete, turning the houses into ovens, despite fans doing slow waltzes on ceilings. Outside, the tarmac roads turned to treacle. The adults were at work and Elvis and his friends were playing in the orchard. Apart from Oye, dozing in her wicker chair on the veranda, her snores loud enough to keep flies from settling on her open mouth, the house and compound were deserted. Efua was staying over, as she often did, and was asleep inside, as she was feeling ill. Elvis left the others playing and headed for the outhouse, one of those bucket affairs that had to be emptied regularly. Despite the powdered disinfectant scattered after each use, it stank in the heat and was home to tomb flies as big as helicopters.

He banged out of the toilet, not seeing the man who emptied the bucket standing waiting for him. Elvis leapt back, startled. Dung men were understandably aggressive and bad tempered, and the dung man was not smiling.

"Do you have my money?" he asked Elvis through the handkerchief that muffled half of his face. Elvis nodded. They all knew where the dung man's money was kept, because if he wasn't paid on time, he left a stinky gift on the front step.

As he dashed for the house to get the money, Elvis noticed Uncle Joseph's car in the drive. He got the money from its place in the top drawer of the sideboard and on his way out heard whimpering and what sounded like a strangled sob. It was coming from the room he shared with Aunt Felicia. Efua shared it with them when she stayed over. He gently eased the door open. Efua was lying on the bed, legs spread wide, while Uncle Joseph grunted away between them. Efua stared straight at him, her teeth biting her lower lip. Apart from the tears streaming down her face and the soft birdlike mews coming from somewhere in her throat, her face was impassive.

Hatred and revulsion filled his nostrils and head, leaving a harsh taste on his tongue. But he felt something else too, underneath the reflex to retch. Little snakes of sensation crawled all over his body. And though he wanted to rush in and scream at Uncle Joseph, push him off and beat him to pulp, he watched instead, his breath coming in short,

Elvis didn't do anything?!?! (handwritten)

rapid bursts. And the saddest thing was that he knew Efua could see the lust in his eyes. He shut the door gently and left.

Later, when Uncle Joseph had gone, Elvis stole back into the room. Efua was curled up in a fetal position on the bed. In one hand she clutched a hug cloth while she sucked the thumb of the other. Tears still streamed down her face, and her left leg was trembling badly. She looked up when he came in, and he felt his gut twist.

"Elvis," she whispered.

He sat down beside her on the bed, face averted, afraid to look at her. He felt her hand on his face, tracing his features.

"I'm sorry," he said, tears running down his face as he turned to look at her.

She seemed surprised by his tears and reached out her hand to wipe them away. Putting the hug cloth down, she reached up and pulled him to her tiny body, all the while humming a lullaby softly under her breath.

"Sssh, it's not your fault," she whispered. *She's comforting him?* (handwritten)

Elvis burst out of a crowded alley in the market straight into the arena occupied by the magicians. He was still disoriented and disturbed about what had happened to Efua the day before; otherwise he'd have known better than to come this way. The arena was packed tight with a crowd that was rippling and alive. A parked van with roof-rack-mounted loudspeakers blared out loud, garish music.

Two boys in high wigs, dark sunglasses and white long-sleeve shirts, gloves, trousers and white canvas shoes danced to the music, bodies fluid. Sweat streamed down their faces and their shirts stuck to their bodies in a wet embrace. Rings of red dust formed around their trouser cuffs, kicked up by their feet. These Ajasco dancers moved to Elvis Presley's "Hound Dog." Watching, mesmerized, Elvis realized then what he wanted to do more than anything else.

Mouth open in wonder at the dancers' dexterity, Elvis moved his feet along in silent learning. Clumsy, he kicked up too much red dust and got clobbered on the head by angry bystanders. Just then a dwarf broke into the circle of dancers, ringing a bell almost as tall as he was. The music came to an abrupt end with an annoying vinyl-scratching screech. Ignoring the voices raised in protest, the dwarf began announcing the next act, a magic show by the world-famous Professor Pele, whom Elvis had never heard of.

Professor Pele was dressed in red robes like a Tuareg. He was silent, and his eyes were wide and unblinking. The dwarf shouted to be heard above the crowd's murmuring and the clang of the bell that he was still ringing.

"Today, ladies and gentle," he began. "Today, de wonderful Professor Pele is here to show you magic—Arabian, Indian and American magic."

For emphasis, Professor Pele threw a fireball conjured out of thin air. The crowd gasped in fear and stepped back, letting out a collective "aaah."

"American wonder. Come and see American wonder." The dwarf broke into the one-refrain song. "Come and see American wonder, come and see American wonder." There was a hypnotic quality to it that soon had the crowd joining in, echoing the heady chant.

"American wonder! American wonder!"

"Okay, I'll need someone to assist in some magic," the dwarf said.

As one, the crowd shrank back, except for the starstruck Elvis. He found himself being herded forward against his will. Falling away like palm fronds from a sprung, once-concealed trap, the crowd left him alone in the middle of its circle with the magician and the dwarf. Riveted, eyes fixed on the arena, the crowd and even the dancers watched. Meanwhile, pickpockets, part of the magician's crew, worked them.

Professor Pele took out a long and deadly-looking sword and with a wicked smile cut the air a few times. With a grunt and a low two-handed throw, the dwarf sent a papaw into orbit. Pele spun round, catching it in midair with his sword, slicing it in two. The crowd gasped; Elvis gulped.

The magician then ran the blade through his stomach and out the other side. There was no blood, no apparent pain. Smiling, he twirled around. Elvis began to sweat and backpedal as Professor Pele pulled the sword from his belly and advanced on him.

"Now Professor Pele go cut off dis young man head," the dwarf announced, pointing at Elvis. "Den join it back again."

Elvis passed out.

When he woke to slaps from Oye, he was home. He had no idea how he had got there.

"Stupid, stupid boy. Elvis, you want to kill me, eh? What were you doing with those wizards?"

"Nothing, Grandma. How did I get here?"

She slapped him again.

"How did you get here? A distant relative of your father saw you faint and brought you home. Do you know how lucky you are? I sent you to buy me kerosene, not entertain tha town. I heard tha' after you fainted, tha magician cut off your head and put it back on again. And you say nothing. Don't you know they can steal your soul and turn you into anything they want?"

Elvis suddenly felt cold. He wondered if this meant that he was now dead and had become a ghost or, worse, a zombie.

"If people find out, they will run away from me, Grandma. I will become like Mr. Jonah," he said tearfully.

Jonah had been a rich rice trader, with several wives. He had been revered and admired. Then he was in a car accident and lapsed into a coma for a few days. Thinking he was dead, his family took his body from the hospital bed late at night. It was important, they said, to ensure his soul could pass over with dignity, though of course the savings on the hospital bill wouldn't go amiss. His family was starting the funeral rites when Jonah came to and banged on the coffin, demanding to be let out.

They let him out, but everyone avoided him after that, saying he was now a demon who could only live by killing others. People walked straight past him on the road, eyes averted. He lost his business. His wives left him. Every day he got a little more invisible, until one day he just faded away completely. He could still be seen when the light was just right, sitting outside his hut sucking on an unlit pipe, muttering to himself.

"You should have thought of tha' before you made a spectacle of yourself in front of tha whole town," she said. "What do you want me to do? Cast a spell to make everyone forget?"

"Would you?"

She glared at him.

"Boy, don't make me knock your head off for real," she said. "I just hope he hasn't initiated you into witchcraft," she continued, forcing a disgusting unguent down his throat.

Afraid, he began mumbling prayers while she made passes over his head with eagle feathers and chalk. His prayer and her incantations interwove in the gathering dusk, calming them both.

BRYOPHYLLUM PINNATUM *S. KURZ*
(*Crassulaceae*)

The common name for this herb is "Never Die." It has opposite trifoliate leaves, which are almost rounded, but are larger towards the apex. The flowers are greenish yellow, with a purplish tint at the base. Their arrangement is loose and sometimes drooping on the common stalk.

This plant has several medicinal uses, which are not to be confused with its ritualistic applications. These medicinal uses include compresses for abscesses or swellings. In this case the leaves are crushed and mixed with shea butter or palm oil before being applied. It can also be used on ulcers and burns. It is used as a cure-all for young children when they are ill, and is believed to draw out bad humors when rubbed all over the body.

SEVEN

3:00:59

))))))

When the star is early on the King's head, the number is two. This is the number of most people. The lobes split between their heart and mind, the constant struggle.

Just like the kola nut, people have distinct lobes of energy. These determine their life plan. Four is the highest number, the King nut. The sorcerer. Three is the seer, the singer, and the shaper. Two is, for most, the struggle to learn love.

))))))

Lagos, 1983

Elvis is about 16

Elvis shaved hurriedly. He hated shaving, which was odd, considering that as a child he used to drench his chin in alcohol and mentholated spirit because he had been told it would help his facial hair grow. Having heard it worked on pubic hair too, he began to drench his crotch in it. He only stopped when the teacher reported him to his father for smelling of alcohol in school, the report coinciding with his father's discovery of an empty bottle of White Horse whiskey—one of his best bottles. Naturally he was severely caned. At least he hadn't had to live with the constant teasing his cousin Obed got. Not realizing exactly how pubic hair grew, Obed had taken the skin from a squirrel's tail and stuck it, fur side out, along the length of his penis.

Now here Elvis was, struggling with razors and bumps, trying to beat the clock. He was joined in the backyard by Jagua Rigogo. (Everyone knew that Jagua Rigogo wasn't his real name, yet no one bothered to find out what it really was.)

Jagua used to regale Elvis with stories of his astral projections to different planes of existence or, within this one, to different countries. He even claimed he had met with aliens on Venus who planned and controlled the future of the earth. His stories were peppered with mentions of arcane masters of wisdom who showed him the hidden truths of the universe. Cosmic mechanics, he called them. Then, just as swiftly, the stories would veer away from the cosmic and you would be back on earth, the story continuing seamlessly.

"India! Dat is a wonderful country. Streets paved in gold . . . almost as lovely as America," he would say.

Elvis would nod, inhaling Jagua's strange incense smell, half scared, half amazed.

"But you were just on Venus a minute ago," he would interject.

"Yes, but astral travel is not encumbered by time and space, you know. De arcane masters or cosmic mechanics who taught me dis were H. G. Wells and his brother, Orson."

"Do aliens even speak our language?"

"Ha, ha, ha. Funny child. Of course not, but I speak deir language, just like I speak de language of angels. Anyway, where was I?"

"India."

"Oh yes, India. Not to mention Australia. You know kangaroos carry de souls of dead aborigines in deir pouches . . ."

The myths and lies tumbled out and Elvis had believed everything, or at least wanted to. The sad thing was, Jagua did too. Now that he was older, Elvis realized there wasn't much truth in Jagua's fantasies.

Jagua yawned as he chomped on his chewing-stick and spat a fine spray of chewed fiber and spittle, scratched his belly and looked at Elvis.

"Good morning, Jagua," Elvis said.

"Elvis. You go late for work, you know. A punctual man is a spiritual man," he replied.

"I'm just leaving now," Elvis said.

"Good."

Elvis was about fifteen minutes late, and as soon as he got to work he sensed the tense atmosphere. It was the way nobody would meet his eyes. His feeling of unease grew as he walked through the large compound to his station. He had been late before, so what was the big deal now? As he bent to lift a freshly mixed pan of cement onto his head, the chief mason stopped him gently.

"De site manager want to see you," he said, his calloused palm gently rubbing Elvis's arm.

It didn't sound good. It was bad enough when the foreman wanted to see you; but the site manager, well, that was a different matter altogether. Elvis had only seen the site manager from a distance, and there had been no reason for them to speak. Elvis set the head pan down and crossed the compound to the site manager's caravan, tapping quietly on the door.

"Come in!" a voice barked.

Elvis opened the door and stepped into the cool air-conditioned interior. The floor was covered in plush carpeting and he instinctively took off his mud-splattered shoes, even though he did not step off the rough hemp doormat into the room. The site manager was a young man, in his early thirties. When Elvis came in he was reading a James Hadley Chase novel. He put it down and regarded Elvis through bored eyes.

"Yes?" he asked.

"You asked to see me," Elvis replied.

"See you?"

"I am the laborer from section six, sir."

"Oh yes, section six. So you are de habitual latecomer?" As he spoke, he flipped through some papers on his desk.

"Sir?"

"De habitual latecomer," he repeated.

"No, sir. I have been late only once or twice before. I am sorry, sir. It will not happen again."

The site manager stared at Elvis for a long time. He hated having to deal with these people. Firing and hiring laborers was not his department, but since he had fired the foreman that morning, he had to do this dirty work now. His father, who owned the construction company, had called and told him to lay off as many people as he could, starting with the foreman—something about being over budget.

"I am terminating your appointment. As from now."

was fired?

"Please, sir . . ."

"Don't beg. Don't waste my time. Just get out."

"But my wages for—"

"Before I count five you should be gone, otherwise I will have some of de boys eject you forcibly. One, two, three . . ."

There really wasn't a lot Elvis could do, so he shuffled out of the compound. None of the other workers looked at him, partly from shame, partly to avoid contagion from his bad luck. He didn't blame them. He would have done the same in their place.

As he waited at the bus stop, he noticed that the traffic had come to a complete standstill and people were running, pursued by policemen, soldiers and local government officials in their dirty brown uniforms. A crowd gathered round a bonfire that was steadily growing in size.

"What happened here?" Elvis asked a groundnut-and-banana hawker who dashed past him.

"It is task force," was the curt reply. It sounded ominous, connoting horror so strong that Elvis shivered and looked up quickly, half expecting to see some malevolent manifestation.

A man came running toward him, carrying some clothes on hangers, a policeman hot on his heels. Just before he got to where Elvis stood, the man tripped and fell. The policeman pounced on him and snatched the clothes away, carrying them to the raging bonfire and throwing them in. As they crinkled and burst into flame, Elvis, drawn to the fire, walked over and stood watching.

The heat slowly crumbled the fuel and the flames reflected off the face of the fallen man. Still prone from the policeman's tackle, he watched the fire slowly turn his goods into a mass of hot ashes.

"But I get ten children," he mumbled over and over. "How I go feed dem?"

Unsure why, Elvis put his arm around the man's shoulders and helped him to his feet.

"Take heart, brother," he said.

The man turned to him.

"I try to make money begging, but my spirit wan' die. So I borrow money, begin to sell dese Okirika."

Elvis nodded. He knew the man was referring to the secondhand clothes smuggled in from Cameroon through the port town of Okirika.

"Every day I go walk up and down, ringing one small bell make people see me," the man continued, his voice breaking. He stared into the blaze and the flames ripped through his heart, the fire entering him. His mind reached back and, like a dead star, collapsed upon itself. He screamed. It was sudden. The sound startled Elvis, who let go of the man and jumped back. It also startled the crowd of strangers and other spectators gathered round the fire, and they turned to look. The man screamed again and tore his clothes off, dancing around the fire naked, emitting piercing calls, bloodcurdling in their intensity.

Before anyone could react, he jumped into the fire. As the flames licked around him, it seemed the fire smacked its lips in satisfaction. And in the fire, he continued to yell as he wrestled with it. The last thing Elvis heard before the man died was his terrible laugh. Its echo hung in the air. He never thought to ask the man's name.

"Ah, madman," someone sighed.

Elvis got off the bus and trudged past the buka where he normally ate. He lingered hungrily outside, but he couldn't shake the smell of burning flesh or the sight of the man writhing in the flames. He wondered why he hadn't helped. Instead, he had just stood rooted to the spot, staring.

A quick count of his money made it quite clear that he couldn't afford to buy a meal even if he could face it.

He turned away and headed home. It wasn't even noon yet, he noted. How was he going to spend the rest of his day? He had been fired from the building site, and his long absence from Iddoh Park and the beach had cost him his spot there. He needed money to buy a new spot, money he didn't have. He felt a little ashamed at how quickly the practical pressures of living had usurped the image of the burning man.

"Elvis!"

He spun around. A man stood in the open door of the buka,

dressed like Superfly. Elvis did not recognize him, and the man, noticing his confusion, explained.

"It's me. Okon."

It hit him. It was the man he had fed barely a week ago, at this same buka. Okon was the man who had scrabbled in the dirt for rice. How come he was so kitted out now? Had he taken to a life of crime? Elvis smiled at Okon, straining to mask his thoughts. He really wasn't in the mood for company, but his hunger got the better of him, so he went back. They sat facing each other, caught in an awkward silence broken only by Okon's occasional repetition of his name—"Yes. It's me. Okon. Okon"—as if this mantra would bond them. Finally he offered Elvis a drink and some food.

"Take anything you want—extra meat, stout, anything."

Elvis smiled uncomfortably and ordered some eba and egusi sauce.

"No big stout?" Okon asked sounding a little offended.

"No thanks. A Coke will be fine."

"Are you sure?"

"Yes."

Elvis ate in silence as Okon studied him. The buka's radio sounded like someone had drowned its speaker in muddy water; still, Elvis could clearly hear the Wings singing, "Please catch dat love dat is falling on you . . . Don't let it drop, it is not made of wood . . ." Elvis sang along in his head, wondering if it would be rude to ask Okon how he got the money he was spending.

"So why are you home so early?" Okon asked.

"I was fired."

"Oh. I'm sorry to hear dat. Why? You are a good person."

"You hardly know me," Elvis protested.

"I know you better dan you think."

He went back to drinking his stout, which, Elvis noted, seemed milky and thick, unlike any stout he had seen before. Noticing his confused look, Okon explained:

"It is concoction."

"Sorry?"

"Concoction; condensed milk and stout. Very good for your blood."

Elvis nodded. It sounded disgusting, he thought.

"I know you dey wonder how I manage get all dis money," Okon said.

Elvis shrugged, embarrassed.

"Dat's okay. I don't want you to think I am a tief, dat's why I tell you."

"That's quite okay, really," Elvis replied. "You don't have to explain anything to me. I don't think poorly of you."

"You are really a good man, but I'll tell you anyway."

Elvis was a little worried; he didn't want to be an accessory to any crime.

"Blood." Okon said simply.

Elvis was by now visibly agitated. Blood. Did that mean Okon was an assassin for hire? Lots of business rivals had turned to that as an effective system of beating competition. Could it be blood money? Elvis suddenly felt nauseous. Okon noted his expression with alarm and explained.

"Blood. De hospital, dey pay us to donate blood. One hundred naira per pint. If you eat well, you can give four pints in four different hospitals, all in one day. It's illegal, of course, but it's my blood, and it's helping to save lives, including mine. Right?"

Elvis smiled in relief. Okon smiled too.

"You can come too, now dat you don't have job," he urged.

"No, I don't think that's for me."

"But if you change your mind, let me know and I'll connect you."

Elvis finished the rest of his meal in silence and, getting up to leave, thanked Okon. As he began to walk home, he heard Okon call out: "Don't forget. Okon, dat's me."

Back in his room, Elvis sat in the rust-crisp metal chair facing his desk. Flakes of rust, like red dandruff, fell to the floor. With a sigh he unlocked the metal box he had just placed on the desk. It used to be his school box, holding his books all through primary school. He ran his fingers along the top and down to the handle, remembering the groove it had cut in his hand. It was still there, a hard calloused line.

Opening the box, he adjusted the mirror he had taped to the inside cover. Then, methodically, with the air of ritual, he laid out the contents: a small plastic compact of hard, pressed face powder, a few tubes of lipstick in different colors, a plastic case with eye shadow in several shades of blue, a small bottle of mascara with a brush hardening in it, an eye pencil and a tin of Saturday Night talc. He held up the tin of talc, admiring the image printed on it—a white couple in evening dress dancing under a sky full of stars. That was the life, he thought. Also laid out next to the box and its contents were a wig and a pair of sunglasses with wide frames studded with rhinestones.

The old battery-powered record player scratched through "Heartbreak Hotel," a stack of coins keeping the stylus from jumping through the worn grooves. Elvis nodded along, singing under his breath as he mixed the pressed powder with the talc. The lumpy powder crumbled in cakes of beige, reminding him of the henna cakes Oye ground to make the dye she used to paint designs all over her body. Satisfied with the mix, he began to apply it to his face with soft, almost sensual strokes of the sponge. As he concentrated on getting an even tone, his earlier worries slipped away. Finishing, he ran his fingertips along his cheek. Smooth, like the silk of Aunt Felicia's stockings.

With the tip of his index finger, he applied a hint of blue to his eyes, barely noticeable, but enough to lift them off the white of his face. Admiring himself from many angles, he thought it was a shame he couldn't wear makeup in public. That's not true, he mentally corrected himself. He could, like the transvestites that haunted the car parks of hotels favored by rich locals and visiting whites. But like them, he would be a target of some insult, or worse, physical beatings, many of which were meted out by the police, who then took turns with their victims in the back of their vans. It was exasperating that he couldn't appear in public looking as much like the real Elvis Presley as possible.

Drawing quickly and expertly with the black eye pencil, he outlined his eyes, the tip of the pencil dancing dangerously close to his cornea. Pulling the mascara brush free, he knocked the dried goop off before dragging it through his already dense lashes. Again he examined his hard work intently before selecting a deep red lipstick. Not satisfied with its shine, he rubbed some petroleum jelly over his lips and then smacked them. Much better, he thought.

He got up to change the record, which was dragging its stylus reluctantly and noisily across the label. He put it into its sleeve carefully and checked the sharpness of the needle by running a fingertip across it. This also cleaned the dust on the needle's point. Selecting "Jailhouse Rock," he blew imaginary dust off the record. He was careful as he put it on, knowing from experience that the thick, heavy vinyl would shatter like a china plate if he dropped it.

He walked back to the table and pulled the wig on, bending to look in the mirror. Elvis has entered the building, he thought, as he admired himself. This was the closest he had come so far to looking like the real Elvis, and he wished he had a camera.

Pushing back from the table, he began to dance around the room. By the time the record had come to an end, he was perspiring heavily. Not wanting the makeup to run, he sat on the bed and put on the table fan he had bought from Redemption, a recent acquisition made possible by his job at the construction site. He let his fingers linger over the buttons as the truth of this day returned to him. From the bed, he could see himself in the mirror on the desk, and he stared hard. What if he had been born white, or even just American? Would his life be any different? Stupid, he thought. If Redemption knew about this, he would say Elvis was suffering from colonial mentality. He smiled. It spread across his face in fine tendrils that grew wider as he laughed until his skin showed through. I look like a hairless panda, he thought. Without understanding why, he began to cry through the cracked face powder.

Elvis stepped out of his room onto the front veranda and looked around, rubbing his sleep-crusted eyes with a couple of knuckles. He wiped his hand down his face and realized he had slept with the makeup on. After that heavy lunch with Okon, he had napped for a couple of hours.

Across the street, in the weak shade cast by the odd tree or veranda canopy, a few women lounged like melting toffee on the stoops. They sat with bored eyes, fanning themselves with magazines, newspapers or raffia fans. One or two chewed on sugarcane stems, mandibles crunching slowly, pausing only to spit sucked-out husks into the street, peppering the black asphalt in yellow-white blobs like tired snowflakes. A couple sat plaiting hair and chatting brightly as though to dispel the heavy air. A few very young children chased a football halfheartedly across the street, upturned empty paint tins serving as goalposts.

Taking a pack of cigarettes from his breast pocket, Elvis shook one out and lit it, his movements slow and deliberate. He scanned the street slowly from behind hands cupped around a flaming match, knowing he too was being watched, studied even. Smoking was a rediscovered pleasure for him, a way to make the day go faster. The smoke felt harsh against the back of his throat and he coughed discreetly. He had not smoked much since he was a kid watching old movies in the motor parks.

Pitching the still-smoldering stub into the street, he walked through the house and out into the backyard, which was walled in by the low building that housed the bathrooms, toilets and kitchens. To his left stood the iron staircase that led to the upper floors. Built in the fashion of an American fire escape, it looked rickety and unsafe and was covered in a rash of rust. Several stairs had been eaten away by the rust, giving the illusion of a gap-toothed mouth. The doors to the toilets stood open, aerating in the heat, walls adorned by drowsy bluebottle flies.

With a tired sigh, he sucked in his breath and slammed into one. As he squatted, he wondered how long he could hold his breath. On one wall of the toilet, the landlord, in an attempt to clean things up years ago, had painted a mural. Faded now from years of grime and heat, the river scene, with a mermaid holding a baby in one hand and a staff of power in the other and a python draped around her neck, was still discernible. A crown hovered over her black hair, and stars gleamed in the air around her blue body. Her face, however, was scratched out. He wondered who had done that, and how they could have endured the stench long enough to do it.

Grabbing a pail of water from the water drum, he headed into the bathroom to wash. He washed his face first, watching the makeup-colored water run onto the concrete floor. The water was pleasantly hot from the sun, and he felt refreshed when he got out. He returned to the veranda and waited for the sun to set while he flicked through his mother's journal and listened to music on the radio, absently wondering if any of the herbal remedies in the book actually worked, and if they did, why Oye hadn't used them to cure Beatrice's cancer.

With nightfall, the veranda became busy, as was the routine most evenings. The men were draped on the veranda while the women huddled in the corners. They were all gathering: Jagua; Sergeant Okoro; Joshua Bandele-Thomas; Abigail, Okoro's wife; Beauty, the single primary-school teacher whom Joshua had a crush on; and Comfort. The men played checkers or argued loudly, all the time munching on some snack and drinking beer or palm wine. The women sat like shadows behind the men and seemed to use the fact that they needed the light to darn, or shell melon seeds, to justify their presence. For the most part, the men ignored them. Those brave enough to call their husbands' attention to something were rewarded with a gruff and impatient answer, as though they were keeping the men from some important philosophical breakthrough.

Elvis, on the other hand, loved flirting with the women. Getting up, he went into his room and returned with the record player and a clutch of records he had inherited from his mother. While the men watched, he turned the machine, with its spinning plate, on, and wound the women and the records into a frenzy of released pressure, dancing with each in turn, laughing loudly, happily. The men sniffed, silently disapproving. When his father and Benji arrived back from the bar, Elvis packed up the records and the record player.

Not like the other men.

"Ah, my son de useless dancer!" Sunday announced as he watched Elvis putting things away.

Comfort, sitting with the other women, watched silently. Elvis ignored his father and walked into his room. Moments later, he came out, dressed, and headed for Redemption's place.

▼▼▼▼▼▼▼▼▼▼▼▼▼▼▼▼▼▼▼▼▼▼▼▼▼▼▼▼▼▼▼▼

ROAST YAMS AND PALM OIL
(Igbo: Ji Ahuru Ahu Ya Manu)

INGREDIENTS

Yams
Chilies
Salt
Ahunji
Palm oil

PREPARATION

Cut the yam into square chunks, leaving the skin on. Place inside an open wood fire amidst the hot ashes. Roast until crisp on the outside and soft and well cooked on the inside. Mix the chilies, salt and chopped ahunji into the oil. Dip the yam in the sauce and eat.

This simple fare is considered the food of the poor, or those serving an intentional penance. The latter group comprises mostly women who have been unfaithful to their polygamous husbands. In these cases, the punishment meant they had to cook mouth-watering dishes daily for their husband and family, but themselves eat only roast yam and palm oil. The minimum penance is usually seven days; the most extreme can last several months.

EIGHT

||||||

When the star marks a fork on the King's head, we have three. This marks the turn.

The study of the relationship of the number of lobes on a kola nut and its relationship to the petitioner is akin to numerology. The number of lobes indicates the energy pockets that the petitioner has and these in turn will determine the nature of their life walk and talents. The more lobes on the kola nut they choose, the more energy pockets they have, thus the richer and more complex their life-walk.

||||||

Afikpo, 1976

Elvis about 9 years old

Oye stood at the bend, near the edge of the road, waiting for the postman. He showed up, on time as usual, with a handful of letters for her. They came from her many pen friends all over the world.

Sunday prowled the length of the porch watching Oye nervously. Big lorries came hurtling around the bend at incredible speeds, and he lived in fear of Oye getting crushed. He would not admit that his concern had anything to do with love, mumbling instead about the high cost of burying the old. Still, Elvis suspected it was love, like the time he cut himself on a rusty knife and got tetanus and there was the possibility of him dying. His father had ranted at him angrily, calling him a wicked and thoughtless child to play so roughly and cost him so much in hospital bills. Yet when he recovered, there was no more mention of the cost of his cure, astronomical as it must have been.

It was only a combination of luck and driving skill that kept the lorries from plowing straight into the house. Some of these lorries were coming to the nearby fish market, bringing traders from the towns. Others came from the brewery in the next town, delivering their quota of oblivion, their drivers tipsy enough to swig beer from open bottles as they drove, in clear view of police at the checkpoints dotted all over town. Others were crammed with market women screaming conversations above the bedlam of the engine, squabbling chickens, snorting goats and barking dogs in cages. Crying children were casually thrown in the direction of a breast to suckle quietly. They roared past, scattering dust and shouted greetings.

The frames of the lorries were built of timber. Elaborate motifs of flowers and climbing vines sprawled over them in vibrant colors, and their tailboards boasted murals: Hercules pulling a lion's jaws apart, a mermaid sunning herself on a beach, King Kong swinging from the Empire State Building. Along the sides ran slogans: SLOW AND STEADY . . . HE WHO LIVES BY THE SWORD SHALL DIE . . . TO BE A MAN IS NOT A DAY'S JOB . . . SUFFERING AND SMILING . . . THE WICKED SHALL NOT PROSPER . . . THE YOUNG SHALL GROW.

Oye stood watching the postman's bicycle fade into the horizon, as though she expected him to turn around at any moment and return to deliver more letters that he had somehow overlooked at the bottom of his bag. Satisfied that he was gone, Oye walked back to the house, her letters tucked carefully under her arm. When Elvis read them later, they would give off the slight scent of talcum powder.

It was summer and schools were on holiday, and Elvis was home, so she summoned him and together they made a pot of too sweet, too milky tea. While she carried the tea, he followed closely, holding the envelopes.

She couldn't read, but trusted only Elvis to read to her. She figured he was still young enough not to be judgmental or tell too many lies. Oye had never learned how to read or write, and before Elvis was old enough, Beatrice read the letters to Oye, taking her dictated replies down in a beautiful copperplate.

Elvis enjoyed Oye's trust. It was one of the few times when he felt needed. That sense of importance was nearly threatened when he began to come across the letters written in foreign languages. The most regular came from someone called Gretel and seemed to be in a language that could be German. When he explained the situation to Oye, she laughed heartily at his discomfort and took the letter from him.

"There's more than one way to skin a cat," she said, holding the letter between her palms.

"What are you doing?"

"Reading it."

"How?"

"Ach, laddie, with magic of course," she said impatiently. "When I hold it like this, I can make out what it's about."

"Then why don't you read all the others like that?" he asked.

"Tha thing with magic, lad, is tha' it always has consequences."

She settled back into her wicker chair, Elvis seated at her feet. She sighed and took the letters from him. With practiced casualness, she flicked through them, choosing one. She ripped the envelope and shook out the letter, which she passed to Elvis.

"Read, laddie," she said slowly.

He took the letter, smiling at the elaborate ritual she had evolved. He wondered what she did on school days; he imagined she prowled the house restlessly until he got back. Clearing his throat, he began.

"Dear Oye . . ."

Mr. Aggrey took the entire kids' dance class to the cinema to watch Fred Astaire.

"See how he floats," he explained. "If you want to be good at dis, watch as many of dese kinds of films as possible."

"What about Elvis Presley films?" Elvis asked.

Mr. Aggrey smiled. "Elvis Presley too. And Indian films. Watch. Learn. Practice."

Elvis took the advice to heart. Since the free movies never showed what he wanted to watch, he began to pay to get into the Indian cinema in the next town to watch Elvis Presley, Gene Kelly, Fred Astaire and nameless Indian film stars in order to study, close-up and firsthand, the moves of great dancers. He liked the female dancers too, but was afraid to ask Mr. Aggrey if he should learn their moves.

Elvis approached Oye days after the Professor Pele incident and asked her if he could learn the dance moves he had seen performed by the Ajasco dancers. She asked him to find out how much it cost, and if it was not too expensive, she would think about it. Two days later he accosted her as she was sweeping the yard.

"Three naira for each lesson," Elvis blurted out.

"Watch yourself, boy! You nearly gave me a heart attack."

"I'm sorry."

"What is three naira?" she asked.

"The dance lessons I told you about," he said, launching into an impromptu routine, arms flailing wildly.

"Hey!" Oye interrupted him. "Are you blind? You canna see this broom? Or are you just going tae watch me sweep with my old bones?"

"Sorry, Granny," he said, taking the broom. "Well?"

"Well, finish sweeping and we'll talk," she said, walking off.

Mr. Aggrey was old, with a shiny bald patch and two hedgerows of hair on either side. He was kind despite the walking stick he brought crashing down on knuckles, elbows, knees and anything else with a joint bone. He circled them as they practiced, hawk eyes watching for a missed beat or a hesitation. He was bent a little, and when he hobbled in time to the music, he looked like a large, misshapen turtle.

In addition to the children, Mr. Aggrey also taught adults the waltz and the tango. These were mostly mid-level civil servants preparing for their promotions and the anticipated social evenings that came along with them. Elvis had heard rumors that those selected for promotions were often tested for their ability to handle such social events, so Mr. Aggrey insisted they dress formally for the lessons.

Elvis often stayed back to watch them, hidden by the tall congas standing in the shadows at the back of the open yard where all the lessons were held. They reminded him of the scenes from Chinese films where monks learned martial-art moves in the courtyards of mountain temples. He thought the adults looked funny in their ill-fitting clothes, which ran the gamut of formal dress from tuxedos and evening gowns through to traditional lace lappas and babanrigas.

Mr. Aggrey worked them hard, tapping out the tempo on the floor with his cane and counting the moves. "Left leg shimmy, right leg shimmy, den turn, left shimmy . . . No, no, no, Mr. Ibe—left leg. Left leg. Left leg! What are you, Mr. Ibe, an orangutan? Is dis how you will disgrace me at some high-society ball? And you, Mrs. Ebele, dis is not Salome's Dance of de Seven Veils. If you keep grinding your waist like dat, your partner will have an embarrassment on de dance floor. Okay, from de beginning. Left leg shimmy . . ."

Elvis watched every day, mentally adding the moves to the ones he already knew. He shuffled along in the shadows, unseen, knowing he would get a beating for not returning home on time after the dance lesson, but not caring.

It was Friday, and as usual, Elvis hid to watch the adult dancers instead of practicing with the other children. Mr. Aggrey waited for the adult dancers to stow their bags before speaking. Elvis observed as several of the dancers noticed twenty rickety wooden crosses leaning on the west wall of the yard. They exclaimed in alarm, and soon a murmur filled the room. None of them wanted to be part of any Satanic rites. Some even backed toward the door, whispering prayers under their breath.

Mr. Aggrey calmed them, explaining that the crosses were there to help them dance. The cross beams would provide support and straighten their backs, providing the stiffer upper-body comportment required in formal dance. With a lot of trepidation, the dancers allowed themselves to be tied to the crosses.

As he watched entranced, Elvis knew what he needed to do to reproduce the Presley hip snap, which he loved dearly, but somehow he couldn't re-create it, as his movements were more fluid than his hero's. The first chance he got to practice alone behind the outhouse, he decided he would lash double splints down the side of both legs from the knee down, giving the stiffness needed to get the snap going.

While he finished off the children's lesson out front, Mr. Aggrey put on some music and left the adults alone to get used to their crucifixion. When he returned, they seemed to be quite happy, whirling around merrily. His breath caught in his throat as he realized that it had worked. They were waltzing, and gracefully. Beautiful black dancers, stapled to wooden crosses that pulled them upright and stiff like marionettes; a forest of Pinocchios, waltzing mug trees, marching like Macbeth's mythical forest.

▲▲▲▲▲▲▲▲▲▲▲▲▲▲▲▲▲▲▲▲▲▲▲▲▲▲

AERVA LANATA *JUSS.*
(Igbo: Okbunzu Nonu)

A straggling, hairy herb found mainly in humid regions, it has elliptic leaves covered with slight hairs and white flowers that grow on the common stalk. The leaves, eaten in soup, are great for sore throats. They induce a heat, exacerbated every time one swallows, which is where the Igbo name comes from. It means literally "to smith in one's mouth." The heat caused by the swallowing is likened to that produced by the bellows of the smith. ·

It can also be used effectively to cast a spell on someone to speak the truth, in which case an unbearable burning is produced each time the person lies. Or it is used to seal one from speaking the truth by creating the same effect, only reversed.

NINE

))))))

Three lines on the King's head mark the turning. These people, rarer than the two, bring new things, sing new songs.

The Igbo have a very abstract mathematical system. Recent anthropological data suggests that they knew about and used π before the Greeks; that they had in fact begun to explore ideas that we now call quantum mechanics. Though there are many treatises on this, it is hard to determine what was there and what has been brought to this thesis by modern scholarship.

))))))

Lagos, 1983

The club was packed, and Elvis and Redemption had a hard time squeezing their way into the room. The band members were lounging by the bar drinking, having already set up their instruments. Loud highlife blared through the house speakers, and most of the crowd shuffled to the fast-tempoed music.

Onstage, King Pago, the house dwarf, tiny next to the instruments and microphones, danced. He whirled like a dervish, his small feet barely touching the ground. He jumped up and spun some more. Stopped. Then started a calmer, more recognizable dance. The audience cheered at this display.

A female dwarf got up onstage and began to gyrate erotically with him, their groins sending up a heat that caused them both to perspire heavily. The crowd jeered, urging them on, and they ground together, trying to outdo each other. Suddenly the woman's boyfriend, a huge

six-foot-tall motorbus conductor, broke through the crowd and, to angry boos, carried his girlfriend off the stage, tucked safely under one
arm, pelvis still gyrating.

Redemption laughed and walked over to the band and was greeted
familiarly. He introduced Elvis and said that he was a great dancer and
that maybe they could use him. The bandleader nodded and said they
would speak during the intermission, as they had to be onstage in a
minute or so.

Elvis stared about him. Everything seemed brighter, better, in here.
It was his second time in a nightclub. The first time, he got drunk way
too soon into the evening and missed much of it. Tonight would be
different, he thought. Besides, Redemption was trying to get him a job
as a dancer, and he wanted nothing to jeopardize that.

Elvis sank into a mock leather seat, stiffened and cracked by sweat
and abuse, and looked out at the crowd. Onstage, King Pago was a
small fireball of energy, a pure elemental, like a rabid gnome. He
jumped, somersaulted, cartwheeled and danced across the unstable
wooden elevation of the stage. Sweat flew off him in a fine spray,
anointing the worshipful crowd.

"Redemption!" Elvis shouted over the music.

Redemption turned from the girl he was chatting up. "Yes?"

"Are you sure they will hire me to dance here? I mean, the only
dancer onstage is that pygmy," Elvis said.

"Dat is not a pygmy. King Pago is a dwarf. Don't worry, you go
dance. Now let me talk to dis girl, okay?"

Elvis nodded and went back to people watching. In a corner, a fat
woman crammed into a red sequined dress several sizes too small
drowned in the waves of music. Her head hung limply from her neck,
arms reaching for air, waving weakly. Her body was a quivering mass
swaying along to the music, shedding sequins like old skin that collected in a pool of light by her feet. Makeup ran in riotous color down
her face, and her mouth was open in a surprised "ooh." The floor in
the corner was not concreted over, and her heels sank into the soft
earth, rooting her to the tempo.

A skinny man stood in front of her, motionless apart from the lewd movements of his twisting pelvis, which he thrust bonily out at the woman. His eyes were closed too, arms raised in adulation, a bottle of beer firmly clasped in one hand. Intermittently, he let out moans, gentle "shshsh"s and "aaaahhh"s.

The record changed, the music slowing to a gentle calypso—Harry Belafonte belting out "Kingston Town." King Pago slowed to a slow shuffle, and the crowd followed his lead and began to swanti.

"Elvis!"

He turned. Redemption stood on the dance floor with two women.

"You won't dance?"

Elvis shook his head.

"Come and help me—come," Redemption said.

Reluctantly Elvis got up. He did not want to be off dancing on the floor when the bandleader came looking for him, but he did not want to annoy Redemption. He joined the group and began to swanti. He learned the dance quickly and easily.

The swanti—or swan-tease, as he later found out—required the men to shuffle forward in a two-step hop, arms spread out to the side, palms open like ruffled wings, while the women, arms raised up, hands curved to sloping beaks, breasts pointing forward, moved back slowly by wiggling their backsides in time to a subtle two-step. When the men stopped, bobbing in place, the women moved forward, breasts teasingly brushing chests. When the men moved into them, they danced away, elongated arms dipping gracefully. To Elvis's left, a couple argued. The man, not content to do the swanti, was trying to press the woman against the wall in a grind. But the woman was having none of it. The musicians began making their way back to the stage, and soon the sound of retuning instruments filled the club.

As the band began to play, the bandleader motioned to Redemption and whispered something to him. Nodding, Redemption returned to Elvis and led him to the back of the club.

"Okay, you done get your first customer," Redemption said, pointing to an Indian woman in her late twenties.

"Customer?"

"Yes. De band, and dis club, attracts rich patrons, mostly Indians and Lebanese, and de band has to find good, well-mannered men and women to dance with dem all night. You will be paid well, don't worry."

"To just dance?"

"Well, dat is up to you," Redemption said with a short laugh.

Stopping before the young woman with beautiful long raven hair and black eyes flecked with the slightest hint of honey, he introduced them.

"Elvis, dis is Rohini. Rohini, Elvis."

Her twin-dimpled smile was pearl white and excited Elvis. To her left stood her silent, towering golem, a eunuch her father employed to chaperone his daughter. He bared teeth in a snarl at Elvis's approach.

"Relax, Prakash," Redemption said.

Rohini was Upanishad Tagore's eldest daughter. Upanishad, a shrewd businessman, had inherited a couple of medium-sized provision shops from his father, Davinder Singh Tagore. Tagore senior had come to Nigeria in 1912 to help build the railways, and stayed on. With an uncanny head for business, Upanishad had turned those two shops into fifteen huge department stores scattered all over the country. They sold everything from dry cell batteries, Swiss Army Knives, groceries and toys to cars and tractors.

"Hello," Elvis said. "Would you care to dance?"

Prakash laid his big hand on Elvis's shoulder in warning. Redemption picked it off and turned to him.

"If you lay your hand on my friend again, I go take you outside and give you de beating of your life, you bastard."

Prakash hesitated. Redemption had a mean reputation, and this club did attract a lot of local gangsters—disgruntled, angry men who would jump at the chance to work over a much-hated Indian. Prakash backed off.

"Hello, Elvis," Rohini replied, her voice like treacle. "Yes, I would love to dance."

With a smile, he led her off and, holding her lightly, swung her through a waltz as the band played "This Is a Man's World," though the singer sounded nothing like James Brown with his high-pitched falsetto.

"So how are you, Rohini?" Elvis asked.

"I'm fine, although life is pretty boring for me at the moment."

"Oh? Why?"

"I am fighting with my father."

"I know all about that," he said with a short laugh.

She smiled. "Really?"

"Yes. Tell me about your father. I mean, why do you fight?"

"You are getting awfully personal for a person hired to dance," she said.

"I am sorry. This is my first time. I meant no offense."

She looked at him in the dim light. He seemed genuine enough, so she told him about herself.

Rohini had been educated at Oxford and graduated at twenty with a first in classical studies. Returning to Lagos, she had spurned every suitor her father had lined up for marriage. Running short of men, he pressed her to return to India to be married off. She refused, defying him in a gentle but firm assertion of her independence. She turned down the offered post as company finance manager, opting instead to take a job teaching comparative philosophy at the University of Ibadan. In deference to her mother's tearful pleas, she lived at home, even though that meant a two-hour commute each way. She also allowed her father to hire Prakash to protect her from the unbridled and scurrilous advances of the native blacks.

"My father is very disapproving, and cares only for money. As he says, 'Vot else I can du? A cock crows; me? I make money."

They both laughed, and Prakash looked on disapprovingly. Remembering the money Redemption had slipped him earlier, Elvis said: "Can I buy you a drink?"

"I think you have got it wrong," Rohini said, leading him back to her table. "It is I who buy the drinks. What can I get you?"

"Beer, please," he said.

She nodded and whispered to Prakash, who grabbed a passing waiter.

"Are you all right, Elvis?" she asked. "You look a little uncomfortable."

"I'm fine." Beaming, he turned to Prakash, taking in his sour countenance. "Don't you ever smile?"

"Smiling is for prostitutes and fools," Prakash said.

"Captain on deck!" Redemption shouted, getting up and snapping to mock attention as Elvis walked into the buka.

"Oh, shut up, you," Elvis said, suddenly self-conscious.

"According to my watch"—Redemption began consulting it with a flourish—"it is now four a.m. Reliable sources—dat is, me—tell me dat de club closed at two a.m. So, Mr. Presley, where did you take Ms. Rohini, you hound dog? Beach motel? No, dat is too cheap, too visible. Eko Palace Hotel?"

"We went for a walk on Bar Beach."

"Bar Beach? Walk?" Redemption sounded confused. Then his expression relaxed into a smile. "You dirty dog. De old beach fuck."

"No, we just walked by the sea."

Redemption shrugged. "Her choice, you know. But tell me how much you made."

"One hundred and fifty naira," Elvis said, counting it and handing Redemption a twenty.

"Ah, no now, Elvis. Not twenty—forty."

With a sigh, Elvis handed over another twenty.

"Now, buy me breakfast and tell me all about it," Redemption said, stuffing the notes into his back pocket and sitting down. Tired speakers leaning in the corner belted out Donna Summer's "Spring Affair."

"There is nothing to tell. She is a very nice girl, and we talked."

"About?"

"About her father and how hard he is making it for her to be her own woman."

Redemption took a sip from the lukewarm tea in front of him. He began to speak but thought better of it when the waiter brought over a plate of eggs, fried meat, fried plantains and bread. Yanking off a piece of bread and digging a pocket in it, Redemption filled it with eggs and fried meat. He took a bite and chewed thoughtfully. When he looked at Elvis, the concern was clear on his face.

"Listen, tell me what you think dis thing you are doing is?"

"What thing?"

"Dis gig I got for you at Sonny's? Listen, dese women are way out of your reach. You are dere to keep dem entertained, no more, no less. You have to move from woman to woman. You are disposable and dey will never care about you. Dey will go on to marry rich foreigners like demselves. And if for any reason she liked you, and you hurt her, well, I think you saw Prakash? De best you can hope for is to make a decent living while things last and maybe get in a good fuck or two—for which you must charge extra."

Elvis put down his cup of tea.

"Where is all this coming from? I just took her for a walk along the beach. I know how to play this game, okay?"

"If you say so."

"I do. But listen, Redemption, I need more work, though. This escort work does not seem like regular work to me."

"Hah, Elvis, you are a true Igbo man."

"I need this, Redemption."

"Don't worry, I'll look into things."

"Elvis!"

Standing in front of the buka was the King of the Beggars, Caesar.

"Who is dat bastard?" Redemption asked, clearly irritated.

"My friend Caesar," Elvis replied, motioning for Caesar to join them.

"You have strange friends," Redemption said, finishing off his tea and standing up. Stuffing a piece of meat in his mouth, he made to leave. "Me, I like only regular guys like me. See you later."

Caesar and Redemption inspected each other as they passed at the door. Caesar nodded; Redemption spat and looked away.

"Your friend is not very nice," Caesar said, sitting down.

"We all have our faults. I'll talk to him later," Elvis replied. "Breakfast?"

"What is bothering you?" Caesar asked Elvis.

"What makes you think anything is bothering me?"

"Because."

"Because?"

"Mmhmm."

"I have a bit of an ethical dilemma."

"Easy now, Elvis. Not so much big words, eh?"

Elvis laughed, and as the King of the Beggars finished the breakfast Redemption had left over, Elvis filled him in on his new gig and the reasons why he needed to earn money fast, ending with his conflict over the right thing to do.

"Listen to dis story," Caesar began.

"Oh, please, not another story. Why can't anyone in this place just give it to you straight?"

"Because de straight road is a liar. Now listen. My broder built a birdcage when I was small. One week, he is building de cage, every day, eh? Den he take two whole days of careful stalking with bait and weaver trap to catch de bird for de cage. I remember dat bird, yellow like dis, eh? Every day I watch dat cage, dat bird, eh? Every day.

"Den one day, rain just fall finish and de air dey heavy with de smell of fresh wet earth and spilled kerosene. I sit dey watch. My spirit move me. My head just begin wild. What would happen if . . . ? Why should de bird be trapped? Could it speak?

"It's like my broder know something is up, because he come dere and watch me as I watch de bird. Den my mother's call my broder away. 'Don't touch de cage,' he warn. I nodded.

"But as soon as he go, my hand was on de cage and suddenly de weaver was in de air. It beat its wings against my face and was gone. I was surprise to hear myself laughing. I was free and I stood in de small rain dat began to fall again. I was powerful, aaah."

"Then what?" Elvis asked impatiently.

"De slap caught me square across de lips, drawing blood, and I start to cry in de rain. 'I told you not to touch de cage!' my broder shout."

"So what is the moral?"

"Why must you mock, eh? It is simple. Choose whether you are me, de bird or my broder. Only you can choose."

story

interesting way to get your point across.

▼▼▼▼▼▼▼▼▼▼▼▼▼▼▼▼▼▼▼▼▼▼▼▼▼▼▼

OIL BEAN SEED SALAD
(Igbo: Ugba)

INGREDIENTS

Ugba (sliced oil bean seeds)
Akanwu
Palm oil
Salt
Fresh chilies, chopped
Smoked fish
Stockfish
Eggplant

PREPARATION

Boil the oil bean seed slices until tender (or buy already boiled in a bag). Using a big wooden bowl (wood helps seal in the flavor), mix the akanwu and palm oil until you have a smooth paste. Add a couple of dessert spoons of water. Next, put in the oil bean seeds, a pinch of salt and the chopped fresh chilies. It is best to use one's fingers to achieve the best mix. Fresh chopped onions are an option for some people. Add strips of smoked fish and stockfish and chopped eggplant. Serve the dish cold (or lukewarm) with cold beer, wine, palm wine or soda.

4:09:00

TEN

))))))

There is danger here. These people can go mad easily. The muse that in-
spires can, when turned counter, become madness. These people are gri-
ots, truth talkers.

Numbers, for the Igbo, had several applications, not entirely limited to mathematical in-
quiry, one such use being to differentiate people by energy configurations composed of
numerical, quantifiable vibratory frequencies. These provide the key to decoding individ-
ual personalities, abilities and the vocation best suited for the petitioner. The Igbo believe
that if one does not follow the life pattern determined by their energy grouping, they are
living outside the dictates of their chi, or personal god.

))))))

Elvis is about
10 years old

Afikpo, 1977

"Are you sure we won't get into trouble?" Efua asked.

They were standing in line to get tickets for the matinee showing
of the latest Bollywood release. Though at thirteen she was three years
older than Elvis, in this situation he felt as if he were the older one.

"Don't worry. Everything is fine."

"But Oye will find out dat you are using your dancing money to
come to de cinema with me."

"She won't."

It was a real dilemma; balancing the cost of the dancing lessons
with their increasingly frequent visits to the cinema. There was the cost
of the ticket, sweets and the obligatory bottle of cold, sweating orange
Fanta—doubled; since he nearly always had to pay for Efua, it came to

a significant amount. He was convinced that his dancing was improving more from studying the moves in the movies than from anything Mr. Aggrey taught him. The films also had soundtracks that ranged from the full orchestral grandstanding of the 1939 Technicolor hit *Gone With the Wind* through to the Bangra pop of Bollywood flicks. This music contrasted with the soul, jazz and highlife that filled his days, blaring from loudspeakers outside record stores or from neighbors playing their sound systems too loud.

He was getting really good as a dancer, and even the cynical Oye whooped with delight the night he staged an impromptu concert for her and Aunt Felicia on the front veranda. He could not afford to stop now, yet he could not afford to continue. The plan to get more money, when he hit on it, was so simple he didn't know why he had never thought of it. Of course its execution required subtlety and time if it had any chance of succeeding, but he felt good about it.

First he offered to collect Oye's letters from the post office on his way home from school. She hesitated initially, because waiting for the postman brought a special feeling to the day. But both Elvis and his father managed to convince her of the danger of waiting near that bend around which the lorries came barreling. It also made sense since he took her replies to the post office.

When she got used to the new system and began to let him open the envelopes for her, he moved on to the next stage of his plan. He stopped mailing her replies, using the postage money instead to pay for his movie adventures. He never failed to feel the pang of guilt, but the candy and Fanta assuaged that and he was soon lost in the movie, hardly aware of Efua breathing gently beside him. He was no longer strictly seeing movies that helped his dancing, although he did learn a few moves from the Bollywood flicks. But he was hooked, and the cheap, jerky silent movies of the motor park had lost their appeal.

The one hitch to his plan was that Oye would be expecting detailed replies from her pen pals from all over the world, a problem compounded by the fact that she received between one and five letters a week. To cover up, he would have to write the replies she so looked forward to. It proved harder than he had thought, and the need to keep varying the voices and contents soon exhausted him.

Desperate, he began using scenes from the films he watched to make up the letters.

Oye's Argentinean pen pal moved from the city to the pampas and began to ranch cattle as a pampas cowboy. He was a tough customer who kept the rustlers at bay with mild threats.

"'Don't make me shoot you, pilgrim'?" Oye asked, alarmed. "What does tha' mean? When did José buy a gun and become a cowboy?" she continued. "He was a priest a few weeks ago."

Elvis swallowed hard and kept his head down. And so the lies rolled off his pen. Scenes from *Casablanca, Breakfast at Tiffany's* and *Gone With the Wind* were rewritten to fit his letters. Oye's suspicions seemed to him to have been allayed too easily and quickly, though, and he couldn't shake his unease, convinced that she was setting him up. It niggled at him all the time.

And the stories he could cook up from the movies were finite, and with the constant reruns, Elvis was fast running out of material. When he started his scam, the plan was to still mail off a few letters so that Oye would receive some genuine replies and wouldn't grow suspicious at the change in tone of the forged ones. He then meant to build up slowly until he wasn't posting any of the letters from her. Things got out of control too quickly, and he stopped posting all her letters too soon. He would still go to the post office, stand in line so that he would be seen by any neighbors or relatives that might just happen to be around on their own business; then he ducked around the corner and out the back door. Hidden by the rampant bush that grew almost up to the back door, he shoved the letters into his schoolbag. Then, in the shade of a leafy tree branch right there behind the post office, he would begin forging the replies. He needed more input. Television was out of the question, as Oye might catch him out. There were all the books he read, like Enid Blyton's Famous Five and the Hardy Boys adventures, but somehow he couldn't bring himself to plagiarize an actual book.

He finally turned to his own imagination. And what a colorful place that turned out to be! A dog that spoke to its owners and saved them from every mishap resigned and bought shares in a beachfront bar called Sharky's, run by a dolphin. A Sri Lankan pen pal was ab-

ducted by aliens in the middle of some secret ceremony performed by
Arthur C. Clarke. A Catholic priest performed an exorcism on a home
in Poland overrun by goose-stepping, machine-gun-toting goblins. A
Cuban Santería priestess regularly turned into an invincible tiger to
rout Castro's secret police. An American pen pal, tiring of her job in
the Department of Motor Vehicles, retrained as an astronaut and took
a rocket to Mars, where she found out that the locals were blacks with
a penchant for playing jazz on moon-rock saxophones.

The more elaborate the story, the more Oye enjoyed it and the
more his conscience nibbled at him endlessly. At first he tried to deny
the prods, masking them as a stomach ulcer. But then he began to have
sudden and inexplicable vomiting attacks. Owning up to the truth, he
decided to turn himself in. The next time Oye settled down with her
tankard of sweet tea to listen to him read, he decided to test the waters.

"Gran, you don't believe the stories these people have been writing to you, do you?" he asked.

"Why? Are you changing what is written there?" she demanded
suspiciously.

"No, no," he protested quickly. "But I mean surely you did not
believe the story about the priest exorcising the goblins."

"Why not? I have seen goblins."

"Okay," he said, taking a deep breath. "What about the woman
who met black people on Mars?"

"What about it? We are everywhere. Why all tha questions, eh? For
so long my pen pals held out on tha good stories. Instead they wrote
boring letters about how well their flowers were blooming and tha'
their local supermarket now had shark and crocodile steaks. What do I
care about all tha', eh? Stop wasting my time, boy, and read," she said.

With a sigh he unfolded a letter from Russia and began.

Afikpo, 1978 *Elvis is about 11 years old*

"Not every hoose is a hame," Oye said. "And since your mother died,
this hoose is no hame. Not with him here, tha way he is."

She balanced her considerable bulk on the tired sway of a wicker chair and began shelling pumpkin seeds into a silver bowl. Occasionally, she would nibble on some of the sweet soft flesh, but for the most part, she saved it. The seeds would be ground into a soft paste on the flat grindstone later and were the main ingredient of egusi soup. In between shelling, Oye sipped on endless cups of too milky, too sweet tea and doled out snippets of wisdom to passersby, who invariably stopped to talk to her.

"Here, lad, go and grind these on tha' stone in the corner," she said, passing Elvis the bowl. Then, just as quickly, she snatched the bowl back from his very reluctant hands. He was pleased at the reprieve. The grinding stone was the worst chore. But it turned out to be only a temporary reprieve. "Better start with those peppers over there," she said instead.

Elvis ground the dry chilies, trying to make all the seeds vanish, mixing in water to thicken it into a paste for the soup.

"I've finished," he called over.

"Already, laddie?" she asked, hauling herself creaking to her feet. "Here, let me see."

And she spread the paste around on the stone with a wet knife, like jam on toast. Then, with an exasperated sigh, she scraped it into a pile.

"More, more. Like egusi, tha chilies have to be a smooth paste."

"But I am a boy," Elvis argued.

"Nobody said boys had to be stupid, did they?"

With a sigh Elvis went back to the grindstone, muttering under his breath.

"What's tha', laddie?"

"Nothing."

"Doesn't sound like nothing to me. Spit it oot."

It was just his luck to be born into the only home in the small town with a psychotic father, a dead mother and a Scottish-sounding witch for a grandmother, he said, and he wished his life were different. She nodded sympathetically.

"Ach, lad, but yer canna paint a canary yellow," she said.

Elvis looked up at her. On the table next to her was a tray that held several pots, jam jars and bottles of herbs and infusions. All day, people came up to Oye complaining of some ailment or the other. She would reach into one of the jars or containers and pass out some dried herbs or a combination of such. Other times, she would nod and just listen, still as a statue except for when, every few minutes, she would bend down and feed some carrots or lettuce to the turtles in an earthenware bowl of water at her feet. When she was alone, she laughed and talked to the turtles *sotto voce*, as though they shared some joke.

"How come you don't talk to the turtles when people are about?" he had asked.

"Because I know tha difference between a gift and insanity."

Finally Elvis finished grinding the chilies into a grade-A paste. Oye usually had a treat for him, a bottle of soda or, even better, a malt drink. This time was no different and, drinking straight from the bottle, he finished it in a few gulps. He looked at her hopefully, but before he could speak, she said, "No, laddie. No more, it'll give you piles. You dinna want to be penny wise, do you?"

Elvis smiled. Oye had a talent for using clichés wrongly. Only the other day she had complained about not having green fingers. Sitting on the floor at her feet, he read through his mother's journal while he waited for the long line of petitioners to be attended to. When the last of them had left and she looked down at him, she saw he was lost in thought, stroking the cracked binding of the journal.

"Thinking about your mother?"

He started.

"Yes. Tell me about her, Granny."

"Have I taught you nothing, lad?"

"Please?"

"Tha's better. I've told you about her so many times."

"Once more. Please?"

"You are going to be here for a while, so you might as well make yourself useful," she said, passing him a handful of dried melon seeds and a sheet of newspaper.

He grimaced but knew there was no getting out of it, so he began to shell.

"Beatrice was a stubborn one, like you. She always had to have her way. Ach! But she was beautiful, even more so than a mermaid, and dark. Probably as dark as tha antimony women use to draw patterns on themselves. She never could wear makeup, your mother. She was so dark it never showed. I always said she was like a photo negative!" Oye broke into a laugh that soon became a hacking cough.

He felt a pang of worry go through him, even though he knew she only had a cold. Oye was getting older each day, and he always worried when she showed the slightest sign of illness. Torn between concern and his impatience for her to continue, he asked:

"Are you okay?"

"Ach," she continued. "Where was I? Oh yes, Beatrice. She loved to dance, your mother. She danced all tha time, and I would watch her spin like a leaf caught in tha wind. I was so afraid for her, she seemed to have no substance, you know? Like she was made out of air, or a dream."

He tried to imagine his mother as made out of air. All of his memories of her were sketchy and had been supplemented by the fantasies he built around the things he read in her journal. Oye had once told him that he had been old enough when Beatrice died to remember her clearly and that it was just his pain that was keeping him from fully remembering. He didn't know if she was right or wrong. He concentrated really hard to try and call up an image of his mother. The only one that came up was of her standing over him in her garden, the sun behind her, a tall, dark, smiling presence. Not wanting to miss anything, he returned his attention to Oye and her story.

"She loved music. She sang for hours while she did all tha chores— and what a voice, ach! She could not have goat it from me, I dinna sing, lad. No. But her father, he could hold a tune. Tha' was your grandfather. He died when I was still a young lass."

"How old were you when you were married, then?"

"Eleven."

"Eleven?"

Oye laughed through her cough. When she caught her breath she said, "Aren't you precious, wee one! If you could see your face—ach! Things were different in those days, you know. By fifteen, most of us had already had three or four children. It was tha way."

"But that doesn't seem right. You were only a child."

"I dinna say it was right, lad. But I dinna say it was wrong, either. I said it was tha way then.

"Anyway, your mother loved music, and when your grandfather died, she inherited his gramophone. It was a beastie of a thing, and you had to keep winding it up or tha people singing sounded like they were drowning. Ach! I never cared much for it myself. She stopped using it though and bought tha' new record player. Your mother loved Elvis Presley . . ."

"So that is how I got my name," Elvis said.

Oye gave him a stern look.

"You know tha'. Act yer age, lad, not yer shoe size. Enough of tha' story, time you went inside and ate your supper. You must have your homework ready before your father comes home or else it will be another night of carrying on. Now go."

Elvis got up reluctantly and left, but not before he poured the shelled seeds carefully into Oye's bowl. He wrapped the newspaper around the shells and took them to throw in the compost heap out back.

EMILIA SONCHIFOLIA *DC*

(Asteraceae)
(Igbo: Nti-Ele)

This is a straggling herb common to open places in the forest or farmland, and frequently at roadsides. Its leaves are irregularly lobed and triangular in shape, resembling the ears of an antelope, which accounts for its Igbo name. These leaves are arranged alternately along the stem, with small pink flowers.

Medicinally, the leaves are eaten cooked in soup or added fresh to a salad to ease fevers. When the fresh leaves are rubbed and squeezed, they produce a green liquid which, when dropped into the eyes, eases soreness, cataracts and generally improves vision and clarity of sight.

ELEVEN

Four lines on the King's head mark the destination; the moment of royalty, the full crown. This star, spread like a child's smile or the reaching of four fingers, is rare.

The four-lobed kola nut is the King nut. Rare, it is always a good omen. Four, in Igbo cosmology, is the number of completion, of dominion over the physical universe. It is also the number of energy pockets that true sorcerers and sorceresses need to perform their sacred duty.

Lagos, 1983

Elvis stared at the mound of grey powder. It wasn't white—at least not in the way he had expected cocaine to be. He rubbed a little between his fingers. It felt coarse, not smooth like icing sugar, the way he had imagined it.

"Careful," Redemption warned. "Dat is big money."

"Sorry," Elvis mumbled, brushing the grainy stuff from his fingers back onto the pile. "Redemption, this is serious business. It is—"

"I know what it is. Are you in or out?"

"I don't know."

"Your trouble too much. Every time I see you, you say 'Hook me up with some money deal.' Den when I do, you say you don't know."

"But—"

"Anyway, it is not you I blame, you see?" Redemption interrupted. "I blame myself for involving a boy in a man's work."

Elvis heaved a sigh and took a swig from his beer.

"This is dangerous, we could go to prison for this."

"In dis country you can go to prison if some soldier does not like you. At least with dis you can make some money."

Elvis drank some more. He seemed to be sweating inordinately, and his throat felt unusually dry. He wiped his forehead with the back of his hand and then ran his wet hand over his trouser leg.

"Haba, Elvis!" Redemption exploded. "It is not like I am asking you to hawk dis stuff, okay? I am just asking you to help me wrap it. Ten naira per wrap—now are you in or out?"

Elvis picked up the sample wrap. It was about an inch and a half long and as thick. He could probably wrap a few hundred in a night, and at ten naira per wrap, it came to a lot of money.

"I'm in."

"Good. Now see how I do it. You take dis small spoon and you measure one—not full, okay? Den you empty it into de fingers of dis glove. One by one, one by one. Dat is one spoonful per finger. Okay, see?"

Elvis watched Redemption measure and deposit five spoonfuls into the five fingers of the glove.

"Next you cut it like dis, one inch above the powder, and only one at a time. Den you tie each packet closed, tight, tight like dis. Make sure you finish one packet before you cut de next, okay?"

Elvis nodded as Redemption tied a series of knots that would have made Baden-Powell happy to know that his work in bringing the Boy Scouts to Africa had not been wasted.

"Den you take each tied packet and roll it like dis, hitting it with dis small hammer like dis, so dat de powder is packed tight, okay? Den you put it inside dis condom like dis and tie it closed, cut, and again use de hammer like dis, see? Den you put it inside dis small plastic bag like so, den again use de hammer, see? Den take dis black electrician's tape, cut it like dis and wrap it around and around and around at least twelve times, see? Den use the hammer again, see?"

Elvis could hardly believe it; the packet looked like a small pellet, no bigger than the sample. Redemption bounced it a few times on the coffee table.

"See? It is strong. Next you put de five packets inside de fingers of another glove and cut and tie, den it is ready. You see dat de glove is de kind used by doctor? Dat's because it is strong but light, you see?"

Elvis picked up the five packets that Redemption had made in what seemed like ten minutes.

"You work fast."

"And good," Redemption said. "Don't worry, you go learn quick. See, Elvis, dis is new business for me, and if it go well and I get plenty job, den you don't have to work in dat club again, eh? When we go to de club we go go as rich men."

Elvis rolled the packets contemplatively between his palms as though he were a psychic trying to guess at their contents.

"Okay," he sighed, and hunched over the coffee table. He reached for a glove and began to make packets like Redemption. It was slow and tedious work and he felt himself getting lightheaded. Noticing the glazed expression beginning to drop over Elvis's face, Redemption sent him out for some fresh air and to buy beer.

They worked all night long, and by the time the city was waking up they had finished the last of the powder in the bowl. In a small black leather bag were the tied packets. By Elvis's count there were at least five hundred. He had not worked as fast as Redemption and had made only about one hundred and fifty of them. Without saying anything, Redemption took a wad of money from his pocket and counted out fifteen hundred naira. He secured the money with a rubber band and handed it to Elvis, who took it and sat there in a daze, weighing the money in his hand. He had never made this much money for less than a month's work. Now, in one night, here it was.

"Next time I go deduct money as per my cut, but dis time is beginner's dash," Redemption said.

Elvis nodded and sat back.

"Put dat money away."

Without a word, Elvis shoved the wad into his pocket. He lit a cigarette and stared at the naked lightbulb in the ceiling. Insects were buzzing around it even though it was losing its power in the face of the sun stabbing its way through the slats of the window louvers.

"Can I ask you something?"

"You can ask, I might not answer."

"How do the people who own the cocaine know that you won't fill the packets with sugar and keep the real stuff for yourself?"

"Elvis? What is dis? Don't go getting funny ideas," Redemption replied sternly.

"Me? What do I know about cocaine? But why do they trust you?"

"So you are saying I am a thief?"

Elvis laughed. "Of course not. Just wondering."

"Listen, Elvis, don't wonder. Don't even joke about dis. Dese people, dey can kill you like dis." Redemption snapped his fingers for emphasis. "Dey don't have to trust me. Dey know I know what will happen if I cheat dem. So please don't even joke about it."

Elvis smoked in silence, while Redemption sat staring into space. Finding a sudden spurt of energy, Redemption stood up. He cracked his knuckles, complaining about how sore the work made his hands. Picking up the bag, he headed for the door. He stopped when Elvis did not seem to be moving.

"Listen, Elvis, I have to go and deliver dis stuff."

"Okay," Elvis replied, still not moving.

"And you need to leave."

Elvis got up reluctantly. He was tired and did not want to battle the buses to get back home, but he had no choice.

Outside, Redemption hailed a taxi.

"You better get a cab too," he warned. "You are carrying a lot of money."

"Sure," Elvis replied. "Redemption?"

"Yes?"

"Why did we have to tie those packets so securely? How will people who buy them open them?"

"Dey are for export; to States. A courier will swallow dem. Depend on de person capacity dey fit to swallow like between two hundred and four hundred. Dat's around two to four kilos. Dat's why we packed dem like dat. So dey don't burst in de stomach, and de last glove make it easy to swallow. Ah, here's my cab."

Redemption opened the door, then hesitated.

"Do I need to tell you not to tell anyone of dis?"

Elvis shook his head.

"Good."

Then he was gone. Elvis stood for a while watching the taillights of the cab disappear in the early-morning Lagos fog. He then turned and headed for Maroko on foot. He needed to think.

The molue did not come to a complete stop, but Elvis jumped off anyway, running for a short distance with the momentum. The huge sprawling area in front of him, full of the cry of commerce, was Tejuosho Market, one of the biggest in Lagos. Armed with a few hundred naira from the fifteen hundred Redemption had given him, he was on his way to buy some new clothes, as the ones he had were falling apart and not really suitable for his nightclub gig. He paused and lit a cigarette before entering the crush.

The market was for the most part comprised of open-air stalls. Everywhere, traders squatted or sat on floor mats. The closed stalls further into the market, housing the electronics and clothes shops, were known in local parlance as imported side.

He navigated the colors—yellow gari, red tomatoes and chilies, purple aubergines, brown and even orange bread, dun groundnuts, yellow-green guavas and red-yellow mangoes. Stalls with children calling in husky voices "Coca-Cola! Is a cold!" while hunkered over wooden boxes housing chunks of ice nestling bottles of Coca-Cola, Fanta, Sprite and plastic bags of cold water under wet blankets of jute sacking.

Pausing by a cart selling secondhand books, he rifled though, looking for something to buy. There was a set of dog-eared Penguin Classics. Elvis pulled a Dickens out, *A Tale of Two Cities*, his favorite, and read the first line: "It was the best of times, it was the worst of times." Smiling, he closed the book. That was the perfect description of life in Lagos, he thought. There were also novels by West African authors: Chinua Achebe's *Things Fall Apart*; Mongo Beti's *The Poor Christ of Bomba*; Elechi Amadi's *The Concubine*; Camara Laye's *The Radiance of the King*; Mariama Ba's *So Long a Letter*; and thrillers like Kalu Okpi's *The Road* and Valentine Alily's *The Cobra*. He'd read them all and ran his fingers along their spines nostalgically. He settled for a torn copy of Dostoyevsky's *Crime and Punishment* and a near-pristine copy of James Baldwin's *Another Country*. He paid the asked price without haggling. Books, he felt, were sacred and should therefore not be bartered over.

Elvis's attention was captured by a bookseller in a stall to the left of the cart. The bookseller was a short man, with a bald patch and round stomach that made Elvis think of Friar Tuck from Robin Hood. He smiled. Bookseller Tuck, as Elvis mentally christened him, was calling out to passersby: "Come and buy de original Onitsha Market pamphlet! Leave all dat imported nonsense and buy de books written by our people for de people. We get plenty. Three for five naira!"

Elvis drew closer. A small crowd was gathering, and some were already buying the pamphlets. The bookseller's assistant, a slight boy, looked harried as he tried to keep an eye on the inventory and operate the cash register. These pamphlets, written between 1910 and 1970, were produced on small presses in the eastern market town of Onitsha, hence their name. They were the Nigerian equivalent of dime drugstore pulp fiction crossed with pulp pop self-help books. They were morality tales with their subject matter and tone translated straight out of the oral culture. There were titles like *Rosemary and the Taxi Driver*; *Money—Hard to Get but Easy to Spend*; *Drunkards Believe Bar As Heaven*; *Saturday Night Dissapointment*; *The Life Story and Death of John Kennedy* and *How to Write Famous Love Letters, Love Stories and Make Friend with Girls*. The covers mirrored American pulp fiction with luscious, full-breasted Sophia Loren look-alike white women. Elvis had read a lot of them, though he wouldn't admit it publicly. These books were considered to be low-class trash, but they sold in the thousands.

"For dose of you whom are romantic, dere is *Mabel De Sweet Honey Dat Poured Away* and *How to Avoid Corner Corner Love* and *Win Good Love from Girls*," Bookseller Tuck called. Spotting Elvis holding the books he had bought from the secondhand vendor, Bookseller Tuck turned to him.

"You, sir, you look like educated man. Here, try dis one," he said, passing Elvis a book.

Turning it over, Elvis looked at the title: *Beware of Harlots and Many Friends.* Smiling, Elvis flicked it open at random, stopping at "24 Charges Against Harlots." He scanned them quickly, jumping numbers.

> *1. The harlots live dirty and dangerous lives.*
> *2. They corrupt young men, make them live immoral lives and feed them chronic disease . . .*
> *4. Almost all that had married left their husbands without sufficient reasons, and the unmarried ones have refused to marry in preference to harlotism . . .*
> *11. No single harlot is healthy in this world, that is why they are smelling.*
> *12. Harlots drink beer too much and smoke cigarettes in like manners, and no single harlot is beautiful, that is why they always paint themselves with beauty make up's and yet you can easily know them. Wash a pig, comb a pig, dress a pig, it must be a pig.*

Elvis shuddered and closed the book and handed it back, opting instead for *Mabel the Sweet Honey That Poured Away.* Paying for the book, he hid it between the Dostoyevsky and the Baldwin and headed deeper into the market.

He passed the smell of trapped antelopes, and of savannahs coming from the basket and rope weavers. The melee of buyers and sellers haggling loudly, trading insults and greetings and occasionally achieving a trade, was thick around him.

As he made a turn and entered the imported side, he could see behind the market, sprawling away into the swamp, a rubbish dump: a steaming compost of vegetables, broken furniture, jute sacking, discarded hemp ropes, glass bottles, plastic bags, tins; the usual. And perched on top, cawing awfully, hunched like balding old men, were vultures.

He stopped in different shops, feeling the fabric for something that was stylish yet promised to be cool, ignoring the rude calls of the traders.

"If you dey buy, buy—if not, move on!"

"Hey, dis man, why you are rubbing my cloth like dat? Dis is not towel, it is fine Italian silk. Move away!"

Haggling was not his strongest suit, but he did his best when he saw a nice black shirt-and-pants combo that would be perfect.

"How much?" he asked.

"For what?" the trader replied, uninterested.

"For this," Elvis said, pointing.

"Is not for sale."

"Then why is it hanging here?"

"Ah, see dis man O?! Is dis your shop?"

As Elvis made to move off, the trader stopped him with a hand on his arm.

"Where you dey go?"

"You said the item is not for sale, so I am going."

"You mean dis one? Haba, I thought you meant de oder. Come, come, I will give you special price."

"No."

"Are you not my customer? Okay, pay fifty naira."

"Fifty? Is it made of gold? I can't pay more than ten."

"Ah! Is dis pricing or daylight robbery? Even de person who make it does not sell for ten. Den me I have overhead, eh. Okay, pay forty."

"Twenty."

"Thirty, last price."

"Twenty-five."

"Thirty."

"Twenty-five."

"No."

"Okay," Elvis said walking off.

Again the trader pulled him back. He was already wrapping the clothes, a smile on his face.

"You dis oga, you can haggle pass Egyptians O!" he said as he folded the twenty-five naira into his pocket and handed Elvis the wrapped clothes.

Moving on, Elvis soon spotted a nice pair of shoes to go with the clothes and bought those. He then made his way back to the open-air stalls and bought some groceries for the house. Satisfied, he headed off

to the bus stop and caught the bus home, stopping at Madam Caro's
for a beer.

The King of the Beggars counted the money again. The amount had
not changed from his last count: one hundred naira.

"Where from dis money, eh, Elvis? Where from?"

"Do you not want the money?" Elvis asked, and reached for the
pile.

The King swatted his hand away.

"Easy. I just ask where it is from."

"None of your business, but don't worry. No one died for it."

Elvis lit a cigarette, drawing the harsh, cheap tobacco deep before
exhaling.

"Dat cigarette you are smoking like you are drinking water will kill
you. You just quench one five minutes ago," the King complained. He
put the money away.

"Please don't nag."

"Respect my age, eh, Elvis? Respect my age," the King said.

"I'm sorry," Elvis muttered, stamping out the cigarette.

"So tell me where dis money from."

"I told you, Redemption and I have a job."

"Dat your friend Redemption, he appear dishonest to me," the
King warned.

"No more than you are."

The comment, meant as a barb, only made Caesar throw his head
back and laugh heartily. "Den you must be criminal mastermind if we
are all your friend," he said.

In spite of his growing irritation, Elvis laughed.

"How long have you been a beggar?"

"Long time."

"And before?"

"I was . . . Look, my young friend, de past is in de past, tomorrow
is all we can hope, eh? Leave all about dat. Give me one cigarette."

"I thought you didn't smoke."

"Why? Because I say it is bad? I tink de money you give me is bad, but I take it. You see, Elvis, life is funny thing. Now give me de cigarette."

Elvis passed the King a cigarette and held a light for him. The King sucked greedily at the other end, and the stick was soon burning. Lighting another one for himself, Elvis leaned back and watched life unraveling in the ghetto settlement under the bridge. He and the King were sitting on the pedestrian path of the freeway bridge, legs dangling over Bridge City below while, behind them, traffic roared past. It wasn't the wisest place to be, but the King liked to sit there and gaze down at his subjects, his domain. Absently, Elvis tried to add up all the ghettos in the city. There were Maroko, where he lived; Aje, where Redemption lived; Mile Two; parts of Mushin and Idi Oro and several other unnamed settlements under other bridges like this one scattered across Lagos. All in all, he thought, there were over ten. Throwing his still-smoking stub over the edge of the bridge, he checked his watch and swore softly.

"I have to go now."

"To your job with your friend?"

"One of them, anyway."

"Be careful. When a car hits a dog, its puppy is never far behind."

Elvis laughed.

"Again with the stories," he said, and headed for home.

"Elvis," Comfort began as soon as he walked in. "Help me carry dis box of cloth to my shop."

She had a shop somewhere across town. He had never been there and had no idea why she would suddenly ask him to do this. It wasn't the chore itself; it was the fact that she had seemed determined to keep that part of her life totally separate from home.

"I'm sorry," he said. "I'm in a hurry."

"Is dat Elvis?" Sunday called out. Without waiting for a reply, he came to the veranda, where Elvis stood talking to Comfort. "Where have you been, my friend? You treat dis house as a hotel, but let me tell you, it is not a hotel."

Elvis stared at him, unsure where his father was going with this line of logic. Deciding the easiest way out would be to apologize, he did.

"I'm sorry."

Sunday grunted. Comfort had ignored the exchange, choosing to spend her time trying to recruit one of the unemployed men in the building to carry the box for a small fee.

Elvis entered his room, remerged shortly after with a towel and headed for the backyard. He washed, changed into his new clothes and shoes and headed over to the nightclub on Victoria Island. Perhaps Rohini would be there again tonight, he thought. He hoped so.

Redemption was waiting for him at the door of the club. He touched Elvis's clothes. "Nice threads."

"Thanks, man," Elvis replied, pulling out some money to pay the cover charge.

Redemption stopped him.

"You work here now, so you no longer pay de cover. But you should buy de gate man some beer now and den," he said.

Elvis nodded and followed Redemption into the bar. The same band was set up and playing a cover of Nigeria's most popular song, "Sweet Mother," by Prince Nico Mbaga. Released in the seventies, it was still on the charts. Elvis glanced at his watch. They were on early. They usually didn't come on for another hour. As he pushed across the crowded floor to the bar, he realized why. There were several high-ranking army officers, in full uniform, sitting in the corner, drinking and talking. The band was probably playing for them. Beer in hand, Elvis made his way to the back of the room where the foreign patrons sat. He did not see Rohini, but within minutes Redemption approached him and led him to where an overweight Lebanese woman sat, cooling herself with a hand-held electric fan. She regarded Elvis with hungry eyes, then waved Redemption away.

"Sit," she said in voice that could crack gravel.

Wiping the sweat from his palms, Elvis sat.

Dancing with his Lebanese client was a little difficult for Elvis, as she seemed to completely enfold him. His face was pressed so close to her sweaty cheek he could smell the funk from her unwashed hair. Her hands were kneading his buttocks with all the expertise of a master baker, her groin rubbing against his hungrily.

"Are you okay, lover?" she breathed at him.

The smell of alcohol was nearly overwhelming, and her bear grip around his ribs made breathing awkward. From a distance, it looked like she was a huge ape devouring him.

"I'm fine," he managed with difficulty.

The band was playing Jimmy Cliff's "Many Rivers to Cross," and he focused on the words, singing under his breath, trying to take himself away, at least in his head.

" 'I've got many rivers to cross, but I still cannot find my way over . . . ,' " he crooned almost inaudibly. Thinking he was singing for her, his client kneaded his back and buttocks even harder and swung him around. Just then, one of the heavily medaled soldiers danced their way, and Elvis bumped into him.

"I'm sorry," Elvis mumbled as his client swung him around in the opposite direction.

The soldier stopped dancing and grabbed Elvis, pulling him out of his client's arms.

"What are you doing, my friend? Assaulting a soldier?" the soldier demanded.

Pulled up by the lapels, Elvis wondered why he was being manhandled so much—first by his client and now by this soldier.

"No, sir. I said sorry, sir," Elvis said.

"Sorry? What am I to do with sorry?"

Elvis didn't answer immediately, distracted by the many medals the soldier had. He couldn't determine the man's rank, but he couldn't help wondering how he had earned so many medals, considering the military saw so little action.

"Oh, you are playing tough, eh? Assault an army officer and play tough, is dat your game?"

"No, sir."

The music had stopped, and the band was watching apprehensively. The dance floor had cleared, as people tried to put distance between themselves and the situation. The Lebanese woman, drunk, grabbed at the soldier's arms, trying to dislodge his grip on Elvis. All the while she slurred: "Release my lover."

"Is dis woman your lover?" the officer asked Elvis scornfully.

Elvis was unsure how to answer in order not to exacerbate the situation and at the same time to appease the woman, as she had not paid him for his two hours of, in this case, hard labor. He chose the diplomatic approach.

"We were dancing together," Elvis replied.

"Dancing, or collaborating to assault an army officer? Do you know dat I am a full colonel?"

"It was an accident, sir."

"So you admit that you assaulted me intentionally?"

Before he could answer, the front door of the club slammed open and six soldiers, who had obviously come with the officers and had been waiting outside, came in at a fast trot. The other officers had gone back to their chairs and were busy drinking and laughing with their dates. The girls were doing their best to pretend they were not terrified. The six soldiers seemed controlled by a collective mind and stopped in front of the Colonel, saluting.

"Shall we take care of dis dog, sir!?" the leader, a sergeant, barked, eyes ahead.

By now, people were beginning to sneak out of the club, and the band members were packing up their instruments. Elvis's terror grew. He had heard about encounters with the military before, but he had been able to steer clear of any until now. The shock of the moment had worn off, and the severity of his position began to dawn on him.

"I don't know, sergeant," the Colonel said. Turning back to Elvis, he asked: "Do you think I should let my men handle you, dog?"

All the while he was shaking Elvis, who was getting dizzy as his head bounced around. Pictures of the scar running down the King of the Beggars' face flashed before him. What if this colonel decided to open him up like a choice cut of beef? Shit, he thought. Double fucking shit.

"Good evening, Colonel, sir," Redemption said, walking slowly over to the Colonel.

"Redemption, what is it?" the Colonel said.

"I know dis man, sir. He just came to Lagos; he is suffering from bush mentality, sir. He does not know any better, sir. Please forgive him."

"You know dis man?" the Colonel asked.

"Yes, sir. He is confuse, sir. Forgive, sir, I beg."

"Maybe I should get my boys to beat de confusion out of him," the Colonel said, laughing.

Redemption laughed along politely.

"He is not worth de trouble of a big man like yourself, sir. Don't waste your time on his type," Redemption said.

The Colonel laughed and let go of Elvis, who collapsed at his feet.

"Only because you know him."

"Thank you, sir."

"You," he said, turning to his men. "Go and find dat band and bring dem back. I feel like dancing."

Snapping to attention as one, the group ran out to get the band. The Colonel turned to Redemption.

"Get him out of here. Him and dat woman."

"Yes, sir," Redemption replied, already helping Elvis to his feet.

As they made their way to the exit, the Lebanese woman kept pulling at Elvis.

"Where are you going, lover?" she kept asking.

"Leave us!" Redemption said tersely.

"She still owes me for at least two hours," Elvis said.

"Forget it, man. We have to get out of here before dese army guys kill you."

"What did I do wrong, anyway?" Elvis asked.

"Shut up and don't even look at dem. Don't even think it. Let's just go," Redemption said.

The back door banged shut behind them as the band was being forced at gunpoint back onto the stage to set up their instruments.

"Dat was close," Redemption said, leaning against the alley wall.

They were in the narrow dirty alley at the back of the club. Elvis looked around. Like tendrils of a spider's web, other alleys ran off the one they were in, connecting each other in a network that probably traversed the entire city. Whatever reply he was about to give died in his throat when he saw three of the soldiers from inside walk down the alley.

"Redemption!" the sergeant called.

"Ah, Jimoh, dat was close O!" Redemption replied, laughing.

The soldiers joined them.

"You get ciga?" Jimoh asked.

Redemption tossed a packet of cigarettes to him. Jimoh passed it around to the other two soldiers. They each took three cigarettes, tucking one behind each ear and lighting the third. Jimoh tossed the packet back to Redemption, who lit two and passed one to Elvis.

"Dis your friend is a lucky man. The Colonel has killed people for dis kind of disrespect," Jimoh said.

"But I did nothing," Elvis protested.

Redemption and the soldiers laughed.

"Dis your friend is a hothead. He did not learn his lesson, I see," Jimoh said.

"What lesson?" Elvis asked.

"Dat dere is no right or wrong with soldier. Just what we want," Jimoh replied.

"Who is the Colonel, anyway? Do you really think he would have shot me in a crowded nightclub?"

"Where did you find dis man?" the soldiers asked, laughing. "You better get him out of here."

Redemption nodded and pulled Elvis along. "Come," he said.

Elvis followed silently as they kept to the side streets and alleys.

"It is better we are not stopped by army patrol, eh? One problem with army people is enough for one night," Redemption explained.

Their route showed the city to be as untidy as the remnants on a half-eaten plate of food. Elvis mused at how personal it seemed, specifically adapting itself to meet each circumstance. On his way to the club, the streets he had traveled singed straight and proud, like a rope burn or a cane's welt. Now every alley with its crumbling walls, wrought-iron gates, puddles of putrefying water and piss and garlands of dead rats was just as unique. Yet, though each square inch was distinctive, the city remained as general as an insult shouted on a crowded street.

Finally they arrived at Redemption's place.

"I think you should spend de night here."

"Sure," Elvis said.

He lay on Redemption's couch smoking until late, the thick smoke

from his cheap cigarettes mixing with the fog from the mosquito re-
pellent burning in the corner. Nothing about his evening made any
sense. And though he had felt the sharp edge of danger, the full enor-
mity of how close he had come to being shot eluded him. It seemed
too surreal. The only thing he could hold on to was the fact that Redemption had risked a lot to save him. Why? He couldn't figure it out.
Absently he wondered how Redemption knew the Colonel, but was
afraid to ask in case he found out. Since the night they wrapped the cocaine, Elvis had come face-to-face with just how dangerous Redemption might be. For the second time that night, he thought of the King
of the Beggars and his warning.

"Elvis."

"Yes."

"Sleep—your ciga is keeping me awake."

"Sorry."

"Sure."

"Redemption?"

"Yes?"

"Thank you."

"Sleep."

FROM MABEL THE SWEET HONEY THAT POURED AWAY

My Sweet Honey,
No tongue can speak what I have suffered this afternoon. Despite the fact that
we were disturbed, the way you delayed and teased me, while I suffered and
burned like a flame inside me, it was so painful. Oh! I don't think I can forgive
you.

Look I promise you everyting you can choose to ask of me. Even I will
give you my life willingly, provided you first let me before I die. What are you
afraid of? I have sworn that you won't have any trouble.

Please my honey, I am coming down there by seven this evening and as
your mother is away we can go out and see a picture or to another hotel or
even walk about and back.

Please reply this letter through the bearer.
I am longing terribly for you.

Gilbert

My Sugar,
You think you are suffering more than I do. But you are wrong. The thing is
this: my heart is strong for you, but my body is weak.

I love you three times more than you love me. But there is one thing
wrong. I do not know how we shall do that thing. You know it will be my first
time and that is why I don't know how to start.

That afternoon I wanted it more than you but I was very much afraid.
Don't blame me for what you say you suffered for I was not free from agony.
I wait for you.

Your Sweet Honey,
Mabel

Who are these
People?

TWELVE

))))))

These people are true Kings and Queens: makers, breakers, saviors, devils.

Sorcerers, dibias, are born with dreadlocks, or dada. Several rites have evolved to allow parents to shave off the natty locks and hide the truth of their child from itself and the world. The power they hold is feared, as it is believed they can unmake the universe and remold it to their own designs.

))))))

Afikpo, 1979

Elvis is about 12 years old

He fetched water from the tap in the yard for his evening bath, whistling the theme song from *Casablanca*. Aunt Felicia cleared her throat loudly and, when he didn't stop whistling, spoke.

"Elvis, stop dat! You know it is taboo to whistle at night. You will attract a spirit."

"Sorry," he said.

Afraid that the gathering shadows were now full of spirits and ghosts, he washed hurriedly, out in the yard, as close as possible to where she polished storm lanterns, soaking the air with the scent of kerosene.

"Wash behind your ears and scrub dose muddy feet," she called out without looking up from her work.

"I have," he replied.

But a stern look from her soon had him doing as he was told. Drying quickly, he scampered toward the house.

"Bucket!"

How did she always know? And without even looking, he mumbled to himself. Retracing his steps, he noticed a movement in the bush and his breath caught in his throat. There it was again, a ghostly movement from behind the outhouse, where the generator was kept. He willed the scream to erupt, but just before it did, the generator thumped crankily into life. The shadow waved. It was Macaulay, the electrician.

Back inside, Elvis began to shiver in the slight chill of Harmattan. Aunt Felicia, not knocking, marched in on his nakedness, and he hastily stuffed a towel in front of him.

"A thimble would have sufficed. Here, let me help you rub lotion," she said, grabbing the jar of yellow pomade and pulling the unresisting Elvis toward her.

He watched her unscrew the lid slowly, the sickly smell of the cheap pomade making him lightheaded. Deliberately, she scooped the thick yellow goop into her palm, fixing him with a look that made him catch his breath sharply. The chirping cicadas outside seemed to shrink the room around them. She rubbed the pomade between her palms, smiling when she saw him lick his lower lip.

"Why are you licking your lips? Are you hungry?"

He shook his head, not taking his eyes off her nipples, which had hardened through the thin fabric of her blouse.

"Come closer," she said, parting her legs, skirt riding up her thighs.

He shuffled toward her.

"Closer."

He was standing in the V between her thighs—so close, her knees brushed the sides of his legs slightly. He shivered: the way he did when he had gone for an inoculation and the nurse brushed his buttock with a sterile swab before pushing the needle home. Even the sharp jab of it had not made the tightness go away. He felt the same now.

She ran her hands over his arms, torso, head and legs, leaving a thin film of grease and goose bumps rashing across his body. Somewhere in the night, a bird called loudly. As he turned to the sound, his towel slipped off and his erection stood swaying between them with the weight of its wrong and the need of it. She ignored it until his whole body was gleaming like a gladiator ready for battle, then, with a gentle stroke, oiled his penis from root to tip.

"Naughty boy," she chided with her breathy laugh, and left him to the sweetness of his agony.

▼▼▼▼▼▼▼▼▼▼▼▼▼▼▼▼▼▼▼▼▼▼▼▼▼▼▼▼▼▼▼▼▼

AGERATUM CONYZOIDES *L.*
(Igbo: Akwukwo-nwosinaka)

This branched herb is hairy, scented and very common to old farmlands and open spots in the forest. Its oval leaves have sawtoothed edges that grow from the hairy stalk. When it does have flowers, they are violet and crowded in cluster heads at the end of the stem.

A decoction of this plant is used as a lotion for scabies and drunk as a remedy for fever. The leaves are juiced and the juice used to cure eye inflammations. The leaves, crushed and mixed with water, are used as an emetic for poison.

Every dibia knows that with the right words, the purpose of any medicine can be changed, so when the right words are spoken over the emetic solution, it causes one to vomit up bad luck and other things such as charms implanted deep inside the body by evil sorcerers and enemies. These charms take many shapes: odd coins, nails, pins, razor blades, small bottles with murky decoctions, even locked padlocks.

The right words spoken over the juice before it is dropped into the eyes will open one's psychic sight. This is to be used with care, for if one sees things others do not and speaks carelessly, or without the office of the dibia, he or she may be considered insane.

THIRTEEN

))))((((

They are sorcerers beyond power. They are the star's end; the star's beginning.

Great care is taken not to provoke these children, because their angry words have real consequences. There is a ritual to circumscribe this power, called the clipping of the tongue, and parents of these children are advised to perform it as soon as possible, preferably hours after birth.

))))((((

Elvis is about
Lagos, 1983 16 years old

Sunday looked up suspiciously as Elvis set a small keg of palm wine down at his feet. Elvis had slept in and had only left Redemption's place an hour before. It had given him plenty of time to consider the incident with the Colonel the night before. He was still a little surprised that he had not known about the Colonel's existence, even as a rumor. Redemption explained that there were many things about Lagos, and in fact Nigeria, that most of the people who lived here were blithely ignorant about. Still, Elvis argued, it was odd.

The two things that stayed with him most about the night before were the fact that he could have died and that Redemption had risked his life to help him. "For friendship, dat's all," Redemption explained this morning. Armed with this new sense of mortality, Elvis decided he should try and talk to his father, mend things, before it was too late. By the time he set off for home, however, it was already late afternoon and night was not far off. Just outside Redemption's house he saw a palm wine seller who had fresh palm wine, so he bought some as a gift for his father.

"What is dis?" Sunday demanded.

"A son can't buy his own father a drink?"

"Since when?"

Elvis did not reply. Instead he reached for his father's empty glass tankard. He filled it and passed it to him without saying a word. Blowing specks of tree sediment off, Sunday took a deep draught and sighed happily.

"It is fresh," he said, surprised.

"I bought it straight from the tapper an hour ago," Elvis replied, lighting a cigarette.

"Must you?" Sunday asked, nodding toward the cigarette.

"I must."

Sunday emptied his tankard and filled it up again. Without a word he passed it to Elvis, who took it, blew the head off and took a deep drink. The alcohol tasted cool and sweet, like a yeast drink. He could see how easy it was to become hooked on this wine.

He remembered how, when he was a child, his father would send him to buy wine fresh from the tappers. He would scamper into the forest of palm trees, the money clutched tightly in his sweating palm, feeling important. He would watch the wine tappers climb trees three, sometimes four stories high with nothing more than a creaky vine harness, to fill their gallon jugs from clay pots tied to the trees' jugulars, where they collected the wine slowly. It was a dangerous job, and when the tappers fell, as they invariably did, they sometimes died.

Waiting at the bottom of the trees with his jug, Elvis would watch the tappers come down, choosing whom to buy from by playing rock, paper, scissors with himself. Having chosen, he would give them the money and wait for them to fill up his jug from theirs. But they would always pour a little wine into the drinking gourds they carried tied to their waistbands first.

"Drink, little man, otherwise you will sour our market," they would say.

At first he resisted, because the wine made him feel queasy, but his father explained that the tappers believed that if their first customer did not drink some of the wine, they would not be able to sell it and it would go sour. With time, Elvis found the wine easier to tolerate, until it became enjoyable, and a part of the errand that he looked forward to.

"What are you thinking about?" Sunday asked.

Elvis told him and Sunday laughed.

"Finish your drink. I want de cup," he said.

Elvis drained the tankard and shook the dregs out onto the ground with one fluid snapping motion. He passed the empty tankard to his father and lit up another cigarette.

"Dere was a time you respected me enough to not smoke in my presence," Sunday said.

"Feared."

"What?"

"Feared, not respected. I was afraid you would beat me. I never really learned to respect you."

"You think I can't beat you now?"

"Please, don't start," Elvis said.

Sunday emptied the contents of his tankard and the keg onto the swamp. Elvis watched him impassively, drawing deeply on his cigarette.

"I cannot drink de drink of a man who does not respect me."

"Your loss," Elvis said

"Why are you even here?"

"I live here."

"No, I mean, why are you here, now, with me, de wine, why?"

"Your wife asked me to speak to you. To be a son to you."

"Your mother spoke to you?"

Elvis laughed at the hope in his father's voice. "No. Comfort, your wife."

Sunday did not speak. He looked at the puddle of wine as though he regretted spilling it.

"She said she was afraid you were drinking yourself to death," Elvis continued. "To be with my mother."

Sunday still said nothing, though Elvis noticed his hands were trembling—whether from anger or something else, he couldn't tell.

"Talk to me," Elvis said. "Dad," he added, almost as an after-thought. It was the first time he had referred to his father as Dad. Ever.

If Sunday noticed, he showed no sign. "Talk to you? Talk to you?! Who do you think you are? Do you think you are a man now, because you have begun to earn some money? Do you think dat is what being a man is? Talk to you. Why? You never listen. You have never listened. All your life I have told you things dat will help you find your way in dis world and you did de exact opposite. You don't listen. I have tried for you, Elvis. But now I am tired. Tired, you hear?! I wash my hands of you, like Pilate. Before I used to think it was your fault, dat you were just hardheaded. But now I don't blame you. Everything for us fell apart when your mother died. I blame de death dat took her. Talk to you? How could you understand my pain? My shame? Do you think dis is who Sunday Oke is? Wanted to be? Do you think dis is how I planned my life? Get out of here, stupid, arrogant child. De day I talk to you is de day death claims me. Get lost! Go!"

Elvis sat silently through Sunday's tirade, flinching at each word. He had spent so much time hating his father that he had forgotten how easy it was to be hurt by him. Standing up, he walked to the edge of the veranda and flicked the stub of his cigarette into the darkness.

"I will go," he said. His voice scared him. It sounded final. Empty and final.

Sunday said nothing. He simply turned his chair around so that he had his back to Elvis.

"I will go," Elvis said again. This time his voice had died to a whisper.

He took a few steps forward to where Sunday sat. Gently he laid his hand on the wooden backrest of the chair, the tips of his fingers, like an undecided breeze, barely grazing his father's shoulder. His tears surprised him. Wiping his face furiously, he walked into his room and closed the door behind him. As he leaned against it, he heard his father's chair scrape around.

"So where are we going exactly?" Elvis asked.

"You need an alternative to de world dat Redemption is showing you," the King replied.

"That doesn't answer my question. Besides, you don't know the world Redemption shows me."

"Well, dis one is different, and better."

"But where is it? We have been walking for over an hour," Elvis said.

"De new Rex cinema."

Elvis stopped mid-stride.

"The cinema?"

"Yes, de new Rex. It is nice O! Air condition, cushioned seat. Very nice."

"I have not been to the cinema in years, but even given that, I don't think it qualifies as an alternative world. I know all about the cinema. Believe me."

"You speak too much English for a high-school dropout," the King said. "Well, Mr. Know-It-All, how many European film have you seen?"

"They make films in Europe?"

"See how you foolish? I learn about dis from one man dat use to teach us night school one time. He say dat film with subtitle will help us learn good English. Anyway, follow me. Dis film will open your eye."

"What is it called?"

"*Love Film,* by one Yugoslavian like dat."

"Not the type, the name."

"*Love Film.*"

"Well, I only see action films," Elvis sneered.

The King of the Beggars set off at a fast trot.

"Den consider dis a new education," he threw over his shoulder at Elvis, who was struggling to keep up.

Bad "How can *you* educate me?!" Elvis muttered under his breath.

"I heard dat!"

It was useless arguing further. It was clear the King had his heart set on it, and he could see the theater's neon sign ahead. It might be fun, Elvis thought. He hadn't been to a film since he arrived in Lagos. There never seemed to be any time or spare money.

"Two ticket for *Love Film,*" the King said, counting out dirty one-naira notes.

"Let me get this," Elvis said, pulling out a handful of crisp notes.

"No," the King said, pushing Elvis's money away firmly.

"Listen, one of you pay me!" the ticket seller said.

Elvis paid. As he handed the King his ticket, something in his eyes caused him to shrink back.

"What?"

"Why do you think we walk here?" *The King cares about Elvis*

"To save money?"

"Because?"

"You wanted to . . ."

"Yes."

"I'm sorry."

The King nodded and stalked into the cinema. Elvis followed, but lost him in the sudden darkness. Minutes later, the King turned up and sat next to Elvis. Without saying a word, he handed him a cold Fanta and a bag of sweets. Elvis took them silently. He sighed when the film started. It looked like it was going to be long and boring, but since it was important to the King, Elvis decided to try and get into the mood.

He wasn't wrong: it was long. But he was utterly mesmerized, forgotten Fanta sweating in his palm, mouth slightly open, eyes glued to the screen.

When they got out, the sun had dipped over the horizon and lamps chased the darkness in thin lines and pinpricks of light. Elvis stood outside the cinema blinking. He couldn't seem to adjust to this world outside.

"Did you enjoy dat?" the King asked.

"Yes, sir," Elvis said. "I loved it."

They walked in silence for a while. Then the King noticed a small bar tacked onto the corner of a building.

"Drink?"

"Sure," Elvis replied, following the King inside.

The bored barkeep looked up.

"What you want?"

"Two beers," Elvis said.

The barkeep walked over and dumped the two bottles down, opening them with such force the caps flew across the room.

"Easy," the King said.

The barkeep just kissed his teeth and walked back to the corner, where he was watching a streaky black-and-white television with the attention of a lobotomy patient.

"What are you watching?" Elvis asked.

"De Price Is Right."

"What?" the King asked.

Elvis shrugged and picked up his beer.

"So tell me what you like most."

"About the film?"

The King nodded and reached for his beer.

"Well, it reminded me of my grandmother."

"How so?"

"Just the way she would tell stories. In a way that let the characters enter your skin, you know?"

The King laughed.

"What?"

" 'I only watch action films,' " the King mocked.

Elvis laughed too.

"What did you learn most from de film?"

"There was the opening line. 'People are important.' "

"Good, good," the King chortled happily, like a man who had just converted a jihad-bent Muslim to Christianity.

"You know people are important. Dat is de message of my theater group."

"When am I going to see you perform?"

"Soon come."

"So how will this be an alternative to Redemption's world?"

"Easy, Elvis. Rome was not built on all roads, okay? It takes time. Have patience."

They sat drinking in silence for a while. Outside, the foot traffic was thinning out. No one else had come into the bar, though opposite it, Elvis could see, several temporary snack stalls had opened and were doing a great trade in cigarettes sold by the stick, fried yams, roast corn and suya. By one of the fires, a group of children huddled around a slender girl playing a wooden flute. There was something disturbing in her melody that called to Elvis, like a buried memory that would not yield itself and yet wouldn't stop nagging.

"Anything else you like about dis film we just see?" the King asked.

Elvis remembered the scene at the end where so many different people stood at a street kiosk in Budapest writing postcards. In that scene, he could see himself.

"Nothing," he said. "Let's go."

"Well, hello, Pilgrim."

"Hey, Redemption," Elvis replied, sitting down next to him.

"Ciga?" Redemption asked, holding out the pack and a book of matches.

"Sure."

Elvis lit up and inhaled deeply, letting the smoke out reluctantly in a thin blue stream. Silently he passed the pack back to Redemption. They sat on a bench behind Madam Caro's buka, less than a foot from a sheer fifty-foot drop into the swamp below. To the left, a tired sun threw halfhearted reflections on the green water. Sunny Ade was belting out a song on the loudspeaker hanging precariously above their heads.

"So have you heard?"

"Heard what?" Elvis asked, reaching for Redemption's glass and taking a swig of beer.

"You know you should be careful drinking from oder people's cup. You can be poison like dat. Even juju can be done to you."

"Heard what?" Elvis repeated.

"Dat I have moved into Maroko."

"This Maroko?"

"Dis Maroko."

"But why?"

"My landlord raised de rent again. Anyway, I thought you would be happy, no? I mean, I have two-bedroom house over dere," Redemption said, pointing vaguely behind them. "Nice, nice place, and I was going to ask you to live with me, but you have dirty attitude, so now you can forget it, man."

"Why should I be happy? Did I win a prize?"

"Ahah, Elvis! Are we not friends? I want to help you leave dat your father."

Smart

Elvis smoked quietly. The King's warnings about Redemption played through his head. While he was tempted to beg for a second chance, he didn't want to live with Redemption's criminal side. It was too dangerous. What was it Oye used to say? If one finger is smeared with palm oil, it soon stains the others. With surprise he realized that he had not thought of Oye, or his mother, for so long. Was he getting too sucked into life in Lagos? He wondered how Oye was. She had declined Sunday's offer to come to Lagos with them. With a guilty pang, he reached into his backpack and touched his mother's journal. He hadn't read it in a while, hadn't even shown it to Redemption. Why was that? he thought. Still, to be away from his father and stepmother would have been wonderful.

With a sigh he got up and walked into the bar, returning to Redemption and the bench with two sweating bottles of beer.

Drinking + Smoking A LOT Lately

"Now you are talking!" Redemption said, reaching for the fresh bottle. "Is dis your way of begging for forgiveness?" he continued, emptying the contents of the bottle into his beer mug.

"For what?" Elvis replied, lighting another cigarette.

"'For what?'" Redemption chuckled. Realizing Elvis was serious, a frown crossed his face.

"What is wrong?" he demanded.

"Nothing," Elvis replied.

"Sure?"

"Sure."

They drank in silence, occasionally swatting at a mosquito or fly. Elvis reached into his backpack and took out his mother's journal.

"What's dat?"

"My mother's journal," Elvis replied.

"You mean like a diary?"

"Yes."

"Why are you carrying it about?"

"It reminds me of her."

Redemption nodded. "Let me see," he said.

Elvis passed the book and Redemption rifled through the pages. "She liked to cook," he said, handing it back.

Elvis took it and returned it to his backpack, thinking it was funny Redemption should have said that, because he couldn't remember his mother ever having cooked. Showing the journal to Redemption made him feel like he had a secret worthy of sharing, like Redemption's passport and visa. They lapsed into another silence, watching the sun sink beyond the horizon as night rolled across the water like black velvet. A few generators thudded around them, and Elvis absently wondered why anyone who could afford a generator would live in Maroko. To their left, through a skirt of trees, was the road, and across the lagoon from it, on the distant shore, were lights.

"Is that Ikoyi?" Elvis asked.

Redemption squinted.

"Oh yes," he replied. "Dis is why I like Lagos."

"Why?"

"Because though dey hate us, de rich still have to look at us. Try as dey might, we don't go away."

Elvis laughed, triggering Redemption, and soon they were gasping for breath.

"Ah, Redemption, you are funny O!"

"True talk, true talk."

They heard someone pull the needle off the record that was playing and an argument ensue. The record that had been playing, Sir Victor Uwaifo's "Joromi," was really popular. One of the patrons no doubt disagreed. Moments later the needle crackled hesitantly before the new song belted out. It was an old Bobby Benson classic called "Taxi Driver," and Elvis and Redemption heard the patrons inside singing along, their initial resentment forgotten.

"Dat na song O!" Redemption said.

"Uhu," Elvis answered, joining in with the singing. "'If you marry taxi driver, I don't care.'"

"'Marry market woman, I don't care,'" Redemption sang. "Who play dat sound?" he asked as the tune came to a stop.

"Bobby Benson, although I think Wole Soyinka wrote it for him in the fifties."

"Wole de man of letters?" Redemption asked.

"Yes."

"Wonderful."

They lapsed into an easy silence, while the record player in the buka went back to playing "Joromi."

After a while, Redemption spoke. "So listen, Elvis, time for serious talk. De people who we wrap de cocaine for, well, dey have moved onto anoder business."

"Which kind?"

"I don't know de details too well. But dey want us to follow with some people and deliver something to Togo."

"Togo? That is two countries away! I don't even have a passport."

"You no go need it. Trust me."

"So what will we be delivering? I am not swallowing any cocaine," Elvis said.

"I don't know what it is, but is not cocaine. Dat dey send to States and oder places, and anyway dey have left de cocaine business."

"Is it that you don't know, or that you don't want to know?"

"Dey are paying five thousand naira each for us to follow deliver something. I don't need to know what it is, neider do you."

"I want to know what I am delivering," Elvis said.

"We are not delivering. Just following, like escort."

"Even escorts are liable if there is trouble."

"Which kin' of trouble, eh? Dat is why we are dere. To stop de trouble."

"So in fact we will be bodyguards."

"Escort."

"As they say in States, 'You say potato, I say putahtoh.'"

"How do you know what dey say in States?"

"I saw it in a movie. Relax. Just because I don't want to follow you blindly does not mean you should bite my head off."

"Who is biting? Anyway, it is better we are all blind, because in de land of de blind, de one-eyed man is mad."

"Fine."

"Okay, your loss."

"Fine."

"Damn dis shit. Look O, Elvis, you have change towards me, why?"

"I don't know what you mean."

"Every time you speak too much grammar, I know you dey lie. Why can't you trust me?"

"Why should I trust you when you want me to take a risk without telling me the whole story?" Elvis said.

"Only a dead man tells everything, only a fool asks."

"Are you threatening me?" Elvis asked.

"Use your teeth to count your tongue."

"The King was right about you!"

Redemption paused, beer halfway to his open mouth. Putting it down slowly, he turned to Elvis.

"Dat dirty beggar?" he asked. "What did he say about me?"

"Promise me you won't hurt him," Elvis replied.

"You should worry I don't hurt *you*. What did you guys talk about me?"

"Nothing."

"Elvis."

"Nothing."

"Don't make me call your name again," Redemption said softly.

"He warned me about you and said you were leading me to a life in crime."

"Are you a child to be led? What did you tell him?"

"Nothing."

"If you told him about dat cocaine . . ."

"I told him nothing. He said he knows you from around and he is trying to show me a different path."

"A different path? Dis is how you repay me for trying to help you? Betraying me to some crazy beggar? How does he know me, eh?"

Elvis took a deep breath. "I know you are trying to help me, Redemption. But he is trying to save me."

"Really? He is trying to *save* you?"

"Yes."

"Well, what do you know about your savior? Who is he? Where does he come from? Why is he so willing to save you? Why can't he save himself from de street? Answer me!"

Elvis remained silent, wishing he hadn't brought it up.

"Dis man who is trying to save you does not tell you about himself? And yet you say I want you to follow me blindly? You are already blind."

"I know his name, and that he is part of a theater group. I know that he got cut along the face while doing an antigovernment play—"

"Dat scar on his face has been dere since I was small boy," Redemption interrupted.

"What?"

"Listen, Mr. Blind Man. I know dat beggar better dan you. He was my master one time."

"Your master? I don't understand."

"You are a small blind boy. Dere are many things you do not understand."

"About what?"

"Me. De King. Lagos. Life," Redemption said, sounding tired.

"Then tell me. Why is everybody keeping secrets from me?" Elvis asked.

"Drink your beer."

"No, tell me!"

"I told you before. Only dead people tell everything."

"At least tell how he was your master?"

"Ask him yourself. If he is trying to save you, let him tell you. But dis I will tell you. De King is not your father, he cannot be, will not be. One day you will become a man and stop dis small-boy behavior."

Redemption stood up to leave.

"Tell me what to believe," Elvis said.

"Tell yourself. If you want to get involve in de job I told you, find me before next week. If not, den it is fine. But you must choose."

"That is what the King told me," Elvis said.

"Den maybe he is trying to save you after all."

▼▼▼▼▼▼▼▼▼▼▼▼▼▼▼▼▼▼▼▼▼▼▼▼▼▼▼▼

BLACK-EYED BEAN POTAGE
(Igbo: Ji Na Agwa)

INGREDIENTS

Black-eyed beans
Yam
Salt
Palm oil
Crayfish
Hot peppers
Cooked beef or chicken and its broth
Utazi
Dried fish

PREPARATION

Wash the black-eyed beans and leave to soak overnight. This will lift the skins off. Most people don't know about the skins, but if left on, they turn the food black and can cause too much gas. Sift the skins off. This should be easy, as they would have risen to the top of the water. Peel the yam and chop it into medium-sized chunks and wash the starch from it.

Next, put the beans in a pot and leave on a medium heat for about half an hour, checking the water level to prevent burning. Also put the yam in a separate pot with enough water to cover it. Sprinkle in some salt and leave to cook until yam is soft, checking always for water level.

Take the pot of beans off the flame and pour the beans into a colander. Wash under a cold tap, then put them back in the pot and return it to the flame. Add a couple of dessert spoons of palm oil and add the crayfish, salt and the peppers. Also add the broth from the cooked meat with some water and the yam.

Leave on a medium heat for about fifteen minutes before adding your spices, such as the utazi.

Last, add the meat (which should have been precooked) and the dried fish. Leave to cook for another twenty minutes. Serve with spinach boiled with spices and onions. Gari (fried cassava powder) steeped in water, milk and sugar makes an excellent side dish.

FOURTEEN

〉〉〉〉〉

This is how the kola nut must be presented.

The actual ritual of the kola nut is as complex as the Japanese tea ritual. Not that one needs to compare the two in order to validate the one, but there is something about old cultures and their similarities that bears mentioning.

〉〉〉〉〉

Afikpo, 1980

Elvis never took his eyes off the glove. He was standing in the middle of his father's bedroom. From the window, the stretch of broken asphalt yawned in the midday heat. Houses on either side crowded together as if to revive it. A soft breeze blew a plastic hairdresser's glove, and it trailed its fingers along the hard surface as though in massage before dancing lightly through the grass at the edge of the road, styling it. The breeze picked it up and slammed it against a wire mesh fence bordering one of the houses. It hung there waving, empty, before slipping lifelessly down into a puddle, sinking from sight.

He had only been inside his father's bedroom a few times, and then only to clean, which was in itself an invariably bittersweet experience. Tins of smoked kippers, baked beans, corned beef and exotic fruits all sat stacked, unused, unopened. Some, contoured into tortured shapes, were well past their use-by dates. Bought for some special moment that never seemed to come, they were eventually thrown away. Shirts, still shrink-wrapped, mocked the holed one he wore. Vials of holy water, collected from every gifted Catholic bishop or priest between home and Timbuktu, stood in a shaky pyramid in the corner. A sip, taken with a couple of aspirin, worked miracles on headaches, his father swore. In the corners, ornamented tea services leaned against stacks of *Reader's Digest*s and newspapers.

Everything was thickly coated with dust before he was summoned to clean. He not only had to dust, but also had to move things and sweep under them. The trick was to pack them back precisely where and how he had found them; otherwise he would not get the reward: crumbling, stale, rice-weevil-infested cookies that always left him feeling cheated.

"What did you say?" his father asked.

"Uncle Joseph raped Efua," Elvis repeated.

"Who told you?"

Elvis was silent. He couldn't tell his father that he had seen it happen. Not once, but several times. Nor could he tell him that it had started a long time ago. How could he? That would mean having to explain why he had never brought it to his father's attention before now. It also meant that he had to face up to parts of himself he didn't want to. This last time, just a few days before, Uncle Joseph had been so rough, slapping Efua around. Even though she was visibly hurt, with one eye closed off, everyone just assumed that it had been a disciplinary beating that got a little out of hand. That happened sometimes, and so no particular attention would be paid to it. Elvis had deliberated whether to tell his father for a long time. And now he did not want to talk about it any longer. Something in his father's tone and manner brought it home to him. This had been a mistake.

"Who told you?" his father repeated, voice hard.

"She did," Elvis lied.

"Has she told anyone else?"

"No, sir. Just me."

His father nodded and reached under his pillow, beckoning Elvis over at the same time. Elvis approached slowly, nearly pissing himself when he saw his father's old service revolver appear in his hand. The smile was tender as his father placed its barrel against Elvis's temple.

"If you ever repeat what you have told me now, I will blow your brains out. Do you understand?" he whispered, his face so close to

Elvis's ear, Elvis felt stubble graze his skin. Elvis tried to answer. He even opened his mouth, but nothing came out. His father twisted the gun barrel hard against his temple and said harshly: "Do you understand?"

"Yes," Elvis croaked, farting simultaneously.

His father smiled, took the gun away and, with his back to him, said:

"Get out, stinking liar!"

Elvis stood still. He heard the words but did not understand.

"Get out!" his father shouted.

Coming to life, Elvis bolted for the door. He fumbled with the lock for too long, and his father was behind him. Elvis's fear spread wetly down the front of his trousers as a slap connected to the back of his head. There was another silence and Elvis froze, unable to look around. I'm dead for sure now, he thought. Instead, his father leaned over and opened the door.

"Stupid as well," he muttered as Elvis raced out.

He circled the house all day, far enough from his father to avoid any direct contact or conversation, yet close enough not to be missed. He haunted the edges of the mango and guava orchard his father had planted in a fit of hope when Elvis was still a toddler. "My Elysian Fields," he had called it.

But here in the orchard, nature had its own designs, and whatever the initial order or plan had been, it soon gave way to a tangled mass of red and white guavas, oranges, mangoes, soursops and bright cherry shrubs. Squirrels outnumbered the fruit, it seemed, and Elvis was reminded of his early childhood when he had hunted the squirrels with the intensity usually reserved for bigger game, armed with his unpredictable catapult that backfired with the sting of rubber or, worse, the lumpy pain of a stone.

Shady and cool, the air was heavy with the scent of rotting fruit and the buzz of tomb flies. The orchard had spread from the west side of the house, where Elvis and Felicia's room was, all the way around to the front. It had been cut back several times, but the odd guava and mango tree survived in the front yard.

He had brought his mother's journal with him and he turned the pages, reading with difficulty the curved, spidery handwriting. All these recipes, and yet nobody he knew cooked from recipes. That was something actors did on television and in the movies: white women with stiff clothes and crisp-looking aprons and perfect hair who never sweated as they ran around doing housework for the husbands they called "hon."

Bored, he closed the book and distracted himself by peering through the window, watching Felicia change. Hidden by the thick foliage, he was invisible. The occasional glimpses of bra, breasts, panties and the anticipation caused his sex to throb. He knew it was wrong to lust after his aunt, but he couldn't help himself. As soon as it was dark, he slipped out, confident that his father would soon go out and not miss him.

Elvis was headed for the local motor park, where silent westerns and Indian films with badly translated English subtitles were shown after dark. He hardly went to these anymore, preferring to attend matinees in the new Indian cinema, but he was broke. Besides, at thirteen he was far too young to be out alone at night, and his father would kill him for sure if he found out. But the thrill of it was enough to make him disregard the risk, and he felt that it was a secret easy enough to keep. There was no danger of running into relatives there—at least not relatives his father fraternized with. Free movies in the dusty motor park were beneath them.

The films were shown courtesy of an American tobacco company, which passed out packets of free cigarettes to everybody in the audience, irrespective of age. That was half the fun; what could be better than free cigarettes and a free movie? If they could get that here, in a dusty end-of-the-highway fishing town, they thought, America must indeed be the land of the great.

While he waited for the main film to come on, Elvis wandered over to where some of the older boys were playing a game of checkers for money. At fifteen and sixteen, with no parents or interested relatives, these boys eked out a living, either as apprentice mechanics or motor-park thugs. Elvis idolized them and wished he could live their lives. Tonight's main gamblers were Able-to-do, an apprentice car mechanic and part-time muralist, and Confusion, a sprinter, who made a living playing football for the town's team.

"Come on, scram!" Able-to-do said to Elvis. "Do you see any other children here?"

Elvis hesitated. A record store about a block up from them was open late, and two huge speakers propped its doors open, throbbing loudly with Isaac Hayes singing the "Theme from *Shaft*."

"Well, well. Dis one has heart," Confusion said.

Elvis glowed. Confusion was his true hero. Of all the people he knew, Confusion was the only one who dared to try and make a living at something he loved. That, coupled with the way these boys adopted such confrontational nicknames, defying a culture where your name was selected with care by your family and given to you as a talisman, was the thing rebellion was made of, as far as Elvis was concerned.

"He will soon have a broken head. Heart or no heart, he should not be here," Able grumbled.

"Don't be so hasty, Able. Everyone has deir uses," Confusion said. Turning to Elvis, he held out some money. "Go over dere and get us a couple of beers."

Elvis headed off in a trot.

"And make sure dey are cold!" Able shouted after him.

When Elvis came back with the sweating green bottles, Confusion let him keep the change. He watched, fascinated, as they both opened their bottles with their teeth. They were deep in an argument about the merits of John Wayne versus those of Actor. Confusion was squarely on the side of Actor, whom he believed to be a true hero.

Elvis loved Actor too, and thought he had the best role: part villain, part hero. Women preferred him to John Wayne and men wanted to be him. His evil was caddish, not malicious, and Elvis knew that though most people dared not step out of the strict lines of this culture, they adored Actor. He was the embodiment of the stored-up rebellions in their souls. But as with all things here, even these archetypes were fluid. Halfway through a James Bond film, Dr. No could change from Actor to John Wayne in the viewer's minds, and James Bond could become Actor.

"Dat John Wayne is suspect O! Hah! Me I think he is just establishment guy O!" Confusion said.

"How can a rogue be a hero?" Able-to-do countered. "In your

small town or dis one, eh? Impossible. Anyway, John Wayne always wins."

"No sir. How many bags full? None. Actor is simply de best. And remember, in every cinema, average bad guy and even John Wayne can die. But Actor cannot die."

From the sound of the crowd in front of the makeshift screen, Elvis figured the main feature was about to start and scampered off. He scanned the crowd. The audience for the most part comprised those of the working class that didn't find their release in religion: motor-park porters and touts, market men and women, the usual motley mix that was the large yet invisible heart of any city. The mostly illiterate audience was unable to read subtitles, but Elvis knew they did not let that ruin their fun. They simply invented their own stories, resulting in as many versions as there were people. Still, for him, it was magical.

The screens were dirty, hole-ridden, once-white bedsheets stretched between two wooden poles. The projectors, archaic and as old as many of the silent stars, sounded like small tanks. Moody, they tended to burn films at the slightest provocation, melting the plastic into cream-and-brown cappuccino froth. They vibrated so badly, the picture often blurred and danced insanely from side to side, sometimes spilling out onto a nearby wall.

At first, Elvis found it was dizzy work just trying to keep focused, until he learned that the popular trick was to sway from side to side while squinting off to the left. Barring the occasional bout of motion sickness, this worked quite well, and Elvis often wondered what it would be like to stand above and look down. He was sure the crowd made quite a sight: hundreds of people swaying from side to side, chattering away like insane birds, worshiping their new gods. They drowned out the commentary provided by the projectionist, who, undeterred, continued his litany on a battered megaphone.

As the film opened, Elvis read the title under his breath. *The Good, the Bad and the Ugly.* He smiled. This was a good one, plenty of action, though it started slowly, with two men waiting for a long time, one of them occasionally glancing at his watch, before shooting at each other. It didn't seem like a terribly efficient way to kill someone. As soon as the last note of the watch died down, the projectionist was off:

"Actor is shooting John Wayne Wayne has dodged Oh No! Actor is down actor is down actor's horse is down Oh No! John Wayne is in action John Wayne is a powerful medicine man He cannot be killed by bullets Oh Look! Indians are running running with many cutlasses and knives bows and arrows they are dodging bullets too as Cowboys fire them . . ."

The projectionist's monologue would have been the same if it were an Indian movie, except of course the characters and the stories were different, most of the time anyway. But on the nights the projectionist got drunk, genies rode horses in pursuit of cow-rustling mermaids, and Ganesh sported six-shooters and the name John Wayne, while the Duke morphed into Krishna or the big-belt-buckled, flared-pant-bottomed star of one of Bollywood's finest productions. Elvis tried to smile, but the projectionist was so loud, he annoyed him. Suddenly, all around him, the audience's voices rose in argument. Here we go again, he thought.

"What do you mean she poison him? I say she is a witch. Witches don't just poison ordinary poison, dey use magic poison."

"Shut up! You always like to show you know something even when you don't."

"Keep quiet! Some of us are listening!"

"Listening? To what? Look at dis old goat! Who is talking to you?"

"Goat! Where is de goat? Are you confusing dat horse with a goat? I don't see any goat on de screen."

"See Actor, see Actor!"

"Dat's not Actor, dat's John Wayne."

To Elvis, the plot lines were simple and were about the eternal struggle between the good of John Wayne and the evil of the villain, known simply, mysteriously yet profoundly as Actor. John Wayne acting as the villain in a film was Actor, and Clint Eastwood as sheriff was John Wayne. These films showed another aspect of that eternal war Father Macgettrick told them was being fought daily between the fallen angels led by Lucifer and the army of Christ, commanded by the armor-wearing, sword-wielding Archangel Michael. And just as in that story, the hordes of demons were dark-skinned.

Running the length of the motor park was a low cement wall where Elvis and his friends usually sat smoking and trying out conversations

Already smoking at page 13 (handwritten)

from the films. American English was exotic and a treat for the tongue, unlike the stricter grammar of England's English, which they learned at school. Whistling a tune from *The Good, the Bad and the Ugly*, Elvis strolled over and took his place on the wall.

"Elvis, enjoy de film?" Hezekiah asked, passing him a cigarette. Elvis accepted it in spite of the lit one smoldering between his fingers.

"'Darn these here rustlers.' That projection man, why must he talk even when the film has sound, eh? 'Shuh likes you, Annie,'" he nodded, sucking on the cool menthol smoke.

"Yup," Titus agreed. "Rawhide. 'Reach for it, sonny.' You know dese people don't hear American."

They puffed and squinted off into the night, afraid of being caught smoking by the adults.

"'If you want to shoot, shoot, don't talk,'" Obed said, getting up and walking off.

"Yup," Hezekiah agreed.

Somehow it all made sense to them, like some bizarre pig latin. And there was a power in the words that elevated them, made them part of something bigger.

It was late as Elvis snuck up the back path to the house. Thankfully the window he had propped open with a dry cell was still ajar. As he approached, he thought it odd that all the lights were still burning. They ran on a generator that his father shut off when the nine-thirty news was over. After that, it was back to kerosene lanterns like everyone else.

Elvis wasn't sure how late it was, but he had left the motor park at ten and it was a good fifteen-minute trip, even at a fast jog. He paused in the shadows of the guava trees out back. Had he been found out? Was his father sitting on his bed right now, waiting for Elvis to climb through the window? Was he weighing a cane to beat Elvis with, seeking the balance of its heft, trying its springiness against the air and whining mosquitoes?

Elvis's mind raced. Best to carry out a proper rekky. That was one of his favorite words, learned from Uncle James, who had been a captain in the Biafran war, where he'd carried out many recon missions, or rekkies, and who was forever carrying out, or asking someone to carry out, a proper rekky.

Melting from shadow to shadow, Elvis approached the front yard, pausing to note several unfamiliar cars parked there. The front door was wide open and light from inside spilled out, cutting a swathe in the darkness, patterning the parked cars with shadows from the hibiscus shrubs that grew along the front of the house. Voices raised in argument spilled out onto the wood of the veranda, which, adjusting in the cool of night, creaked in response. These were all good signs. It meant his father was still up because he had guests, not because he had found Elvis out.

Curious, and using the hibiscus as camouflage, he peered over the windowsill. His father, Uncle Joseph and several men he did not know were arguing. In the corner, tied hand and foot, was his cousin Godfrey. Watching over him, eyes alert and hard, was another cousin, Innocent.

While Godfrey, Efua's brother, was his first cousin, Innocent was one of those relatives that English terms could not properly identify in the tangled undergrowth of the Igbo extended family: distant enough not to be a real cousin yet close enough to be a brother.

Elvis absently wondered why Godfrey was tied up. No doubt the heated debate revolved around him and was probably an attempt to come up with a suitable punishment for something he had done. Godfrey was a real troublemaker, and his fighting and stealing shamed the family. There were few crimes more heinous than bringing shame to one's family, and Elvis was used to seeing him tied up and beaten.

Well, that settles it, he thought. He was not about to miss a beating, seeing as he was not the one getting beaten. Beatings were Uncle Joseph's specialty. He had an unerring accuracy with the cane, which meant that it landed on the same welt repeatedly until you felt like a hot wire was buttering through your flesh. And he always sent you out to cut the cane for your own whipping.

"A bad cane doubles de punishment," he would call out cheerfully to your dead-man-walking figure.

Retreating to a tree that afforded a direct view into the parlor from a comfortable yet out-of-sight perch, he settled down to watch. Plucking a guava, he wiped it on his shorts and bit into the sweet flesh. Around him, in the other trees, he could hear bats feasting on the ripe fruit. They kept away from his tree, repelled by his human odor and the scent of cigarettes.

He must have dozed off, because the muffled sound of people talking underneath the tree woke him. Innocent and Uncle Joseph were huddled in some kind of negotiation. Though he could not hear the words, there was something sinister in their manner that disturbed and frightened him. Sitting, barely daring to breathe, he strained to hear, but their voices were too low, as though the men were afraid the shadows might hear. The conversation was short and both men returned to the parlor, but not before a bundle of money changed hands. Shortly after, Innocent and a now untied Godfrey walked out and headed quickly into the night.

Climbing down, Elvis hastily worked his way around to the back of the house. He was just about to climb in through the window when he heard his father calling his name from the open door of the bedroom. As his eyes adjusted to the dark, he stared straight at him, but his father had no idea that Elvis was outside, only a few feet away. Changing tactic, Elvis stumbled around to the side door, yawning.

"Yes, sir," he answered.

"Where have you been?" his father demanded, filling the doorway. "Why are you not in bed?"

"I went to piss, sir." Elvis's face and eyes were still sleep-swollen from his nap in the tree, and it was an easy sell.

"Get back to bed now, stupid child," his father snarled before heading back down the corridor to the parlor. With each step his disposition changed, until with a cheery "Where were we?" he returned to his guests.

Elvis shook his head and slipped into his room.

"You have de devil's luck," Aunt Felicia muttered from her cot across from him. They shared a room, but she had wisely kept out of the exchange with his father. "But even de devil runs out of luck. Lucifer fell. Remember dat."

Elvis crawled into bed silently and fell asleep as soon as his head hit the pillow to dream of cowboys and superheroes and naked angels who teased his lust cruelly.

▲▲▲▲▲▲▲▲▲▲▲▲▲▲▲▲▲▲▲▲▲▲▲▲▲▲▲▲▲▲▲

SABICEA CALYCINA *BENTH.*
(Yoruba: Jiri)

This is a slender plant found mainly in forests that exhibits creeping and climbing characteristics. The leaves are pointed at the apex and heart-shaped at the base. It has white flowers and blue-black berries.

Ground, the leaves are applied to the limbs of young children to help them walk on their own. Crushed and added to palm wine, the leaves serve as a laxative. They can also be used on cuts and wounds. Drunk in infusion, the leaves are said to improve memory. Sometimes ginger is added for taste, and to sharpen the edge of the recollections.

FIFTEEN

))))))

The oldest man in the gathering must offer it to the guests.

One does not rush into the kola-nut ritual either. There is a strict protocol to hospitality.
The guest is first offered a glass of water. Next, he is presented with the nzu, or white
chalk spoon. This is a large wooden spoon covered by rubbings from the ritual white
chalk, or nzu, with a residual piece of the chalk left on it.

))))))

Lagos, 1983

Tinubu Square, nicknamed Freedom Square, was milling with people.
There were the usual students, poets, musicians, actors, liberals, lec-
turers and plenty of hippie types. They sat in groups talking, drinking
or eating. Elvis hung on the edges of these groups, looking for an opportunity to join one, all the while scanning for the King.

Freedom Square also supported plenty of hawkers, selling everything from alcohol, kebabs, suya and cigarettes to bars of soap and
decks of cards. Hovering on the fringes, hugging the shadows, were
the drug dealers. They sold reefers of marijuana, amphetamines and
other tablets to addicts. But the trade was conducted curiously. The
buyer and the seller never faced each other. The entire transaction was
carried out back-to-back, and the two parties appeared to be totally
unaware of each other's presence.

The King of the Beggars got up onstage and began plucking reluctant chords from a battered out-of-tune guitar. The crowd grew
silent as he performed a series of tone poems. He was talking about the

beauty of the indigenous culture that had been abandoned for Western ways. It was essentialist, maybe even prejudiced, because the culture he spoke of was that of the Igbo, only one of nearly three hundred indigenous people in this populous country. He spoke of the ancient systems of governance that were like a loose democracy, leaning more to a socialist system, a governance based on age-grades that gathered to discuss the way forward in any crisis. This system produced a tight-knit community, where the good of the group was placed before individual stake. He spoke of the evils of capitalism that the United States of America practiced—a brand of capitalism, he said, that promoted the individual interest over the communal. It was a land of vice and depravity, infested with a perverse morality based on commercial value rather than a humanistic one. The King called for everyone to return to the traditional values and ways of being. Elvis wasn't completely convinced, though. The King's rather preachy sermon sounded a lot like the ideas of Obafemi Awolowo, an independence advocate from the early days of the nation. Elvis's main problem with the King's theories was that they didn't account for the inherent complications he knew were native to this culture, or the American. As naive as Elvis was, he knew there was no way of going back to the "good old days," and wondered why the King didn't speak about how to cope with these new and confusing times. But Elvis was mesmerized by the richness of the King's voice. It was seductive, eliciting the listener's trust, and he soon forgot his concerns and began to believe the King was right.

When the King finished, a nervous-looking young man in round glasses got up onstage and began to recite a speech. Though he tried to shout over the noise of the now animated crowd, Elvis could only make out snatches.

". . . A country often becomes what its inhabitants dream for it. Much the same way that a novel shapes the writer, the people's perspective shapes the nation, so the country becomes the thing people want to see. Every time we complain that we don't want to be ruled by military dictatorship; but every time there is a coup, we come out in the streets to sing and dance and celebrate the replacement of one despot with another one. How long can we continue to pretend we are not responsible for this? How long . . ."

Elvis lost the thread again as the King materialized beside him.

"Good evening," Elvis said.

"Sshh, listen. Dis speaker is good."

"But I can't hear him . . ."

"Sshh!"

Elvis strained to hear the young man over the crowd. In the distance somewhere, someone was playing a radio loudly, and he could hear Fela Kuti blowing a saxophone riff. It was an amazing thing to hear, a saxophone player in full flight. He had to really struggle to focus on the young man's words.

". . . Malcolm X once said America is a prison. So is this country and we are both the jailer and the inmates, imprisoning ourselves by allowing this infernal, illegal and monstrous regime of military buffoons to continue. They continue to play us like fools, buying off our allegiance with money, or with force when they cannot pay the price. I am calling for a rebellion . . ."

Controled by military

"Let us move away," the King said. "He is getting carried away, and de army go soon come."

"I thought you wanted to topple the government! So let them come."

"Have soldiers ever beaten you?"

"No."

"Den let's go."

"Okay," Elvis said, following the King out of the square and down to the CMS motor park. "It is good because I need to talk to you anyway."

There was a cart selling tea, bread and fried eggs. Customers jostled for space to sit and eat on the long wooden benches set around the cart in a quadrangle. Elvis noted the mixed crowd: late-night workers, policemen, security guards on break and the homeless, including a large number of street children.

"You wanted to talk?" the King asked as they sat down on a bench in the far corner of the motor park.

"Yes," Elvis replied.

He nervously lit a cigarette and passed the pack to the King, who took one.

"Still smoking too much," the King said.

"What of you?"

"I am too old for dat to matter. You still get chance."

"Tea?" Elvis asked, nodding to the cart. The tea had a eucalyptus smell that carried to where they sat.

"Okay," the King said.

Elvis got up and walked over to the cart. He returned a few minutes later with two mugs and a packet of animal crackers, walking slowly so as not to spill any of the scalding tea over himself. He handed the King a mug, then sat down, blowing heartily on his own. The packet of animal crackers sat unopened between them, like the questions Elvis was almost too afraid to ask.

"So what is it?" the King asked.

"I was talking to Redemption the other day."

"Uhuh?"

"And he told me that you were his master once."

The King put his steaming mug down carefully between them. Picking up a twig, he began to pick his teeth with it. Elvis watched warily. There was something disturbing about it. If the King had pulled out a long blade and begun cleaning his nails with it, Elvis couldn't have been any more afraid than he was then.

"Did he explain?"

"No. He said I should ask you."

The King laughed loudly, his manner affected and insincere.

"Dat Redemption is a real rascal, eh? I warned you about him," he said.

"How were you his master?"

"I am de King of de Beggars."

"But . . ." Elvis began. Then it clicked. "Oh!"

"Yes. I used to use small boys to beg for me. People like dem more, you see. Me, I look after dem. Dat's what he means."

Elvis let out his breath. "I see," he said.

"Anything else?" the King asked, dropping the twig and picking up his tea.

"Your scar."

"What?"

"How did you get that scar?"

The King's hand shook a little and some tea slopped over the tin mug's side, landing on the table with a loud smack.

"I told you. Soldiers did it."

"Because of a play."

The King did not answer.

"Redemption tells me you had the scar even when he was a child."

"So?"

Elvis was silent. The King let out his breath in a long, drawn-out sigh. Again he set the mug down, though this time he did not reach for the twig.

"You ask questions like police," he said.

"I am sorry."

The King nodded.

"So how did you get the scar, really?" Elvis asked.

"Soldiers."

"Because of a play?"

"No."

"So you lied."

"About de play."

"And the soldiers?"

"Dey did dis to me. I used to live in de north before de war. You were not even born dat time. I work for de Public Works Department, laborer special class. Den de Hausas begin to kill us like chicken. Plenty, plenty dead body scatter everywhere like abandoned slaughterhouse."

"My father told me about it."

"Mhmm." The King nodded. "I manage escape, heading for south, I hide inside train like dis. Just before de train cross Lokoja to safety, soldiers, Nigerian army soldiers, stop de train. Plenty of us dey hide in de train—men, woman, even childrens.

"Anyway, de soldier commander, small boy like dis, maybe lieu-tenant, drag us all come down. Den he make us sing de Muslim call for prayer. Dose who cannot sing it, like myself, he call us to one side. Den he release de oders, say make dem climb inside de train and wait. De rest of us, my family included, he give shovel say make we dig trench.

As we dig, I see de people on de train watching us with pity. I dig well, as a laborer special class. I begin to supervise, telling dem to dig straight and clean, thinking dis will please de officer and he will release us quick, quick."

The King paused to drink some tea. He was not looking at Elvis, looking away instead into the darkness of Balogun Market, as though the deserted stalls were thriving with a ghost trade only he could see. Elvis followed the King's gaze, wondering if this was the market where Comfort had her shop.

"When we dig finish, de young officer make us stand to attention in front of de trench for inspection. So we stand, man, woman and childrens, even my wife and childrens too. De soldiers take aim so dat we must stand and not run. Den de young officer begin walking down de line, shooting everybody one by one for head. I fear, I craze, I vex! I take my shovel and try to hit him. One soldier next to me take his bayonet and cut me like dis. I shout and fall inside de pit. Dey leave me so, to die slowly. When he done shoot everybody, de officer take out camera and begin to snap us photo. Den he send de train off and leave with his men."

"Oh, God," Elvis said.

"Yes, it is only God dat save me," the King said. "When everybody leave, I drag myself fifteen mile to de next small town, where dey take pity on me. When I done well finish, I go join Biafran army. Every day, I try find dat young officer, but God save him."

"I don't know what to say."

"Well, I hope you are satisfy as you drag up sleeping dogs for me."

"I'm sorry."

"You know how to sorry, but not how not to sorry. Tanks for de tea. Greet Redemption for me," the King said, getting up and walking away into the darkness.

"Auntie," Elvis said. "Long time no see."

If that was not quite the welcome she had envisioned after two years of absence, Felicia did not show it.

"Elvis. You've grown so much," she said.

They were standing in front of Madam Caro's.

"How did you find me here?"

"Comfort said you would be here."

The way she said "Comfort," it sounded like a curse instead of his stepmother's name.

"So where are you staying?" he asked.

"At a friend's place."

"Oh. When did you get into town?"

"Last night."

"I see. Can I buy you a drink?"

She laughed.

"No thank you. I just wanted to see you one more time before I leave for States," she said.

"That's right. You leave, when?"

"Tomorrow night."

"Ah. How is everybody back home?"

"They are fine."

"What of Efua?"

"Nobody is sure. She left home shortly after you moved. No one has seen her since."

"Why did she leave?"

"She was fighting with her father. You know she has always been strange."

"Strange?"

"Yes, strange. Don't act like you never noticed. Anyway, why don't you come and see me at my friend's house later tonight? I have to go and see your father now. Then visit some of my husband's people."

"How is your husband?"

"You never returned for my wedding."

"I am sorry."

"It is okay, I don't blame you," she said, making it quite clear from her tone that she did.

"Sorry," he mumbled.

"You're all dressed up. Where are you off to?"

"I'm going to a club."

"Listen, I will be at my friend's place later. Here is de address," Felicia said, handing Elvis a slip of paper.

"Sure, sure," he said, taking it and slipping it into his back pocket.

"Elvis," she said, taking hold of his hand.

"Yes?"

"Come later."

He looked from her hand to her face and nodded.

"Good," she said, letting go.

"Okay."

They stood facing each other for a moment; then both leaned in for an awkward hug.

"Okay, see you later," Felicia said, turning to leave.

Elvis returned to the table out front where he had been drinking with Okon and a few others. He missed Redemption, but he was not going looking for him.

"Ah, Elvis, dat woman fine, well, well," Okon said as Elvis sat down.

"Shut up!" Elvis said.

"Ah, sorry O, not to me make your life so," Okon replied sulkily.

Elvis had suddenly lost interest in the conversation and the company. Finishing his beer, he got up.

"Elvis? Where to?" Okon asked.

"To the club."

"Okay, see you later." Okon shrugged.

Elvis was pensive as he caught the bus to the club. First there had been the confrontations with Redemption and the King, and now Aunt Felicia had arrived, bringing memories and guilt from his past. This was turning out to be a difficult week.

"Elvis, long time," the doorman at the club said in greeting.

"Alaye, how now?"

"Fine, ma broder. Just pushing de day, you know?"

Just then a sleek black BMW pulled up and Rohini got out, flanked by Prakash.

"Rohini, hi," Elvis said.

She looked at him blankly. He was surprised. He knew he had only danced with her the one time, but there had been the walk on the beach, and they had made out.

"Rohini," he repeated.

Prakash stepped up to him and Elvis stumbled back. Rohini put her hand on Prakash's arm in restraint.

"What is it?"

"It's me. Elvis."

"I know. Listen, I don't mean to be rude, but I usually keep my club business inside the club," she said.

"I see," he said. "But we are right outside."

"So we should take it inside."

"Right."

"So are you coming in or what?" Rohini asked.

"Ah, Elvis, I cannot allow you," the doorman said, laying his hand gently on Elvis's chest.

"Alaye? What is this?"

"Sorry, Elvis, but orders is orders. If we allow you in, de Colonel go close dis place."

"Even if he is with me?" Rohini asked.

"I am sorry, madam, but orders is orders."

"Is the Colonel in there tonight?"

"Elvis, I no fit let you."

"Well," Rohini said with a shrug.

"Can't you help me?"

Rohini looked at him for a moment; then, as if making her mind up, she said: "Wait here. I'll see if your friend is inside."

Elvis nodded.

When Rohini and Prakash had entered, Elvis approached Alaye. "Alaye, you sure you cannot allow me to enter?"

"I done tell you, Elvis. De Colonel give me de order personally," Alaye replied.

"But how will he know?"

"Ah, Elvis! De Colonel knows everything. Everything."

"How? Is he God?"

"God? No. Devil? Yes. Ah, Elvis, you are funny. Don't you see all dose black GMC truck dat just pull up and arrest people?"

"Yes."

"Dose are de Colonel's boys. He is chief of security to de head of state. He hears everything, see everything. Haba, let me tell you, he is original gangster."

"So his boys are everywhere?"

"Yes. As far as I concern, you can be working for him."

"If I did, why would I want you to disobey him and let me in?"

"To test me. Look, Elvis, I am sorry."

"He is right, you know," Redemption said from behind him.

Both Elvis and Alaye jumped.

"Ah, Oga Redemption, you surprise me!" Alaye said.

"Better me dan de Colonel."

They both laughed heartily at that.

"So you agree with this?" Elvis demanded, rounding on Redemption.

"See you, small club ban and you want to shit yourself. Relax. I don't agree, but I warn you, you don't know de Colonel."

"Then tell me."

"Come," Redemption said, walking away from Alaye. "You don't know who can be working for him."

As they walked, Redemption explained to Elvis that the Colonel ran the state security forces and that all other security agencies were under him, including the police. He was behind the disappearances of famous dissident writers, journalists, lawyers, musicians, teachers and thousands of nameless, faceless Nigerians.

"Dey rumor dat he personally supervises de tortures, taking pictures throughout," Redemption said.

"Who are they?"

"Dey have no name. You are like dose white people in ghost film. Instead of running, you are asking questions. De man is bad, dat's all."

"You seem to know him quite well."

"Yes, I do. But don't worry, not many people know about de Colonel, and even though dey don't know, dey should thank God every night dat dey don't."

"Why take pictures?"

"Dey say it is because he is an artist, looking to find de beauty of death."

"The beauty of death?"

"Yes. Like de spirit, you know. He takes de picture just as de person die too, maybe he want to get de ghost on film," Redemption said, laughing uncomfortably. "But he is never satisfy, so he arrange de dead body many ways, sometime he cuts de leg or head off."

"That is sick."

"It is just now you know?"

"So has he ever found it?"

"Found what?"

"The spirit—or is it the beauty of death?"

"How can he, when he don't know what to look for?" Redemption said, stopping. They had arrived at the bus stop. "Go home, Elvis. Go and see your auntie. I hear she come to see you today," he said as a bus pulled up.

"How did you find out?"

"Maybe de Colonel told me," Redemption said, walking back to the club, his mocking laugh following Elvis onto the bus.

Elvis stood on the balcony looking out over the dark water of the sound. Behind him, to his left, Felicia sat at a round metal table.

"Is that Maroko?" he asked, pointing out across the sound.

"I'm not sure. I only arrived in Lagos last night."

"It is nice, the way the rich live," he said, turning back to her, indicating the entire condo with a sweeping gesture. On the way there he had been stunned by the smooth tarred roads, well-laid-out grounds, huge villas and mansions in white, high metal fences patrolled on the inside by stone-faced guards armed with automatic rifles.

"Come and sit down," she said. "Are you full or should I fetch you more food?"

He sat down opposite her and pushed away the still-half-full plate.

"No thanks. I haven't eaten so much in so long."

"Does she starve you?"

Elvis looked away.

"She does, dat bitch!"

"Let's talk of other things," he said.

"Fine. Your father says you dropped out of school."

"Can we drop that subject?"

"De way you dropped out of school? I don't think so."

"I wasn't learning anything useful there."

"You know, education is de only chance here. If I dropped out I wouldn't have studied nursing in de university and I would not be going to a good job in America."

"You are going to a husband in America."

"And a good job—don't sass me, boy, before I . . ."

"Before you do what? Can't you see I am all grown now?"

"Elvis, still so stubborn, still so proud," she said, shaking her head.

"So what is his name?"

"My intended?"

"He is your husband now."

"You're right," she giggled. "I still haven't gotten used to it."

"These things take time. Are you looking forward to going?"

"Not really. I am afraid. America is so violent and I won't have my family."

He snorted. "Well you better make *him* your family. This one fell apart a long time ago. As for the violence, you will be fine as long as you don't sleep with some white woman's husband. That's why people get shot there."

"Dere is no danger of dat," she said with a laugh. "Anyway, Patrick, my husband, is a doctor in a hospital in Las Vegas."

"How did you meet?"

"He wrote from America saying he wanted a wife from home, and mutual friends hooked us up and we began writing to each other. Den he came over for six months and we had a good time. When he went back, I was sure he would forget me, but he didn't. He wrote regularly and came back within six months to marry me."

"Then he left again?"

"Yes."

"So how much time have you spent with him, in total?"

"A few months."

"And how much time have you been apart?"

"Longer than we have been together."

"So why did you not just follow him back?"

"Their immigration people make it really hard, Elvis. Dey are not convinced dat we are married. Dey even said dey wanted us to have a child first to prove it."

"They are mad," Elvis said, getting up and walking over to lean on the metal rail. He shook out a cigarette and lit it.

"May I have one?" she asked.

"Trying to become an American lady?" he joked.

"No," she said, laughing. "I got into de habit working night shifts. It seemed like everybody died at night and I needed something to burn de smell from my nostrils."

They smoked in silence for a while.

"Have you got a photograph of Patrick? I'd like to see what he looks like, if I may."

"I thought you'd never ask. I'll be right back," she replied, getting up and going indoors.

She returned with a photograph album under one arm and a small paper bag in the other.

"Pull up a chair," she said, sitting down, moving plates to one side and laying the album open on the table. He sat next to her and she explained who was who, turning pages excitedly.

"Dere," she said, snapping it shut on the last page.

"Nice."

"Here," she said, reaching for the paper bag. "I have gifts for you."

With a flourish, she laid a Bible on the table in front of him.

"A Bible? I don't want to disappoint you, but I am not much of a Christian," he said, not touching it.

"It was your mother's," she said.

He picked it up gingerly, as though it would bite. Touching it brought back memories of his mother: how she would say her rosary every night before a statue of the Virgin of Fatima and then read a passage of the Bible before bed. Or maybe she hadn't. It was getting difficult to separate the imagined from his real memories. He wondered why Oye hadn't given it to him when she gave him his mother's journal. He opened the Bible; scrawled in his mother's cramped, spidery

Mother
was
religous

handwriting were her name and a date. There was also a handwritten
dedication: "Sweet Lord Jesus, all that I am, all that I have, is yours,
Lord, now and at the hour of my death." He flipped through it
quickly, the pages fanning out in a ripple. The book seemed to stay
open a little longer at a section that was heavily underlined.

"Dat is an omen," Felicia said. "Dat was her favorite psalm."

"It opened here because constant use has cracked the spine. It's
not an omen, just bad binding."

"You of little faith!"

"The Lord is my shepherd . . ." he began, but stopped.

"Go on," she urged.

"No," he said, shutting the Bible and putting it back on the table.
"What else have you got for me?"

She reached into the bag and pulled out an envelope and handed
it to him. He weighed it in his hand. It was thick.

"What is this?"

"Just a little money to help you, but don't open it until you get
home," she replied.

"Okay."

She reached into the bag again and pulled out a postcard. Elvis
took it and stared at it for a long time. It had four panels on the front.
In one, the word "Vegas" was spelled out in lights. The second panel
framed a nighttime shot of the Strip, all lit up. The third panel featured
an Elvis impersonator, while the fourth was a photo of the Graceland
chapel. This is an omen, he thought. This is it. He turned it over and
over. On the back Patrick had scrawled a note, and the date stamp
showed it was nearly six months old.

"Dis is where I am going," Felicia said. "I wanted you to have it.
My address is on de left-hand corner."

"Thank you."

"As soon as I am settled, I will send for you. It will probably take
some time to get you a visa, so you must be patient. Okay?"

He nodded and lit another cigarette.

"Dat is, if you want to come," she added.

"Sure—who doesn't want to come to States?" he said.

"You smoke too much," she said.

"Oh, not you as well!"

"I am worried about you, Elvis. What do you want to do with your life?"

"You know."

"I don't. Tell me, please."

"I want to be a famous dancer. Like Elvis."

"He was a singer too."

"I can sing."

She sighed. "Listen, Elvis, dis is a difficult world. You have to let go of childish dreams. You can't get by dancing, at least not here."

"Thanks for believing in me."

"I want you to go back to school."

"School? At my age?"

"And what age is dat? You are only sixteen. If you had stayed in school, you would be graduating dis year. If you work hard, it will only take you a year to catch up."

He turned back to the sound. Below in the garden, fireflies decorated the shrubs in lights. Cicadas called. Soft music came from an adjoining condo. On the street, an occasional car swished past silently, headlights picking out a buoy or an anchored boat.

"Why does nobody listen to me? I am not going back to school. I want to be a dancer, period. I am really good at it, have worked hard at it."

"At least think about it."

"In America I can become very famous doing what I do."

She got up and began to clear the plates away. He watched silently, not offering to help.

"You won't help?" she asked.

"No. You need to practice your wifely duties before you join your husband."

"You are a fool," she said, stalking off with the plates.

He laughed and followed her to the kitchen. He opened the fridge and helped himself to a beer while she soaked the dishes.

"Take it easy on de beer," she said.

"They can afford it."

"Madam, let me," the house girl said, relieving Felicia of the dishes she still held. Reluctantly she let them go. Elvis watched the exchange, and kissing his teeth disdainfully, he went back out on the balcony.

"What is it?" Felicia asked, following him.

"Why do your friends need a servant?"

"Oh, get off your high horse. We had servants when you were younger. You are so angry all de time. What happened to your joy?" she said, taking the beer bottle from him and swigging.

He wrestled it back from her. "I don't remember us having servants."

"It seems dere is a lot you do not remember," she said.

"What do you mean?"

"When are you going to ask me about Oye?"

He said nothing, looking away.

"Elvis. She was your grandmother. You two were inseparable when you were a boy."

"You said 'was.'"

"Yes. She died last year. Didn't you know she was ill?"

"I did, but my father wouldn't let me come."

"Just like with my wedding."

"That is not fair."

"She kept asking for you. Asking if you still remembered her."

"Of course I remember her!"

"Don't snap at me. Anyway, she wanted me to tell you she forgave you for all the tricks you played on her as a boy."

"So she knew all along," he said.

"Of course she knew. She was a witch. She told me everything."

"If she knew, then why didn't she say anything?"

Felicia shrugged. "I never understood my mother. Maybe she liked what you made up, your stories. Perhaps she needed dem, who knows? De important thing is she forgave you."

"How did she die?"

"Like your mother. Peacefully, in her sleep."

"That is good."

"Yes it is. Dere is something else. She believed Efua was here in Lagos. Dat she came looking for you. I think it would make Oye happy if you tried to find her."

"Lagos is big. She could be anywhere," he said. "Was it her dying wish?"

"Why?"

"Because then I have to do it. You cannot refuse the dying their last wish," he replied.

"Where do you get dese things? You are just as bad as her, inventing de world," she said, glancing at her watch.

He caught the look. "It is getting late," he said.

Lifting his shirt, he opened the Fulani pouch hanging there and put the postcard and envelope into it next to Beatrice's journal. The Bible was too big to fit.

"What is dat?" she asked.

"A Fulani pouch—the cowherds carry their valuables in them. My friend Redemption has one."

"And cowherds wear it with such a thick chain?"

"This is Lagos," he said with a shrug, picking up the Bible.

She walked him to the door and hugged him for a long time.

"I will miss you."

"Me too."

Letting go, she watched him walk out and down the stairs to the street door. He turned and waved one last time before opening the door and stepping into the darkness.

His mothers
favorate psalm

PSALM 23

The Lord is my shepherd; I shall not want.
He maketh me to lie down in green pastures: he leadeth me beside the still
    waters.
He restoreth my soul: he leadeth me in the paths of righteousness for his
    name's sake.
Yea, though I walk through the valley of the shadow of death, I will fear
    no evil: for thou art with me; thy rod and thy staff they comfort me.
Thou preparest a table before me in the presence of mine enemies: thou
    anointest my head with oil; my cup runneth over.
Surely goodness and mercy shall follow me all the days of my life: and I
    will dwell in the house of the Lord for ever.

SIXTEEN

))))))

We have always done things this way.

The kola-nut ceremony is part hospitality, part etiquette, part protocol and part history lesson. Unlike the Japanese tea ceremony, women take no part in the kola-nut ritual. In fact, female guests are never presented with kola nuts.

))))))

Afikpo, 1980

Rushing to get ready for school, Elvis sidestepped his aunt Felicia's constant nagging.

"I've told you before to stop staying out so late," she railed. "One of dese days you will get caught."

"Especially if you keep announcing it so loudly," Elvis replied.

"Watch your mouth, boy, before I watch it for you," she warned sternly.

"Sorry," he mumbled, stepping into the starch-stiff, tarplike green shorts. Though he was thirteen and she only nineteen, she treated him like he was six. When he complained to Oye, she laughed and told him not to worry.

"She's your mother sister. She's trying to make you forget tha' you lost your mother so young."

Oye always had an explanation for everything, but they were seldom satisfactory to Elvis.

"Leave your shirt off until after breakfast so you don't stain it," Felicia cautioned as he slipped on an undershirt.

wasnt Makeup dangerous?

"Okay," he said sitting on the edge of the bed, watching her putting on her makeup, fascinated by the deep flake of her powder-patted cheeks, the cherry pout of her lips and the heavy blue eye shadow that made her look older. He was amazed not just at how much makeup made her aware of herself, but by how much he wanted to wear that mask. It would be the perfect remedy for his painful shyness. She smacked her lips together over a piece of tissue to blot the lipstick, making him squirm uncomfortably. It seemed to him like she smiled knowingly, but he couldn't be sure.

Her cheap perfume was acrid, and he sneezed as he watched her check her reflection one last time in the cracked mirror. He envied her this ability to prepare a face for the world. To change it any time she liked. Be different people just by a gentle hint of shadow here, a dash of color there. She could even change her hair to suit her mood: sometimes wearing huge Afro wigs that scoured the sky's underbelly; other times, the elegant plaited stalks called mercy, as though they were stakes in a hunter's trap, or the playful run of cornrows—his favorite.

"Why are you sitting dere daydreaming instead of going to breakfast?" she demanded in a shrill tone, shocking Elvis from his reverie. She was already at the door on her way out. "Come on!"

"I'm coming."

As she clacked out on six-inch platforms, riding on the echo of her teeth kissing, he reached into the wastebasket for the tissue that wore her lip shape in distinct red. He pressed the paper lips against his, eyes closed, inhaling all of her. Dropping the tissue back into the wastebasket, he fingered her wig on its wicker stand.

"Elvis!"

"Coming!" he replied, grabbing his schoolbag and shirt and heading for the dining room. His father sat at the table reading the paper. The headline caught Elvis's attention: MILITARY TO STEP DOWN. That was strange; Elvis could not remember when the military had not run the country. His father spoke often and nostalgically about his days as a member of parliament in the first republic, but to Elvis it sounded suspiciously like all his father's stories. Like the one about being made to walk forty miles each way to school every day as a child. Or the one about hunting a lion with his father, Elvis's grandfather, armed with

nothing but native broadswords. Of course his father did not know
that in general science, Elvis had learned that lions had been extinct in
this part of the country since the twenties. But he never challenged
him. That attracted an angry telling off, at best; at worst, a slap. His father could slap well too. The initial impact stung, and for hours after,
a strange heat persisted, reminding you of your transgression all day
until it burned out as a lumpy bruise.

"Who will run the country if the army steps down, then?" Elvis
asked, stuffing a large piece of yam in his mouth and chewing noisily.

"Stop eating like a goat, lad. You have no manners," Oye said.
"Sunday, speak to your son."

"Do what your grandmother says, boy, unless you want a beating."

"Must you always threaten the lad, Sunday, eh?"

"I thought you wanted me to talk to him?"

"Talk. Not threaten."

"Ah! Women!"

Elvis ate slowly, scrunched down in his seat, reading the back of his
father's paper.

"If civilians take over, will that be better?" Elvis asked nobody in
particular.

Sunday Oke put down his paper, shoveled a piece of yam into his
mouth, chewed contemplatively, then spoke:

"Good children do not concern themselves with adult problems."

Elvis opened his mouth to speak, but Aunt Felicia got there first.

"Elvis, time to leave if you want me to walk you to school."

As Elvis hurried out of the compound to join the other children
streaming to school, he thought he saw Innocent lurking in the bushes
outside. He looked unkempt, and even from a distance it was easy to
see the blood on his clothes. Just then his father's car nosed out of the
gate, and Innocent vanished.

Voices, disembodied and distant, floated in to Elvis, waking him. He
got up and stumbled outside to pee. The moon was full, washing
everything in a white fluorescence. It was bright enough to see by, and

he didn't need the safety of the storm lantern he clutched in one hand while the other directed the piss stream away. Aunt Felicia's nurse's uniform, left out to dry overnight, flapped on the line, triggering his fear of ghosts. He scurried inside and hid under the covers.

The voices he heard earlier were still deep in conversation. They came from the parlor and meant his father had guests. He wondered who they were. Curiosity overcame his fear and he crept out into the dark corridor, heading as close to the curtained-off parlor door as he could. Light from the lanterns cracked through the gaps around the curtain; still, Elvis repeated the Lord's Prayer softly to himself.

"We will cover all de campaign costs," one of the men said. "It will cost you nothing."

Another: "It is just dat you are de only one from dis town with a chance of winning. We really want a representative in de House of Assembly."

"You have done it before. In de first republic": still another.

The hand over his mouth smothered any screams, and the arm wrapped around him pinned his limbs tight. He was lifted bodily and carried down the corridor, fear locking him rigid. But Oye's voice soothed him.

"You shouldn't eavesdrop on conversations tha' dinna include you," she said, plunking him down on his bed. "Now sleep."

"Come and vote for Chief Okonkwo and de People's Party. De People's Party is de party for de people and by de people, led by de people."

The election campaigns had begun in earnest, Elvis noted as the van sprouting loudspeakers drove past the house.

"Where shall we put our mark? Next to de People's Party! What shall we spit upon? All de other parties."

The song was catching, and Elvis soon found himself repeating it. He hated when that happened. With a sigh, he returned to the paper. Reading the paper had begun as part of a homework assignment from Sunday. His initial resentment with the work was balanced by his happiness that his father was spending time with him, even if it was to ask questions about what he had read. But now his pleasure was singular and he looked forward to it.

The editorial, about one of the presidential candidates, claimed that he held the key to the Atlantic Ocean and that if provoked, he could unlock the sea and flood the whole country. Elvis laughed out loud. He thought it might be funny if the sea actually did flood the country in a couple of days. That would surely freak out the newspaper's editor.

"Elvis! Where is your father?" a woman asked him.

"I don't know," Elvis replied, wondering who she was.

"Elvis, do you know where your father kept de flyers for de rally?" a man asked him.

Elvis shrugged and headed for the peace of a tree branch. Shortly after his father resigned his position as superintendent of schools and announced his plans to run for office, their home became a madhouse of thugs and media and other nondescript hangers-on, and it seemed like Elvis could never find a moment for himself. The cost of politics meant that they were swamped by hundreds of people who come by for free food and drink and to offer their support or services. Oye managed to hold a circle of sanity, though. Her reputation as a witch frightened even the vicious thugs that Uncle Joseph had hired.

The campaigns were held during the Harmattan, which was Elvis's favorite season. Chilly winds from the Sahara blew a fine red dust that clouded everything in a shimmering mist, making the air dry and harsh. Everyone went around with chapped lips, and in some extreme cases, cracked soles. But there were also the heady scent of dry grasslands, new discoveries, bush fires and Christmas.

Harmattan fell between December and January, when the sun burned the cool season into a crisp before February. It was the season of rest. The harvests were over, and the next planting season would not begin until April or May, when the rains returned. It was as if everyone were on a long siesta.

From his perch in the tree, Elvis could see clearly over the wall of the compound. The campaign truck was still visible, lurching down the potholed street to the small town square. The voice over the loudspeaker was distorted by the wind and the words were unintelligible, but loud nonetheless. He could also see a lot of adults lounging in the public square under huge umbrella trees. Well, he thought, the campaigners will have an audience.

Some children ran after the truck, lost in the cloud of dust it scoured up. They shouted and tried to jump onto the bumpers and running boards. He waited for the sound of tears that would announce the inevitable accident. Surprisingly, there was none.

The party truck had stopped in the square, but the group of adults seemed not to be listening. They were carrying on animated conversations or playing board games. Seeing that the commentator's adulation for the candidates was getting them nowhere, a bunch of thugs climbed down from their perch on the roof of the truck and began to offload heavy jute sacks from inside the truck. They then approached the nonchalant crowd.

From what Elvis could make out, they were handing out drinks, snack packets, money, T-shirts, bags, mugs and trays, all with slogans printed on them. The square had suddenly come alive with people jostling for the gifts. He dropped from his perch and ran out of the compound. If he hurried he might get a free T-shirt with an opponent's slogan and photograph. That was bound to piss off his father, something that brought him immense pleasure.

By the time he got to the square, it was a melee of arms, legs and raised dust as adults shoved children aside for access to some token. All the time, the commentator was shouting over the noise, wild promises chasing the gifts: "Dis is from Chief Okonkwo, your candidate for Congress. Chief Okonkwo is an erudite son of de soil educated in de USA, and his money is uncountable. He does not want to join government for embezzling money but to dash you all money. Dis small sample will show you de riches and benefits you will enjoy by voting Chief Okonkwo for Congress."

Suddenly the sky was full of the sound of a helicopter. The whoomping of the big bird drowned any commentary from below and held everyone's attention as it swirled dust into every bodily orifice. Everyone stopped fighting, standing stock-still. Who knew if it was the police—or even worse, the army? Elvis noted real fear on some faces old enough to remember the reality of helicopter gunships from the war.

"Vote Abrake for president!"

The voice from heaven startled everyone. Then a shower of small notes and coins fell from the hovering craft.

"Vote Abrake for president! What did I say?!" the disembodied heavenly voice repeated.

"Vote Abrake for president!" the crowd cheered in unison as they fought through the dust storm to retrieve coins and notes. There was much hair pulling, punching and swearing.

Even the personnel from the other party abandoned their duties to fight for the money. Then just as quickly as it had come, the helicopter rose and vanished, leaving behind dust-teared eyes, torn clothes and an arena swept clean by scrabbling fingers.

As he trudged home, pockets full of retrieved coins and sweets, a dusty T-shirt that announced OKONKWO FOR GOVERNOR clasped firmly in hand, Elvis smiled happily. His father, though contesting, was unable to afford much of a campaign team or gifts.

Elvis did not know why his father bothered. He was bound to lose with his intimate approach of house-to-house calls where he appealed passionately to kinsmen and women who listened patiently until he finished before asking: "Yes, Sunday, dat is all well and good, but are you offering as much money as de oder candidates?"

The forest fire had raged for days, and was still quite dangerous, threatening to spread to nearby homesteads. Elvis sat on the roof of the still-unfinished two-story house his father was building to replace their current bungalow. With Sunday's resignation from his job to run for office, all construction had stopped on the new house, all the money diverted to his campaign. Elvis stared at the distant magnificence of the fire. These fires raged every Harmattan, set by farmers to clear the bush from land they intended to cultivate come the rains.

Traffic was backed up on the road running through the dense forest. Flammable cargo meant trouble. Petrol tankers often exploded like bombs, scattering debris everywhere, further fueling the fires, and he could see the police turning them away. The fire brigade truck was parked helplessly while the firemen lounged about watching the fire, some crouching by burning roadside twigs to light cigarettes. This fire was too big for them to fight; they only had one truck, and besides, it was common knowledge that their water supply had been cut off for days—something to do with a broken generator at the pumping station.

Updrafts, sparks and even volatile oils within some plants, like the oil bean tree, fanned the flames. The fire had cut them off from neighboring towns, as there was just one road in and out, so most of the campaigning had come to a halt, which for Elvis was a mixed blessing. It was a relief not to keep hearing the trucks and helicopters, but it also meant that his father and his new thugs hung close to the house.

Hezekiah was sitting next to Elvis, watching the fire. He had brought a couple of sodas and a bag of peanuts and was happily munching away as if he had never seen one of these fires before. Elvis turned to look at him. They weren't really friends and had only spent time together on the smoking wall after the movies. Perhaps it had been a mistake to invite him over.

"Dis is a good time to hunt," Hezekiah said.

"Why?"

"All de animals and reptiles are fleeing de fire. So just wait on de road and kill dem as dey come out. Easy."

Elvis imagined antelopes and deer running straight into the roads to be hit by cars. Or the grass cutters, cousins of the rabbit, roasting as they ran and reaching safety well-done. He wondered if there were people down there by the fire, collecting ready-cooked game.

"Well, it gives a whole new meaning to fast food," he replied, and they both laughed.

"Peanuts?" Hezekiah asked, passing the bag.

"Look," Elvis replied, pointing.

Birds, on fire, tried to fly from the flames. Little sparrows and finches ricocheted like flaming Ping-Pong balls. Lovely white egrets flapped their wings of fire, hovering like phoenixes before crashing to be consumed in a whoosh of flame. Those that escaped one part of the forest only spread the fire to another.

"If dose things crash into a roof, dey can set de thatch on fire," Hezekiah said.

"My father says that the only creatures who love forest fires are kites. He says they soar above the flames and ash, razor-sharp eyes hunting for prey, swooping down on confused creatures, snatching them up to some distant height where they can eat their catch in peace."

"Aah."

"My father says they are the politicians of the forest: the only ones to profit from everyone else's loss and pain."

"Ha, Elvis, dat your father is deep."

They sat in silence for a long time, until darkness began to creep up on them and the Christmas lights began to come on in houses. For Elvis, there was nothing as comforting at night as the gentle winking of Christmas lights in some distant window.

"So, are you getting new clothes dis Christmas?" Hezekiah asked.

"With this election? Not likely."

"But surely you people will be killing at least one or two goats."

"I guess so, but with all these thugs and party supporters around, I doubt I will get to eat much."

"Well, dere is an easy solution. You kill de goat. I'll help you. You know de butchers always get a choice cut."

"Why are you so eager to help? Aren't you killing a goat?"

"No, we can only afford a chicken."

"Chickens are easy enough to kill, certainly easier than rubber-necked turkeys. Or goats," Elvis said.

"But as you know, de hardest thing about chickens is catching dem. Dey weave and bob like crazy, running in a straight line, den veering off to de right or left suddenly, sending everyone crashing into walls."

Elvis laughed. He was very familiar with chasing chickens.

"So what do you say about de goat? Have you never killed one before?"

"No," Elvis said.

"What of a chicken? At least tell me you have killed a chicken."

"One," Elvis said in a voice that betrayed the freshness of the memory. Having caught the chicken, he had grasped it firmly by its wings and laid it on its side, trapping both its legs and wings under-foot, all the while following the instructions Aunt Felicia was shouting at him. Lifting its neck tenderly, he plucked a few feathers to reveal its pulsing pink neck.

"Now comes de real test," Aunt Felicia had said. "If your knife is sharp enough it will sink through de neck like butter, severing de head completely."

But that chicken did not die easily. Even when they immersed it in a pan of scalding water to ease the plucking, headless and all it sprang up and sprinted off before beating itself into an acceptance of death on a tree stump.

"What is it?"

Elvis told Hezekiah about his chicken.

"Don't feel so bad—if dey could, chickens would kill us. Dat's de way it is."

"Have you killed a goat before?"

"Many," Hezekiah said.

"Are they easy to kill?"

"No. Goats are a different matter. Dey have eyes dat watch you, not letting you get away with anything. And dat bleat, so childlike. It's not easy. But den being a man is not, abi?"

"I don't want to kill anything."

"Sometimes we have no choice."

▼▼

FRIED YAM, PLANTAIN AND BEEF STEW
(Igbo: Ji Egerege, Unine Ya Stew)

INGREDIENTS

Yam
Plantains
Vegetable oil
Cubed beef
Diced onions
Curry powder
Fresh bonnet peppers
Salt
A tin of chopped tomatoes
Sugar

PREPARATION

First, peel the yam and plantains and slice them into thin slivers. Next, wash yam and plantain slivers and pat dry with paper towel. Put two dessert spoons of oil into a frying pan and bring it to heat, and then add the yam and plantain slivers. Fry until crisp. Leave to drain on a large plate with a paper towel.

Put the beef to cook. When tender remove from flame. In a deep pot, bring two dessert spoons of vegetable oil to heat. Add the onions, curry powder, fresh bonnet peppers, salt and the tomatoes. Leave on a low flame to reduce. Put in a pinch of salt. When the tomatoes have reduced, put a pinch of sugar in to take away the acidity. Pour in the stock from the beef, stir in the meat and leave to cook for thirty minutes. Arrange the yam and plantain slivers in a nice pattern and drizzle the stew over it.

SEVENTEEN

∭

The youngest male must carry the wooden kola bowl and show it to all of the guests in order of seniority and in order of clan.

The youngest male brings the ornate wooden bowl with the kola nut in it. Carved in the shape of an animal, the bowl has a center dip of peppered peanut butter, which the kola nut is dipped into before eating. In the absence of this, and sometimes even in its presence, alligator pepper is presented as well.

∭

Lagos, 1983

Elvis approached the veranda, where his father sat sipping meditatively on kaikai. The local gin had herbs and roots steeped in it, and the once clear liquid had taken on a murky mud color. He stood for a while in the doorway looking at his father, trying to assess his mood. Aunt Felicia's visit had stirred up questions that he had buried deep inside himself, and now he wanted answers.

The street outside was busy with people hurrying past. A few threw casual greetings at Sunday. With a sigh, Elvis walked out and sat down on the low wall enclosing the veranda. It was waist-high and built of decorative cinder blocks that interlocked in a ladder pattern. Elvis hooked his heels into some of the holes to keep his balance. His position put him squarely in front of his father.

"Evening, sir," he said.

"Evening."

"Can I speak to you about something?" Elvis asked.

"If it is about my drinking, dis is medicinal."

Elvis smiled.

"No, it's about something else."

"What?"

"You remember when Godfrey disappeared?"

"Uhuh."

"Well, Efua came to see me saying she overheard her father and Innocent talking about money."

"You remember dis?"

"Yes."

"Never mind. What is your point?" Sunday asked.

Elvis noticed that his father's eyes had hardened, but Elvis cleared his throat and pressed on.

"She said Uncle Joseph was discussing paying Innocent for killing and burying Godfrey in the forest somewhere."

"Was I dere at de time?"

"In the room with them? No."

"So why are you asking me? Go and ask Joseph, good-for-nothing brother dat he is. Here I am suffering while he is rich, but he cannot offer to help, eh? After I put him through school, gave him de money to start his business, made him de man he is today."

"Why don't you just ask him for help?"

"You know nothing, eh? I am de senior brother. No, he should know what to do. After all, did he ask me to help him? No! I knew what I had to do as his brother and I did it."

Elvis considered the logic for a while, then realized that if he tried to explore it, he would be led away from what he wanted to talk about.

"Efua said that Uncle Joseph and you paid Innocent one thousand naira each to kill Godfrey. You paid the first installment and Uncle Joseph was to pay when the job was done."

"I don't know what you are talking about."

"Do you know what happened to Godfrey?"

"How should I know? Dat boy was a criminal, a disgrace to de family. Maybe he got killed stealing from somebody. For all I know, he is in prison in Katsina-Ala!"

"So Efua was lying?"

"Is it not de same Efua dat said Joseph raped her?"

"He did."

"What are you talking about? Are you mad? I thought we had dis conversation years ago?" Sunday was yelling now.

"Easy—we don't want the neighborhood to know," Elvis cautioned.

Sunday swallowed a glassful of kaikai and shuddered. The alcohol cut the edge off his anger.

"If not dat I have been drinking, I would beat you to an inch of your life, you bastard!" Sunday hissed.

"Listen, I am grown now. I am no longer afraid of you," Elvis said, unhooking his feet from the wall in case he needed to get up in a hurry.

"How can you say dese things about your own family?" Sunday asked.

"I saw Uncle Joseph raping Efua. I saw him."

"So does dat make us murderers?"

"That is why I am asking you if you had anything to do with it."

"And I said no."

Elvis rubbed a hand across his face and looked out into the street. They lived in one of the few places where Maroko made contact with the ground. Halfway along, the street sloped up into a plank walkway. But outside their house, the street was muddy and full of potholes. In the abandoned uncompleted building across the street, the makeshift buka was turning a good trade in fried yam and dodo. He watched the crowd coming and going and absently made a note to get some before it closed.

In the middle of the street a taxi idled, the driver's door open. The interior light was on and Elvis could see the driver talking to a young woman in the passenger seat. He couldn't make out what they were saying, but everything about the man's manner indicated that she was his lover. Soft highlife music from the car radio leaked into the night.

"I don't believe you," Elvis said, turning back to his father.

"Who are you to believe or disbelieve me? Look at dis mad child, dis world has spoiled!"

"Innocent came to my room a few nights after the murder," Elvis said, pausing at the word "murder." That was something, to call it that, but what else was it? he thought.

"I gave him food and he seemed very afraid. He mentioned Godfrey, then fled in terror," he continued.

"So you harbored a known criminal in my house?"

"What do you mean, 'a known criminal'?"

"Well, you said Efua told you dat Innocent killed Godfrey. So you knew he was a criminal and yet you harbored him in my house."

Elvis stared at his father, mouth open. This could not be happening, he thought.

"Shut your mouth before a fly enters it," Sunday said. "All your life, you have been like dis, eh? Never having a grip on de real world. You are just like your dead mother. Touched."

"Leave my mother out of this!"

Sunday stood up threateningly.

"Are you shouting at me? Are you crazy? I will—"

"Sit down, old man, before you fall down," Elvis said, rising to his feet.

They stood staring each other down for a few minutes; then, unexpectedly, Sunday folded, his rage gone, replaced by a look Elvis took to be shame.

"Dis world has spoiled," Sunday muttered under his breath as he sat down.

"Dad."

Sunday looked up. It sounded strange to hear his son call him Dad, but he liked it.

"Dad," Elvis repeated.

"What?"

"Did you pay Innocent to kill Godfrey?"

"You don't understand de difficulty of trying to be a man in dis society. So many expectations, so much pressure. You will see."

"So he is dead."

"I never said dat."

"You didn't have to. Dad, did you have anything to do with it?"

"Do you know what people ask you when dey meet you as a young man? Who is your father? First, dey want to know your father's name, de stock you come from, before dey decide whether to bother talking to you."

Elvis was silent. He reached for the kaikai. With trembling hands he put the bottle to his mouth and took a deep drink. The liquor burned through him in a series of hacking coughs.

"Easy," Sunday said.

"So what does that mean?" Elvis asked. His was voice tight and his eyes were tearing from the harsh liquor.

"In dis place, it used to be dat all you had was your name—before dis new madness with money started. De measure of a man was his name. It will be again. It took me years of pain, suffering and hard work to build a name people could respect. My father was a houseboy to de white priests. We were nobody. To de whites we were their servant's children, mini-servants. To de traditional world, we were white people's slaves, a curse, so we were disinherited of land, clan, everything. I built our name up with honor until it became a force to be reckoned with. I have never had much money, but I had a name dat opened doors. A name people spoke with respect."

"He was killed for a name?"

"No! He was killed because he was a threat to all we had. De only inheritance I had to give you was a name of honor. His actions were muddying de only thing of value we had to give you."

"So he *was* killed for a name."

"No! He was killed for honor."

"What kind of honor does that? Kills its own?"

"Can't you understand? I did dis out of love for you."

"So now you did this for me?" Elvis asked.

Sunday took a deep breath and a gulp of the gin almost simultaneously. He didn't respond.

"That is why your backers pulled out of your campaign. That's why you drink, to drown your conscience. I used to think that it was my mother's death that pushed you over the edge. But this was part of it too. I'm sorry for you," Elvis said.

Sunday put down the gin bottle.

"Don't be sorry for me, be sorry for yourself. Do you know why we have a lot of deformed children begging? Because their parents know dey have no future. So at birth, before de child knows pain, dey deform it because it increases its earning power as a beggar. Do you see de love? All dey have to give de child is its deformity. All I have to give you is my name, your name, Elvis Oke. And when I die, it will continue to help you build something for your children. Dat's why I don't want you to be a dancer. It will spoil your name."

"What are you talking about? Your name is associated with failure. Where is the honor in that? How can I carry this name knowing that it belongs to murderers and rapists?"

"Dis was not murder! Dis was a mercy killing. It was only a matter of time before de police caught Godfrey in some crime and executed him publicly. Dat would have killed all of us."

"I could forgive you if I tried, you know. But Uncle Joseph? This was his son. First he rapes his daughter, then he has his son murdered?"

"Why do you insist on dis rape story?"

"You think I made that up? That Efua made it up?"

"She is a harlot, you know. Here in Lagos. I have seen her."

"Liar!"

"And you can't know for sure dat what you think you saw dat time was Joseph raping his daughter. Maybe you were confused."

Elvis finally had to accept that his father would never believe that Joseph was capable of rape. Or maybe he didn't want to. He had some-how deluded himself into believing that murdering Godfrey was an act of honor. He had not even considered the effect it would have on In-nocent, who had to carry out the crime. This was all shit, all shit. Isn't that what Redemption always said?

"He raped her."

"You can't know for sure, unless it happened to you," Sunday said. His tone was conciliatory, as though he was subconsciously begging Elvis for it not to be true.

"He raped me too," Elvis said, surprised at how calm he sounded as the memory of that day in the chapel came rushing back with a pain so fresh, he instinctively clenched his buttocks against it. But whatever had held him up all this time collapsed in the face of his admission, and his tears were followed by body-shaking sobs. He cried, loud and hard, mouth open, snot running down his nose. Sunday stared at Elvis, mouth open, searching for the possibility of a lie. But there was none. The sound, when it came from him, was nothing Elvis recognized. It was a howl. All animal, all death. It propelled Elvis off the veranda. This was not the comfort he wanted, needed. He could deal with all his father's anger, but not this. He stumbled down the street to the bus stop, ignoring the curious stares of passersby, wiping furiously at his face with his sleeve. As he walked, he realized, the only way out of this life was Redemption.

"Redemption! Redemption!" Elvis called, banging wildly on Redemption's door. The room was dark and there was no answer.

"He done move," one of the neïghbors said, opening a door. "Now stop de knocking, eh? I cannot hear myself thinking."

Shit, Elvis thought. Of course Redemption had moved, to Maroko, where he had just come from. In the confusion of the confrontation with his father, he had fled by instinct to this place where he had always felt safe.

"Elvis?"

He spun around. Redemption was standing in the doorway to Kansas's room. "Why you dey find me here? You know I moved."

"I forgot."

"What is it?"

"Can we talk?"

"Is dat Elvis? Elvis, come and join us, we are eating," Kansas called from inside the room.

Elvis crossed the courtyard in seconds. Redemption stood aside to let him in.

"Dere is beer in de fridge. Help yourself, den wash your hands and join us," Kansas said.

Elvis opened the miniature fridge and helped himself to a Gulder.

"Isn't this the stuff that blows up in your face if you smoke while drinking it?" he asked, popping the top.

"Dat is plain rumor," Kansas said.

Elvis sat down on one corner of the love seat. Redemption occupied the other. Kansas sat on the bed facing them. On the coffee table between them was a meal of fufu and egusi sauce. Redemption and Kansas were working up a sweat eating. To their left, too big for the compact room, was a television set. They were watching a video on it.

"Ah, Elvis. Wash your hand, de food is going fast," Redemption said.

"Thanks, but I am not hungry."

"Dis food sweet, man. My girlfriend cook it," Kansas said.

"Thank you, but I am fine," Elvis insisted. "What are you guys watching?"

"*Dirty Harry*. Dat man is too bad. Real Actor."

Elvis nodded and sipped at his beer. He really wanted to talk to Redemption alone.

"Hey, that's John Wayne!" he said, excitedly pointing to Clint Eastwood. He knew fully well it wasn't, but he wanted to be part of the conversation, defaulting to the ignorance he expected of the other two.

"John Wayne? You dey mad. Dat is Actor. John Wayne is not in movies anymore," Kansas said.

"But . . . what?" Elvis said, sounding confused.

"Is okay, Elvis," Redemption explained. "Things change, you know. Now dere is only Bad Guy and Actor. No more John Wayne."

"Why?"

"Because de type of movies done change. Dat's all. Now let us watch de movie in peace."

Elvis lapsed into silence, drinking several bottles of beer as he watched images flicker across the screen. The color needed adjusting, and everything had a garish red tint to it that made him nauseous after a while.

"Do you have ciga?" he asked Redemption.

Redemption passed a packet of Marlboros to him.

"This is not my brand," Elvis said, looking disdainfully at the pack.

"Okay, give my ciga back."

"You don't have any Benson & Hedges?"

"Give me my ciga back," Redemption repeated.

"Easy," Elvis said, taking one and lighting it before passing it back.

"Take it easy. Gulder is strong beer, don't drink too much."

"Humph."

Elvis had no recollection of falling asleep, but woke groggily as Redemption shook him roughly.

"Wake up. Dis is not your house. I told you to easy on de beer. Wake up, we have to go."

Elvis yawned and stretched. He sat up and wiped drool from his mouth.

"Where is Kansas?"

"He go pick his girlfriend. Come on, we have to go before he return."

Standing up, Elvis noted that the place had been tidied since he fell asleep. The empty beer bottles were gone, as were the remnants of the meal. Kansas had even changed the sheets.

"Boy, you guys work fast," he said.

Redemption smiled.

"It is Kansas, my broder! De tings a woman can make you do is wonderful."

Elvis laughed. They staggered out of the room, the latch locking home behind them. Elvis felt a moment of panic and checked under his shirt for his Fulani pouch. It was still there, he noted, opening it. As were his mother's journal and a copy of *The Prophet* by Kahlil Gibran, one of his favorite books.

"I hope he has not forgotten his keys," Elvis said.

Something about the comment struck them both as funny and they fell about laughing.

"Dat will be one angry broder if dat is so," Redemption gasped.

"Am I still drunk?" Elvis asked, swaying dangerously.

"No. It's de ground dat is moving," Redemption said, laughing.

"So how are we getting home?" Elvis asked.

"I bring machine. I go ride."

"Which kind of machine? Ha, Redemption! Are you in any condition to ride?"

"How you go know de difference, drunk as you be?"

Elvis giggled. "I guess you are right."

They approached a burly black motorcycle. Redemption straddled it and kicked the stand up. He swayed for a moment, then found his balance.

"Okay, Elvis, climb aboard. Maroko straight," he said.

"Are you sure you can operate this?" Elvis slurred, as he settled into the passenger seat, arms firmly wrapped around Redemption's midsection.

"Hey, Elvis, are you homo? Release me small," Redemption said. Elvis relaxed his grip.

"Sorry, I am holding on for my life," he said.

"Ha! Elvis. Relax, you know I am Easy Rider," Redemption said, revving up and releasing the clutch. The bike shot off at an incredible speed, swaying from side to side.

"Easy!" Elvis shouted.

"One-way trip to heaven!" Redemption shouted back.

They roared down the Isolo freeway, weaving between cars like a bobbin threading yarn, barely managing to stay upright.

"Whose bike is this?" Elvis yelled over the roar of wind and traffic.

"Dis machine? It belongs to de new people I am doing business with," Redemption yelled back.

"Hey, slow down. That is a police checkpoint ahead. You don't want them to open fire," Elvis said, pointing ahead to the makeshift barricade of oil drums and car tires that sat in the middle of the free-way like a pimple. Redemption ignored him, clutched down, revved up and cut across four lanes of traffic to an exit.

"Redemption!"

"Easy, Elvis. Dis is not States. Dey have no car to chase us."

"Just don't kill us."

"Relax, you fear more dan woman. Listen, punk, do you feel lucky?"

"What?"

"Well, do you?"

"Stop speaking in riddles. Just stop, it will only cost us a couple of bucks in bribes to get past."

"Number one, we no wear helmet. Number two, I don't have de papers for dis machine. Number three, I no get license. Plus I hold gun in my pocket. Dat is too much bribe dan I can afford. I no fit to pay!"

Redemption shouted as they gunned up the exit ramp and made a sharp right.

"Gun?! Gun!?"

"No dey shout 'gun' like dat. People can hear."

They made a left and were soon traveling down a dirt road skirting the lagoon.

"Where are we?"

"Near Mile 2. One more left and we go dey back on de freeway."

As they bumped over the road at high speed, a tall column of dust kicked up by the tires chased after them. To their right, the water was a black presence, reflecting the moon. In the distance, Elvis could make out small fishing canoes bobbing on the swell, the lanterns burning in their prows dancing like fireflies.

"Yeee!"

Redemption's shout was the last thing Elvis heard before the bike skidded out from under them and they were free-falling. They came to a stop about twenty feet down the road. Behind them, the motorcycle's engine roared for a while, the tires spinning in the air, before spluttering to a stop. The single headlight burned through the silent dark.

"Elvis?"

Silence.

"Elvis?"

"Shit, I think I am dead."

"No, my friend. Wounded, but not dead. Are you okay? Complete?"

Elvis got into a sitting position. Redemption was already standing up. He lit two cigarettes and passed one to Elvis. Elvis accepted the cigarette and took a deep drag; then, pulling himself slowly to his feet, he checked for broken bones. He was fine aside from a few bruises and a torn shirt.

"How are you?" Redemption asked.

"Apart from some bruises, I am fine. You?"

"Man no die, man no rotten."

Elvis laughed. It felt good.

"What happened?"

"Who knows? Too much drink, bad road, witchcraft. Choose one."

"Do you realize we could have died?"

"But we didn't. So dis is an omen dat we will both live long," Redemption said, walking back to the prone bike. As he righted it, Elvis called out:

"Be careful of spilled fuel with that cigarette."

"Shut up, my friend. Dis is not a movie," Redemption said, climbing back onto the bike and kicking the throttle. After a few abortive attempts, the bike came alive.

"Excellent. Not even a scratch. Dis is good omen. Okay, Elvis, all aboard."

Elvis hesitated.

"You want to spend de night here?"

"Shit," Elvis muttered, climbing on the back.

As they left, he was glad to notice that Redemption had cut back on the speed.

"So why did you come to see me? You must have been upset to forget I moved."

"Is that deal you offered me still open?" Elvis asked.

"Yes. And after dis accident, I am confident for both of us. It will go well. Trust me."

Elvis's reply was swallowed up by the wind as they gained the freeway and Redemption opened the throttle.

▼▼▼▼▼▼▼▼▼▼▼▼▼▼▼▼▼▼▼▼▼▼▼▼▼▼▼▼▼

SPIGELIA ANTHELMIA *L.*
(Yoruba: Ewe Aran)

As in most herbs, this is common to abandoned farmlands and clearings in the forest. It is a small erect herb with a rounded smooth stem. Its leaves are oval and broad at the base, tapering to a fine point at the apex. It has pale pink flowers with dark stripes and its fruits are small, round, warty and two-lobed.

The plant is boiled and drunk to expel worms. Its fresh leaves are considered especially poisonous to domestic animals and can cause their death in two to three hours. An overdose of the extract of the leaves is capable of killing a human. In the past, witches used it to exact revenge on their enemies either by mixing it in with the feed of domestic animals or by pouring a large dose of the decoction into a soup or drink.

EIGHTEEN

))))))

This is the first step. This is the way it is done.

The protocol is followed strictly.

))))))

Elvis is about 13 years old

Afikpo, 1980

Invariably the talk turned to sex. Obed and Titus had seen blue movies, and although they didn't understand much, they tried to convey what they had seen to the others.

Titus, in hallowed silence, told of how a woman took a man's penis in her mouth and sucked out his soul while he yelled in pain. The others were not convinced at first, but he insisted he had seen it, white and lacy, dripping from her mouth. Elvis, in Obiechena's *Biology for Beginners,* had read differently, but he knew better than to be a nerd by arguing. Besides, Obed was suggesting that they experiment on each other. Elvis wasn't sure why, but this was something that he wanted to do, so he wasn't as vocal as the others in his protests.

Maybe Elvis is gay?

"Dat is evil, Obed!" Titus shouted.

"Yes, we will surely go to hell for dat," Hezekiah agreed.

"Dat is homo. It is taboo, forbidden," Elvis interjected weakly.

"But I saw it in de movies," Obed insisted.

That one stumped everyone. They sat in the Anglican chapel, a simple bungalow in white at the bottom of the hill, where the cashew groves ended abruptly in a pant of hot white sand. It was nothing like the elaborate Catholic church they attended, and it had less of a religious impact on them. They often came here to gorge on the fruit they had picked from the grove. In the daytime, the chapel was a cool sanctuary from the sweltering afternoon and was always empty except for the bats that infested the roof by the hundreds, and whose dank smell hung in the air just below the musk of angels. At dusk they streamed out in a dense black squeaking cloud to feast on the cashews.

But to Elvis there was an unspoken thing, an air of sacredness that tugged at him. He often lay on one of the pews inside, waiting for an angel to reveal itself to him. The air here was light, unlike in the Catholic church, where the air was oppressive with taboos, guilt, incense, prayers and portents of magic. There were no crucifixes here, no statues, only an oil painting of a brilliant sunrise over the altar. An uncomplicated relationship that he would not dare admit.

"Was it John Wayne doing it?"

"Or Actor?"

"No. Dese were two men I do not know, but dey were doing it and it must be all right because dey do it in de movies," Obed insisted.

"But we might get caught. You know grown-ups are always dropping in here to pray," Elvis said.

"Not by dis time. Dey are at work."

They paired off, alternately lying on top of each other, humping through their clothing. As the afternoon wore on, they became a little more adventurous and were soon down to their underwear, then nothing. Lost in effort, they did not notice an adult appear at the door of the chapel.

Titus saw him first. Though the man did not speak, they knew he had been there a while. Leaping up, they made a run for it, but Elvis had been underneath the heavier Obed, and as he struggled to his feet, fumbling with his shorts, he felt a slap connect with his face. His head jerked back and he fell.

Elvis opened his mouth to speak, but the man put his finger to his lips. He couldn't focus on any details—what the man looked like or what he was wearing. All he was aware of was the man's sweaty, hot smell, choking him.

He opened his fly and Elvis saw his huge erect penis pop out. He was petrified.

"Come here," the man said gruffly.

Zombielike, Elvis went to him. The man placed his hands roughly on his shoulders and forced him down on his knees. His penis was level with Elvis's face, a twitching cobra ready to strike.

"Suck it," the man hissed.

With a shudder, Elvis remembered Titus's story about the woman who sucked the man's soul out. That would make him a vampire, Elvis thought, and that was for some inane reason more frightening.

"Suck it," the man hissed again, thrusting his hips forward so that his penis brushed Elvis's mouth. Reluctantly he let the tip in, sucking on it slowly, as though eating a stick of sugarcane. The man trembled, making guttural noises in the back of his throat. Elvis stopped, afraid the man's soul had already started to leave his body.

The man did not speak, just pulled Elvis's head back into his crotch, ramming his penis down his throat so hard he gagged. Tiring of this, he dragged him up. Thinking it was over, Elvis started to turn to run, but the man slapped him hard again, stunning him. Elvis could taste the warm rust of his blood mixing with the man's musk. Without speaking, the man spun Elvis around, forcing him over the edge of a pew. Holding Elvis's squirming body down with one hand, the man yanked Elvis's shorts down with the other. For a second everything seemed to stop. Elvis felt the man hard against his buttocks, and then a burst of fire ripped him into two. The man tore into him, again and again. The pain was so intense, Elvis passed out. When he opened his eyes, he was on the ceiling looking down on their bodies spooned together. The man had stopped moving and lay sweating and heaving like a farm laborer on break. Elvis closed his eyes and drifted into darkness.

When he came to, he was alone. As he pulled up his shorts, he felt the wetness on his buttocks. Fearing it was the dreaded juice of the soul, he tried to wipe it away. An examination of his hand revealed blood. Dazed, he stumbled to the front of the altar and sat on the floor for hours, staring up at the picture of a sunrise.

Night filled with the screeching of bats streaming out of the roof. Still he sat, staring impassively at the painting, willing Jesus to reach out of the sun and heal him. Inside the chapel, darkness became denser, the only source of light a dim bulb on the porch. Becoming aware of a presence at the door, he turned to look but could only make out the vague outlines of a body. Not too tall.

"Elvis."

"Yes?"

The figure was still fuzzy as it approached, but soon his eyes came into focus.

"Elvis," Efua called again.

"Yes," he replied softly, glad that it was she who had come looking for him.

Efua sat down beside him and held his hand. For a long time neither spoke.

"What happened?" Efua asked, her voice so soft it was almost inaudible. He told her. In the darkness he felt her tense up and wince.

"He's done dat to me too," she whispered, afraid to speak too loudly.

"I tried to tell my father about you," he began, and paused.

"And . . . ?"

"He didn't believe me."

"Grown-ups do not believe children. Are you cold?"

He shook his head in the dark and felt her smile, and the warm saltiness of his tears surprised him.

▼▼▼▼▼▼▼▼▼▼▼▼▼▼▼▼▼▼▼▼▼▼▼▼▼▼▼▼▼▼▼▼▼▼▼

JOLLOF RICE WITH DRIED FISH

INGREDIENTS

Rice
Palm oil
Salt
Hot peppers
Dry powdered crayfish
Onions
Maggi cubes
Dried fish

PREPARATION

Wash the rice several times in warm water, then put it on to boil for about fifteen minutes. Wash it again and then put it back on to boil. Pour in some palm oil (only a little, because though palm oil soothes the interior like an inner poultice, too much can also clog the veins and cause fevers). Add salt, hot peppers, the powdered crayfish, onions and a couple of Maggi cubes. Add the dried fish, previously softened in hot water. Fried meat is optional, but dried or smoked antelope goes particularly well in this dish. Top up with water to keep from burning. After about thirty minutes, turn the heat down and wait for all the liquid to dry up. Serve. For the best taste, cook in an earthenware pot over a wood fire.

NINETEEN

He does this by arranging the kola nuts on the wooden kola bowl, and saying "Honored guests, kola is here."

This is to determine two things, the person's clan and whether they come in peace. If they come in peace, they rub the chalk across their left wrist. The reverse applies if they do not come in peace. Then with the residual piece of chalk, they draw their family and clan marking on the floor, usually a symbol of eight lines: four for the personal, four for the clan.

Lagos, 1983

Sunday Oke woke with a start. It was not a noise that woke him. Nor was it the silence. It was something moving between, deep inside him. Strains of classical music reached him from a radio somewhere in the night. Sunday couldn't place the song, but he knew the program well. It was called *Music of the Masters*. The music rode on an undercurrent of static, as though the radio playing it wasn't tuned properly. In the distance, the early-morning cargo train screamed past. For some reason he thought of the image of a bullet-ridden corpse lying across train tracks. Was that what had woken him? No, he muttered under his breath, remembering that the image came from last night's news.

It seemed that a lot of bodies were turning up dead on the train tracks in the early-morning hours, riddled with bullets. There must have been a lot of bodies found that way for one to finally make the news, Sunday thought at the time. He remembered laughing when the reporter said the police maintained that the cause of death, in each case, was "the impact of early-morning trains hitting the bodies."

He got up, swinging skinny legs out of bed, flesh wrinkled and sagging. He yawned and stretched. Beside him, Comfort snored loudly. Her youngest child slept on a mat in the corner of the room. The things that child must see, he thought.

He slept naked, and his sex swung pendulous and full, heavy with regret for a life of too much sex and not enough love. Yawning, he pulled on a pair of babanriga pants and a loose jumper. Unlocking the door, he felt his way down the dark corridor to the backyards and the toilet. He peed, staring at the amber liquid collecting in the bowl as though he expected to divine what had woken him. As he poured the bucket of water in to flush it, he felt like his life was going down the drain.

He felt his way back to the door and stepped into the living room, standing there confused for a moment. Elvis, that was it—he wanted to talk to Elvis. He let himself out again and knocked on Elvis's door, which opened straight out onto the veranda. The architecture in Lagos never made any sense; maximizing rent seemed to be the main design consideration. There was no answer. Still not back, he thought. Coming back into the living room, he stared at Comfort's other two children sleeping on the cushions spread out on the floor. The thought of sitting on bare chair springs did not appeal to him.

Deciding to go back out onto the veranda, he pulled a sweater over the jumper, as he felt the cold a lot more acutely these days, and fetched a beer from the fridge chugging in the corner, giving off heat. He spotted Beatrice's record player sitting on the sideboard where Elvis kept it. He picked it up, holding it tucked in the crook of one arm, while under the other he held some records. Balancing everything carefully with his beer, he walked out to the veranda.

After he set everything down, he put on Miles's *Kind of Blue*, sat back on the bench, sipped his beer and let the music wash over him. The sky was oversalted with stars and he traced Orion's hunt and Pegasus' winged flight. A shooting star streaked across the sky, stirring an epiphany that disappeared out of reach as quickly as the star, leaving him with only the sense of having imagined it. He reached for his beer and took one more swig.

He played record after record, relaxing until he had no more cares than a rag flapping gently to night's rhythm. With each record played, he seemed in search of something; the "Blue in Green," the treads in the shoes of "Giant Steps," musing about the true meaning of "Epistrophy," squeezing juice from "Naima."

That was how Elvis found him when he got home, snoring gently to the Everly Brothers. It was raining.

Back to Elvis' thoughts

Elvis rescued the needle from its endless rasp over the inside track of the record. He lifted the vinyl disc off the still-spinning plate and, holding it gingerly between fingertips, blew off imaginary dust. He replaced it in the sleeve that showed the Everly Brothers wearing 1950s coifs. He watched the record player slowly spin to a stop before he shook his father's shoulder.

"What?" Sunday said groggily.

"Go inside and sleep. You will catch a cold," Elvis said.

Sunday yawned and stretched, coming awake.

"What time is it?"

"Three a.m.," Elvis replied, glancing at his watch.

"Where have you been?"

"Out." Elvis headed for his room, throwing a "Goodnight" over his shoulder.

"Wait."

Elvis paused, his hand on the doorknob. He didn't turn around.

"I have been waiting for you."

Elvis turned around. "For me? For what?"

"Sit down. I need to talk to you."

"If it is about Godfrey, forget it. There is no need."

"It's not about Godfrey. Sit down."

Elvis walked over and sat on the bench next to his father. They did not look at each other, both choosing a point in the darkness to gaze out at instead.

"Benji just gave me some disturbing news yesterday."

Elvis didn't respond.

"He told me you have been hanging around with dat man dey call de King of de Beggars," Sunday continued.

"Yes, he is a friend of mine."

"What type of friend? What would make a young, well-brought-up man like you associate with beggars?"

Elvis was silent.

"De company one keeps tells a lot."

"What does your friendship with Benji tell?"

"Elvis! I am still your father, respect me!"

Elvis looked at his father scornfully but said nothing.

"Look, Benji told me dat de King, or whatever he is, is a dangerous man."

"How would Benji know?"

"Benji knows things. Just listen. Dey say dat de King was discharged from the army for crazy behavior."

"When?"

"After de civil war."

"That was a long time ago. He seems fine to me."

"But what kind of man begs for a living?"

Elvis looked pointedly at his father.

"I am unemployed, not a beggar!" Sunday nearly shouted.

"He's just trying to do what he thinks is right."

"We all are. I've always tried to do just dat. I ran in de first free elections in nearly twenty years, as you know. Den dose army boys came back and toppled de new civilian regime. Of course, de good thing about dat was dat Okonkwo never got to enjoy his victory."

Elvis remembered the military coup that had removed the civilian government two months into power. As always, there was the national radio broadcast, usually by a northern officer: "My pellow kwontrymen, I wish to ashwar you dat dis hasu been a bloodless coup. Dere will be no bloodshed, but we are imposing a dusk-to-dawn kerfew . . ." Even as the announcement was being made, army platoons would be taking out the corpses from the bloodless coup and burying them in unmarked graves. The thing that baffled Elvis the most was that everyone came out to have parades to welcome the new reigme in, as though this time for sure things would get better. But Sunday was still talking, so he tried to focus.

"It's not because nobody tries but because de reasons are complicated. And your King, how is he fighting? By begging?"

"No. He is a poet and a regular speaker at Freedom Square. He is also an actor and uses theater to fight the government."

"Maybe you should have run for office, not me," Sunday said with a smile. "But de point is, how will staging plays defeat a military government? Bigger men, like Wole Soyinka, have tried, but nothing changes. If he cannot do it, how can a beggar?"

"I don't know. I think everyone is just trying to find their way."

"Are dey finding de way, dese people you speak of?"

"I don't know, but I do know some people are trying very hard and others are not."

"So?"

"So they will eventually find a way."

"Who are 'dey' dat you speak of? Do you even know?"

Elvis shrugged and looked away. Sunday chuckled.

"What?" Elvis asked.

"You sound grown. Like a man; yet you are not a man, and so dis is only de voice of others speaking through you."

"What?"

"Elvis, sometimes even good people use us."

"Who is using us?"

"I am saying dat dis King is using you."

"To do what?"

"Who knows? But Benji says all dis political agitation is a front, dat it is to help him find and kill de officer dat killed his family during de war. Dis is not for change, but revenge."

Elvis lit a cigarette and took a deep drag. Part of him knew his father was speaking from fear. Everybody around him was afraid of change, of rocking the boat, in case they disappeared. Yet part of him had begun to doubt the motives of everyone around him, so he could not totally dismiss his father's concerns.

"The King does good work. I support him."

"Den you are a bigger fool dan I thought. Don't you know dat when de King is next arrested you can be implicated by association? Elvis, try and understand. I am doing dis as your father, not as a stranger. I am trying to help you."

"The way you helped Godfrey?"

Sunday's wince was audible and Elvis immediately felt a pang of guilt. Maybe his father *was* trying to help him. But it seemed too convenient. He had alternated between ignoring and bullying him all these years; yet now, hours after being confronted with the murder of his nephew, he was suddenly concerned for Elvis.

"You have a bad mouth," Sunday said. "You get dat from your mother."

Elvis said nothing, lighting another cigarette instead.

"Dis is why I don't talk to you. Every time I try, you shut me out with your rude comments," Sunday went on.

"I think you should go and sleep off your guilt instead of putting it on me. It's not working," Elvis said, tossing his half-smoked cigarette into the street and getting up.

"Elvis . . . I . . ."

"Goodnight," Elvis said. On impulse, he bent down and kissed the top of his father's head before walking briskly to the door of his room.

As he went inside, he looked back. Sunday had not moved from his seat, except to run his finger meditatively over his bald spot where Elvis had kissed him.

▼▼▼▼▼▼▼▼▼▼▼▼▼▼▼▼▼▼

ROAST VENISON
(Igbo: Ele Ahurahu)

INGREDIENTS

Venison
Vegetable oil
Apples
Allspice
Fresh bonnet peppers
Diced onions
Salt

PREPARATION

Dig a hole about two feet square and build spit support from two forked tree branches. Fill the hole with coals, wood and kindling. Light the fire and hang the venison over the flames to burn off the fur. Scrape hide regularly with a knife to clear the fur.

Spread large banana leaves out on the floor and lay the venison on them. Wash the soot off with water, then cut the skin of the animal in several places and stuff with a mix of the ingredients above.

By now the fire should have died down to a steady heat with low flames. Hoist the venison over the fire using a length of metal guided through the animal and suspended from the spit supports. Turn and roast slowly for about seven hours. Best served communally on trays with salad, palm wine, music and dancing.

1:52:46

TWENTY

))))))

This is the journey the kola must make. The eldest man, in presenting
the kola nut to the gathered guests, must say, "This is the King's kola." The
youngest boy in the gathering then takes the bowl and passes it to the
eldest guest and says, "Will you break the King's kola?"

*The complexity of the kola-nut ritual comes from the peculiar way that age and lineage
are traced among the Igbo. Certain Igbo groups trace lineage along matrilineal lines,
though others are unapologetically patriarchal. The kola-nut ritual provides a ritual
space for the affirmation of brotherhood and mutual harmony while also functioning as
a complicated mnemonic device.*

))))))

Afikpo, 1980

Elvis is about 13 years old

The call, though soft when it came, terrified him. Panting and sweating, he struggled to see through the darkness. Familiar objects took on
a different life. There it was again, insistent.

"Elvis . . . Elvis."

"Who is it?"

"Innocent."

Muttering curses under his breath, Elvis got up and felt his way to a
candle and a box of matches. He lit the candle and opened the door. Innocent stood shivering outside. His tortured look caused Elvis to gasp.

"Innocent?" he said, the name loaded with questions too hard to
articulate.

"It is me . . . I am hungry," Innocent replied.

Nodding, Elvis led the way to the kitchen out back. On tiptoe, he reached for the key that was always above the door, on the lintel. Carefully, so as not to wake anyone, he reheated some rice and stew for Innocent. Watching him eat, Elvis felt a strange mix of revulsion and pity, yet did not know why. There was something else too—something that had to do with the terrified looks Innocent shot around the room.

"What is wrong?"

"Nothing."

"You seem upset."

Innocent paused in his eating, empty spoon midway between the plate and his mouth. He looked at Elvis as though he were seeing him for the first time. He put the plate of rice down, although he kept hold of the spoon. He held it in midair as if it were a baton and he the conductor of some orchestra. He seemed to be deliberating within himself whether to tell Elvis something. After a while he sighed.

"I used to be a soldier in de Biafran war."

Elvis was a little surprised by that. It just seemed to come out of nowhere.

"I know."

"Yes. Well, dat time na rough time. I was only a child, you know."

Elvis nodded.

The alabaster Madonna wept bullet holes. They traced a jagged pattern down her face and robes to collect in a pool of spent shell casings at her feet. She trampled a serpent underfoot, which seemed to be drowning in the brass waves. Her arms, folded over her Immaculate Heart, kept it from flying out of her chest. Her face, cast lovingly toward heaven, wore a sad smile. Sitting among the shell casings at her feet, a thirteen-year-old Innocent sucked on a battered harmonica. The sound whispered out of the honeycombed back, floating up, past the Madonna to an askew Christ on the cross. It went in through the wound in his side, worming around and out the nails in his feet, condensing on the walls of the pockmarked church in a dew of hope.

In the burned-out skeleton of the church, in the reluctant shadows cast by the walls, a group of soldiers, rifles in arms, bristled. They were young, most no more than fifteen. The sweet smell of marijuana floated past them, mixing with the smell of stale sex, warm blood, burned wood and flesh, rising in an incense offering to God. Cicadas hummed and the very air, hot and humid, crackled with the electric sigh of restless spirits. The smoker, seventeen, the oldest person in the platoon, was known simply as Captain. He stubbed out the spliff he was smoking, grinding it into the dry, crumbly earth. It was 1969 and they were part of the Biafran army's Boys' Brigade.

The harmonica sang breathily as Innocent teased a hymn from it. The notes fluttered hopefully, hesitantly, a fragile thing. But as the sun warmed them, they rose steadily. Some of the soldiers in the shade who were familiar with the Catholic hymn hummed along. The hymn brought back memories of a different time, a different place.

"Hey, Music Boy! Play me another song," Captain shouted.

Innocent stopped sucking on his harmonica.

"Like what?" he asked.

"You know de Beach Boys? Play dat." Captain laughed loudly.

Innocent turned away and went back to playing the hymn. There was no love lost between him and Captain—mostly because out of everyone in the platoon, Innocent was the one he usually chose to bully. Across from him, tied to a tree, were the corpses of the Catholic priests who used to run this parish. Their white soutanes were caped in crimson. On the floor near them, one dead, one whimpering in shock, were two nuns who had been raped by Captain. The dead one had tried to struggle. Innocent had watched, afraid to intercede, afraid of what Captain would do to him. He had stared into the nun's eyes that were as grey as a fading blackboard, watched her implore him as the life ebbed away, steeling himself. Like Captain said, "War is war."

The rest of the carnage—the shooting of the priests, the burning of the church and the slaughter of the congregation who had been worshipping inside it—had been done before they got there. Most of the dead had been refugees fleeing from the advancing federal troops. Innocent could no longer tell the difference between rebel- and federal-controlled territory. The lines kept shifting.

It was Harmattan, and everything was coated in fine red dust. A sloughed-off fragment of another hymn popped into Innocent's head, the words flooding: "Are you washed in the blood, in the soul-cleansing blood, of the Lamb?" He shrugged it away and went back to his playing.

The other boys in the platoon rippled toward Captain. They were hungry and wanted permission to go scavenging. Innocent took the harmonica out of his mouth and gazed past them.

Off to the right was the priests' house: a one-story structure with big, sweeping verandas and a balcony that wore a lovely ornate wrought-iron balustrade. Bougainvillea crept up the walls in green-and-purple lushness. The building's brilliant whitewash surprised the red earth of the courtyard. To the left stood two low bungalows that had been the school. In the middle, behind him, were the smoking remains of the church, its once-white walls mascaraed in black tear tracks. In the quadrangle between the buildings rose the statue of the Virgin, shadowed by the statue of Christ on the cross perched in front of the church. Towering above the Madonna and Christ was a bamboo flagpole. On it white twine beat forlornly in the wind, wishing for a flag.

Some bodies littered the road into the church compound and on the dry grass that was tenaciously holding on to the hard earth. They were mostly women, some men and even a few children. Some of them had been shot; others had been hacked to death with machetes. A few had been clubbed. Blood stained their clothes. The whitewashed stones lining the road were flecked with the dried blood, like teeth stained with pink dental dye. There were still pools of blood, clotting flies into a knobby black crust. The earth was baked so hard it couldn't absorb any more blood. It refused to soak it up.

Even though the enemy had been responsible for this massacre, Innocent knew the rebels weren't much better. He had long since lost any belief in the inherent goodness of the rebel cause and the evil of the enemy. Once he had been driven by deep idealism. Now he just wanted to survive. He had seen Captain commit enough atrocities to realize that they were all infected by the insanity of blood fever.

He looked at the dead bodies. They had probably converged on the church compound believing they would be safe here, protected by God's benevolence and man's reputed fear of Him. How wrong they had been! He could have told them that. There is only one God in war: the gun. One religion: genocide.

He looked up to see Captain studying him intently.

"Oi, Music Boy!" Captain called. "Music Boy!"

Innocent ignored him.

"Oh, Music Boy is angry dat we defiled God's servants. He believes God is going to punish us. Dat's why he is playing his mouth organ, to ease de souls of the dead mercenary priests to heaven or hell," Captain said, bursting into deep laughter.

Innocent stopped playing. He was suddenly nervous; there was something dangerous in the way Captain laughed. Still laughing, Captain got up and walked over to Innocent. Innocent sprang up and walked away.

Captain stopped and turned to one of the boys in the group. "James."

"Sar."

"James, aim at dis bagger and fire on command."

James hefted his Mark IV rifle up, rammed a bullet into the breach and pointed it at Innocent's chest.

"At yar command, sar!" he said.

"Do you see? Do you see obedient, eh? Next time I call you, you jump up, run over and say 'Yes sar!' Do you understand me?"

"Yes sar!" Innocent said, snapping to attention. He knew Captain was a little crazy and capable of killing him.

"Good. Music Boy!"

"Yes sar!"

Captain laughed. Turning to James, he said, "Ajiwaya," a Biafran army term meaning, "As you were." James lowered the rifle. It was still cocked. He held it gingerly. Having no safety catch, it was extremely dangerous to carry once cocked. James spoke up, deflecting Captain's attention from Innocent.

"Sar. Permission to speak, sar!" he said.

Captain gave him a perfunctory nod.

"We are hungry, sar. Can we sarch de priests' house to see if we can find food, sar?"

"Go on," Captain said.

The group broke rank and with whoops of glee tripped their way to the priests' house. It had not been burned, and that made Innocent suspicious. The whole place was probably booby-trapped. He shouted a warning, but nobody listened. They were too hungry. None of them had had anything more substantial than wild fruit foraged in the forest. No meat, since most of the animals had fled deep into the jungle to hide.

Innocent remembered the last time they had meat. One of the boys had shot a monkey. They had done it before—shot monkeys. Cooked them into a pepper soup that smelled delicious. But Innocent could never eat any. The monkey had looked so human, the small hands so like a child's, scraping the side of the container used as a pot. One monkey, obviously not dead, had jumped up after being shot. One of the boys had crushed its skull under the butt of his rifle, cutting off its baby squeal. Everyone teased Innocent about not eating the monkey. Called him a coward. A woman. Not a warrior. He pointed out how much like cannibalism it all seemed. Captain swore at him, saying he would make him eat the next dead enemy soldier they came across. The boys hooted with laughter. The last time, however, only a few weeks ago, he had given in to the taunting and taken a piece of the meat. Later he was sick, but he couldn't get the taste of it out of his mouth. The frightening thing was, he had enjoyed it.

A few minutes later, the boys emerged with tins of pork, stale bread, bottles of hot beer and altar wine. They had been left behind by the federal troops, who were mostly Muslims. They brought the loot to Captain, and only when he had selected what he wanted did they pounce on the rest. Tins were bayoneted open. Hot beer boiled over roughly opened bottles. Nobody paid any attention to Innocent or offered him any food. There was only one motto here: "We shall survive."

Innocent got up and walked up the three steps into the burned-out shell of the church. The fire hadn't consumed everything. Three walls, the roof—three-quarters of the church—had been burned. In the still-smoking pews he saw the roasted corpses of the congregation. They had been shot, clubbed or macheted to death and then tied to the pews to roast with the church. The air was heavy with the stench of roasted meat, not nauseating, but actually mouthwatering. Innocent wondered if they had all been dead or whether some had survived the shots, clubs and machetes to be consumed screaming by the fire. Did dying in a church guarantee you a place in heaven? he wondered, walking up the aisle crunching soot, ash and charcoal underfoot.

The altar had miraculously survived. It was still set for mass: white altar cloth, chalice, communion wafers still stuffed into the ciborium, water,
wine, candles, flowers and an open missal. Innocent walked round the altar and read the open page. He used to be an altar boy, and the Latin was
not difficult for him to read. "Kyrie eleison, Christe eleison, Kyrie eleison."

Behind the altar, not wearing a single bullet hole and only slightly
cracked from the heat, was a stained-glass window. It filtered the harsh
sunlight in soft blues, yellows, pinks, oranges and greens. Innocent noticed that the floor, the altar, the missal and his own body had become
a patchwork of color. He licked the tip of a blue finger and peeled away
a red page, an orange one and a green one. He paused and read. "Agnus Dei, qui tollis peccata mundi, miserere nobis . . . Agnus Dei, qui
tollis peccata mundi, dona nobis pacem." He smiled at the last line:
"Grant us peace."

His stomach rumbled and he wished he had fought with the others for some morsel. He looked out. The rest of the platoon was now
gorging on papaws plucked from a nearby tree. His eyes took in the
now barren tree—so much for that idea. He turned back to the altar.
Nobody was going to miss the communion wafers, and he was sure
God didn't want him starving to death. Carefully hoisting his rifle onto
his back and dropping his harmonica into his pocket, he picked up the
ciborium and began stuffing his mouth full of the sweet white circles
of bread. Finishing it off, he emptied water into the wine in the chalice. Saying a silent prayer for forgiveness, he reached for the chalice.
Even as he picked it up, he heard the click of the bomb arming itself.
The bastards had booby-trapped the altar.

"What happened?"

"De bomb's arming mechanism was faulty, so it did not explode."

Elvis sat back. How was he to respond to Innocent's story? He had
no idea what to say to him, if anything. But the silence between them
was becoming too strained, so he blurted out: "I didn't know you
played the harmonica."

"Not since den," Innocent said. He picked up the plate of food
and began to eat feverishly again, staring around him in fear.

"Is somebody after you?"

"Why would anybody be after me?"

"The last time I saw you, you were with Godfrey," Elvis said.

Innocent stopped eating.

"What do you know about dat?"

"Nothing."

"Are you saying Godfrey is after me?"

"No. Why? What is going on?" Elvis asked. "I saw you the other day with blood on your clothes. Are you all right?"

"Do you see any blood on me now? Do you see any wounds?" Innocent said testily.

Elvis examined him surreptitiously. There was no blood on his clothes. He was right. But there were several deep scratches around his throat.

"Were you fighting a lion?" Elvis asked, indicating the scratches.

"Mind your business before I slap you," Innocent hissed.

"Maybe I should wake Oye," Elvis threatened, getting up. Oye's room abutted the kitchen.

"No, Elvis. What is wrong with you? You cannot tell I am joking with you," Innocent said, his manner changing instantly. "They are love scratches, you know."

Elvis looked at him blankly.

"Love scratches?" he echoed.

Just then, Innocent dropped the plate with a clatter Elvis felt sure would wake the dead, sat bolt upright and, with a yelp, dashed out of the kitchen into the rain and darkness. Petrified, Elvis stared into the nothingness in the corner of the room that had spooked Innocent, one eye watching the candle burn down to a few stutters, then darkness. He sat there until exhaustion and the sound of the rain took him.

Afikpo, 1981

Sunday Oke paced the living room restlessly, ignoring the calls from his supporters to sit down. The votes were being counted, the polls having closed hours before. The living room was crowded with supporters who had gathered to wait. There were so many of them that they spilled out into the front and back yards.

In the kitchen, Aunt Felicia and others sweated to produce the endless amounts of food demanded by the crowd that gathered. Elvis sat on the front veranda at Oye's feet, watching the thugs yelling up and down the road just beyond the fence and gate. They were celebrating their patron's victory early, hoping to psych everyone else out. Elvis was convinced that they would be overrun at any moment by a mad fire-bearing mob of thugs.

"Don't worry, laddie," Oye said. "Tha's their way of preventing anyone from complaining if they cheat."

That was not comforting to him. Neither was the feeble defense that the only thugs his father could hire looked like they were capable of providing. They sat near the gate looking as frightened as he did.

Oye noted his apprehension with a smile. "I don't think you have tae worry about tha thugs, lad, your dad is not going tae win. He had no money tae start with, you know."

Elvis laughed nervously. "Why do you think he went through with it, Gran?"

"Since your mother died, your dad lost his way, you understand?" Elvis nodded.

"Well, this election gave him back his fire, some direction. But I don't think he took it too seriously. At least I hope not."

"I think he took it seriously, Gran."

"Tha' could be bad, laddie. If tha' is indeed true, I think you should worry more about your father than tha thugs."

Elvis laughed nervously again. The thugs on the street outside were getting noisier, and the reason soon became apparent. Their boss, Chief Okonkwo, was riding past in a large convertible. With one hand he held a megaphone calling out to his opponents, while with the other hand he doled out money to the thugs. His shiny red convertible pulled up outside the Oke home. The generator was on, and in the lights, the car looked like a red wound against the night.

"Good evening," he called through the megaphone. "Sunday Oke, I greet you."

Sunday stepped out onto the veranda flanked by his main supporters. Seeing him standing there, his thugs galvanized into action, making a big show of keeping out Chief Okonkwo and his entourage.

"Okonkwo. How can I help you?" Sunday called back.

"De question, my friend, is how can I help you. It is obvious dat you are going to lose, but being a generous man, I recognize your obvious talents and would like to offer you de chance to work for me."

The megaphone gave the sense of a one-sided conversation to the people beginning to emerge onto their stoops and verandas, who only heard Chief Okonkwo's voice. Elvis watched his father, feeling his frustration and humiliation.

"Get lost, you ghoul! De results are not in, so I wouldn't gloat yet if I were you."

"But dey will be soon, and I will be de winner."

"Well, dat doesn't matter, because we both know dat de army boys will come back with a coup within six months."

Chief Okonkwo laughed. "Is dat a prophecy or are you just a bad loser?" he asked.

"Go to hell!" Sunday shouted back before turning and heading back.

Elvis was glad his father didn't see his supporters cheering for Chief Okonkwo. Some of them left immediately, joining Okonkwo's team. Others would follow later. As Chief Okonkwo and his entourage moved off, failure settled on the compound in a hush. Even the thugs at the gate began to drift off. When, an hour later, the news of Chief Okonkwo's victory was announced over the television, it was anticlimactic.

"So what now?" Elvis asked Oye as they watched people drift off to celebrate at the Okonkwo compound.

"Well, your father thinks he can get anoder job in Lagos and I heard him telling a friend dat if he lost de election he would take it," Aunt Felicia said.

"Lagos? But that is over eight hundred miles away! What about you? Are you coming?" Elvis asked, voice shrill.

"Don't be silly, Elvis. Mother is too old to travel and I am seeing someone, so I cannot come either. But don't worry, you will be fine. You are nearly all grown now."

"I just turned fourteen."

"Like I said, nearly all grown," Aunt Felicia said with a wink that made him blush.

"But my dance lessons, I can't leave," he mumbled.

"Why don't you go to bed and wait until your father decides what he's going tae do before you get so upset," Oye said gently.

Elvis got up and went into the house. Noticing that his father was sitting out on the back veranda, he sat on the window ledge and watched as the night thickened with rain. In his father's hand was a drink; a half-empty bottle of scotch sat on the table beside him. He was sobbing quietly as he listened to the record player spin his dead wife's favorite records.

Elvis watched his father's face in the gathering shadows. He had watched him do this before: play records, drink and then cry into the night, the falling rain muffling his sobs. But tonight it felt different—unremarkable, yet different, like the masks that adorned the walls of the men's cult house.

His father was talking to Beatrice's ghost. Elvis had never seen anyone else account to the dead. Daily, people thanked, cursed, supplicated and yelled at God. But the dead were another matter. They were too unpredictable, too vengeful.

Sunday Oke let out a long sigh and wiped his eyes, completely oblivious to Elvis's gaze. He should never have agreed to get involved in politics, he thought. Never listened to the supporters who had egged him on with promises of money and help, but who had disappeared leaving him with a heavy debt. He certainly should not have taken early retirement from his lucrative job as the district education inspector. The job had offered prestige and a good wage, which he supplemented handsomely with generous bribes from schools and headmasters who wanted favorable reports.

"I mean, look at me," he mumbled to the empty stool next to him. "Oh, Beatrice, look at me, reduced to dis. Now I have to sell off my father's land and dis house to pay dose debts, and to survive I have to take a job in Lagos, running away with my tail tucked between my legs."

He took a deep swallow and grimaced loudly as the harsh liquor burned through his pain.

"My supporters, you ask?" he went on, refilling his glass. "I ask de same. As soon as things got sticky, de tricky bastards decamped to dat thief Okonkwo, who paid them generously. Me? I was left alone to foot de bill for de ambition of others."

He took another mouthful and gargled before swallowing.

"What did you say . . . ? Of course it was my ambition too. But I was stupid to let dem talk me—what? Don't interrupt me, Beatrice. Just because you are dead does not mean I can't slap your face," he grunted.

Leaning back in the chair, he laughed bitterly through his tears.

"Of course you don't understand. You are a woman, how could you? Honor is a secondhand concept for you, earned through your husbands or sons. But for us . . . for us it is different," he continued. "I had come too far to step down. People were looking at me; my honor was naked in public and I had to clothe it."

Sobs wracked his body and he fought to gain control. Meanwhile, the Temptations were "talkin' 'bout my girl, my girl."

Letting out his breath, he continued. "I know I lost. Dat is the consequence of war, Beatrice. Someone wins, anoder loses. But as long as de fight was with honor, both warriors can rest peacefully."

Elvis continued to watch his father silently. Part of him wanted to reach out in comfort, but something deeper told him it would be wrong. This was too private a thing to be shared. Elvis left his perch and crossed the corridor, heading for bed. He noted Felicia's absence with a strange pang. She was probably with her boyfriend, the one he had just found out about. Pulling the covers up to his chin, he let the drumming of the rain on the roof lull him.

Book II

〰〰〰

. . . and above all the never-ending knowledge

that this aching emptiness would be all . . .

—AYI KWEI ARMAH,

The Beautiful Ones Are Not Yet Born

TWENTY-ONE

))))((((

The eldest guest blesses the bowl and says, "We have seen the kola, but the King's kola must return to the King."

))))((((

History is at the heart of the ritual, marked in Igbo by the word omenala, *which literally means "the way we have always done it."*

))))((((

Lagos, 1983

Elvis is about 16 years old

"So we work for the Colonel?" Elvis asked.

"Dat's right," Redemption replied.

"I don't like that."

"Elvis, behave O! Dat's why I no tell you, because I know you can act out."

"But that guy is dangerous."

"So you better behave."

"What does he want us to do?"

"I told you, I no sure, but it is safe business."

"You keep saying that, but I don't believe anything involving that man, or his friends, can be safe. Or legal."

"I no talk say it is legal. But is only a little illegal, you know? Like when something bend, but not too much."

"I don't think there is such a thing as a little illegal. It is illegal or not."

"Haba Elvis! So you are telling me dat stealing bread from bakery to feed yourself and killing somebody is de same? Everything get degree."

"I don't like this, that's all I'm saying."

"Fine. No like am, but do am."

Having slept late, they had only both woken up a few minutes before. They were hurriedly shoving food into their mouths as they waited to be picked up. Elvis was still a little sleepy. After his conversation with his father, he had barely fallen asleep when Redemption had come round, banging on his door. He gave Elvis ten minutes to take a hurried shower before hustling him off. They had taken several buses and were now in a part of Lagos he'd never been to. As they waited, Redemption suggested they get some food in a nearby buka.

"So how long have you worked for the Colonel?" Elvis asked.

"For long time. Even dat last deal we do . . ."

"The cocaine?"

"Yes, dat was him too. Now he is in a new trade."

"I don't know what trade can be more lucrative than drugs. Why the switch?"

"Do you know if it is airplane we are buying and selling? Enough question. Eat."

"But it is illegal no matter what kind of trade, right?"

"Watch yourself," Redemption warned.

Just then, they heard shouts of "Ole! Ole!" from the small market to their left. It was half hidden by a timber merchant's sprawling compound, and Elvis hadn't noticed it at first. A small crowd chased a man out onto the dirt road between the market and the line of bukas. Elvis got up to get a closer look, but Redemption pulled him down.

"Stay out of it," he hissed.

The crowd had formed an angry semicircle around the man, leaving the timber yard as the only possible escape; but the mean-faced workers gathered at the gate ruled out that option. The man didn't look to be more than twenty, though it was hard to tell, partly because his face was dirty and bloody. A tire hung from his neck like a rubber garland, and his eyes wore the look of a cornered animal.

"But I no steal anything!" he shouted. "I beg, I no want to die!"

"Shut up!"

"Ole!"

"Thief!"

"I no be thief! I came to collect my money from dat man who owes me!" the accused thief shouted, pointing at a man in the crowd.

"Which man?" someone in the crowd asked.

"Dat one. Peter."

The man he was referring to, a short, nondescript man, shifted uncomfortably. "Who owe you? Craze man!" Peter shouted, throwing a stone at the accused thief.

It caught him on the temple, tearing a gash, and fresh blood pumped dark and thick.

"I no be thief O! Hey, God help me! My name is Jeremiah, I am a carpenter. I no be thief!"

"Shut up!" the crowd shouted.

"Is he a thief?" Elvis asked Redemption.

"Maybe."

"Or is he a carpenter?"

"Maybe."

"Which one?"

"Either. I don't know and I don't care."

"My name is Jeremiah. My name is Jeremiah," the man kept repeating.

The crowd had grown silent; the lack of sound, sinister, dropped over the scene like a dark presence. Jeremiah was spinning around in a circle like a broken sprocket, pleading with each face, repeating his name over and over. Instead of loosening the edge of tension by humanizing him, the mantra of his name, with every circle he spun, seemed to wind the threat of violence tighter, drawing the crowd closer in.

Elvis watched a young girl, no older than twelve, pick up a stone and throw it at Jeremiah. It struck him with a dull thud, and though she lacked the strength to break skin, the blow raised a nasty purple lump. That single action triggered the others to pick up and throw stones. The combined sound was sickening, and Jeremiah yelled in pain. There was something comically biblical, yet purely animal, about the scene.

"Why doesn't anybody help?" Elvis's voice cracked. This was just like the time that man had jumped into the fire and the time the youths had chased that thief in Bridge City. In both instances he did nothing. Now, again, he did nothing.

"Because dey will stone you too."

Elvis's question had been rhetorical, and he glared at Redemption, who went on blithely:

"Look, Elvis, dese are poor people. Poor people are hungry people, and like Bob Marley talk, a hungry man is an angry man. You get ciga?"

What We talked about in Class

Elvis passed his pack. Redemption lit two, passed one to Elvis and pocketed the pack.

"Hey!" Elvis said.

"Sorry. Habit," Redemption said, handing the pack back with a smile.

"How long can we use the excuse of poverty?"

Although Elvis had not asked anyone in particular, a man sitting across the room responded angrily, not taking his eyes off the scene outside.

"You dis man, you just come Lagos?"

"Hey! Mind your business!" Redemption shouted.

The man returned to arguing with the buka owner. She was standing in the kitchen doorway, attention divided between pots bubbling over on the wood-burning stove and the scene outside.

"He must have molest a child," the buka owner said, voice heavy with wonder.

"If so, he for die by now. I tink he is just a common tief," the man said.

"But he no look like tief," she countered.

"How does tief look?"

"Not like him!" she said.

Elvis turned away from them. He watched Redemption's face. It was clear that his attention was focused completely on the events unfolding in the street outside, even though his face wore a disinterested look. His breathing was shallow, and that intrigued Elvis.

"Where are the police when you need them?" Elvis asked, sucking smoke into his lungs.

"Dere dey are," Redemption said, pointing to the checkpoint a few yards up the street. The policemen were watching the scene with bored expressions.

Outside, the crowd had given up throwing stones and was watching Jeremiah for signs of life. He lay on his side twitching, the tire necklace still in place. Elvis noticed that Jeremiah's hands were tied, explaining why he couldn't fight back. A whooping sound went through the crowd as a man ran up with a ten-gallon metal jerry can.

"What is that?" Elvis asked.

"Petrol," Redemption replied.

"Oh."

The crowd parted slightly to let the man with the jerry can through. He stood in front of the prone Jeremiah for a while, appearing unsure about what to do next.

"Baptize him! Baptize him!" the crowd shouted.

Moving quickly, the man unscrewed the can's cap and doused the prone Jeremiah with the petrol. Jeremiah twitched as the petrol got into his open wounds and burned. A fat woman stepped back and Elvis caught his first good look of Jeremiah's face. It was tired, features reflecting Jeremiah's struggle against the inevitable resignation. The man threw the empty can to the ground and it resounded with a metallic echo. Nobody moved or spoke, not in the crowd, the buka or at the police checkpoint. Everybody was waiting for something to happen. Anything. Peter stepped forward and stood before Jeremiah, who, revived by the harsh smell of the petrol, was struggling to his knees.

"I beg, Peter. You know I no be tief. I beg."

Peter calmly reached into his pocket and pulled out a cigarette lighter. He flicked it on and stepped back from Jeremiah, dropping the lighter on the tire necklace. Elvis followed the lighter's fall. It could not have lasted more than two seconds, though it seemed to take forever. It was hard to tell which came first, the sheet of flame or the scream.

"Aah," Redemption said in a long, drawn-out breath. "Necklace of fire."

It sounded so sensual it made Elvis shudder.

"Every day for de tief," the man across from them breathed.

"One day for the owner," the buka owner completed.

They watched as the screaming, burning Jeremiah struggled to his feet and tried to break through the circle, but men who had retrieved long wooden planks from the timber yard earlier, for this exact moment, pushed him back with the long wooden fingers. The only way out was in the direction of the timber yard, and Jeremiah headed for it. From where Elvis sat, it was impossible to see his limbs; he looked like a floating sheet of flame. The men by the timber yard gate, caught off guard, yelled in alarm and scattered in every direction as Jeremiah crashed through and into the yard. He was still screaming. Within minutes, the timber yard was ablaze and the workers formed a chain, throwing buckets of water and sand at the fire, but it was too big. The mob of lynchers had melted away, as had the police.

"We should help," Elvis said, not getting up.

"What good is dat."

"The fire will spread."

"Not our problem. Anyway, our ride is here," Redemption said, walking out to a black GMC truck that had just pulled up. Elvis hesitated for a second, then followed him. The last thing he saw was the buka owner grabbing all the money from the tin that served as her till. She stuffed bills and coins down her bra and ran out the back, leaving the food still burning.

"Get in," Redemption said, opening the back door for him.

As he climbed into the truck, Elvis was shaking. This scene had affected him more than anything else he had seen, though he wasn't sure why. Maybe it was the cumulative effect of all the horror he had witnessed; there was only so much a soul could take. As they drove off, Elvis watched the spreading fire through the tinted glass. It was horrifying, yet strangely beautiful.

Beautiful?!

Is Elvis changing for the worse?

▼▼▼▼▼▼▼▼▼▼▼▼▼▼▼▼▼▼▼▼▼▼▼▼▼▼▼▼▼▼▼▼▼▼▼

MORINGA OLEIFERA *LAM.*
(Igbo: Okwe-beke)

This small deciduous tree with a crooked stem, often forking near the base, has a dark grey and smooth bark. The twigs and young shoots are densely hairy, and the tree is often found in farmlands and around small-town homes. It has doubled, sometimes tripled, large leaves, and small white sweet-scented flowers and a podlike fruit.

Its leaves and the young pods are used as vegetables for soup or salad, and the kernels yield clear, sweet oil. The root and bark are used as an antiscurvy treatment. The tree is planted on graves to keep away hyenas and its branches are used in a charm against witches.

TWENTY-TWO

)))))

He then passes it to the next in line by seniority.

Yet there is a deeper philosophy to this, a connection to land and history that cannot be translated.

)))))

Lagos, 1983

Elvis is about 16 years old

They left the scene of the fire behind, merging onto a highway that cut into the edge of a cliff, the Atlantic falling off to the right, sheer rock rising to the left. Mountain goats ran across the road, timing the traffic with practiced ease. The sea was an angry crash on rocks, and the landscape seemed too barren even for birds.

Then the road dipped, still hugging the coastline, until it was at sea level and waves swept over the rock battlements to flood the road. The cliff to their left relaxed in gentle gradients, into a rolling plain of windswept grass. They turned off and headed inland, the sea grass giving way to richer, denser rain forest. The road wound between trees that had probably been there a few hundred years, and the vegetation matting between them seemed as impenetrable as a sultan's harem.

"Where are we going?" Elvis asked.

"To collect de merchandise," the driver said.

Elvis studied the two men up front. The driver was short, dark and thick, and he gripped the steering wheel with short, stubby fingers and small hands. He had introduced himself as Anthony, and he seemed garrulous and friendly.

The other passenger was tall and skinny, like an upright mamba, and as dark, his skin shining with a purple hue. He wore a sour expression that seemed apt given that his name was Conrad. His face was patterned with deeply cut tribal marks that would have identified his exact clan a century ago, and might have also saved him from being sold into slavery, because the scarifications would have lessened his market value—unless he ran into slavers so desperate for a trade that they wouldn't care. He was taciturn, barely responding to their greetings, and then gruffly. The only thing the two men had in common were glittering red eyes; probably the result of some drug, Elvis decided.

"Are we going to meet the Colonel?" he asked.

"You ask too many questions. Watch yourself," Conrad warned.

Elvis lapsed into silence, staring out the window at the increasingly rural landscape. Tall elephant grass that reminded him of his childhood and the rhino beetle hunts he went on, wading through the four-, sometimes five-foot-tall grass, peeling the reluctant armored black beetles from their perches on the tips of the grass. He and his friends would tie stiff black hair-plaiting thread, obtained from a female relative, to the beetles' torsos, under their wings. Prodded with sticks by the boys, the beetles would take off, flying in circles controlled by the strings, whirring like small black helicopters.

As they passed the occasional small town, he saw old men and women dozing outside their huts. Dogs slept in the middle of the road, where it was warm, reluctantly getting out of the way for their truck. But Anthony never slowed down or swerved to avoid any, and he left a trail of roadkill behind them.

"Hey, Zorba!" Conrad said every time they hit one.

Elvis conjectured that Zorba was Anthony's nickname. It probably came from the movie *Zorba the Greek*, with Anthony Quinn. In some way, he guessed, it made sense.

They had been driving for about four hours and dusk was settling, but just before it got really dark, they pulled up to a solitary hut. A single kerosene lantern burned from the top of a pole mounted outside. Though there was no sign of any electric lights, a generator thumped somewhere behind the hut. There was only the sound of the generator

and the idle throb of their engine. Even cicadas did not sing. Anthony
and Conrad got out.

"Wait here!" Conrad called over his shoulder.

Elvis and Redemption exchanged looks. Leaning forward, Redemption wound down his window and lit a cigarette, taking a deep,
grateful drag.

"Give me one, man," Elvis said.

"Dis is my last. I go fifty you," Redemption replied.

He took a few more drags that burned the cigarette half down. Reluctantly he passed it to Elvis, who sucked greedily until he burned
through to the stub.

"Dis car big O!" Redemption said looking around the back of the
truck. The GMC truck had two regular rows of seats, and two benches
in the back that faced each other. "I fit take it make good taxi. Carry
plenty passengers one time," he continued.

"I don't trust those guys," Elvis replied.

If Redemption was surprised at the non sequitur, he did not show
it. "Me too," he agreed.

Just then Anthony and Conrad came out of the hut carrying two
giant plastic coolers. Grunting, they struggled to get them into the
back of the truck. Turning in his seat, Elvis offered to help.

"Clever man," Anthony replied cheerfully. "You wait until we
done, den you offer."

Elvis laughed uncomfortably. Conrad had already started walking
back to the hut. He returned with six people. As they got close, Elvis
saw that their hands were tied and that they were a mixed bunch of
kids, boys and girls, ranging in age from about eight to sixteen. Conrad opened the back doors and they filed in silently, sitting facing each
other, three to a side, on the benches, the coolers sitting on the floor
between them.

While Anthony rambled on about the weather and the trouble the
repeated rains were causing his father's farm and their crops, Conrad
chained the feet of their new passengers together. He was about to
slam the door shut when a hard-faced man came banging out of the
hut, lugging a third giant cooler.

"What's dat?" Conrad asked. "Colonel said two cooler."

"Dis is food and drink. It is long trip."

"Okay. Help me load it," Conrad said, lighting a cigarette.

The man grunted from the effort of carrying the heavy cooler by himself, shooting baleful looks at Conrad, who just watched, smoking. There wasn't enough space to get the third cooler in on the floor, so the man sat it on top of the other two coolers already there. With any luck it would upturn and spill the food and drink everywhere, the man thought. But thinking better of it, he lifted it back down and began to move the other coolers around to see if he could fit them all in on the floor. As he was doing that, Elvis turned away from Conrad and the man and focused on Anthony. He was talking rapidly, even more so than he had on the drive up, and he seemed agitated. Elvis could hear the generator thudding away in the background and wondered why it wasn't connected to any lights—at least, none that he could see. Perhaps it powered some other device. He was curious, but knew better than to ask Anthony or Conrad.

"Redemption, you hold your gun?" Anthony asked.

"Sure."

"You get bullet?" Anthony pressed, loading a big revolver.

Redemption took out his automatic, pulled out the magazine and checked it. Elvis looked from one gun to the other nervously. He didn't like guns.

"Bullet dey, thirteen rounds accounted for, sir," Redemption said in mock military style. Both he and Anthony laughed.

"Why you dey always laugh?" Conrad asked, getting in and slamming the door.

"Easy, Connie, you too vex."

"Go, go," Conrad said, slapping the door of the car.

"Okay," Anthony said, grinding gears and accelerating too fast. The truck skidded in the sand before finding a grip and heading off.

Elvis turned to look at the six passengers. None of them were moving. They wore dazed expressions and seemed unaware of their restraints.

"Who are they?" Elvis asked.

"De people you are here to escort. Anthony is driver and I am relief driver. You are de escorts."

"Why are they chained?"

"Dey are crazy runaways from Ghana. Their papa is a big man in Rawlings gofment, so we are returning dem to their parents. Simple," Anthony replied.

Elvis sat back. He didn't believe a word of it, but he knew better than to ask more questions.

He stared out of the windows at the thick soup of night. It was so dark he could barely make out the shapes of trees and huts lying low like sleeping animals. They stopped at several police checkpoints. Each time, Anthony handed some money and cigarettes to a lead officer.

"Esprit de corps," he called each time as they drove off.

"Esprit," the officers always responded.

Elvis looked at Redemption the second time he heard the exchange.

"Army talk," Redemption said. In minutes, he was asleep. Elvis couldn't sleep. He was too scared. Everything was wrong, and yet he couldn't tell exactly what. He didn't believe they were returning the kids to their parents, but couldn't think of anything else they might be doing with them. He sighed and looked behind him. In the gloom, he could make out that one of the kids, a young girl, was staring straight at him, eyes awake, afraid. He wanted to say something to reassure her, make her shift her gaze, but he couldn't think of anything.

"Look, dere is a small town coming ahead. I go stop make we piss and stretch our leg," Anthony said authoritatively.

Within ten minutes they pulled into the dusty motor park of the town that abutted the market. A crooked sign said: WELCOME TO IBARE—THE STRUNGLE CONTINUES. Elvis could see lights staggering up a hill in the distance and assumed it marked the outskirts of the town. It didn't look that small.

"Wait here," Anthony said to Elvis and Redemption. Turning to Conrad, he said: "Go use toilet, den when you come back Redemption dem fit go. Me, I need to call de Colonel."

"Elvis, you be liability," Redemption said as soon as they were on their own.

"Leave me," Elvis said, getting out of the car.

"Where you dey go?" Redemption called after him.

"I want to buy cigarettes."

Shouldn't
be leaving.
Dangerous.

"What of de ciga you had before?"

"I want to buy some more. Is it your money?"

"No. Good, buy all de ciga you want. Dat's more for me."

Elvis headed off, and Redemption became aware that the young girl in the back was sobbing.

"What is your name?" he asked.

"Kemi," the girl replied.

"Are you hungry?"

She shook her head, but he couldn't tell if it was from sobbing or in response to his question.

"Look, you better stop crying before dey come back," he said.

"Please don't kill me, sir," she sniffled.

"Who go kill you? Nobody want to kill you."

"The other man said he is going to kill us," she said.

"Where you learn to blow grammar like dis?"

"I am in secondary school."

"So what are you doing with dese people?"

"They kidnapped me, sir."

Elvis wandered back to the car.

"Sssh!" Redemption said to Kemi.

Elvis unwrapped a packet of cigarettes, lit two and passed one to Redemption.

"Whom were you talking to?"

"Dis girl, Kemi."

"The one crying?"

Redemption nodded.

"So what is really going on?" Elvis asked.

"With what?"

"With these kids. Why are we transporting them tied up to another country?"

Redemption took a deep breath. "As I know it, de Colonel dey supply dese children to white people who want to adopt dem."

"And why are they so silent? Are they drugged?"

Silence.

"Redemption?"

"I no go lie. Me too done begin to suspect dat story. But as you know, dey have paid us five thousand naira each."

"When did they pay us?"

"I have your share. Don't worry."

"So what do you think the real deal is with these kids?"

"Well, maybe slavery."

"Slavery? Who still buy slaves?"

"Plenty people. Dese children can become prostitute in European country or even for Far East."

"Redemption, I don't want anything to do with this. Why didn't you tell me before?"

"Because you for act like dis. Hold yourself, Elvis. Listen, I dey thirsty. Go see inside dat cooler whether beer dey dere."

"Man, this is all shit. I don't want any part of this."

"Elvis! Hold yourself. It is too late now. If de oders hear you, dey can kill you. Make we just deliver dese children wherever and den wash our hands for de future. Okay?"

"No! How can it be okay?"

"Elvis, listen carefully. We dey deep inside dis shit. De best thing is to keep low until we can leave safely. Okay?"

"Okay," Elvis grumbled.

"Now, go check dat cooler for beer."

As Elvis opened the back door, Kemi tried to get up from her seat, but the chains held her fast. The other kids were still stoned, and Elvis wondered why she seemed unaffected by whatever drug had been given to the others.

"Please, sir, help me!" she begged.

"Shut up!" Redemption shouted at her from the far side of the truck, banging on the window. She flinched and watched Elvis with sad eyes. Avoiding her gaze, Elvis looked at the three coolers. Somehow the man who loaded them had gotten them to fit side by side, but Elvis couldn't tell which one held the food. Even though the food had been loaded last, he had seen the man who put them in rearranging them to fit, so the cooler of food could be any of the three. It didn't help that they were all the same color.

"Redemption, there are three coolers here. Which one?"

"How I go know? Check all three. Dere must be beer in one of dem," Redemption replied.

Elvis muttered obscenities under his breath and reached for one of the coolers. He popped the lid, but it was so dark, he could see nothing. The contents gave off a strange rusty smell and he decided against plunging his hands blindly into it.

"You get light?" he shouted at Redemption.

"Light?"

"It is dark back here."

"Dis is government motor, so flashlight must dey glove box," Redemption said, opening the passenger door. The overhead light came on as Redemption opened the door, and Elvis staggered back in disgust. He tried to shout, but nothing came. Kemi, however, let out a piercing scream that had Redemption scrambling to the back. He clocked her on the side of the head with the pistol butt and she fell silent.

"What is it?" he demanded.

Elvis pointed to the cooler, face ashen, hand trembling. Redemption looked inside and recoiled. There were six human heads sitting on a pile of ice.

"Shit!" he swore, popping the covers off the other coolers. The second one held what appeared to be several organs, hearts and livers, also packed with ice. The third held bottles of beer and what looked like food. Redemption took a few steps back, noting that a small crowd was beginning to gather, drawn by Kemi's short but loud scream. He looked for Elvis, who was heaving at the edge of the road, away from the crowd. Moving swiftly, he came up beside him.

"What is going on?" an old man asked.

"I don't know," Redemption replied.

"But I saw you in de car," the old man insisted.

"Elvis, get up," Redemption said, pulling urgently at Elvis's arm. Looking around desperately, he saw Anthony and Conrad making their way back to the truck, clearly unaware of the excitement.

"Listen, young man," the old man continued, tugging at Redemption's shirt. "We hear scream. What is going on?"

"Ask dose men. It is deir car," Redemption replied, pointing to the approaching Anthony and Conrad. Returning his attention to Elvis, he forced him upright and shook him roughly.

"Collect yourself," he hissed. "We get to move quickly."

"Oh my God!"

Redemption turned to the shout. It came from a young man who had gone to inspect the coolers. In his fright he had knocked one of them over, and the human heads rolled across the ground like errant fruit from a grocery bag.

"Shit!" Redemption said, dragging Elvis across the road and into the darkness of the market. They moved quickly, Redemption trailing Elvis behind him like a leashed dog. They threaded between empty stalls, followed by the angry shouts of the crowd. When he thought they had put a safe distance between them and the crowd, Redemption stopped to catch his breath and determine if they were being followed. They were not. The crowd had probably caught Anthony and Conrad and were more than likely beating them to death. Redemption thought he heard one shot, but couldn't be sure, and then the sound of the crowd grew louder. They had no doubt killed the two men and were fanning out in search of Elvis and Redemption.

"Move!" Redemption said, pushing Elvis ahead of him.

They broke free of the market and found themselves on a side street. Redemption scanned the road. It was a residential street and everything was quiet. He passed his gun to Elvis.

"If anybody come, shoot, den run."

"Where are you going?" Elvis asked. His wits were returning, fueled by terror.

"To find motor to steal. Wait here."

Elvis nodded and shrank into the safety of a mango tree's shadows. He held the gun gingerly, afraid it would go off and kill him. Shortly, he heard the sound of a car pulling up; but unsure of who was driving it, he stayed hidden.

"Elvis!"

He got up and looked. Redemption grinned at him from an old Mercedes-Benz. Elvis ran to the car and jumped in through the window, not bothering to open the door. As Redemption roared off, a barking dog chased after them.

▼▼▼▼▼▼▼▼▼▼▼▼▼▼▼▼▼▼▼▼

FISH PEPPER SOUP

INGREDIENTS

Fresh fish
Fresh bonnet peppers
One fresh plum tomato
Palm oil
Uhiokiriho
Utazi
Onions
Maggi cubes
Salt
Crayfish
Akanwu

PREPARATION

You can use any kind of fish for this dish. Just make sure your fish is fresh. The best test for freshness is to put the fish in a bowl of water and watch to see if it moves. It should at the very least twitch, otherwise it is a little too old. Clean and gut the fish; this might include descaling if it is a scaly fish like tilapia.

Put the fish in a pot with a little water and put on to boil. Add all the other ingredients and leave to simmer for about twenty-five minutes. Serve in bowls with fresh basil.

This spicy dish is great for women who have just undergone labor. The heat of it, mixed with the herbs, releases healing enzymes and can even cause stubborn afterbirths to fall out. In some older members of the clan, there is still the belief that fish pepper soup, cooked with the right herbs, can endow the consumer with a fish's abilities in water.

TWENTY-THREE

))))))

And so the kola makes its journey round the room and is seen by the eldest of all the clans.

Every time the ritual takes place, the history of all the clans present, and their connections, is enacted. This helps remembering.

))))))

Abeokuta, 1983

Elvis is about 16 years old

Elvis sighed, unwrapped a Bazooka, and read the fortune on the insert, desperately seeking words of wisdom.

"Bazooka Joe says: 'A friend in need is always a pain.'"

That wasn't much help, so he unwrapped another.

"Bazooka Joe says: 'A bird in hand is worth two in the bush.'"

Still not much help.

"Bazooka Joe says: 'It is never right to do wrong.'"

Another:

"Bazooka Joe says: 'A stitch in time saves nine.'"

Bazooka Joes were pretty big chunks of gum, and by now he could hardly move his jaw. Still, he unwrapped another.

"Bazooka Joe says: 'Time waits for no man.'"

"Elvis, easy, you go get lockjaw," Redemption cautioned.

Elvis laughed and went back to looking out of the window. They had been driving since late the night before. Beyond the window, cornfields rustled in the breeze. He remembered the corn his mother grew in a small area of her garden and how their blond stalks, pregnant

with seeds, brushed him teasingly as he played near them, their pollen
on his arms, itching when it mixed with sweat, his shoes covered in a
layer of golden dust, like sun-yellowed snow. In the distance, leafless,
dried, skeletal trees held up the horizon with bleached silvery arms.
Shading his eyes against the sun, Elvis looked ahead, through the
windshield, absently wondering how Redemption could see to drive.

Finally running out of Bazooka Joes, and not being able to hide
from it any longer, Elvis asked the question.

"What exactly happened back there?"

"I no sure, but I think dat we were trading in spare parts."

"Spare parts? What are you talking about?"

"Spare human parts. For organ transplant."

"What?"

"Light me one ciga and I go tell you," Redemption said.

Elvis lit two cigarettes, passing one on. Outside, the landscape had
changed to a haze of greenery. They had left the savannah and the
cornfields behind and were now surrounded on either side by a dense
forest. Tall palm trees and thick foliage lined the road. Elvis never
ceased to be amazed by the way things changed here. Nothing happened in subtle degrees—not the weather, not the movement of time,
and certainly not nature. It was impossible to see more than a couple
of feet into the forest on either side, and Elvis wondered if it would be
like the twilight of the forests back in Afikpo, near their house, where
he went to escape his father's anger. Once inside, it was easy to lose a
bigger pursuer in the tangle of liana, ferns and other underbrush, and
the darkness: not as dense as night, but a gloom far moodier, far
scarier, penetrated only by the call of invisible animals and birds. Its
safety was tenuous, as though it held a threat worse than a beating
from his father.

"So tell me."

Redemption took a deep breath and looked at Elvis.

"Keep your eyes on the road!"

"You sure say you want to know?"

"Just tell me."

"American hospitals do plenty organ transplant. But dey are not always finding de parts on time to save people life. So certain people in

That's why they were going to kill the kids.

Saudi Arabia and such a place used to buy organ parts and sell to rich white people so dey can save their children or wife or demselves."

"They can't do that!"

"Dis world operate different way for different people. Anyway, de rich whites buy de spare parts from de Arabs who buy from wherever dey can. Before dey used to buy only from Sudan and such a place, but de war and tings is make it hard, so dey expand de operation. People like de Colonel use their position to get human parts as you see and den freeze it. If we had cross de border yesterday, airplane for carry dose parts to Saudi hospital so dat dey can be sold."

Elvis was silent. He stared out of the window, but kept seeing the heads in the iced cooler. He felt strange, like there were two parts of him, each watching the other, each unsure. He watched from another place as his hands trembled and his left eye twitched uncontrollably. He did not want to talk about this anymore, but somewhere he had crossed the line on that possibility.

"How much?"

"It depend on de part. Human head fetch ten thousand dollars."

"But there is no head transplant surgery."

Redemption laughed. "Elvis, eh! Dey can use de eyes and also something dey call stem cell. Anyway, heart is also ten thousand. De oders, like kidney, are like three to ten thousand dollars. It is big money for de Colonel."

"So if we sell them to the Saudis at ten thousand, how much do they sell at?"

"Dat depend. If your only son dey die, how much you go pay for spare part for him?"

"Anything, I guess."

"Dat's right."

They sat in silence, broken only by their breathing and Leo Sayer on the car radio, reassuring them, "You make me feel like dancing."

Finally, Redemption said it. "You no go ask about de children we carry?"

"I was afraid to."

"Well, as I hear, dere is too much damage to de organ as de

Colonel de harvest dem. Also, not all survive de journey. So many of de parts are thrown away."

"Oh my God!"

"Yes, dose children will arrive in Saudi alive, den, depend on de demand, dey will harvest de parts from dem. Fresh, no damage, more money for all of dem."

"And none of the Americans ask questions about where the organs come from?"

"Like I said, if your only child dey die, you go ask question?"

"How could you get us involved, knowing all this? We are as bad as the Colonel and the Saudis."

"No forget de whites who create de demand."

"Them too. But how could you do this to me and claim to be my friend?"

"Firstly, I no know dat's what dis job was. Secondly, dere are plenty people like Kansas who are also looking for money, but I choose you because you be my friend. You can be ungrateful."

"Ungrateful! I—"

"If you want to preach, hold it. I tire," Redemption interrupted.

"Fine."

"Good."

The motion of the car lulled Elvis to sleep. Beside him, Redemption chain-smoked to stay awake, the spiral of smoke blurring his vision. After several hours they came up to a small town, where Redemption slowed and pulled off by an isolated buka. Elvis woke up and looked around. They were in an industrial area, surrounded on every side by warehouses.

"We're lost, aren't we?" Elvis asked, stating the obvious. They had been driving all night and most of the morning, yet Lagos still seemed so far away.

"Make I ask dem inside. You want anything?"

"Anything cold, and some food," Elvis replied.

He got out of the car and stretched. Ahead, the road unwound in a dusty ribbon. A crow called from its perch on a leafless branch, and a snake, probably a viper, basked in the noon heat on the road's edge.

He had no idea where they were. He watched a slim woman sail past balancing a load on her head that defied the frailty of her neck. Two small children followed closely, munching on sugarcane stems, while another was tied to her back by a lappa. It slept, lulled by the sway of her hips and the shade from the load.

Redemption came sauntering back to the car. He held two cold bottles of Coke and a fistful of bread. He broke off some bread and handed it to Elvis with one of the Cokes.

"Any idea where we are?"

"Near Shagamu. If we just continue straight we go meet freeway. Turn left and we go dey for Lagos in two hours."

Elvis nodded and bit into the bread. It was hard and crumbly, but to him it tasted great. Eating quickly, he washed it down with the Coke. He tossed the bottle to the dusty ground and lit up a cigarette.

"Return de bottles," Redemption said, snatching the cigarette from Elvis's mouth. Empty bottles were valuable because the local Coca-Cola factory washed and reused them. To ensure they got their bottles back, the factory charged local retailers a deposit on the bottles, which could only be redeemed when the bottles were turned in. The retailers in turn passed the cost of the deposit on to consumers if they intended to leave the immediate vicinity of their shops with the drinks. The amount varied from retailer to retailer but was usually no less than the price of the drink.

With a grunt Elvis got out of the car, bent down and picked up the empty Coke bottles and walked back to the buka with them. The owner returned the deposit and he pocketed it. By the time he got back to the car, Redemption already had the engine running. Elvis slid into the passenger seat, slammed the door and, as they drove off in a cloud of dust, lit another cigarette.

They traveled in silence for a mile or so until they came across a line of pedestrians dressed in bright red and yellow clothes Elvis had only seen in Indian movies. Unlike the Hare Krishnas who were now a common sight in Lagos, or the Hindus and Sikhs who owned businesses in Nigeria, these Indian-influenced Nigerians wore outfits that mixed ideas right out of Ali Baba and the Forty Thieves and costumes from a Bollywood production, complete with turbans. They had a regal look that was marred only by the sweat staining their outfits darkly, falling in streams down their faces.

"What is this? The invasion of the Raj?" Elvis asked, laughing.

"No, dese are de followers of dat new prophet, Guru Maharaji."

"Guru who?"

"Maharaji. He is a local boy O! I hear say he used to be petty assassin. Den one day he escape on ship from de people whose child he kill and den return six years later saying he is de next prophet after Mohammed and Bahai. Say de Indian people dey crown him savior but dat he wanted to come back here just to help us. Bloody tief, I bet you he only reach Ivory Coast."

Elvis laughed again. "These prophets, eh? How do they get people to follow them?"

"Who else dem go follow? Only prophets fit help us now, we be like de Israelites in de desert. No hope, no chance, no Moses. Who else we go follow?"

"Shit. A nation of prophets and devotees is a damned place."

"Or a blessed one."

Elvis snorted. Just then, one of the women caught his eye. It wasn't just the way her bodice cupped her bosom tightly, or the way the rest of her outfit fell freely around her, swelling with each movement of her hips; not even the lone dreadlock that broke free of her turban and snaked down the side of her face. It was something else.

"Stop—stop!" he yelled at Redemption.

"I no fit, Elvis. We must reach Lagos and make plan before de Colonel find us."

"Shit," Elvis muttered as the line of devotees faded in the dust of their backwash. He felt sure that it was she—Efua. It made perfect sense. She was, after all, the one among them who most needed to believe; plus Aunt Felicia and even Sunday had said that they heard she was in or around Lagos. What good would stopping do? If she had wanted his help, she would have come to him. He was sure that his address was no secret back in Afikpo. Maybe he should just let her be. On the other hand, maybe it wasn't her. After all, he hadn't gotten a very good view. Still . . .

"I think we just passed my cousin Efua."

"Here?"

"She was with the Maharaji people."

"Aah. Maybe is for de best."

"What?'

"Well, as you tell me, she done suffer. So maybe is for de best."

"All her life she has been surrounded by fakes and charlatans who have not helped her. If that was her, I should go back and save her. But it's probably not her."

"Dis Elvis, you dey very selfish."

"What do you mean?"

"Since I know you, you only care about yourself."

"How can you say that, Redemption?"

"Because it is true!"

"But I want to help my cousin, do the right thing—how can that be selfish?"

"Until you see somebody dat you think is her, you never even talk of finding her. You never even think it. Now you say you want to help. Na lie. You dey want be hero, de savior of your cousin. Oh yes, I know your type. I *am* your type. If you can't save yourself, den save others, abi? Dat way you can pretend to be good person."

"I'm not following."

"Why? It's simple."

Elvis was silent.

"Let's take me. Since you have know me, what do you know about me? Nothing!" Redemption continued.

"That is not true."

"Really? Okay, where dem born me, what be my papa name?"

"You've never told me."

"I never tell you, or you never ask?"

"That doesn't make me selfish."

"Close your mouth before fly enter. Everything is about Elvis. I sure say you no even know your papa papa name."

"That's not true."

"When it concerns you, nothing is true. Dere is a saying dat if everybody say you are smelling, better take shower before arguing. Even when you dey vex for your papa, you done ask yourself why tings be as dey are for him? You done try to understand him? Instead, you carry yourself as if nobody can understand you. Please, my friend, you are not so difficult to read."

Elvis had no comeback, no quick retort. Redemption had never spoken to him this way, and it hurt. He kept quiet, lighting a cigarette with trembling hands. As he sucked in the smoke, he couldn't hold back the tears that ran soundlessly down his face.

"Ah, Elvis, no ciga for me?" Redemption asked. "Just because I tell you de really truth?"

He turned to Elvis when he got no reply. Seeing the tears run down his face, he coughed and reached for the packet lying on the seat between them. He put one in his mouth and depressed the lighter on the dashboard. As he lit his cigarette from its glowing tip, he wondered if he had gone too far. Ah, what the hell, he thought, it was too late now.

In a few minutes they hit the tarred smoothness of the highway and were headed for Lagos. With any luck, Redemption thought, they would get there by lunchtime.

Sunday Oke folded the newspaper and laughed.

"What is it?" Comfort asked.

"Dis crazy government. Dey want to bulldoze dis place."

"Which place?"

"Maroko."

"Bulldoze?"

"Maroko."

"Why?"

"Well, according to de paper, dey say we are a pus-ridden eyesore on de face of de nation's capital."

"Maroko?"

"Not only Maroko, but all de ghettos in Lagos. A simultaneous attack on de centers of poverty and crime, dat's what dey are calling it. Dey even have a military sounding name for it—Operation Clean de Nation."

"Maroko?"

"Stop repeating dat word like a crazy person! I say not only

Maroko, but Ajegunle, Idi Oro and all de smaller ghettos under de fly-overs. But phase one is Maroko."

"When?"

"Well, according by de paper, it can happen anytime."

"Anytime? How we go do?"

"Me? Nothing. I am not leaving dis place. We just managed to buy dese few rooms we own, and now dey want to come and destroy it. Why? So dat dey can turn dis place to beachside millionaire's paradise? No! And den we will all move to another location and set up another ghetto. Instead of dem to address de unemployment and real cause of poverty and crime, dey want to cover it all under one pile of rubbish."

"What of compensation? Did de paper talk of dat?"

"Yes, dey say dey will pay compensation, but dat is a pipe dream."

"Why?"

"Dey haven't paid de promised compensation to dose dat lost things during de war. You know how many years dat is? When do you think dey will pay us? In de meantime will we live on fresh air? I am not going anywhere."

"But we can at least try, eh? Maybe dem go pay before de bulldoze."

"Pay first? Dat's like asking prostitute to pay you before sex."

Comfort shot him a very disapproving look. "I no know about dat. But anything is possible."

"Pipe dreams. I know I am not moving," Sunday said. He turned to look at Comfort. She was staring off into the distance, her face furrowed in worry. Her hair was plaited, she wore no makeup and her dark skin seemed to glow. She was beautiful in spite of the toll that three children, a divorce, living with an alcoholic, running a small business, age and living in Lagos had taken. For a moment he thought he might be in love with her.

"I am not moving," he repeated.

"Where Elvis?" Comfort asked, turning to him.

Caught off guard, he looked away shyly, before she could see what was moving in his eyes.

"What?" she asked.

"Nothing. I don't know about Elvis. Dat boy has used up all my patience."

She laughed, and the sound, sudden and uninhibited, surprised him.

"Like father, like son," she said.

"What is dat supposed to mean?"

"Nothing. I just dey wonder. Over two days now, him never reach house."

"He will come back soon. Anyway, why are you not in the market? It is just eleven in de morning."

"I decide to close my shop today."

"Why?"

"Why yourself? I no fit rest or am I spoiling something for you?"

"I only asked a simple question."

"I dey go big market today for Shagamu with Gladys dem to buy new material for sale."

He nodded. He had never taken any real interest in what she did to earn a living, not since she had slept with someone to get him a job. Since then he had only really been interested in what he could lift from her purse to buy palm wine.

"When are you leaving?"

"In about one hour. Gladys dem go come for me. Dem dey charter taxi."

"Hmm," he grunted.

"What?"

He drained the already empty palm wine bottle dramatically. But if she understood what he was hinting at, she said nothing. Deciding not to leave anything to chance, he spoke up.

"A man needs a little something to line his purse, you know. In case of emergency," he said.

"Well den, a man needs a job," she said, getting up and walking inside to get ready.

With a curse, he threw the empty palm wine bottle into the street. It narrowly missed a man in a bad suit cruising by on a high-pitched Vespa. The bottle shattered, raining green gems everywhere.

"Ah, Mr. Oke, watch it!" the man on the Vespa shouted.

"Sorry, Mr. Moneme! How is de insurance business going?"

"Not well," Mr. Moneme replied, the rest of what he said drowning in the whine of the Vespa.

Sunday was still muttering under his breath when the Mercedes pulled up and Elvis got out.

"Come and see me later," Redemption called, reversing and heading back in the same direction.

Elvis waved and walked onto the veranda. His father smiled at him, and Elvis almost fell for it, until he noticed the empty cup on the bench and the thirsty way Sunday licked his lips.

"Just take," he said, holding out a ten-naira note to his father.

Father will do anything for wine

▼▼▼▼▼▼▼▼▼▼▼▼▼▼▼▼▼▼▼▼▼▼▼▼▼▼▼▼▼▼▼▼▼

ALSTONIA BOONEI *DE WILD*
(Apocynaceae)
(Afikpo: Ukpo)

Found in the drier lowland rain forest, this small tree has brown, flaking bark, and when cut secretes white latex that is irritating to the eye. Its leaves are broad, leathery, smooth, glossy and dark green on the upper surface and bluish green on the lower. Yellowish-white flowers cluster at the end of each stem. Hanging in twos, its fruits contain numerous seeds.

Leaves, roots and bark macerated in water are applied externally to ease rheumatic pains. An infusion of the bark alone is drunk as a remedy for snakebites and arrow poison. The latex, smeared on wounds caused by Filaria worms and then bandaged with the crushed bark of the ordeal tree, is an excellent cure. Some women drink a decoction of the bark after childbirth to cause delivery of the placenta. The leaves cooked in a yam potage are an excellent way to prevent early miscarriages.

TWENTY-FOUR

✦✦✦✦

But beware, this is not as easy as it seems.

It also defines being.

✦✦✦✦

Lagos, 1983

Elvis is about 16 years old

Elvis emerged from his room a few hours later, awakened by his father's shouting. Stumbling out onto the veranda, he saw Jagua Rigogo
sitting in a corner, his pet python draped round his neck: a real boa, so
to speak. Confidence, who also lived in the tenement, was arguing
heatedly with Sunday. Confidence kept his distance from Jagua and his
snake. He couldn't stand either. He worked hard at what he did, con-
ning people. It was, he said, his life's work, something he had been
named to do. He thought Jagua was a lazy ne'er-do-well who sponged
off people's good graces and fear of damnation. Jagua was a practicing
druid and held healings and mystic consultations for people daily from
his room at the end of the compound. It wasn't much of a living, but
being the landlord's brother, he had no rent to pay—something
everyone suspected was really at the bottom of Confidence's hatred.
Elvis had asked him about it once and Confidence had replied: "Is not
dat. I just hate people who can't make an honest living."

The hatred was mutual, exacerbated by the fact that Confidence
had tried to strangle Jagua's python with a guitar string. Jagua put a
curse on him as he rescued his snake. Everyone pooh-poohed Jagua's
druidic philosophy and magic spells, but night after night, for over

three months, the snake would wind itself chokingly around Confidence's neck, slowly draining the life from him, until he woke with a start, bedding wrapped tightly around his neck, to find it had all been just a dream. But neither the Gideon Bible under his pillow nor the rosary he wore like a necklace kept him safe, until he apologized.

"Please control yourselves. Dis is not boys' club. We are here to discuss our future. Be reasonable, Confidence," Madam Caro cut in.

Elvis looked at her. What is she doing here? he thought. She didn't even live in the building. He noted that there were in fact several people, some he did not know, gathered around his father.

"Thank you, madam," Sunday said, quickly wrestling control away from her.

"What is going on here?" Elvis demanded.

"Dis your child no get manners O!" Freedom, a teacher from the building next door, said. He had a high-pitched voice and effeminate ways, which included a penchant for short-sleeve shirts that bore an uncanny resemblance to women's blouses.

"Hold it, Freedom," Sunday said. Turning to Elvis, he said, "We are planning revolution here."

"Revolution? For what?"

"You dey dis Lagos? Abi, you never hear dat gofment want to bu'-doze Maroko?"

"This Maroko?"

"Yes," Madam Caro said.

"Here, read de paper," Sunday said, handing it to Elvis. As he scanned the story, Elvis heard them return to arguing.

"So how do we go on from dis point?" Freedom asked.

"Well, my view is that dey should not be allow to get away with it. We must oppose them," Jagua replied.

"But how?" someone Elvis didn't know asked.

"We rally de people around us. Dey do not like it either dat de authorities are trying to demolish deir town," Sunday said.

"It is one thing to think it is wrong, but why do you think they will risk anything for you?" Elvis asked.

"Not for me, my son, but de cause."

"What cause? Who do you think you are, Malcolm X?"

Sunday shot Elvis a withering look.

"Elvis, show some respect," Madam Caro said.

Elvis looked away.

"De boy is right O!" Freedom said. "We need strong leader."

"Like who? De Beggar King?" Sunday asked.

"Weren't you just criticizing him the other night?"

"I still am."

"Ah, de man influential O!" Madam Caro said.

Elvis stared at her in surprise. He didn't know she even knew who the King was.

"Dese people have been treated badly by de authorities all their lives. Dey pay high taxes, get low wages, poor accommodation, no clean water," Sunday argued.

"Okay, chief. We get de point. Dis is not election campaign. Just tell us what to do," Confidence interrupted.

Sunday glowered at him.

"So, Elvis, you will talk to de King?" Sunday asked.

"Talk to him yourself."

"Leave dis your stupid son, I will go and call de King," Confidence said.

"You know where he lives?" Sunday asked.

"No, but I de see him begging near Bridge City for Ojuelegba."

"Return quick," Jagua said.

With Confidence gone, the men started a game of checkers to keep busy until his return. Madam Caro walked hurriedly back to her bar, glad to be able to check on her helpers, whom she was convinced were stealing from her. Elvis sat back and watched the game unfold. If he hadn't grown up in this culture, he might have thought it strange to have walked in on the heated debate about not letting the government get away with their plans and then to see the same people who had been protesting only moments before begin a game of checkers while they waited for something to happen—in this case, the return of Confidence with the King. Yawning, he contemplated going out for a meal and a drink, but he didn't want to miss any of the unfolding events.

Jagua, who had lost early in the round of checkers, was the first to see Confidence returning. He called out, and everyone's attention followed his pointing finger.

"Well done, Confidence," Sunday said as soon as Confidence and the King were within earshot.

Confidence came up onto the veranda, but the King stayed a few feet away in the middle of the street. Jagua studied the King with some distaste, even though, with his matted dreadlocks and lean face, Jagua could have been a relative.

"Where you find him?" he asked.

"Near Ojuelegba, so I tell him dat we want to talk to him about something. But he refuse to follow me until I give him some money. So you people owe me twenty naira," Confidence replied.

"Don't worry about dat," Sunday said. "We are in dis together. Somebody go and call Madam Caro."

Nobody moved, so he turned and yelled for Comfort's son Tunji. When Tunji emerged from the dark innards of the building, Sunday sent him off at a fast trot to summon Madam Caro. "And tell her dat palm wine is needed to smooth dese talks," Sunday added as Tunji scampered off.

The King had been silent all this while, and except for a smile in Elvis's direction, he gave no indication that he knew who he was.

"Hello, people," the King called. "Any chance for food?"

"Help us and den we shall see," Sunday called.

"So how can de King help you?" he asked Sunday.

As he was about to answer, Sunday saw Madam Caro hurrying over, a small keg of palm wine in her hand. He delayed his response until she had found a seat on the veranda, then sketched out the nature of their dilemma as the King listened thoughtfully. While Sunday was explaining, someone had gone to fetch a cold soft drink and a small loaf of bread for the King. Accepting them gratefully, he proceeded to chew loudly throughout Sunday's monologue. He finished the bread just as Sunday finished speaking.

"So what is your advice?" Sunday asked.

The King put the soft drink to his mouth and, without taking his eyes off Elvis, drained the bottle. With a satisfied sigh he put it down.

"Well, as I know, dis gofment is not easy. To put hand for deir eye is dangerous."

"Look, we are not small children. We know de risk. Just tell us how for do," Confidence said impatiently.

"Well, in my experience, marching with placard is de best way to start."

"Marching where?" Jagua asked.

"Like in front of deir office. Dat is de first step," the King replied.

"I go bring de women. We go march to local council office and tell dem our vex," Madam Caro said, jumping in.

"We will march on de council offices on Monday. Dat gives us two days to get things set. I will lead, de men can carry placards and de women can support with singing and refreshments," Sunday said.

Madam Caro glared at him.

"Not dat de women are less important, though, right?" Freedom cut in sarcastically.

None of the men responded.

"I can make de placards quick quick," Confidence said, caught in the sudden optimism of the moment.

"Dere is only one problem," Sergeant Okoro said softly.

He lived in the same building and had been silent for much of the argument. His usual gruff and aggressive demeanor was replaced by a softer, almost fearful side. Occasionally, Sergeant Okoro had been menaced on his way home from work by some of the other residents, as he was the most readily available authority figure. Once or twice he would have been very badly hurt if Sunday hadn't intervened. Even his decision to invite him to this meeting was not popular, but Sunday knew none of the others really wanted to go against him.

"What is de problem?" Sunday asked.

"Well, as far as I know, de police dey come here tomorrow, with bu'dozer. Dere is no time for marching on Monday."

"So what now?" Confidence asked.

"Time for step two," the King said.

"What is step two?"

"It is dangerous. Are you sure?" the King asked.

"Look, we are not playing here," Freedom said.

"Okay. Step two is to stop dem from entering Maroko."

"Stop dem from entering?" Freedom asked.

"Form human barrier at all de entrance," the King said.

"But dere are too many entrances to Maroko." Sunday said. "We cannot block dem all."

"But dere is only four dat a bu'dozer can use," the King said. "Your street here, which has two entrance, and Lawanson Street, which has two."

As the King spoke, Elvis visualized the two streets. The King was right; they were the only two streets with outside access wide enough for any kind of vehicle except a bicycle or a motorcycle. He saw them spread out across Maroko in an uneven cross—a cross that would be held down at each end by human sacrifice, if they did what the King suggested. From the sky, he imagined, the streets must look like two straps straining to keep everything inside the bulky, unwieldy square of the ghetto.

"So simple it might work," Okoro said doubtfully.

"But what if dey decide to drive through us?" Jagua Rigogo asked the question on everyone's mind.

"They wouldn't, would they?" Elvis asked.

"Whatever else dey may be," Madam Caro reassured them, "dey are human." *Why do they think they wont kill them*

"I'm not so sure," Sunday mused, looking at Okoro, who looked away guiltily.

They quickly ran through the plan. Confidence would paint placards using slogans devised by Jagua. Sunday, Madam Caro and Confidence's wife, Agnes, would go and talk to people to try and mobilize enough of them to attend the street blocking the next day. And the King would lead them.

"I am sorry, but I cannot," the King said.

"Why can't you lead? It was your idea," Confidence asked.

"I dey leave town dis evening with my band, de Joking Jaguars. We dey go tour and we no go return for at least two weeks," the King replied.

There was a lot of loud dissension, but the King was adamant.

"Why you no lead?" the King asked Sunday.

"Me?"

"Yes, you," everyone agreed, all desperate to have a leader that was not them.

"All right, if it is de will of de people," Sunday said.

On the veranda, Elvis groaned to himself. What a fake old fart, he thought. But the conversation had moved on now that a leader had been identified. It was decided that the children would join their parents on the picket line as a guarantee that the police wouldn't stampede them. Confidence did not like it. What if one of the children got hurt? He was prepared to let his children join, but he felt he could not ask the same of the other parents. He was outvoted and Freedom was put in charge of mobilizing the local children, as he was so good with them. They were to lug old tires, broken furniture, and empty petrol drums—anything they could find—and build an effective barrier that the police could not bridge. These, the King told them, could also be ignited to create a wall of flame to further frustrate the police assault that was bound to follow their resistance.

"Build dem three by three," the King instructed.

"Three by three?" Freedom asked.

"Three walls, three feet apart, three feet thick."

"Dat's three by three by three. Ju don't know your math," Joshua said, looking up from his calculations.

Everybody glared at him.

"Sorry," he mumbled.

Elvis had hung around wanting to talk his father out of leading what he was sure would be a suicide mission, but the insistent blaring of a car horn pulled his attention away from the meeting. Looking up, he saw it was Redemption, waiting for him in the Mercedes they had stolen from Ibare. As he ambled across the street, he saw that the King had beaten him to it and was talking to Redemption through the open driver's window. As he got closer, he also noticed a soldier in full uniform sitting in the front passenger seat. It was Jimoh. The last time Elvis had seen him was the night the Colonel had almost killed him at the night club. He hesitated for a minute, but Redemption signaled him over frantically.

"Why you never come see me, Elvis?" Redemption asked as Elvis approached.

"I just woke up."

"Dis Elvis, you are something, sleeping at a time like dis."

The King had moved when Elvis came across, and now stood slightly to the left, watching.

"Why are you still driving this car?"

"Dat is small problem. Remember dis man?" he said, pointing at the uniformed soldier sitting next to him.

Elvis nodded. "It's Jimoh."

"De Colonel send him to tie up de loose ends."

"What do you mean?"

"De Colonel send me to kill both of you," Jimoh said.

Unconsciously, Elvis stepped back from the car. Overhearing, the King stepped forward, his hand on Elvis's back, steadying him. Bending to look through the car window, the King spoke to Redemption.

"So what is de plan?"

"Me, I no get plan. I go dey dis town, I no fit run. In a few weeks de Colonel go forget us and everything go quench," Redemption replied.

"But you get to live dat long first," the King said.

"For me dat no be problem, but I worry for Elvis."

"I fit help Elvis. My troupe dey leave town today to tour de country. He can follow me. By de time we return, everything go done cool down."

"Dat's good," Redemption said. "Elvis, you dey hear?"

Elvis nodded. Redemption reached into his back pocket and pulled out an envelope, which he handed to Elvis.

"Elvis, dis na de money. You understand?"

"Yes," Elvis replied, taking the envelope and shoving it into his back pocket.

"Chief," Redemption said, turning to the King and handing him a handful of money. "Dis na for you."

"Don't insult me, Redemption. I no dey do dis for money."

"I know. But I know as things hard for you. Take it."

Reluctantly the King took the money and pocketed it.

"Elvis," Redemption said.

"Redemption."

With a hearty laugh, Redemption drove off and Elvis and the King crossed the street, headed back for the veranda.

"Listen, Elvis, we dey leave from in front of my place by six dis evening. Get your things and be ready."

"Sure," Elvis said. He stopped halfway across the street and turned to the bus stop.

"Where you dey go?" the King asked.

"To think."

"My place at six. We no go wait," he shouted after Elvis.

Elvis rode the bus down to Bar Beach. Getting off, he trekked across the sand, past the tourist beaches with pink expatriates baking slowly in the sun, past the mangy horses, the photographers with monkeys, the kebab, soft drink and food hawkers, through a coconut-palm thicket to a deserted beach. He sat, legs pulled to chin, gazing out at the ocean, watching giant waves crash against the shore. Elvis felt as if he were locked in a time warp, a suspended existence. The sea and the sky blended into one, and the background of sand, hardy grass and coconut palms sealed everything in completely, and the crashing sea became a dull throb in the background.

He chain-smoked, thinking about the children he had almost led to their deaths. He kept hearing Kemi's voice, begging not to be killed. Watching the breeze playing through the leaves of the coconut palms, he wondered if Redemption had lied to him, if he had really known all along what the deal was. How could Redemption lead him down such a path? Now he had to flee from the Colonel, lay low for God knew how long.

It was kind of the King to offer to take him with his touring group, but things were happening here, and part of him wanted to stay and face the Colonel. Jimoh, however, had been clear: he had orders to tie up loose ends, which Redemption pointed out meant killing them. His own cowardice surprised him. He always thought when the moment came he would do the right thing. But going with the King also presented him with another opportunity to dance. The Joking Jaguars, the King's performance troupe, was composed entirely of musicians and dancers. He missed dancing, and here was a chance to get back into it. The music would be highlife or jazz, he knew, and he probably wouldn't get to do his Elvis impersonation, but he was still a good dancer regardless. And there would be an audience, one that had paid to see them perform. He had never had that, only bored and disgruntled passersby who felt his street performing was little more than begging, harassment even.

Elvis stubbed out his cigarette and settled back. Listening to the *clack, clack* of the palm fronds form a percussive background to the oboe throb of the sea, he dozed off. An hour later, he woke with a start and, standing up, dusted off the seat of his trousers. White sand, in fine glittering silicon chips, clung to him, catching the sun, turning him into a patchwork fabric of diamonds and ebony.

▼▼▼▼▼▼▼▼▼▼▼▼▼▼▼▼▼▼▼▼▼▼▼▼▼▼▼▼▼▼▼▼▼▼▼▼▼▼▼

FRIED OKRA AND SWEET POTATO

INGREDIENTS

Sweet potatoes
Olive oil
Strips of beef
Okra (chopped)
Ose mkpi (fragrant yellow chilies)
Fresh plum tomatoes
Onions
Tomato puree
Maggi cubes
Salt
Ahunji

PREPARATION

Peel and slice the sweet potatoes thinly. Heat some olive oil. Salt the slices of
sweet potato and drop into the oil when hot. Fry until crisp on the outside but
soft and powdery on the inside.

Heat some oil in a wok and drop in the beef. Sauté the meat for a while until brown and then add the rest of the ingredients. Fry until okra is a little brown
around the edges, but still crunchy. Serving suggestion: arrange the slices of
sweet potato in the shape of a flower; scoop the okra into the middle.

TWENTY-FIVE

There is peril in this, and the loss of face is not only on the young neo-phyte, it is on his clan, as they have not taught him well.

Igbo clans comprise close kin who settled in clusters. All rights to land and ascendancy are determined by age, with the older males taking precedence. Likewise, the clan de-scended from the oldest relative in the cluster takes precedence over the others.

Is Elvis there?

Elvis is about 16 years old

Lagos, 1983

Joshua Bandele-Thomas was measuring the barricades at one end of the street. He stopped, muttered something and made little notes in a worn leatherbound book. Counting off ten steps, he stood away from the barrier and set up his surveyor's tripod. He bent and trained it on the barrier. Muttering even more, he made notes again.

Sunday watched him and shook his head. Crazy bastard, he thought.

Freedom and the boys had done a pretty good job. The barricades, made of broken furniture, old car skeletons, poles, building debris and other junk, were very secure. There was no way a small vehicle could get past them, much less a bulldozer. Besides, they were three deep. He turned round and watched Freedom directing the boys building the second set of barricades at the bottom of the street, arms waving, head bobbing like a conductor putting an orchestra through its paces. The children responded, laughing at Freedom's high-pitched squeals and commands.

Sergeant Okoro walked over to Sunday.

"What do you think?" Sunday asked him, nodding in the direction of the barriers.

"I think dey are okay. Dey won't keep dem out for long, though. Dey will bu'doze dese barricades in ten minutes."

"Ever de optimist. We were considering placing ourselves between de barriers and de trucks."

"Dat will only slow dem down. You cannot stop dem."

"I don't think any of us are being naive enough to believe we can stop dem. We are only hoping to delay dem for a while. Until de press can make a big story about it."

"You call press?"

"No, but we dey hope say de story will attract dem."

"Fine, because you cannot stop dem."

"Yes, sure," Sunday said, walking away.

Joshua Bandele-Thomas came over and stood beside Sunday. "De measurements do not compute."

Sunday looked at him and shook his head. Joshua, his next-door neighbor, was an eccentric who modeled himself entirely on the classic Jeeves-and-Wooster English gentleman. He wore three-piece suits whatever the weather. For years he had worked as an accounts clerk for the Upanishad Tagore Company, eking out a sedentary and pedestrian existence. But he harbored a not-so-secret ambition: he wanted to go to England and study to be a surveyor. So he scrimped and saved, allowing himself only the luxury of elocution lessons. Unfortunately, the only teacher he could afford and still save enough to go to England was an old Spaniard who had come to Nigeria in the 1920s and stayed. Joshua was quite a character with his three-piece suits, bowler hats and Spanish-accented English.

Some years before, thieves had broken into his room and stolen his life savings, which were hidden inside his mattress. That marked a turning point in Joshua's life. Instead of the mad ranting or raving Sunday had expected, he was quite calm about it. The only apparent difference was that he ate less and spoke only when spoken to. He had been stabbed in the eye during the attack, as he fought to keep his money, and his employer had graciously paid for a glass eye. Joshua accepted the gift gratefully and went back to work at the UTC a week later. Everyone thought he was fine. In fact the neighbors were admiring and spoke complimentarily of him in his absence.

Then one day someone saw him down at the marina on Lagos Island. He was wearing his three-piece suit, but he had substituted his bowler for a hard hat. He also had a surveyor's level mounted on a tripod. He was causing a minor traffic jam as he went about carefully surveying the area, trailing an extra-long tape behind him. Sunday had caught a bus and gone down to bring Joshua home, and when he broached the subject of the surveying, Joshua responded merrily, "Why ju ask, Mr. Oke? Ju want a survey?"

Sunday had looked at him the same then as now, sadly. Madness was a terrible thing.

"The measurements do not compute," Joshua repeated to Sunday, popping out his glass eye casually and rubbing the irritated socket.

Sunday nodded and looked away quickly. He knew what was coming next. Joshua cleaned the glass eye by sucking on it for a few minutes and popping it back in, still wet. Sighing, he went off down the street to measure the second set of barriers.

When the barriers were ready, Freedom sat on the floor by the last one with his exhausted troop of boys. Each one held a sweating cold bottle of Coca-Cola as they laughed and horsed around. Confidence, Okoro, Sunday and some other men from the neighboring tenements lounged on the steps drinking palm wine and chatting in somber tones. There had been some worry that the neighbors would not join them in the protest. The night before, however, employing the campaign tactics that hadn't worked for him during the elections, Sunday had gone from tenement to tenement, home to home, across Maroko, speaking to the men and women he thought would have the most influence over their neighbors. Instead of the resistance or even apathy he had expected, nearly all had responded positively and had come out in force to help construct the barricades and assist in other ways.

"Gentlemen, Confidence has prepared de placards and banners," Sunday announced.

The men crowded round as Confidence unrolled each one. There were twenty banners in all, and the four slogans had been repeated at random. WE OWN THIS LIFE; FREEDOM; RIGHTS TO EXPRESS; NO SA-

CRED COWS. They were all done on old, stained brown-once-white sheets donated by the local clinic located a few blocks away. The doctor who ran the clinic was of dubious qualifications, and his nurse was his wife. After watching footage of the war-crime trials in Nuremberg in the cinema, everyone referred to him as Dr. Mengele. To ensure their plan did not leak, Sunday had asked Sergeant Okoro to stay back from work—not that he did not trust him, but one could never be sure what kind of pressure could be brought to bear on a man.

The police came at seven a.m., no doubt hoping to catch the street unawares. Everyone had been awake for hours, though, waiting tensely. Unsure how many policemen there were, Freedom instructed his boys to run from barricade to barricade, setting the first line alight.

The lone police Land Rover had a fire truck and a bulldozer behind it. The fact that there were only four policemen and two firemen was a clear indication that the authorities had not expected any resistance, and they were easily repelled by the placard-carrying residents chanting behind the walls of flames.

An hour later reinforcements arrived and the fire brigade doused the first line of flames, but with a sneering laugh, Jagua Rigogo set off the second wall. He was every inch the warlock. He had two more friends from his brotherhood with him, and together they looked like they had just stepped out of *The Lord of the Rings*, hair falling in tangled dreadlocks that came all the way down to their waists, flailing madly as they ran from one end of the barrier to the next, setting it alight. Jagua stood with his cronies in white smocks, beards and Medusa hair looking crazy. Arms raised, staffs of office held in the classic spell-casting pose of the Brotherhood of the Golden Dawn, they screamed spells at the police like insane Merlins and Gandalfs, with a touch of Catweasel.

"Ignome gatturbe oringbe javanah!" they screamed defiantly.

His python, aroused by Jagua Rigogo's screaming, unwound itself from his neck, raising itself into a three-foot rod of curiosity. Head cocked at the police, hovering over Jagua, it stared around. The police and fire brigade retreated from this apparition. The crowd pressed forward, all of them singing along to the Bob Marley song coming out of the sound system with the large speakers that they had borrowed from the record store down the road.

"Get up, stand up, stand up for your rights. Don't give up de fight!"

More reinforcements arrived; and a bigger fire engine, with a bigger hose, aimed its nozzle and shot a jet of water over the barrier, right between the druids, catching Jagua square in the chest, breaking three ribs and throwing him fifteen feet back. In seconds the second wall of flame was a hissing wet mass. The police advanced, but so did all the children on the street. They draped themselves over and inside the barrier. Each child carried a candle and sang the hymn "Jesus Loves Me." The fire engine backed off, as did the baton-wielding police. Two hours had passed and an impasse had been reached.

"Listen, you cannot stop us from doing what we have to do," the inspector in charge of the operation called across. "You will only delay de inevitable. You are also senselessly placing yourselves at risk, not to mention dese children. Move back to your homes and I promise no one will be hurt. We will do what we have to and go."

Nobody responded. Angry, he shouted orders at his men, and a couple disappeared to return a few minutes later with the bulldozer rumbling behind them. Sergeant Okoro, keeping well out of sight, whispered a few words to Freedom, who ran over to Sunday and whispered something to him.

Nodding, Sunday got up and raised his voice. "Hello!" he called. The bulldozer stood idling and its engine drowned Sunday out. "Hello!" he called again.

The police inspector signaled for the bulldozer driver to turn off its engine. "Yes?" he replied.

"Can you let us evacuate de wounded wizard?" Sunday called.

"Two men should carry him over to us. We'll see he gets to de hospital. Is dat clear?" the inspector called back.

"Yes, sir."

Walking back, Sunday nominated the two other wizards to carry Jagua Rigogo. As they lifted him, Sunday whispered to him and Jagua nodded painfully. As they neared the barrier, Sunday signaled Freedom. As Jagua was handed over to the police, he began waving his arms painfully about and screaming at the top of his voice.

"Dey are killing me O! Dey are killing me O! Dey are killing me O!"

While everyone's attention was diverted to the screaming Jagua and the two other mad druids, still casting spells, Freedom vaulted over the barrier effortlessly. He crept round to the bulldozer. The driver had jumped down and joined the police and firemen surrounding Jagua. Freedom quickly cut through the rubber pipes that worked the hydraulic system of the bulldozer's blade. By the time Jagua had been calmed down and put in the Land Rover on his way to the hospital, Freedom had finished and stood with the others, watching.

"Hey, you!" the police inspector called to Sunday.

"Yes."

"Ask dese people to move or I will send de bulldozer in and crush your children!"

Sunday turned to Freedom, who smiled at him. Sunday then called to the children, who removed themselves from the barrier and gathered behind the now solid wall of adults.

"Move dis rubbish out of de way," the inspector barked at the bulldozer driver.

No one moved as the huge metal dragon roared into life and rumbled slowly forward. More like a squat rhinoceros than a dragon, it hugged the ground reassuringly, although its movements were more sluggish than before. The driver's face furrowed into a frown as he ground the gears angrily. From behind the third barrier, now burning too, the wall of men looked on. Two feet back from them stood a second wall, made up of women, humming gently, the sound swelling the men's courage. Behind them, the children huddled, candles burning, their faces ghoulish in the fire- and candlelight.

The policemen watched them, faces hard. A fireman sauntered to the far side of the burning barrier and lit a cigarette. He exhaled softly and scratched his crotch distractedly. Yawning, he stretched, wishing he could go back home. He did not see the point of this. It would be easier to come back another day when they were not expected. That would be his plan. Besides, even if the crowd dispersed, how could they demolish the place with the people still in their homes? He glanced hopefully at the police inspector's face, his spirits sinking at the determined look.

The bulldozer lumbered closer to the barrier. Even though it was beginning to skew slightly, some of the men looked worriedly at Sunday. But swallowing their bristly fear, they stood their ground. Sunday tried to smile reassuringly at them, but the sweat on his forehead belied it. He noted the bulldozer's approach warily and glanced at Freedom from the corner of his eye. Freedom stood there without fear, a curious smile playing at the edge of his lips. He was either very confident or mad. Catching Sunday's eye, Freedom flashed him a brilliant smile. Sunday decided to trust him.

Jagua Rigogo's two druidic companions stood with dreadlocks billowing out behind them, beards working with the rigor of the spells they cast, hurling them at the bulldozer as though they were stones, or cannonballs shot from a castle wall. But the roaring metal beast would not stop, so they ran after it, beating it angrily with their wooden staves. The beast rumbled on, skewing even more. Ten minutes after it had come to life, the bulldozer stood two feet from the flaming barrier. It had only crossed twenty feet.

"Destroy dat barrier!" the police inspector shouted at the driver.

Nodding, the driver tried to engage the blade of the bulldozer. The levers groaned under his hands, but the blade only lifted half an inch before crashing down noisily. The next minute, rubber hosing under the metal behemoth ripped apart, blowing steam, hissing and twisting like angry vipers. The driver shouted at the machine and angrily began to yank all the levers in front of him. The bulldozer reacted by spinning round in widening arcs, its blade cutting swathes in the ground, ripping up the end of the barrier, scattering flames and embers everywhere. The policemen screamed and jumped back, as did a couple of men at the far side of the barrier.

With a screech, the bulldozer plowed forward, tearing a hole in the fire engine and coming to a stop amid tortured metal. Druids, driver, police and firemen lay in scattered heaps on either side, where they had dived for cover. The startled crowd had stopped singing and was staring open-mouthed at the spectacle.

"Arrest dose bastards!" the inspector yelled, coming to life and pointing at the two druids.

The policemen pounced on the two druids. Grunting from the exertion of beating them, the policemen shackled and hauled them off to the now returned Land Rover. The inspector approached the barrier and stood glowering over it at the line of men. He was stumped. Twenty years in the police force and he couldn't dispel a simple street protest. The truth was that he had never had the heart for this part of police work, the bullish, brutish enforcing of orders from above. He sighed. His men stood behind him, waiting for orders, waiting for him to redeem this farce. He looked back at them and then turned to the barrier. Taking a big handkerchief out of his pocket, he wiped his face.

"Why are you people so stubborn?!" he called out.

Nobody replied.

"Dis is pointless. In de end, we will break through dis barrier."

Still no one replied.

The inspector was getting really exasperated now. "Someone will get hurt! I don't want dat to happen."

Nobody said anything.

"Dere are children here."

One of the men behind the barrier started giggling. One of the policemen picked it up, and soon the street was ringing with the sounds of laughter. Everyone was laughing except the inspector. Sunday was the first to notice the change in him, the tentative twitch of fingers reaching for his holstered pistol. Then it was out and pointing.

The shot silenced everyone and brought one of the laughing men down. Screams replaced the laughter and people began to panic. Confused, other policemen opened fire. People dropped to the ground, and it was unclear whether they were ducking or had been hit. Sunday stood still as people fell beside him, like rapids shooting a rock. Scanning the prone figures, he realized that only one person had been hit, but the firing hadn't stopped. He screamed, high-pitched and unnatural. The firing stopped abruptly and everyone froze as Sunday approached the pistol-waving, wild-eyed inspector.

"Can we talk?" he asked, his voice soothing.

"Go on," the inspector said, still looking at him warily.

"If you and your men stay here any longer, things are going to get a lot worse."

"So what do you suggest?"

"What if I gave you my word dat we will pull out and let you in later?"

"When?"

"In a few days."

The inspector began to calm down a little, the pistol steadier in his hand.

"But what guarantee do I have dat you will keep your word?"

"You've shot one man. One is in hospital and you have arrested two more. I don't think we want to risk anyone else getting hurt."

"But you don't understand. Dere has been an incident here. Somebody will have to answer for it. Somebody has to be charged with dis. Somebody . . ." the inspector finished lamely.

"I understand. But you have two men under arrest, right?"

"Yes."

"So charge dem."

"But dey are your people. I thought sewer rats stuck together?"

Disbelief, dangerous at this stage, was beginning to creep back into the inspector's voice.

"We will come and bail dem."

"I don't know."

"Dere are children here. Why don't you accept a tactical withdrawal? A dead child is difficult to explain."

The inspector considered it for a while.

"But what can we charge dem with?" he asked.

"I don't know. How about violent disorder and criminal damage?"

"To what?" the inspector argued.

"Say dat dey got in de way of de bulldozer, causing de accident."

"But that will not hold up in court." *Since when do they care about court*

"Probably not. But it won't be your problem anymore. Dis will, though, if it gets any worse."

The inspector deliberated silently, holstering his pistol. With a definitive tone he called his men off. Sunday looked at the bulldozer and the destroyed fire engine. Turning, he took in the burning barricade. Behind it, littering the ground sadly, were the banners and candle stubs. A bloodstained piece of crumpled tissue, broken and small, lay like a dead bird in the corner. At the other end of the street, some men and women were helping the shot man into a taxi. His left kneecap was hanging off, but at least he had not been killed. Freedom stood on a veranda, looking bewildered. Confidence sat on a stoop, head cradled between his hands, his wife making concerned passes over his head. Had it been worth it? Was any of this worth any principle? Sunday was not so sure anymore. Sighing, he walked past Freedom and Confidence into the tenement. Behind him, children were playing a new dare game: who could jump over the still-burning barricade.

Things are getting out of hand

^^^

ANTIDESMA MEMBRANACEUM *MUELL. ARG.*

(Euphorbiaceae)
(Yoruba: Aroro)

This small tree is found mostly in the savannah. Its bark is pale grey and fissured and its twigs and young leaves are covered with a lot of hair. As with most herbs, the flowers are yellowish green. Small and black, the fruits occur along the base of the stalk.

A decoction of the leaves is used as a bath to prevent abortion. Mixed into stream water or seawater, milk and some Jordanian hyssop, it becomes a mystic bath to protect against witchcraft.

Mistake
Adio says
mis carage

TWENTY-SIX

))))))

Mistakes are expected until the boy becomes a man, but still no ground is given.

An example is the town of Isu-Ama, comprised of the following clans set up by the brothers they were named after, in order of age, with Isu being the father. The clans are Isu—father; Anyim—first son; Utum—second son; and Igwe—third son.

))))))

Ijebu, 1983

[handwritten: Elvis is about 16 years old]

The van bearing the legend JOKING JAGUARS stood shedding dust, body vibrating from the grumpy throb of its engine. Dust-encrusted musicians stood sweating in its reluctant shade, sipping on warm Cokes. A small crowd of curious children had gathered, speaking in hushed tones and pointing at the shapes lashed to the roof rack under tired green tarp.

Elvis mopped his brow with a dirty handkerchief and stared around the small town. It boasted one church, one shop with a decrepit petrol pump out front and a junior school. He didn't know what it was called. Hell, maybe. Wherever they were, he did not speak the language. That was the problem with a country that was an amalgamation of over two hundred and fifty ethnic groups, he thought—too many bloody languages.

He walked over to a hawker and with sign language bought a bunch of ripe bananas and a measure of peanuts. Munching on a mouthful of banana and peanuts, he wondered how they found these towns. There were no road maps or signs. He looked at the musicians and tried to imagine what had kept them going all these years as they played small towns where nobody really appreciated the skill required to take years of abuse and turn it into amazingly beautiful melodies; the drain of searching yourself constantly, plumbing depths of nakedness to play that bad-ass solo that was lost on the loud-talking, drinking audience.

The King, the troupe leader, had gone off to see the local chief to get his permission to perform that evening. He also needed the local Catholic priest's permission. Both would cost him money. With luck the gate takings would be good.

"Elvis!" one of the musicians called.

"Yes, George."

"Is dat how your mother raise you? Not to offer your friends food?"

"My mother died when I was a child. What do you expect?" Elvis called back.

George roared with laughter. He wiped a tear and got up from the tree stump he was sitting on and strolled over to Elvis. Yanking a banana free, George peeled it halfway. He took a bite, then threw a handful of peanuts in after it.

"Why do you do it, George? Why are you a musician?" Elvis asked.

George glanced at him sideways. He wondered if Elvis was beginning to unravel at the edges. That is what the road did—ate away at the edges of your resolve until you were nothing but frayed soul fabric. From then on, there was only the music—and the sacrifices it demanded of you. At sixteen, George thought, Elvis was too young for the road. The King felt his youth would protect him. But the road always got you. Of course, he knew nothing about the fact that Elvis had the added pressure of being a fugitive from the Colonel. They had been gone for two weeks already, and George had not expected Elvis to survive the first week. Maybe he was made of sterner stuff. He liked him and secretly hoped the boy was not cursed by the muse. He was a nice kid with good moves and great potential as a dancer, though he had yet to be original. He was too young for that. George hoped this was just a phase for Elvis, that maybe he would have the chance at a normal life.

"I don't have a choice, Elvis. When de muse calls, you obey."

Elvis laughed. Hollow.

"I mean, we have been doing concerts for seven years now as Joking Jaguars. Almost every night we perform in a different town, under a different sky. I have not been at home for more dan six months at a stretch in all dat time. I have twelve children and a wife tired of waiting. And every night I get into costume and get up onstage and I die. I die." George swallowed hard.

Elvis looked away, uncomfortable with this sudden intense display of emotion.

"You see, Elvis, in dis time and place, being a musician is not blessing. It is curse. Listen to my advice. Listen carefully. Do not live dis life unless it is de only thing you can be. Go out and get a nice job. Dere is a nice office job for you somewhere. Find a good wife. Look for a girl with a compassionate smile and fire in her eyes. But not de manic rage of a forest fire—look instead for de gentle glow of a hearth, a girl whose laughter makes de drudgery of life bearable. And when you bury your nose in her hair and draw a deep breath, if you are lucky, de spice of her love will infuse you with de husky scent of wood smoke, de throat tickle of curry leaves, de breathlessness of peppers and de milk burp of still-unborn babies. Draw all of dese deeply into you, until every part of you is infected by her. And if you are lucky, she will purge you of de insanity of de muse, de knife-edge beauty of seeing yourself as you are. As you really are."

Elvis looked away into the distance, eyes following the dancing heat devils.

"The heat is too intense," he said.

"Yes," George replied, stepping back from the lip of the chasm. "You'd think it would burn everything bad to a crisp."

Elvis nodded. This was all too much for him. Seeing a child hawker with a keg of cold water, he called him over. For a penny, he and George slaked their thirst. The sun had moved, and like an old woman tugging at her skirts, it dropped shadows over them. George sighed with relief. He couldn't really stand the heat. His beard and rather corpulent disposition did not help much either.

In the shade of the rickety old van sat Ezekiel "Spectacles" Onyia. Ezekiel's nickname did not come from wearing spectacles, but from the streak of vitiligo that ran across his eyes in a perfect spectacle shape. He was the lead guitarist and a committed musician. Zekeyspecs, as he was also known, was humming a gentle blues, plucking scales from his tired Spanish acoustic guitar. The instrument was so old and battered, it never ceased to amaze everyone how he produced such delightful music on it.

The Joking Jaguars were twenty men strong. Women were not allowed on the road trips because they obviously could not handle the strain. Or so the King said. Elvis suspected it had more to do with the fact that the King was afraid women would prove a distraction and cause rifts between the musicians.

There were several young boys, however, who sang soprano parts. They also played the female roles in the play that was always part of the performance. There were five of them, aged between nine and fifteen, and they were all nondescript, bar one. Esau, the oldest, had a certain air to him that marked him apart. He was stunningly handsome. But what really set him apart was the grace with which he carried himself. When he was dressed in full drag, he made more than a few heads turn longingly, including some of the musicians who knew he was a man. Elvis was fascinated by the conviction Esau brought to his roles. The other boys and men played women badly. There was caricature about it: a certain derision in their acting, an exaggerated femininity that was no more than a reassurance of their masculinity. Esau, on the other hand, brought a simple understanding, something of a shared commonality; nothing more.

Scanning the rest of the group, Elvis was disturbed that he could not remember most of their names. Yet they shared living, eating, cooking, sleeping, performing and even dreaming space together, daily.

There were a tuba player; George on saxophone and clarinet; the King on guitar and vocals; Zekeyspecs on lead guitar; Benson on rhythm guitar; Esau, the four other boys and Elvis on background vocals and dancing; a tall, thin guy on double bass whose nickname was Langalanga; and the others on a variety of percussion instruments from maracas and clap drums through to congas.

One of the drummers played a subtle rhythm behind Zekeyspecs. Another one tapped sharp time on an empty bottle with a rusty nail.

George got up and walked over to them and began to sing in a deep, rich baritone. The four boys supplied the harmony. Elvis's foot tapped to the music. There was a transcendence to the moment.

When they performed for an audience, the musicians played to please it. They searched in themselves for something, no matter how personal, that the audience could latch on to. But now, they sang and played what they wanted, each musician leading, then following, then leading again, until everyone had sung his piece. This was for them. No audience. Nobody. Not even for each other.

Elvis was just about to begin dancing when Esau marched into the middle of the seated musicians. Elvis sat back and watched. Esau stood stock-still for one long moment, then began to dance, his body so fluid it teased a tear from Elvis. The song came to an end abruptly, catching Esau in midstep. They broke up laughing.

Just then, the King came up. He was smiling. Elvis understood him well enough to know that they had got the permission they needed to perform that night.

Some of the musicians drove around the area campaigning, making announcements and playing music through a battery-powered amplifier. Wooden posters advertising their show in lurid colors hanging from the side of the van heightened the effect. Other musicians walked around town, stopping at bars to drink and eat, all the while displaying their instruments and talking loudly among themselves about that night's concert. Elvis walked up to the King to ask what play they were performing that night.

"If You Bamboozle Somebody, He Will Bamboozle You," the King replied.

Elvis nodded; he knew the play well. There were three main characters and some minor ones. The play was short, lasting only two hours, which meant that night's audience would be small. The play's characters were the good-time girl Owumara, played by Esau; the joker, or bob, Johnson the taxi driver, played by Elvis; and the old lady, played by the King. Different people played the other minor characters. The play itself had a simple plot with a didactic thread.

The evening's show always started with a dance during which the band played all the popular tunes of the day. The play followed, and then there was another dance afterwards. For a big audience in a big town, the total number of songs played in one night came to about forty, not counting those played as part of the play. Most evenings began at nine p.m. and finished at four in the morning. Tonight would be different. The town and the audience were small, and Elvis figured they could get away with twenty songs, give or take.

The play itself consisted of an opening and then a scene or play proper. The opening varied between twenty minutes and an hour and consisted of a chorus, an in and a duet. The opening chorus was usually a fox-trot or a quickstep sung and danced by the main characters. Esau excelled at this. The in and the duet were both comedy sketches. The in was performed by a solo stand-up comedian, while the duet was played by two actors. It was within the opening that all of the vaudeville influences were kept. As with all traditional performances, audience participation was encouraged. This varied from applause, weeping and jeering to throwing food and money onstage. A few members of the audience usually joined the actors onstage, improvising with them.

The evening passed uneventfully, and they got away with a five-hour performance, including the dances. Tired but richer, the musicians headed for the van and the local police station. Where they could, they tried to sleep in or near one; it was the safest place for them. While the musicians bedded down on raffia mats in the station's courtyard, the King counted up the evening's takings, which he locked in a small metal safe.

A few of the other musicians, George included, were huddled under a neem tree, smoking beside a fire. The neem wood burned lazily, releasing a cooling eucalyptus scent. Elvis, unable to sleep, joined them. They made room for him. Langalanga, the bass player, sat with a metal saw trapped between his knees. With one hand he bent and massaged the blade. With the other he drew his bass bow across the blunt edge, causing the saw to sing: a deep belly growling hunger that rose to the shrill call of morning angels.

George passed him a cigarette and Elvis dragged deeply, blowing smoke rings before passing it back. Thinking about Redemption, the Colonel, his father and the effort to protect Maroko from destruction, he felt a sudden pang of sadness.

George noticed the expression on Elvis's face and asked, "What is it?"

"I just realized something," Elvis replied.

"What? Are you in love?"

"No. I just realized that it is only a small group of people who are spoiling our country. Most people just want to work hard, earn a living and find some entertainment. Yet it seems that no matter how they try, they remain poor."

"What are you talking about?" George asked, confused. "Where did dat come from?"

"Leave him, he is making sense," the King said, coming over to join them. He laughed deeply and slapped Elvis on the back. "De boy is becoming a man," he said.

Elvis swallowed.

"Dat is exactly what I have been trying to tell you since I met you. De majority of our people are honest, hardworking people. But dey are at de mercy of dese army bastards and dose tiefs in the IMF, de World Bank and de U.S.," the King said.

"But how is the World Bank responsible if we mismanage the funds they give us?"

"Funds? What funds? Let me tell you, dere are no bigger tiefs dan dose World Bank people. Let me tell you how de World Bank helps us. Say dey offer us a ten-million-dollar loan for creating potable and clean water supply to rural areas. If we accept, dis is how dey do us. First dey tell us dat we have to use de expertise of their consultants, so dey remove two million for salaries and expenses. Den dey tell us dat de consultants need equipment to work, like computer, jeeps or bulldozers, and for hotel and so on, so dey take another two million. Den dey say we cannot build new boreholes but must service existing one, so dey take another two million to buy parts. All dis money, six million of it, never leave de U.S. Den dey use two million for de project, but is not enough, so dey abandon it, and den army bosses take de remaining two million. Now we, you and I and all dese poor people, owe de World Bank ten million dollars for nothing. Dey are all tiefs and I despise dem—our people and de World Bank people!" the King ranted.

Elvis didn't know what to say. He looked up at the sky. It was beautiful. Stars. Like so much sand.

"But why don't we revolt and overthrow this government?" he asked finally, unable to keep the exasperation out of his voice.

"Who want to die?" George said.

"We should retire for de night," the King said, squinting at his pocket watch in the half-light. "We leave early for Lagos. We go perform for Freedom Square tomorrow. I hear say de Colonel's boys go dey dere. Time to send a powerful message, eh?"

Nearly everyone laughed heartily. But the King noticed Elvis's terrified look and took him aside.

"Don't worry, Elvis. Your matter go done clear by now."

"How do you know?"

"I don't, but I just feel it."

"I'm afraid. The Colonel is trying to kill me."

"Yes, but by now him go done tire for dat."

"You don't know. I'm not convinced."

"I am sorry, but we must return tomorrow. You can stay."

"Where? Here? I don't know anybody here. I don't even know the language. How can I stay here?"

"Den you must return with us. No worry, I go protect you."

Elvis spent a restless night, dreaming that the Colonel was chasing him with a large machete, slashing at him madly and only just missing.

Dawn left streaky marks across night's face, and the men stood by the idling van, sipping gingerly on hot tea flavored with eucalyptus leaves and munching on hard cassava bread. Farmers on their way to the fields called out greetings to the men. Some congratulated them on a good performance the night before. Elvis, mind numbed from too little sleep, yawned back at them.

George stood beside him. "Tired?" he asked.

"Very."

"Ah," George said. "It is so, coming and going. Never staying. You realize dis is de way your life will be from now on if you continue with us."

"Yes, very exciting."

"Wait a few years. Den tell me if it is still exciting."

"Why are you so pessimistic?"

"Dis life is like an itch. You scratch and scratch, until you chaff your skin to de bone. But still you itch. I'm not pessimistic, Elvis. Just tired," George said, walking off.

MOI-MOI

INGREDIENTS

Black-eyed beans
Onions
Palm oil
Fresh chilies
Salt
Crayfish
Maggi cube
Shredded beef
Dried fish

PREPARATION

Soak the beans overnight, then wash thoroughly to remove outer skins. Put beans in a blender with the onions, palm oil, fresh chilies, salt, crayfish and Maggi cube. Add the shredded beef and bits of dried fish. Pour the contents into envelopes of tinfoil or plastic containers. Next, put four sticks at the bottom of a large, deep pot in a cross pattern and cover with water. Put the wraps or containers in the pot on top of the crossed sticks. Steam over a low fire, topping up with water from time to time, until the moi-moi has the consistency of tofu. Serve with gari soaked in milk, water and sugar.

TWENTY-SEVEN

))))))

This is a journey to manhood, to life; it cannot be easy.

The old Igbo adage is: Manhood is not achieved in a day.

))))))

Lagos, 1983

Elvis is about 16 years old

Sunday stumbled bleary-eyed out of the house, straight into a rush of people, screaming and shouting. He stood on his veranda lost in an alcoholic mist.

"Sunday! Sunday! Dey have come!" Comfort screamed, running past him and dumping a hastily packed bag in the street before dashing back inside.

It was light everywhere, but it wasn't sunlight. The earth rumbled as though thunder shook it. Sunday glanced at his watch; it was four a.m., too early to be dawn. He opened his fly and urinated into the street, narrowly missing the bag and a small group running past with an open coffin packed tight with their belongings. He raked up some phlegm and spat with a plop into the nearby swamp.

"What's matter, eh? What's matter?" he mumbled, staring vacantly into the bright light.

"Sunday, you stand so? Why not help me pack before bu'dozer come knock our house down?"

"What's matter? Which bulldozer? Are you mad?"

"De gofment send anoder bu'dozer," she said, dropping another bag on the ground and going back for more.

"De government can go to hell!" he yelled. "I want to sleep."

Comfort elbowed him aside and stooped to lift the stuff she had salvaged onto her head. Thank goodness the children were staying with relatives, she thought. She didn't think she would have managed with them here.

"If you want to die, go and sleep. If not, help me carry something and let us go!" she shouted at him.

"Go where?"

He tried to focus.

"Look, Papa Elvis, bu'dozer is come. Me, I have carry my gold and expensive lappa and I no fit to carry more. Let's go," she said urgently as the rumbling grew louder.

A few streets away, clouds of dust and sprays of water rose as the dozers leveled everything in their path—houses, shanties, even the swamps.

"Go where?" he asked again. *Does he not get it?*

She took one more look at the approaching bulldozer, stepped into the street and was swallowed by the crowd. He looked for her, but she was lost somewhere in the sea of bodies flowing past him.

"Go where?" he muttered to himself under his breath. "Dis is my land. I buy dis house, it is not dash to me. Why I go?"

The dozers rolled uncomfortably closer. The vibrations from them shook the windowpanes, dislodging a few, which fell, shattering noisily. The lights cut through the sky and the night was bright, and still Sunday stood on his veranda smiling enigmatically. A few yards away a house built of corrugated iron and cardboard crumbled with an exhausted puff, while the old generator in another exploded.

Sunday became aware of another presence on the veranda. Turning quickly, he gasped when he saw Beatrice reclining on the bench. She noted the shocked look on his face and spoke.

"Sunday, don't be afraid."

"Why not? You're a ghost. Have you come to kill me?"

Beatrice smiled sweetly, and something about that smile sent shivers down his spine.

"No, I came to warn you to leave."

"And if I don't?"

"Den you will die."

He turned away from her. If he ignored her, she would disappear. She was, after all, a drunken hallucination. He laughed. Madam Caro must have laced his palm wine with some narcotic. Whatever it was, it was good, and he was glad he was a regular.

"Sunday."

He turned back to where Beatrice had been sitting. She was still there, but there was another presence too.

"You're not really here," he told her.

"Oh yes I am—and so is he," she said, pointing to a leopard curled up in the shadows.

"What is dis? Did you bring a spirit leopard to kill me?"

"No. He is here on his own."

"But what is dis?"

"I am the totem of your forefathers."

Sunday blinked. A talking leopard, his wife's ghost, the bulldozers: it was too much.

He turned back to the scene unfolding in front of him and saw policemen and soldiers driving people off with gun butts and leather whips. "Get out! Go! Go!" they yelled. In the distance a mother stopped in mid-flight, remembering her son trapped in her hut. She ran back for him. "Hassan! Hassan!" she screamed. The butt of a rifle chased her screams down her throat with a mouthful of teeth and blood. She crumbled to the ground and the soldier kicked her aside.

"You are going to die here, you know, unless you get out," the leopard said.

"He's not joking. Listen, Sunday, you still have a son to care for. Leave," Beatrice said.

Sunday was getting worried. If Beatrice and the leopard were only hallucinations, why had they remained even when he wasn't paying any attention?

"You are de one who will die!" he shouted.

"I am already dead," Beatrice said. "And I think de leopard is a spirit."

"You disappoint me, Beatrice, eh. Why must you mock me?"

Beatrice's ghost looked hurt, her lips trembling.

"I came to you in your time of need, but if you like, I can leave."
Sunday shouted and punched himself around the face.

"In the old days, people were close to their totems, who infused
them with their own special attributes, both physical and metaphysical.
Lycanthropy was not unusual in those days when the ancient laws were
kept," the leopard said.

"Go and tell your story elsewhere," Sunday interrupted. "If you
are person or spirit, I don't know and don't care. Both of you just leave
me alone, dat's all."

The 'dozers were only a few yards away and policemen and soldiers
were running past his house. One of the policemen spotted him
slouched on his veranda in only a loincloth, looking for all intents like
a man basking in the noonday sun.

"You dere!" the policeman barked.

"He has seen you. Won't you go, or do you want to die?" the leopard asked.

"Think of Elvis," Beatrice said.

"You dere, go now before I vex!" the policeman yelled again.

"This is the hour of your death. Go out and fight for your honor."

"You deaf? I say move before I move you!" the policeman yelled
again, advancing on Sunday, and cocking his rifle.

"Well, at least die like a man," the leopard said with a bored yawn.

Beatrice, already fading into the shadows, watched tearfully as the
'dozers approached. They were almost upon him and the vibrations
were coming from everywhere. Grabbing a cutlass Comfort had
dropped earlier, Sunday sprang with a roar at the 'dozer. The policeman let off a shout and a shot, and Sunday fell in a slump before the
'dozer, its metal threads cracking his chest like a timber box as it went
straight into the wall of his home. Sunday roared, leapt out of his body
and charged at the back of the policeman, his paw delivering a fatal
blow to the back of the policeman's head. With a rasping cough, Sunday disappeared into the night.

Elvis was halfway through his act when Freedom Square erupted. Soldiers spilled out of trucks flooding the area. There was a stampede.

People, food, furniture—everything was trampled underfoot. The soldiers laid into everyone with tough cowhide whips, wooden batons and rifle butts, and the air was heavy with screams and shouts. As far as they were concerned, the audience was as guilty as the performers.

"My head O!"

"Yee!"

"Move!"

"Stop or I'll shoot!"

"Bastard!"

Elvis, completely confused, was unsure how to react, not fully comprehending what was happening. He felt someone yanking at his arm. He turned. It was the King of the Beggars. He was yelling at him, but Elvis couldn't hear any sound. The King slapped him hard.

"We get to go now," he said while hurrying Elvis off the stage. They ducked behind an army lorry and headed for the edge of the square and the streets that snaked off it into the dark maw of the city. They had almost made it when a soldier stepped out of nowhere. He loomed large and dark, blocking off the light. Elvis saw the King disappear into the distance.

"Identify yourself!" the soldier barked.

"I . . . I . . ."

"Bloody civilians," the soldier said, bringing his rifle butt down on the side of Elvis's head with a resounding crack. From a great distance Elvis heard the soldier call for help to lift him into the back of a lorry.

Elvis hung from the metal bars on the window, feet dangling six inches from the floor, suspended by handcuffs. The pain was excruciating, building up in slow stages, getting worse with each passing minute.

At first all he felt was a slight ache in his shoulders, which spread until his whole body was one mass of pleasant sweet aches. After about ten minutes he felt a headache coming on, nothing serious. Twenty minutes later his arms were shaking and the pleasant aches were replaced by painful spasms as the weight of his body became unbearable.

Sweat was rolling off him in bucketfuls; his arms went numb and his fingers began to swell like loaves of bread. The rest of his body was torn by a searing-hot pain and he stretched downward, trying to bring his feet into contact with the ground. That only made it worse. Then his head exploded, and tears streaming down his face mixed with the sweat before hitting the floor in sheets of protest. His bloodshot eyes began to film over as his face became congested with blood and his tongue, swollen, protruded from the side of his mouth, forcing his teeth apart. Each pulse beat sounded a million times amplified, and he began to mumble incoherently. Pain did not describe what he felt now. Prayer followed.

After half an hour he was ready to deny his own mother. Against his will, a moan escaped his lips. Softly at first, then in a flood, he was begging, swearing, crying and sobbing. He was concerned with one thing and one thing only—stopping the pain. But then, just when he was about to slip into blissful unconsciousness, the beating began.

The inner tubing of a bicycle tire was used to flog him; it left no marks and yet stung like nothing he knew. Then a concentrated solution of Izal, an industrial disinfectant, was poured over the beaten area. This not only increased the pain, it sensitized the area for the next bout of flogging. He screamed until he lost his voice; still his throat convulsed. When his tormentors tired, they left him hanging there, dangling and limp. It went on like this every few hours for a couple of days. No questions were asked; only confessions were heard.

▼▼▼▼▼▼▼▼▼▼▼▼▼▼▼▼▼▼▼▼▼▼▼▼▼▼▼

PORTULACA OLERACEA *L.*
(Potulacaceae)
(Yoruba: Papasan)

An annual herb with bright yellow flowers, small and prostrate. It has oval leaves that narrow toward the base. Uncannily like a bishop's miter, the fruits open to reveal many warted seeds.

Crushed, the plant is applied locally to swellings and bruising and even whitlow to ease pain and promote healing. The juice, dropped into the ear or onto a sore tooth, relieves earache and toothache.

4:54:37

TWENTY-EIGHT

)))))

There is only one path: omenala.

*For the Igbo, tradition is fluid, growing. It is an event, like the sunset, or rain, changing
with every occurrence. So too, the kola ritual has changed. Christian prayers have been
added, and Jesus has replaced Obasi as the central deity. But its fluid aspects resist the
empiricism that is the Western way, where life is supposed to be a system of codes, like
the combinations of human DNA or the Fibonacci patterns in nature. The Igbo are not re-
ducible to a system of codes, and of meaning; this culture is always reaching for a pure
lyric moment.*

)))))

*Elvis is about
16 years old*

Lagos, 1983

The King of the Beggars edged into the police station. He had been
trying to trace Elvis for four days now.

"Who dey in charge here?" he asked the policeman behind the
counter.

"You go see duty sergeant."

"Where is he?"

"He go toilet."

"When he go return?"

"When he shit finish. Why so many questions? If you want to see
duty sergeant, you must wait, dat's all."

The King sat down on a hard wood bench to wait, trying to block
out the shouts and screams from the cells. After a four-hour wait, he

saw a short, potbellied man stroll into the station, idly picking his teeth and belching intermittently.

"You," the policeman shouted at the King. "Dat is duty sergeant," he said, pointing to the short man.

The King went up to him and introduced himself, explaining that he was trying to locate Elvis. The duty sergeant regarded him with two dead eyes and, while belching a cloud of alcohol fumes into the King's face, made a grunting noise.

"Well?" the King asked, suppressing the wave of nausea that rocked him at the odor from the sergeant's mouth.

"Well what? Do I look like missing-persons computer? Please leave my office," the sergeant said.

"I want to see my friend. He was arrested in Freedom Square four days ago," the King insisted.

"Your friend? Who are you? Even if you be president himself, how I go know your friend?"

"Elvis Oke," the King stated.

"Do I look de type of man to mix with your nonsensical friend?"

"Could you please check your records?"

The policeman made a big show of checking for Elvis's name in the log book on the desk in front of him. His brow furrowed in concentration as he ran his finger down the pages. Finally after a few minutes he looked up.

"You sure dis is de station you want?"

"Yes. I'm sure."

"You no sure. His name is not here."

"What do you mean? His name is Elvis Oke and officers from dis station arrest him four days ago. I done go every other police station in dis area. It done take me four days to trace him to you. His name must be dere."

"No curse me, you hear? Who are you? I don't know and I don't bloody care. If you do not hold your mouth I will arrest you."

While he had been waiting earlier, the King had seen the names of the senior officers on duty scrawled in chalk on a blacked-out square on the facing wall. He recalled them, dropping them into the conversation to see if it would help.

"Is Inspector Johnson in?" he asked.

"He is on leave."

"But he was with me yesterday!"

"Den go find him in your house."

"What about Assistant Superintendent Adelabu?"

"What about him?"

"Can I see him?"

"Out."

"So who is in?"

"Me. Duty Sergeant Okafor, and I go soon go to toilet."

Finally frustrated, the King handed the policeman a twenty-naira note.

"Ah! Why you never perform before, sir? You are looking for your friend. Is he . . . ?" the sergeant said, and gave an accurate description of Elvis.

"Dat is de one."

"He was transferred to Tango City."

"Tango City?"

"Yes. Special Military Interrogation Unit. Deir office is called Tango City."

"Why Tango City? Where is it?"

"I don't know. All dis question and you only give me twenty naira?"

"Can't I bail him?"

"You cannot bail somebody who is not charged," the policeman said simply.

"What can I do den?" the King asked, sounding broken.

The policeman stared at the King for a few minutes.

"Pray," he said.

Elvis felt his feet touch the floor. He collapsed in a heap, unable to feel his body. No, that wasn't quite right. He could feel his body—but as a single sheet of flaming pain. He sat awkwardly on the floor in front of a tin plate of rice and reached for the spoon, but neither arm would move. They dangled uselessly in his lap like a pair of broken wings. He had lost any sense of when his last meal had been, but the smell of the food caused saliva to fill his mouth, dribbling over even as he tried to swallow. He struggled onto his knees. The effort took a long time, causing him to gasp for air, dizzy as hell. Slowly the dizziness passed and he hunkered down and ate out of the plate like a dog; every swallow painful. Exhausted, he sank into the food.

He felt himself being lifted and dragged roughly, then strapped to a chair, the rope cutting into his wrists, knees and ankles. Someone was slapping him roughly, but the mists of unconsciousness claimed him again. He dreamed he was standing underneath a fountain. The cool spray was refreshing, yet it stung his wounds. He opened his mouth to drink and felt its ammonia burn. He woke with a jerk and heard laughter. A soldier stood in front of him, urinating into his face. Spluttering, he shook his head vehemently from side to side to get out of the way, making it pound so violently that he slipped into unconsciousness again. When he came to this time, he was hanging from his arms again. He didn't struggle against the pain anymore. It was part of him now. It seemed like he couldn't remember a time when it was not here. It had become essential to him. As long as he was in pain, he was still human.

"Speak," a voice urged.

He stared. It sounded familiar, but its owner stood in the shadows.

"Stupid boy. Do you think anybody cares whether you live or die? Confess and save yourself."

His vision cleared and he realized it was the Colonel.

"Why won't you confess?" the Colonel asked.

Elvis opened his mouth to speak, but his tongue, the size of a thick slice of watermelon, kept getting in the way.

"Beat him some more, Jerome. He is too stubborn," the Colonel said to someone in the shadows.

Elvis noticed for the first time that he was naked and began to struggle against his chains. He saw a stocky man stripped to the waist step out of the shadows, face heavily scarified. He smiled with a mixture of contempt and pleasure at Elvis's squirming.

"I never touch you and you dey cry. Today I go show you pepper," Jerome said.

He walked over to the wall and selected a koboko, the whip about
four feet long. He came over to Elvis and showed him the whip.

"De Fulanis use dese on each oder to test who be man enough to
marry. A hundred lashes, no sound, or else you still be boy."

Elvis closed his eyes and tried to block out everything.

"Are you boy or man?" Jerome went on. "Because a boy no sup-
pose to do a man's job," he finished and laughed loudly.

Then, whistling softly under his breath, he began rubbing a cool
white paste all over Elvis's body. It felt good, soothing almost. Jerome
smiled as he noted his expression. Still smiling, he took Elvis's penis in
one hand and gently smoothed the paste over it, working it up and
down. Elvis felt himself swell. Jerome laughed and massaged Elvis's penis faster and faster. It was not long before Elvis shuddered and shot
semen all over his torturer's hand.   *Proof?*

"So you be homo," Jerome said, laughing breathlessly.

Tears of shame streamed down Elvis's face.

"De thing is you dey stupid. You think say I dey rub you cream?
You must be mad. Dis is chemical and it go burn like nothing you
know and when I flog you, you go think say your skin dey burn."

Already Elvis could feel the slow heat of the concoction burning
through the coolness. Jerome brought the whip up and sent it snaking
round Elvis's body. He screamed and Jerome laughed and pulled the
whip back, flaying a thin line of skin off. Elvis screamed again.

"Tell me who dis King of de Beggars is. We know you are one of
his boys," the Colonel urged.

"I don't know him!" Elvis screamed.

The Colonel chuckled.

"You sound like Peter denying Jesus," he said.

Elvis stared at the Colonel. It was clear he did not recognize him
from the club that night, nor did he seem to know that Elvis had been
part of the group smuggling the human parts. The beating had
stopped. Jerome looked worried and the Colonel approached him and
asked what was wrong. Jerome whispered something in his ear and the
Colonel nodded and replied. With surprise, Elvis realized that his body
was jerking in spasms, probably from the pain. Jerome rushed out and
returned shortly with an Indian doctor, and together they brought

Elvis down. The intelligence sector chose Indian doctors because it was assumed they had no allegiance to the tortured and so wouldn't try to kill them, to ease the pain. The doctor felt for a pulse, a heartbeat. There didn't seem to be any. Elvis couldn't understand it, because he was wide awake. With a slight frown, the doctor raised a huge horse-sized syringe and stabbed an adrenaline injection straight into his heart. Elvis's eyes slowly opened.

"Well?" he heard the Colonel asking from a distance.

"He'll live. But he must rest now," the doctor said.

When Elvis woke up, he was lying on a mat in a corner of the same room. He sat up slowly, his arms tingling with pins and needles as blood returned. He became aware that in the shadows to his left, Jerome and a couple of armed soldiers stood silently. The Colonel was sitting in a chair. On the floor in front of him, shackled hand and foot, was a man, whimpering.

"Can you speak now?" the Colonel asked, his manner abrupt.

Elvis was not sure if he was talking to him or to the bound man at his feet.

"Answer me when I speak," the Colonel said.

Before either Elvis or the bound man could speak, the Colonel moved his hand almost imperceptibly and the bound man screamed. Then Elvis saw the blood. The Colonel got up and walked over to Elvis and dropped the bound man's bloody ear on the floor in front of him.

"Dis is what happens when my questions are not answered," he said gently. "You look young and confused, and frankly you are not de type I like to torture. I like to break people who think dey are hard. But I will cut you up if I have to. Do you understand?"

Elvis began sobbing and the Colonel rubbed his head tenderly.

"Listen, stop crying, okay? Tell me where de King is?"

"I don't know. We were running and we got separated."

"Okay, tell me where he lives."

"Under the bridge."

"Which bridge?'

"By Ojuelegba."

The Colonel laughed. It sounded like wet rope rasping on dry wood.

"Dis one is just a child. Throw him back," he said, walking out.

*   *   *

They threw Elvis out of the van before it had stopped. He hit the rough road surface and rolled painfully, coming to a stop by the base of a wooden electric pole. He used the pole to pull himself up and pulled down the blindfold. He could see the army truck speeding away in the distance.

He was on a back street that was deserted except for the corpses of hundreds of dead rats that littered the roadside. The sound of children playing carried out to him. He stood up and covered his nakedness behind cupped hands, nude except for the Fulani pouch hanging from his neck. He stole some clothes from a line and started walking. He didn't know where he was or where he was going. He just walked. It wasn't clear to him if he was really free or whether it was just an illusion. All day long he just walked, on and on, like a man possessed. The sun dipping on the horizon cast long shadows behind him. Cars whizzing past him blared their horns angrily as he wandered into the road. He stumbled on a rock jutting out of the ground and fell with a thud at the foot of a brazier that burned bright. The children roasting corn and pears for sale with their mother screamed in shock.

"Get up, madman!" the woman yelled. "Shut up!" she threw at her screaming children.

Elvis raised his head and tried to focus on her but saw only the leaping flames. Sitting beside the corn seller, hunched and chewing on a corncob, was an old woman who reminded him of Oye.

"I said get up—are you mad?" the corn seller shouted at him. "You are blocking my market, get up!"

She swung a firebrand at him. It crackled through the air and hit him on the leg. The burn felt good, brought him back into his body. He laughed as he got up and stumbled away into the night.

▏▎▎▎

SYNSEPALUM DULCIFICUM *DANIELL*

(Sapotaceae)
(Igbo: Udara-nwaewe)

A small tree of the rain forest, it has a green bark and elliptic leaves that are somewhat wedge-shaped. Small pink-and-brown flowers cluster around the axils of the leaves, and it has an oval, purplish fruit.

The pulp of the fruit, around the seeds, is sweet and has the lingering aftereffect of making acid substances consumed within three hours of it taste sweet.

5:12:50 (handwritten)

TWENTY-NINE

))))))

There is only one history: Igbo.

But there are things that cannot be contained, even in ritual.
The Igbo have a saying: Oya bu uto ndu. That is the joy of life.

))))))

Lagos, 1983

Elvis is about 16 years old (handwritten)

The King marched at the head of the mob, singing in a deep baritone. Immediately behind him were the three druids. The rest of the mob was comprised of the curious, thugs looking for some trouble, market women and students. They all sang at the top of their voices as they marched on Ribadu Road, the seat of government.

"Who shall be free?" the King sang.

"Nigeria shall be free," the crowd responded.

Like a strange pied piper, he picked up more and more people as he marched. No one had any clear idea why they were marching or where they were marching to. But that did not seem to stop them. The King, like Gandhi on his salt march, was resolute. Even the press joined the march. They had covered the Freedom Square raid, but this was much bigger.

Predictably the army soon got wind of the approaching mob and set up a barricade. The Colonel was there in person, having decided to put a stop to the irritation that the King had become. For the past few months, as the King's media profile grew, the Colonel's bosses brought the King up at every briefing.

The Colonel walked up to the barricade of tanks. "Who is in charge here?" he asked.

"Lieutenant Yar'adua reporting for duty, sir!"

"Listen, if you want to survive de day with your rank—when dat mob reaches here, do not open fire until I give de order. Understand?"

"Yes sir!"

"Good," the Colonel said. He walked back to his car, a black BMW, and came back with a sniper's rifle. He picked a spot ahead of the tanks and settled down to wait for the crowd.

They soon came around the corner, singing. The King was well ahead of the mob by at least ten yards. The Colonel was impressed by the size of the crowd that the King was able to muster. Raising the sniper scope to his eye, he held the King in a perfect cross. But then he noticed the news cameras. It would not do to have an assassination taped, especially by the BBC. It would affect foreign investments, and his bosses wouldn't take kindly to that. The Colonel put the sniper rifle down and walked back to the tanks.

"Do you have a megaphone?"

The lieutenant nodded and passed the megaphone. The Colonel walked out front to the face the crowd.

"My fellow countrymen, I wish to assure you dat dere is no need for dis demonstration. If you disband now and return to your homes, we will forget de whole incident."

"And if we don't?" the King demanded.

"Nobody wants dat," the Colonel said. He was losing patience with the whole situation, and he would soon order his men to stop the mob, cameras or no cameras.

"We get legitimate concerns. We want democracy."

"Yes, democracy, no more army!" the mob chanted.

The Colonel took in the agitated crowd and the media and felt his rage building. He had one nerve left, and this King guy was jumping on it.

Lieutenant Yar'adua came up to him. "How do you want us to proceed, sir?"

"I'm not sure. Radio de General and ask him what he wants. Dese journalists are my main concern, otherwise I would just kill everybody here," the Colonel said.

"Yes sir," Lieutenant Yar'adua said, saluting and making his way back to the tank to carry out his orders.

The Colonel watched as some younger members of the crowd began to gather stones and rocks, anything that could be used as a projectile. The Colonel turned to the soldiers behind him and, identifying a sergeant, motioned for him to come over. He pointed out the troublemakers to the sergeant and asked him to have a few men armed with tear-gas launchers aimed at the edges of the crowd. They would need to keep the crowd contained in one place if they were to maintain control.

Lieutenant Yar'adua walked back to where the Colonel stood smoking a cigarette and watching members of the press creep closer.

"Sir!"

"Proceed."

"De General said to send some men to remove de press while you talk to de Beggar King. He wants you to calm him down and remove him from dis place with minimum damage."

The Colonel swore under his breath.

"How? By magic? Okay, take a group and begin to round up de press, starting with dose one over dere," the Colonel said, pointing to some members of the press who had crept forward.

"Yes sir!"

"Lieutenant."

"Sir?"

"Handle it yourself. Don't send junior officers."

"Yes sir!"

The Colonel turned back to the crowd. "You—come forward," he said, pointing to the King.

"Make we meet halfway."

"Sure," the Colonel replied.

The two men advanced on each other. As he approached, the King felt trepidation. Something was not right here. The army never talked. He suspected the press had something to do with this sudden offer to talk, but there was something else. He had been around enough rats in his life to know their smell. Looking around, he scanned the rooftops for snipers. The Colonel walked toward the King, keeping a fake smile plastered to his face for the press. No need to appear menacing to the world, he thought. Underneath it, however, he was cursing the King, wishing he could handle this his way: walk straight up to the King, draw his Collectors' Edition 1911 Colt .44 automatic and blow the bastard's head right off. Better than his morning shot of gin with a coffee chaser. He cracked his neck and swallowed hard to keep his anger in.

The crowd of protestors stood watching the King and the Colonel get closer. Whatever group mind had held them together before seemed to have deserted them. They began to break up into clumps of twos and threes, drifting to buy things from the ever-present hawkers, who, sensing a possible trade, had followed them. They stood munching on fruit or cookies and downing soft drinks. The Colonel saw the crowd begin to break up and smiled. It never ceased to amaze him how quickly mobs lost focus if their leader was separated from them. He glanced at his watch. In this instance, it had taken less than two minutes. Seeing the Colonel smile and glance at his watch, the King stopped and stared around him, convinced that he was walking into a trap.

"What's wrong?" the Colonel asked.

The King shook his head and resumed walking. This was it, he thought. Well, at least there would be television cameras to record it all. If he died now, he died a hero of the people.

Drawing closer, the King recognized the Colonel as the officer he had been searching for all this time. This was the man who had murdered his family so long ago. He was older, but it was the same sneering smile and the eyes that the King could never forget.

What happened next would be described differently later. Some would mention butterflies surrounding the King; others, cats; others still, dogs; others said eagles. Some also said that a hand reached down from heaven and handed him a sword with which to smite the unjust army.

The King reached into his dashiki and pulled out an ugly dagger. Before the Colonel could release his pistol, the King sprang and sunk his knife deep into the Colonel's throat. The soldiers at the blockade opened fire and the bullets lifted the King bodily into the air. He soared, arms spread, before falling to the ground in a broken rumpled heap.

The crowd scattered in panic, bullets and angry soldiers chasing them. The three druids stood their ground, bullets buzzing about them like angry hornets. Tired of spells, with Jagua in the lead, they were swatting at soldiers with their magic staffs, knocking them out. The protective bubble they believed their spells wove around them broke when a soldier they missed stopped and shot them all, point blank: Jagua in the face, the other two in the chest.

Madam Caro took four bullets in her ample backside but didn't slow down, the pestle she used to pound amala and eba at her buka held high, pounding army heads into submission. An unknown man ran toward the oncoming soldiers wielding an old Igbo sword called an akparaja. Short, wide and double-edged, it cleaved heads off with ease, littering the floor like a pineapple harvest. He took ten soldiers before running out of luck on the end of a bayonet.

The youths who had been gathering rocks and stones earlier hurled a fusillade at the soldiers, but they hit the helmets and riot body armor without doing much damage. Tear-gas canisters were fired at them. Apart from the choking smoke, the canisters of gas caught a few by surprise, tearing holes through them. Cameramen sought shelter and continued to film. The street was too narrow, and the bulk of the crowd jammed each other tight. When the shooting finally stopped, there were bodies everywhere. Conservative estimates by the press put the casualty figure at about two hundred. What no one could have guessed was that when the film of the King jumping the Colonel and stabbing him was broadcast, he would be deified, turned into a prophet, an advance guard, like John the Baptist, for the arrival of the Messiah.

Elvis felt the hot sun burn his face, and with it the first stab of a headache. He opened his eyes and glanced around him, taking in the wilderness of crumbled and derelict buildings. To his right a pole rose up out of the ground, marking the site of what used to be someone's house, a silent sentinel, a beacon.

"Hassan! Hassan!" a woman called out in a voice hoarse from effort, but only the howling of the wind greeted her.

All around, scavengers, human and otherwise, feasted on the exposed innards of Maroko. They rummaged in the rubble as bulldozers sifted through the chaos like slow-feeding buffalo. Here some article of clothing still untorn; there a pot; over there a child's toy with the squeaker still working. There was a lot of snorting coming from a clump of shrubs as a pack of hungry dogs fed. The hand of a corpse rose up from between the snarling dogs in a final wave.

Elvis took it in and tried to recall what had happened before he came to be there. He vaguely remembered the dreams and walking. He searched around for clues as to where he was, and then it dawned on him that he was lying in the rubble of what used to be his house. By his foot a piece of paper stuck out from under a concrete block. He could see it was torn from an almanac. It bore the legend JESUS CAN SAVE. He shut his eyes and hoped this was another dream. He opened them but it was no dream. He struggled to his feet and stood swaying while he tried to gain his balance. Where was his father? Had he slept through all the destruction? When had it happened? Where had he been? Where were Comfort and her children? Jagua? Confidence? He searched frantically for any sign of his family, and one of the human scavengers, seeing him scramble about, called out: "No worry yourself. I done search dere. Nothing dey, only dead body."

Elvis stared at him uncomprehendingly. Corpses? Whose? Where? But the man was gone. Elvis scrambled over a final pile of rubbish and rubble and stopped short when he saw a piece of colored cloth sticking out from the mud of the swamp. He recognized his father's lappa. He stood still for a long time before he approached it. In that time he experienced nothing. Thought nothing and felt nothing. He wondered whether he would be able to weep for his father's death. If he was dead, that is. It was more likely that Elvis would feel relief, though.

He scrambled down the pile of rubble, half falling, half sliding, until he came to the bottom. He was brought to a halt by his father's foot poking out at an odd angle. He clawed the debris away and exposed the body. There was a hole the size of a saucer in his chest, ribs crumbled like a cracker into lots of pieces, as if a large object had rolled over them. Sunday's eyes were popping and his mouth was forced open into a silent laugh. Elvis's glance took in the body of a policeman lying not

far from his father's body. It only took a minute for him to work out
the general sequence that must have led up to his father's death. What
puzzled him, though, was the policeman. What had killed him? He approached the body. The entire back of the head was missing and there
were claw marks all over the body. It looked like he had been mauled
by some large predator. That was really strange, because there were
no animals of that size anywhere near Lagos or Maroko. It certainly
wasn't the work of a ghetto rat.

Elvis sat there in the rubble and tried to figure out what had really
happened. He wished his head would stop pounding for just one
minute. The inside of his mouth was furred and tasted like an old slipper.
It bothered him that his father was dead and all he could feel was relief.
Dead. That word fell with a thud like a mango loosened from a tree.

He gazed at the bodies of his father and the policeman and then he
took in the whole of Maroko. What would he do now? He had no
money, and all his worldly possessions had been in their house. Whatever had survived had already been looted, and he didn't think he
could get anything back from the scavengers. He didn't know what he
was going to do about burying his father. Whatever happened, there
was no way his father was going to get an elaborate funeral. No cows
or dogs slaughtered to ease his passage into the next world. He had to
find a way to take his father's body back to Afikpo. He tried to wrap it
in a scavenged length of cloth. He had almost succeeded when he was
interrupted by the harsh bark of a voice.

"What are you doing?"

Elvis glanced up and saw the uniform of a soldier with a big shiny
gun standing over him.

The uniform barked at him again: "I said, what are you doing?"

"He is my father."

"So what? Where are you taking dis body?"

"To bury him."

"No! Government say no dead body can leave here without clearance from HQ. You get clearance?"

"I . . ."

"Do you want me to arrest you?"

"But . . ."

"If you annoy me I will kill you and add you to your father."

"So what happens to my father?"

"You answer soldierman with question?"

Elvis didn't see the slap coming, but the blow knocked him over. He tasted blood.

"I'm sorry . . . but my father . . ."

"All right, since you have apologize, I can let you have de body for some money."

"I have no money . . ."

"No what? Get out of here now," the uniform said, descending on Elvis and pounding him repeatedly with his rifle butt.

Elvis stumbled away. The tears that wouldn't come for his father streamed freely now as he felt worthless in the face of blind, unreasoning power. He could return later, when it was dark, but he knew the body would be gone.

Elvis started walking again, unable to accept his situation. One minute he had a life—not much of one, but he had one. And the next, everything fell apart. He walked for hours. He had no plans, no ideas about what to do or where he was going, he just walked. He wasn't going anywhere in particular, but at least he was not standing still.

He kept walking until he found himself underneath one of the many dusty flyovers that littered the city. Another ghetto had been growing here for a long time, but now it just exploded as the influx from Maroko brought more life flooding into it.

All around him, everywhere, there were people: food sellers, soft-drink hawkers, tire vulcanizers, small-time car mechanics, women and men lying on top of their belongings and hundreds of beggar children. Over to his left a child slept on a broken chest of drawers and another huddled in a basket once used to store yams.

Some of these children had always lived here. Others, here with their parents, had been displaced from other ghettos by Operation Clean the Nation. His eyes caught those of a young girl no more than twelve. She cut her eyes at him and, heaving her pregnant body up, walked away. He glanced at another child and saw a look of old boredom in his eyes. Elvis read the city, seeing signs not normally visible. A woman sat by the roadside begging for alms, her legs as thick as tree stumps, her arms no more than plump plantain stems clutching the air vainly. Her torso was a lump of soft dough kneaded into shapelessness and swollen by the yeast of shame which she inhaled daily. Her body was covered in ripe yellow and red sores, throbbing with the pus of decay. She sat there as if her pain had taken root.

Some distance away from her, a man stood, then sat, then stood again. Now he danced. Stopped. Shook his head and laughed and then hopped around in an odd birdlike gait. He was deep in conversation with some hallucination. It did not seem strange to Elvis that the spirit world became more visible and tangible the nearer one was to starvation. The man laughed, and as his diaphragm shook, Elvis thought he heard the man's ribs knocking together, producing a sweet, haunting melody like the wooden xylophones of his small-town childhood.

In another spot, a young girl hawked oranges from a tray on her head. She had just got out from school and had barely had time to put down her books before snatching up the tray and heading for the streets. In a poor family everyone had to earn their keep. She sometimes let her male customers feel her firm breasts for a small fee. She marveled at the sweet stickiness she sometimes felt between her legs. She was saving up to go to secondary school.

Elvis traced patterns in the cracked and parched earth beneath his feet. There is a message in it all somewhere, he mused, a point to the chaos. But no matter how hard he tried, the meaning always seemed to be out there somewhere beyond reach, mocking him.

He found a quiet spot that didn't seem to have a claim staked on it. Curling up, he covered himself with the torn bit of cloth he had been wrapping his father's corpse in, and settled down to sleep.

Elvis woke up in Bridge City, feeling more than slightly confused. His stomach rumbled noisily but he was too broke to eat. He got up and stretched. He wondered what to do for money, remembering Okon telling him something about selling blood in hospitals. But which hospital? Just then he heard someone call his name. He turned round and, sure enough, there was Okon.

"I was just thinking about you."

"Den I will indeed live long."

They both laughed.

"What are you doing here?" Elvis asked.

"I should be asking you. I live here."

"Since Maroko was demolished?"

"No. For months before den. You?"

"I just got here last night," Elvis said. "But I'm not ready to talk about it yet."

Okon nodded sagely: "Words cannot be force. When dey are ready dey will come. Have you eaten yet? No? Come den."

And over breakfast Elvis probed Okon about what he did. Whether he still sold blood for a living.

Okon laughed. "No. I stop dat long time. For a while we hijacked corpses from roadsides and even homes which we sold for organ transplants."

Elvis shuddered. Okon noted it.

"I know how you feel," he said. "It is bad for a man's soul, waiting at roadside like vulture, for someone to die, so you can steal fresh corpse, but man must survive. When dey start to demand alive people, me I quit. I am not murderer. Hustler? Survivor? Yes. But definitely not a murderer."

Elvis had stopped eating and had been studying Okon's face.

"But your face tell me you know about dat type of thing," Okon continued.

"And now?" Elvis asked.

For the first time he really saw Okon for what he was: a tired man. His eyes were bloodshot and rheumy and fought hard to suppress any glimpse of the soul beneath. His face was weathered dark-brown leather with fine lines all over it.

"I am caretaker."

"Caretaker?"

"Don't rush things, my friend—gently, gently. Watch, look, learn. If you like things, den you can join. Until den, just come here and eat. I will square de owner. Okay?" Okon said softly.

Elvis nodded.

"Why are you helping me?" he asked.

"Because nobody help me."

Elvis looked away, suddenly guilty that he had questioned Okon's intentions.

"Have you heard anything about the King?" Elvis asked.

"So you never hear?"

"Hear what?"

"De King done die."

The days passed quickly, and Elvis felt he had always lived in Bridge City. Time lost all meaning in the face of that deprivation. In Bridge City the only thing to look forward to was surviving the evening and making it through the night. Elvis soon got into the swing of things with the help and guidance of Okon. He became a caretaker, guarding the young beggar children while they slept.

Bridge City was a dangerous place, and when darkness fell, it was easy to be very much alone in the crowds that milled everywhere. Hundreds of oil lamps flickered unsteadily on tables, trays, mats spread on the ground and any other surface the hawkers who flocked to Bridge City at night could find to display their wares. Yet even all that light could not penetrate the deeper shadows that hung like presences everywhere.

Young children who had been out all day begging were prime targets for the scavengers spawned by this place. They were beaten, raped, robbed and sometimes killed. So they came up with the idea of "caretakers." The children paid one set of scavengers to protect them against the others—simple and effective. Just thinking about the degradation made Elvis's skin crawl. He watched the children huddled on rubber sheeting exposed to the night and the vampire mosquitoes. On rainy nights they slept standing up, swaying with the wind as the rain was blown everywhere, flooding their sleeping places.

The two things Elvis missed most were books and music—not the public embrace of record-store-mounted speakers, but self-chosen music, the sound of an old record scratching the melody from its hard vinyl, or the crackle of a radio fighting static to manifest a song from the mystery of the ether. He often thought about teaching these children

to dance. He didn't expect it to save them, but it would give them
something in their lives that they did not have to beg, fight for or steal.

He had come to terms with the King's death; but he hadn't come
to terms, and probably never would, with the way the King had been
deified. He was spoken of with a deeply profound reverence, and the
appendage "Blessings be upon his name," usually reserved for prophets in Islam, was being used whenever his name was invoked. A
group of Rastafarians even claimed he was the Emperor Selassie, Christ
himself, the Lion of Judah, returned to lead them home.

He hadn't heard from Redemption for a while and though he
asked repeatedly, nobody seemed to have heard from him.

Elvis ran into Madam Caro a week after arriving in Bridge City,
where she had already set up a thriving bar. She gave him a bottle of
beer on the house and expressed her condolences at his father's death.
When he asked how she knew, she explained that she had run into
Comfort a few days after Maroko was razed.

"Did she find his body?" he asked.

Madam Caro nodded.

"But he was not complete. We can only hope he can still find peace
on the other side."

Elvis smiled sadly.

"And Comfort?'

"She done move to Aje. Her shop still dey Balogun side. If you
want to visit her, I get de address."

"Thank you, but no," he said, shaking his head.

"What of Redemption? Any news?"

She said she hadn't heard from him but that she would keep her
eyes and ears open. She went off to serve another customer. Aside from
her limp, she was no worse for wear.

That had been three weeks ago, and hardly a day went by without
Elvis wondering if Redemption had survived the Colonel's men, and if
so, where he was. In a few weeks he had lost everyone in Lagos who
meant anything to him—his father, the King, Redemption, even Comfort. He was occasionally tempted to ask Madam Caro for Comfort's
address, but always decided against it. Sunday had been the only thing
they had in common and now he was dead. Elvis didn't see the point

of contacting her, but it was hard not to give in to the loneliness and feel sorry for himself.

He walked to Madam Caro's and bought a beer. Bringing it back to where the children slept, he sat watching over them. He pulled the Fulani pouch from under his shirt, unzipped it, took out his mother's journal and stroked the cover repeatedly. He was lucky that it had survived prison. Next to it was Aunt Felicia's postcard. Suddenly the idea of America didn't seem so bad. He lit a cigarette and, looking up, caught the eye of one of the kids. She smiled at him. Her eyes were round and glowed strangely. Her teeth were small, white and even, and he wondered in an abstracted way where or when these children washed. There were no bathrooms, yet their skin glowed with a lovely sheen, and apart from the odd one, they never smelled.

The girl stood up and approached him. She was wearing a loose smock and he could see through it her barely formed breasts, their nipples grazing the material. She was only about twelve, maybe thirteen, and yet when she walked she swayed with knowledge far beyond her years.

She stood before him and he stared at her transfixed. Her lips parted slightly and her tongue darted out to lick her upper lip and he followed her every movement, his tongue licking in sync. She knelt before him and the movement made her sleeve drop, exposing one of her small breasts. His eyes grew big and he fought the spell, but the wave seemed to drown him in its power. She reached out and stroked his sex, and despite himself he felt his lust swell.

She smiled and took his hand and placed it on her breast and he watched while, with no help from him, his fingers began to move, stroking her nipple. It hardened and her breathing grew shallow and hoarse and she stroked him faster and faster and suddenly he let out a strangled cry and staggered up and away from her.

"Stop! Stop!" he yelled.

She stood up, confused and a little afraid. No one stirred except for one child, who glanced in their direction for a moment before looking away, uninterested. He wondered why his body had not cringed, why he had enjoyed it, desired more.

Okon sauntered over from behind the shrubbery in the shadows, which served as a toilet. He had heard Elvis's cry and thought he was fighting off scavengers. Now he felt irritated because he had cut himself off to come and help and felt the familiar discomfort of unfinished business.

"What's de matter?" he asked Elvis harshly.

Elvis opened his mouth but no sound came. Speechless, he pointed to the half-naked girl.

Okon understood and laughed. "Don't start your shit. Different laws apply here. She wants it and dat's all dat matters," he said.

"But she is a child," Elvis stammered.

"You go learn. We call her Oliver Twist because she no fit to get enough. I was her first, you know—did a good job, didn't I?"

Okon looked past Elvis to the girl, who had developed a coy and seductive manner. Elvis looked from Okon to the girl and back again, something in his gaze causing the girl to drop her eyes. Okon yanked her roughly to him, pressing her close. Although Elvis held his hands over his ears, he could still hear the sounds of their coupling, crude and lusty: her delicate whimpers and his deeper, harsher grunts. He wondered why he sat there with his hands over his ears, his sex throbbing, doing nothing. As they both staggered out into the light, Okon was adjusting his trousers. The sleeve on the girl's dress was still down, showing her breast. Her eyes held a curious mix of satisfaction, shame and pity when she looked at Elvis.

"You must learn to enjoy more. Dese are de fringe benefits of dis job," Okon said, reaching out to pat Elvis on the back.

Elvis shrank away from his touch. "How could you?"

"No start your shit. We are who we are because we are who we were made. No forget."

"Yes, I'll never forget," Elvis said softly.

He turned round. The girl was still standing there looking at him. He reached out on impulse and pulled her sleeve up, covering her breast. She smiled, suddenly shy, and hiding her face behind her hand, she giggled.

"You be fool," she said tenderly.

He smiled. "Yes. A fool."

Later that evening he felt a chill come upon him. Within days he was ill, his fever raging so hard that he passed out into a place of spasms and hallucinations. When he regained consciousness, the young girl was mopping his brow and Okon was nervously smoking a cigarette. Elvis sat up and wrapped the hole-ridden lappa tighter around himself, cowering away from the thundering rain. It came down in solid sheets, and in minutes the ground under the bridge was flooded.

The beggar children slept standing up, gently swaying with the rhythm of the rain. He had been given the only dry spot there was, on top of a pile of tires, as he was the sick one. Besides, he was the gentlest caretaker, taking only what was actually offered to him and in many cases handing it back when he didn't actually need it.

Okon looked at him. "You worry us," he said.

"How long was I unconscious?" Elvis asked.

"Four days."

"Four days?"

"Yes. But you are back."

He felt the young girl arranging cardboard boxes around him to fend off the spray carried by the wind, and he looked up and his eyes met hers.

"Go and sleep," he whispered hoarsely.

"Shh," she said, and wiped his fevered brow.

"I'll never leave you," he promised her rashly. He knew somewhere in him that of all the promises ever made, that was the one most likely to be broken. What circumstance did not steal, time eroded.

"Sleep now," she said gently.

Her fingers, like butterfly wings, cooled his brow. She then climbed up beside him and, wrapping her little body around him for warmth, she slept, and this time he was not aroused.

The rain came down in one solid, unyielding sheet. It had been like this for days now, and few had been able to leave their homes as the city flooded. Shops closed and everything had slowly ground to a halt. No cars moved, because the streets had become canals. The only people about were the beggar children, who were making a fortune by fetching buckets of clean water to housebound people.

The young girl whispered the news to Elvis. Religious leaders, Muslim and Christian, had come together to urge their followers to pray together for the rain to stop.

Across Lagos, in another slum, Comfort waded through the ankle-deep water that flooded her home. She was lucky that the flooding was minor. The new man she was living with sat in a wicker work chair with his feet on top of a stool, reading a newspaper. He stopped to bawl out that he was hungry and then went back to reading.

Dinner was served in watery silence, broken only by the occasional slosh as some undercurrent disturbed them. Tope, her youngest child, paused in her meal to watch a rat that had just swum into the room. Taking careful aim, she hit it on the nose with a lump of fufu. It shrieked in anger and swam out hurriedly, muttering under its breath about the indignities of mixing with the poor. Tope laughed so much that she dropped her small piece of meat in the water. In a flash she was down on the floor, rooting in the water for it. Her brothers, Tunji and Akin, laughed at her loss, but with a triumphant yelp she held up the piece of meat, inspecting it critically before plopping it into her mouth. Her mother regarded her with a bored stare and went back to her own food.

The storm had not eased up for days. Almost as if they were symbiotically bound, Elvis's fever still burned. Through the film of rain, hazy and unclear, Elvis saw a young boy standing around at a public tap waiting for his bucket to fill up. The public tap was situated directly below a high-voltage power line. Picking up a thin piece of metal, the boy rapped out a tune on the metal beak of the tap, dancing in the puddles, laughing. Suddenly the girl jerked up. Eyes wide, she reached out a trembling hand and pointed. Elvis saw it too. More than four thousand volts of electricity arced from the overhead cable in a beautiful steel-blue hue, like ice reflecting the sun, and hit the upturned bicycle spoke the boy held with the grace of a cat.

There was a brief flash like a bolt of lightning and then, scarcely disturbing the heavy air, its fragrance alluding to death, a choking smell filled the nostrils as only the smell of burning flesh can. Elvis watched the boy's body float away in the deluge, while another took his place and took the full bucket of water to whatever destination would pay for it.

Elvis shut his eyes and went back to sleep. He was woken by the smell of cigarette smoke and the slap of checker tiles on a wooden board. He sat up and stared uncomprehendingly at the sight of Redemption and Okon playing a game of checkers. He thought he might still be asleep and dreaming.

"Redemption?"

Redemption looked up, saw Elvis and sprang to his feet, scattering the checkers everywhere, the board falling to the floor with a thump.

"Elvis!" he said, giving Elvis a hug. Standing back, he pulled Elvis to his feet. "Make I see you." Redemption continued, examining Elvis critically. "Well, you done lose weight but not too much."

Elvis was still confused and a little lightheaded, so he sat down, leaning back against a bridge support.

"Redemption. How? When?"

"I find him," Okon said from the floor, where he was picking up the checkers.

Just then the young girl rushed up to Elvis from where she was buying some food, with a cup of strong eucalyptus-flavored tea. He took it with a smile and sipped it slowly.

"You sleep well?"

He nodded, embarrassed by her attentions and the smile on Redemption's face.

"How long did I sleep this time?" he asked the girl.

"Two days."

"Two days?"

"Yes."

The rain had stopped, though the sky was a troubled grey. Elvis realized that his fever had abated. As the young girl fussed around Elvis, Redemption was busy sending another child off to buy them beer and some more cigarettes from Madam Caro's.

"What is your name?" Elvis asked the young girl.

"Blessing," she replied.

He smiled. He finished the tea and watched her take the cup back. She reminded him so much of Efua, and he wondered why all the women in his life had to take care of him—even those he should have been taking care of.

Blessing came back quickly and tried to make him lie down again.

"Aren't you losing money by staying to take care of me?" Elvis asked her.

"Sleep, you never strong," Blessing said.

Yes, he thought, dozing off, sleep.

He woke up to someone slapping him gently.

"Redemption," he said as his eyes focused.

"Yes, how you go sleep again. Two days sleep never do?"

Elvis yawned and sat up again, back against the same bridge support. "Beer?"

Elvis nodded and took the offered drink from Redemption. He took a cautious sip and let out his breath in a satisfied sigh.

"I see you done better. You want food?" Redemption asked.

"No."

"So, Okon told me of your deal here. I see dat I teach you well."

"Whatever."

"Elvis, your words dey cut me."

"Sorry."

"So, what's making you sick?"

Elvis shrugged.

"Well, even though I am not a doctor, make I guess. Dis life you are living?"

"Ah, Redemption, no mock our life," Okon protested.

"I hear you. But not de life I dey talk of. Na Elvis here. He is not able for dis type of living. Abi?"

Elvis nodded.

"So what do you want to do?"

Again Elvis shrugged.

"De sickness affect your tongue?" Redemption asked angrily.

"No, but I don't have answers for you."

"I see you never change. Always big grammar for lie."

"I am still trying to understand what happened to you. How you managed to escape the Colonel. Why you disappeared for so long. What you are doing back here. So forgive me if I am a little tongue-tied."

"Make I tell you what happened. After you and de King leave, de

Colonel begin chase me bad, bad. People begin talk say I cheek him and him no fit to do anything about it. De Colonel vex well, well. But I manage join some traders to Cotonu in Benin Republic."

"You left the country?"

"Yes."

"No take am brag. Benin Republic is next door. It is not like say you go overseas," Okon said.

"Shut up!" Redemption said.

"So when did you come back?" Elvis asked.

"When I hear three days ago say dat de King killed de Colonel. I wish dat I hear sooner. I would have been back since."

The three of them were silent, sipping from their beers.

"Why did you agree to come back here with Okon?"

"Ah, Elvis. You get suspicious mind O!"

"Experience has taught me that you always want something."

"Elvis, your words dey wound me because I come here with gift for you."

"Gift?"

"Here, take my passport."

Elvis took the proffered passport.

"What is this?"

"My gift to you. Use it to go to America, go join your auntie."

"But I cannot—it's your passport, Redemption."

"Dose white people no go know de difference in de photo."

"Why not use it yourself? Why would you give it to me?"

"Elvis, take de passport. You know I myself no go ever go America," Redemption said.

"Why?"

"Because dis na my home. I be area boy, alaye. I no go fit for States."

"I'm not sure I want to go, either."

"Take it. If I was going to use it, I for done use it by now."

"I don't understand," Elvis said.

"Sometime you just hold something like dat for dream. For believe. No worry, I go find anoder thing!"

"I don't want to go!"

"It is America, Elvis! Take it. You know how many people are planning for dis and can't get it?" Okon said.

"When did we start thinking of America as a life plan?" Elvis asked.

"When things spoil here. Don't blame me. I no spoil am," Okon said.

"Even during your father's time we dey plan for abroad. Dat time it was London, now it is America," Redemption said.

"But remember all the things the King said about America?"

"You never believe dat. It is your fear talking. America is better dan here. For you. Your type no fit survive here long," Redemption said.

"But this country is just as good as America."

Redemption shook his head. "Not for you. Go."

"I promised Blessing that I would never leave her."

"Go," Blessing said. "Go, den you send for me."

Elvis stared from Redemption to Okon and then to Blessing. He knew they were right, but the thought of leaving for America frightened him. Even though it had become painfully clear to him that there was no way he could survive in Lagos, there was no guarantee he would survive in America.

"Fine. I'll go. But I am not well."

"You well enough to travel. It is plane, you no go take leg," Okon said.

"Okay, Elvis done leave de country," Redemption announced with a laugh.

Elvis stood at the floor-to-ceiling glass windows of Murtala Mohammed International Airport, staring down at the runway. He wasn't sure how to feel. On the one hand, he had the opportunity to get away from his life. On the other, he felt like he was abandoning everything that meant anything to him. Oye, Efua, his father, the King, Redemption, Okon, Blessing, even Comfort. It wasn't like he couldn't make it in Lagos. Plenty of people did it every day, and they lived full and happy lives. But Redemption had been right: not him. He knew that what he thought he was leaving behind wasn't that much, and after all, his aunt Felicia was in America. No, what he was leaving had nothing to do with quantity; nor, in spite of Redemption's protestations, did it have to do with quality. This was something else, something essential.

He sucked on his cigarette, blowing meditative smoke rings. Wiping his brow, he silently cursed the broken-down air-conditioning system. Soldiers, armed for battle, crawled everywhere like an ant infestation, and Elvis watched them nervously, still haunted by the specter of the Colonel. Putting as much distance as he could between him and them, Elvis found a row of seats in a corner. They were flush against the wall and offered a view of the entire departure lounge. The ashtray next to him was stained with tobacco-colored spit; and gum, half melted from the heat, dripped down the side like wax. He stubbed out his cigarette delicately, trying not to make contact with the ashtray.

Efua. He had tried not to think about her. Tried to pretend that the things Redemption had said to him that day when he thought he had spotted her with the Maharaji's devotees weren't true. But Redemption had been right. Elvis was selfish, or self-centered, or self-obsessed. Efua had been as much his victim as she was Uncle Joseph's, even if he hadn't raped her. Elvis had never known her, at least no more than he wanted to. Perhaps that was what Redemption had meant.

Not wanting to think about it anymore, he reached into his bag and pulled out a book, one of the only luxuries he'd allowed himself before leaving. All the naira he had left after buying three hundred dollars on the black market, and his ticket, he had given to Blessing. Thirty pieces of silver, Redemption had called it. He touched the shiny paperback cover: James Baldwin's *Going to Meet the Man*. Opening it at the turned-down page that marked his place, he began to read. Jesse had just come on the lynching scene with his father. As he read, Elvis began to see a lot of parallels between himself and the description of a dying black man slowly being engulfed by flame. The man's hands using the chains that bound him as leverage to pull himself up and out of the torture. He flinched at the part where the unnamed white man in the story cut off the lynched black man's genitalia. He closed the book and imagined what kind of scar that would leave. It would be a thing alive that reached up to the sky in supplication, descending to root itself in the lowest chakra, our basest nature. Until the dead man became the sky, the tree, the earth and the full immeasurable sorrow of it all. He knew that scar, that pain, that shame, that degradation that no metaphor could contain, inscribing it on his body. And yet beyond that, he was that scar, carved by hate and smallness and fear onto the world's face. He and everyone like him, until the earth was aflame with scarred black men dying in trees of fire.

A soldier came up to him. "What are you doing here?"

"Waiting for my plane," Elvis said.

"Ticket?"

Elvis handed it over, even though this soldier had no legal right to do this, to demand anything of a man sitting by himself in a corner reading.

"Passport?"

Elvis obliged. The soldier inspected both documents for a long time. He passed them back to Elvis. Everything was in order, but he was clearly not satisfied.

"Staying here is suspicious," the soldier said. "Move."

"To where?"

"I don't bloody care! Just move," he insisted, poking Elvis in the chest with the ugly snout of his rifle's barrel.

Elvis shoved the passport and ticket into his bag and got up. Under the soldier's supervising gaze, he sauntered over to the café in the middle of the departure lounge. He bought a Coke and found an empty table. The match he dragged across the raspy box edge to light another cigarette illuminated his face as he watched the soldier move on to other victims. Reaching instinctively for the Fulani pouch around his neck, Elvis felt a momentary panic when he realized it wasn't there. Remembering that Redemption had made him take it off, he relaxed. It was bound to attract unwelcome attention in both Nigerian and American customs. It was good advice, and he had ditched it, after transferring his mother's Bible and journal to his bag. Reaching into the bag, he pulled out the journal and flipped through it. It had never revealed his mother to him. Never helped him understand her, or his life, or why anything had happened the way it had. What was the point? Nothing is ever resolved, he thought. It just changes.

In the manner of all garbled airport announcements, he heard his flight called and, finishing his Coke, he got up and walked toward the boarding gate. He stood in the line of passengers waiting for his name to be called. He thought about his father and felt guilt wash over him. Nearly every night, in his dreams, he saw Sunday's ghost wandering aimlessly, searching for his house and Madam Caro's buka, long gone under the tyrannical wheels of the bulldozers. He mused at how the King, with all his imperfections, had become the icon for freedom and spiritual truth.

"Redemption," the airline clerk called.

Elvis, still unfamiliar with his new name, did not respond.

"Redemption!" the clerk called louder.

Elvis stepped forward and spoke.

"Yes, this is Redemption."

ACKNOWLEDGMENTS

Percival Everett, who read every draft and without whom this novel would still be a vague idea. Ron Gottesman, Carol Muske-Dukes, T. C. Boyle, Steve Isoardi, Jeanette Lindsey, Viet Nguyen and PB Rippey for reading, feedback, support, friendship and satsang. Sandy Dijkstra for believing and for brokering the best deals, and everyone at The Agency. My family always—Daphne, Mark, Charles, Greg, Stella, Nnenna, Simone, Philomena, Bruno and Delphine. Friends every writer needs—Titi Osu, Helena Igwebuike, Jennifer Dobbs, Wendy Belcher, Elias Wondimu, Amy Schroeder, Ava Chin, Sholeh Wolpe, Kim Burwick, Sylvester Ogbechie, Musa Farhi, Tanya Heflin and Bridget Hoida. Ayesha Pande—my friend and a wonderful editor. Stacey Barney, Cary Goldstein, Jeff Seroy and everyone at Farrar, Straus and Giroux.

R. C. Agoha's book *Medicinal Plants of Nigeria* was an invaluable resource, as were:

Beware of Harlots and Many Friends, J. Nnadozie (Onitsha: J.C. Brothers Bookshop, rev. ed., 1965).
Mabel the Sweet Honey That Poured Away, Speedy Eric (Onitsha: A. Onwudiwe & Sons, 1960).

If your name isn't here, it's not because I don't love you or that your kindness has been forgotten.

Thank you all.